LEGION

WILLIAM ALTIMARI

IMPERIUM BOOKS

"Legion," by William Altimari. ISBN 0-9728726-0-4 (softcover), 0-9728726-1-2 (hardcover).

Library of Congress Control Number: 2003106222.

Manufactured in the United States of America

IN MEMORY OF
WILLIAM C. ALTIMARI, BOATSWAIN'S MATE SECOND CLASS
AND VETERAN OF THE PACIFIC WAR,
AND TO ALL THE MEN AND WOMEN OF THE AMERICAN
ARMED FORCES,
GUARDIANS OF FREEDOM AND LEGIONARIES OF THE
MODERN WORLD

TO RULE NATIONS WITH YOUR POWER, ROMANS, THESE
WILL BE YOUR ARTS: TO IMPOSE THE WAY OF PEACE, TO
SPARE THE VANQUISHED AND SUBDUE THE PROUD

VIRGIL

FIFTEEN YEARS BEFORE THE BIRTH OF CHRIST

1 EVERY MADMAN THINKS EVERYONE ELSE IS MAD.

Publilius Syrus

German horsemen broke from the copse and thundered down the slope. In the clearing, three men lay twisted in impossible poses.

One of the Germans reined up before the human tangle. The two other horsemen rode up beside him.

The sunlight slipped through the trees and dappled the tall warrior. Thick hair and a golden beard that could have dulled the edge of Celtic steel made his head seem enormous. His hair was drawn up into a knot at the top.

He slid from his saddle, a blanket with a leather cinch, and approached the chopped men. He laid aside his shield and made a gesture, and his men dismounted.

"Romans bleed well," Barovistus said. He flung back the cloak he had worn to cut the morning chill.

"They are small men," one of the others said.

"So they are." Barovistus placed a hand on the hilt of the sword at his hip. "But they are wise to the ways of war. They must be dealt with wisely."

Yet the carrion at his feet had never known war. The Roman traders had come to barter goods, but had fallen to the demand of a more primitive need.

Barovistus glanced at the purses beside them. "Our men did well. We don't slay Romans for silver coins. We'll show the men of the Tiber that they are rotting flesh on the banks of the Rhenus."

"But will they back away?" one of the other Germans asked.

"We must test the temper of their blade," Barovistus said. "Will they fight for the honor of three nameless men? We shall see."

"And if they do?"

"Then we'll cut the flesh from their midget limbs and the ravens will feast."

The two other warriors laughed.

"And," Barovistus added, "the rest of them can return to their olive groves and their feminine Greeks. They can leave the lands of the Rhenus to us."

He grabbed his shield and sprang to his horse, and his two men followed.

The scavengers returned. Ears that had once heard stories of heroes at a mother's knee, or perhaps whispers of love, were now peeled like the skins of grapes. As black beaks tore at the morsels, beyond the forest the Germans, too, feasted with pleasure.

Centurions ruled the Roman world. Augustus knew this better than any man. The First Citizen — he avoided the hated words king and emperor — referred to them as *"my* soldiers." Ever distrustful of legionary commanders, he knew the danger of unsheathed iron in the hands of ambitious men. Had not even the Divine Caesar erred here? Had not some of Caesar's own commanders, flush with the victories of his genius, turned on him and sided with the faithless Pompeius? And was it not true that others — both old comrades and pardoned enemies — had gleefully felt Caesar's hot blood shower their hands as they tore at him on the fateful Ides? Caesar's trust had brought his fall, a crash that had shaken the world.

Diocles reflected on these and other matters as he rode through the countryside with the centurion and the twenty recruits. During the journey from Rome, he had gotten to know Probus to a fair degree. Twenty years of service throughout the Empire had earned the centurion much experience to lighten the load of wounds and scars. An air of accomplishment clung to him as naturally as did his dark brown cloak. Diocles had known people of many lands and races, but he had never known anyone who wore pride as well as a Roman.

Though a Greek, Diocles was treated correctly by the centurion. Neither slave nor freedman, Diocles was a freeborn citizen of Rome summoned to these Gallic fastnesses by his powerful patron — the commander of Legion XXV Rapax. Diocles had made certain Probus knew that from the outset. Yet what even Diocles himself did not know was why he had been summoned here at all.

"You ride well," Probus said as he glanced at Diocles before checking the position of the late morning sun. "We should be at the fort by midday."

Diocles looked over his shoulder at the recruits strung out behind him. "They don't ride so well."

Every one bounced along on his saddle.

"We're not a race of horsemen. But we make do. They will too."

Probus was about forty, but he wore it heavily. He might once have been handsome, but most of that had been scoured away by service in savage outposts.

"So how does Gaul seem after Rome?"

"Clean," Diocles said, smiling.

"A slave's navel is cleaner than Rome. But what of the Gauls? How do you take their measure?"

"I've not seen enough of them to make a judgment."

"Why is it that Greeks give every answer like they might be taken to court for it?"

"Natural contrariness."

Probus scratched at the stubble on his chin. "Then let me educate you. The Gauls are a great race."

"You served here before?"

"Long ago I was posted here with Legion XVI Gallica. Of course, Caesar had broken the Gauls years before. But there were still rebellions here and there. And by the gods, could they fight!"

"But not as well as you. . . ."

"No discipline, the Gauls. There's no sense to the way they make war. They hit the line like runaway stags. In two months I could train these skinny lads to cut down any onslaught of Gauls. Discipline. No barbarous race can stand before it."

Diocles studied the eyes and gestures of Probus but said nothing.

"A Gaul fights like he and his enemy are the only two men on earth. No Roman would make that mistake. But man on man they fight like Titans."

"Were you posted to this fort then?"

"Oh no. This one hadn't been built yet. We had temporary camps and we moved about."

"Is it true that—"

"And the women! Gallic women would make Venus rage in envy. When the heat is on them they can burn you to a cinder."

Diocles laughed.

"The women wear trousers here, and when they cut that thong and let them drop, thank the gods and take a deep breath. They can ride you to death."

"But you still live . . . ."

"But I've definitely shortened my life," Probus said with a smile.

The group rode on, with Probus offering an occasional word of encouragement to his tiring recruits.

"How long have you been with the legion?"

"This will be my first day. I was with II Augusta in Spain, but it seems my talents are needed along the Rhenus. I was on leave in Rome when I was ordered to take these skeletons with me to Gaul."

"So today you're coming home, in a way."

"I suppose. A soldier does what he's told."

A movement in the distance caught Diocles' eye, but he saw that Probus had already noticed. On a ridge to the east, a blonde warrior, spear and shield visible, sat astride a small horse.

The centurion lifted his helmet from a saddle pommel and pulled it on. The warrior observed them as they rode by, then jerked his mount around and disappeared down the far side of the ridge.

"Let's bring it up," Probus shouted to his men.

They tightened the line and brought their pack mules closer in.

"A Gaul?" Diocles asked.

"No." Probus knotted the thongs beneath his chin. "I didn't know the Germans were on this side of the river. I don't like it."

"He didn't seem hostile."

"Germans are born hostile. They tumble from the womb reaching for a sword."

Diocles scanned front and back but saw no others.

"They war on Romans, on Gauls, on each other. They have all the ferocity of the Gauls. And none of the grace."

"But we're not at war with them now, are we?"

"My friend, Germans are at war with mankind."

They rode on in silence.

Soon they came upon cultivated areas being worked by a man or two. Occasionally one of them guided a plow behind a trudging ox. The fields were sparse compared to the lush holdings Diocles knew from Italy. Yet whatever sustenance the Gauls drew from these patches seemed enough. They were big and muscular, with fair complexions nicely set off by colorful shirts and trousers.

"We'll skirt the village," Probus said. "These wide-eyed lads can gape at Gallic maidens some other time."

To the east, round wooden buildings with conical thatched roofs spread out among the farmland.

Probus picked up the pace. Roman soldiers became the primary features of the landscape. Probus waved to them on the way by. Sometimes on horseback, but mostly afoot, the soldiers gibed at the lanky recruits. Weighted down more with tools than with weapons, most groups were apparently work details sent out to cut timber or to repair roads. The track on which Diocles' roan mare stepped was not some Celtic rut, but a metalled road of hard stone. Each piece had been set with precision, and a stone curbing held the roadbed in a tight embrace.

Diocles noticed that Probus's expression had changed. The centurion's eyes had taken on a keenness he had not anticipated in the veteran soldier. A new posting, new friends — possibly new battles — lay ahead. Though a centurion had a greater right than any man to be jaded by life — or numbed by death — Probus refused.

"I want to thank you for letting me travel with you. I —"

"You were no trouble. You're not too talkative like most Greeks."

"I think instead."

He looked at him with a half-smile. "Now you *are* trouble."

"Perhaps we might share food together sometime."

"I'll be commanding the First Century of the Third Cohort, as well as the entire cohort. You can find me there."

"I'll look for you. It'll probably take both of us some time to get our bearings."

"Not this old cock. Have you ever been to a legionary fort? Every one is arranged almost the same throughout the Empire. Sometimes the shape varies — depends on the terrain. But the inside is the same. I could find the Third Cohort blindfolded."

Diocles admired the peculiar Roman genius for organization. Forts the same everywhere — what a simple thing, but how efficient, and how powerful.

"The fort might seem confusing at first, but it's built on a grid and you should master it easily. It still dazzles the Gauls."

"I'm sure it does — what must they have thought when they first saw it?"

"Thought? The Gauls don't think — they feel. Not such a bad way to spend a life — if you happen to be a Celt."

"And a Roman?"

"Destined for greater things." Probus quickened his horse's gait. "Come and I'll show you the greatest men in the history of the world."

2 CHANCE, NOT WISDOM, GOVERNS HUMAN LIFE.

Roman saying

Diocles urged his horse up a slope, and when he reached the top he stared in wonder. A meadow spread before him like a carpet, the stone roadway streaking through it in a hard white band. Beyond it lay his goal. On rising ground, a quarter-mile off, sprawled the timber fort of the Twenty-fifth Legion.

It was, indeed, an awesome thing. In the midst of the Gallic wilderness, it rose as a silent statement of Roman power and resolve. Rectangular, it must have been fifteen to twenty hectares in extent. Diocles approached it with Probus and the recruits, and they rode over a wooden bridge. A manned gate, now open, spanned a pair of ditches surrounding the fort. The first ditch, about fifty feet from the wall, was V-shaped and nine or ten feet deep. The second ditch, some ten or twelve feet closer in, was cut in an oddly distorted V. The slope nearest the fort was shallow and inviting to any would-be attacker. However, the outer slope of the ditch, which an attacker could not see until he was in the ditch itself, was nearly vertical. If a shower of javelins rained on him from the wall of the fort, he would turn to flee up the sharp grade. There he would struggle and die, pinned to the scarp like an insect.

Diocles glanced at the soldiers in the ditches who were cleaning out the loose soil and clumps of weeds. Then he followed Probus and his recruits up to the fort.

The wall was as surprising as anything he had yet seen. Not wood — which could be set alight — the wall was a massive turf rampart. The earthen blocks were about a foot and a half long and a foot wide and a good half-foot thick. They must have weighed sixty or seventy pounds apiece. Not only were they immune to the torch, but they would be impervious to the ram, though Diocles suspected that what the Gauls or Germans knew about ramming would fit in a sparrow's eye. Yet it was characteristic of the Romans that if they expected a light rain, they built for a storm. Unlike fatalistic Greeks, these men left nothing to the gods — or to chance.

The sloping rampart rose about eleven or twelve feet and was surmounted by a five-foot wooden parapet. Soldiers were leaning against it and watching as they approached.

A pair of wooden lookout towers loomed above the oaken gateway. Probus and Diocles passed beneath these and entered the recessed gate area. Probus spoke for them both and one of the men on duty checked a papyrus sheet on the table in front of him. He exchanged some words with Probus that Diocles could not hear.

"We're cleared," Probus said and signaled his recruits to follow him in. "I have to report with these wretches. You'll want the headquarters building, too, so we'll go up together."

They rode into the fort and a metalled street stretched out before them.

"This is the Via Praetoria. We'll take it up to the Principia."

Diocles looked right and left to orient himself. Sunken into the ground on either side of the thoroughfare were timber-lined drains flushing with wastewater, to be carried under the walls and away. Lining both sides of the street were low buildings that were apparently barracks. Soldiers came and went in considerable numbers here. The barracks were timber, with plastered and whitewashed exteriors, and the sun striking them caused Diocles to squint as he rode by. Roofs of wooden shingles angled off them, and a few lounging soldiers found shade beneath the overhangs.

The traffic ensured that little attention was paid to the newcomers. Most soldiers went about on foot, though occasionally a horseman threaded in and out.

"This is the Via Principalis," Probus said at a wide intersecting street. "That's the Principia."

Diocles had not known what to expect, but he had not expected this. Easily a hundred feet across, the building extended along the opposite side of the Via Principalis. It might have been mistaken for a Roman country villa were it not sited here in the core of a legionary fort. A long portico with ten or more columns graced the front of the Principia and flanked an arched gateway in the center. Here, too, all was plastered and whitewashed to a dazzling purity. The angled roofs of the portico and of the building beyond were fitted with terra cotta tiles that contrasted with the bright walls. Who could ever have dreamed that this exquisite arrangement was the pulsing heart of the Roman military animal?

Probus and Diocles rode to the headquarters and dismounted, while the recruits brought the mules up behind.

Diocles followed Probus past a plinth supporting a bronze sundial and went into the entrance hall. Several soldiers were on duty. After identifying himself to one, Diocles was told the Legate was out of the fort at the moment. However, a tribune would be along to escort him to the Praetorium, the commander's residence.

He turned to Probus, but the centurion had already gone on. Suddenly he heard a commotion outside. Had he arrived an hour later he would have missed it. Had he and Probus lingered a bit longer over meals or rest stops, all this would have passed before he had reached the fort of the Twenty-fifth Legion at Aquabona on the Rhenus. Yet Fortuna had rolled not other dice, but these.

He went out and saw several soldiers hurrying past and buckling their sword belts. They were quickly joined by others, and all ran off down the Via Principalis. Diocles looked around and saw a pair of horsemen racing toward him up the Via Praetoria. They turned left in front of him and galloped down the Principalis. Their tense faces startled him.

"What is it?" he asked as he snared a soldier running by.

"A Greek slave grabbed a weapon and took a hostage down by the stables."

Diocles released the man's sleeve and bolted down the road.

He knew well the story of Spartacus. Ever since the revolt sparked by the Thracian gladiator a few generations earlier, the Romans were nervous to the point of obsession about slave risings. He knew they would crush even the whisper of rebellion.

Diocles followed the crowd to one edge of the fort. Next to a bank of stables, some bales of stale hay left from the winter had been piled up. The defiant slave stood atop a tall stack. At his feet on a lower bale crouched the terrified hostage. The slave held a drawn bow, the arrow pointed at the other man's skull.

A young soldier with an air of self-importance was demanding the slave come down. The Greek was having none of it.

Diocles spotted the man he had just spoken to outside the Principia. He pushed his way through the clump of soldiers and came up next to him.

"What's going to happen?"

"The Greek is finished, the fool. There's no going back now."

"Is that man a Gaul?"

"Yes. He's one of the workers in the armory."

"And the man below?"

"Ulpius Crus. The laticlavian tribune."

Diocles had no idea what that meant, but it clearly meant something.

"The slave is his," the man said with the kind of smile that a common soldier reserves only for the agony of his officers. "Crus looks the fool and he cannot see a way out. No matter how this plays, he knows his rocks are in the crusher."

All the soldiers standing around appeared to be relishing the tribune's discomfort.

14

"I'm a Greek," Diocles said to the soldier. "I'll try to get him down."

Though he was younger than Diocles, the soldier gazed at him like an indulgent father. "Save your pain. By tomorrow the Greek will be nailed to a cross. If he's lucky, they'll cut his throat after an hour or two."

The sound of a horse behind them caused the cluster of men to split in two. A black stallion brushed Diocles as it went by.

The horseman approached the tribune. Instantly Diocles sensed something odd about him. He did not seem to be a man on the back of an animal. There was an intuitive communication between the two that created an eerie fusion of disparate spirits. Diocles got the feeling not of tacit cooperation between horse and man, but rather of the taut threatening energy of a centaur.

Diocles was unsure if he was a soldier. Instead of the off-white tunic most soldiers wore, his was a rich bright blue. He had no weapons, but wore at his waist just a leather belt with tinned decorative plates. He was of medium height and build. The sun striking his silver hair made his head seem like it was covered with spun metal. From where Diocles stood, he could not see the man's face.

The horseman stopped a few feet from the tribune and spoke to him in a soft voice. Eager for advice, Ulpius Crus answered with a tone of humility that seemed forced.

The silver-haired man extended his right leg forward, raising it over the horse's neck and sliding from the animal as fluidly as a raindrop rolling off a leaf.

Diocles moved closer.

The man in blue approached the bales of hay. Confidence empty of all arrogance graced each stride.

"Tell me Greek," he said, looking up, "why this idiocy?"

His voice was as hard as burnished steel.

"He wants to sell me to a slave dealer. I'll not be sold again! Ever!"

"Why not? A slave does what he's told — just like a soldier."

"And a slave can be willing to face death, too — just like a soldier."

The silver-haired man turned around. Diocles was surprised to see he was only about forty. Black eyebrows recalled hints of lost youth, and a pair of marks that might once have been dimples sliced through each cheek in vertical grooves. He still had the traces of a smile in his eyes from the slave's quick answer, and Diocles was drawn to the attractive face. He wondered if he might be one of a group of traveling actors here to earn some coin by performing for the soldiers. But why he would interpose himself in this crisis Diocles could not imagine.

"You'll get your wish!" the tribune shrieked. "Death as slow as a night watch!"

"And I'll take some of you with me. I have five arrows — the last for you."

"What does this wretched Gaul have to do with it?" the man in blue asked.

"I needed to get your attention — and I have it."

It was a petty triumph, but all he had left.

The Gaul buried his head in his arms. The crotch of his trousers was wet.

A bearded man burst through the crowd and ran toward the tribune. He babbled in Celtic and gestured toward the Greek and the Gaul. His arms were as hairy as a bear's but blotched with burn scars. Years at the forge had not prepared him for this. He was trying to hide his fear for the life of his friend behind Gallic bluster.

The man in blue laid a hand on his shoulder and spoke to him in the man's own language. The gentle voice calmed him.

Perhaps, thought Diocles, he was not an actor but some kind of priest.

"This comedy has played long enough," the silver-haired man said to Crus. "I can end it, but you must do something for me. . . ."

"What is it?" he asked, desperate for a resolution.

"Give this miserable Greek to me so I can deal with him in my own way."

"The dog is yours, centurion. But I want to be there when he breathes his last rank breath."

"Did you hear that, Hercules?" the centurion said. "You're my toy now."

"Perhaps I can help," Diocles said without thought.

"Who are you?" the centurion asked.

Diocles recoiled under the weight of that gaze and for a moment he forgot his own name.

The centurion turned away. "Greek, move that arrow from the Gaul and aim it at me."

"Why should I do that?"

"Because if you don't, I'll come up there and break your spine."

Diocles watched the two men take each other's measure. Across some black gulf they eyed one another for centuries.

The young Gaul peered around, but the arrow was still pointed at his head.

The centurion raised a foot onto a bale of hay.

The slave jerked the bow away and aimed the arrow at the Roman.

The burly Gaul on the ground moved forward.

"Stay where you are, you fool!" The centurion looked at the other Gaul and made a sideways gesture. The young man scampered to the side and began to come down.

"We'll trade hostages," the Roman said to the Greek. "The Gaul for me."

Reeking of urine, the young Gaul at last reached the bottom. The older man threw his arms around him and hugged him until he almost crushed him. They turned together to thank the centurion.

"Go!" the Roman ordered without taking his eyes from the Greek.

They moved away but stared back over their shoulders as they went.

The Roman began climbing the hay bales, the arrow aimed at the center of his blue tunic.

Diocles moved closer so he could hear. He noticed the centurion wince in apparent pain as he made the climb.

When the Roman neared the top, the slave gestured to him to keep his distance. The centurion sat on a bale about ten feet away.

He allowed the tension to eat at the Greek.

His arms were shaking from keeping the bow drawn for so long, and he eased the taut gut forward to rest a bit. With a quick pass of his hand he wiped the sweat from his face.

Still the Roman did not speak.

"Shall we stay here until we die of old age?" the slave said.

"At this point, old age is not your worry." The Roman gestured toward the arrow. "Who is the better for this?" he asked in a weary voice.

"I'm without hope, so what does it matter?"

"No one is without hope." The centurion stood up.

The Greek drew the bow.

"I've looked into the eyes of many killers," the Roman said, "but yours are not familiar. Will you loose that shaft into my lung and watch the blood spew from my mouth?"

Sweat poured from the slave's face and his arms trembled.

Almost indifferently, the centurion strode forward and swept the bow and arrow from his hands. He threw them aside as though they had been meaningless, as indeed he had proved they were.

"I never misread eyes," he said so softly Diocles could barely hear him.

The slave fell to his knees, tears of dread running down his cheeks. He started shaking uncontrollably.

"Why cry for tomorrow?" the centurion said with a hard voice. "The sun hasn't yet set on today."

3   IT WILL BE PLEASANT TO LOOK BACK ON THINGS PAST.

Roman saying

A cheerful tribune, Titinius by name, led Diocles through the vestibule of the Praetorium. Rectangular in plan, the commander's residence sat behind the Principia. A courtyard opened the center, providing shade and cool air and betraying its origin in a warmer climate than this one. Wooden posts supported the overhanging roofs. The two men crossed the courtyard and entered a range of rooms on the right. Diocles was taken to the commander's bathhouse, where he was allowed to scrape away the remnants of the journey from Rome.

Afterward he was shown into a room with a long table and several couches. He wore a new white tunic for the occasion and waited by one of the couches.

A pair of slaves came through a doorway to the right, each man bearing a tray of food he placed on the table.

"Diocles!" said a familiar voice from behind him.

He turned as the commander came striding through the other doorway.

"Hail, old friend!" the Legate said and gripped Diocles by both arms.

"Hail, Sabinus!" he answered with a smile and greeted the person whom he loved more than any other, except his own wife.

"Sorry I wasn't here to meet you. " Sabinus laid down his bronze helmet and reached for a glass goblet of wine from one of the slaves. "Too strong," he said after a sip, and he held out the goblet so the slave could add more water. "Do you believe the Gauls drink wine without water? Primitive race."

Far more handsome at thirty-five than the gods would usually allow, Marcus Aemilius Sabinus gazed at Diocles as he sipped his wine.

"Why are you standing?"

Diocles stretched out on one of the couches.

"I had to meet with the Gallic chieftain this morning," Sabinus said. "He's nervous about the Germans. I broke precedent and went to him instead of demanding he come to me. Some of the old centurions didn't care for that" — he shrugged — "but so be it."

He signaled to one of the slaves to help him with his armor.

The commander was wearing a bronze muscle breastplate, encircled above the waist by a white sash as a symbol of rank. Beneath this he wore a linen doublet. Leather strips, dyed white and trimmed with yellow fringe, hung from this at the shoulders and waist. The slave removed the doublet, and Sabinus stretched out in his simple red tunic.

"Eat." He reached for a bowl of mushrooms and olives. "Let's indulge before we speak of matters of substance."

Diocles smiled and dipped into a plate of cold pork.

"Sometimes," Sabinus said, "the Legate of Augustus wearies of substance and hungers just for the pleasure of old friends."

———

Finishing with sweet cakes he did not need, Diocles lounged on his side and sipped at a goblet of warmed honey wine.

"So why have I summoned you? That's what you want to know."

"And that's what you delight in not telling me."

"A fair rebuke, young Greek, but take care — I have five thousand armed men at my elbow."

"Sabinus, please...."

Suddenly serious, Sabinus leaned forward. "I have a great task for you. I want you to give these men immortality." He made a gesture that seemed to take in the entire fort.

"Who? What men?"

"The soldiers of Rome."

"How?"

"I want you to walk in the footsteps of your great countryman Polybius. What he did for the legions of Scipio, you shall do for the army of Augustus."

Startled, Diocles leaned back on his couch. "I am no Polybius."

"No one I know writes more beautifully than you."

"I don't understand."

"My friend, I've been here four months, and I now know that these men are like no others on earth." He reached for a honey cake and one of the slaves brushed a fly from it just before it touched his mouth.

"But what—"

"Sometimes I even regret I was born a patrician—that this command is just another step in my political career. In the dark of the night, I envy these scarred centurions and wish I could stay here as long as I please." He pushed his fingers through his thick black hair. "Of course, they're not the tenderest of mortals. They're no Vestal Virgins. But, by Jupiter, they're the sharpest salt in a world being made soft by sweet cakes and honey wine."

"What would you have me do?"

"Stay with me this summer. Record for posterity the story of life in the legions. Tell our children's children what these men have done for Rome—and for the world."

"This is a sobering task."

"Would you prefer a childish one?"

"What of my wife?"

"She was in on my plan. No doubt she seemed especially affectionate before you left. She knew you'd be away for some time." He smiled. "And consider—when you return, she'll be exquisitely keen."

"My patron is a rogue—do his soldiers know that? And what of your son? His tutoring is my true task."

"He'll profit by a respite from your rhetorical flourishes."

"You leave me no open door."

"A free man always has an escape. He can walk away from the request of an old friend who wishes for nothing but to see his words become immortal."

"And I thought my wife was the cleverest person I know!"

"Cornelia is a Roman. Need any more be said?" He stood up. "Let's walk off some of this meal."

They strolled out to the sunny courtyard.

"How am I supposed to do this?"

"That I leave to you. After all, you're a Greek—where is the vaunted Hellenic ingenuity?"

Diocles scowled in reply.

"Surely, nothing is difficult for the son of a race that divides all mankind into two—Greeks and barbarians."

They walked in silence. Finally, Sabinus laid a hand on his left arm.

"Old friend, you needn't stay if you really don't wish to. I know I wouldn't care to be away from Cornelia for so long . . . ."

"No, no, I was thinking of something else. Did you hear about the incident today with the slave?"

"No, I was with the Gauls. Tell me."

He told in detail what had happened.

"This is a very serious matter," Sabinus said. "Where's the slave now?"

"With the man who ended the crisis."

"You say he was a centurion?"

"So he was called by the tribune."

"He doesn't sound familiar. He must be new here."

The commander turned away and walked off by himself.

"Sabinus," Diocles said, hurrying after him. "Can the man be spared? He's a Greek and—"

"No. An example must be made. The centurion knows that. I'm sorry, but the Greek is probably already dead."

4 THOSE WHO CROSS THE SEA CHANGE THE SKY, BUT NOT THEIR SPIRITS.

Horace

I have decided to keep a record of my reflections as I undertake the task Sabinus has set before me. My patron does not realize the difficulty of this commission. He is a man to whom everything has always come easily. His appearance, his talents, his connections in Rome — all assure his ease of passage. He sprints like a deer around life's obstacles. Now he wants a scholar, a man of sedentary ways, to write an account of the fighting men of Rome. The only thing more idiotic than the request is that I have acceded to it. No experience could prepare me for the remoteness I feel among these men. I will have to place my finer sensibilities in a cedar box and hope that prolonged storage does not rot them. I will find no men here eager to argue about literature or philosophy. I will find no one who will know even the meaning of those words. It is fortunate for Sabinus that I love him. If I did not, I would be on my way back to the fora of Rome. The air there may not be as sweet, but the talk is always heady and wise. I expect the next noble talent I will acquire is how to confront an enemy as I prepare to disembowel him.

Sunlight glancing off the lake lit the soft grass under the trees. A hillock beneath an oak formed a natural seat, and to this the centurion pointed.

The Greek sat. He had stopped shaking. The greatest terror finally brings its own release.

The centurion carried no sword, but his dagger hung at his right hip.

"What's your name?" he asked and folded his arms across the front of his blue tunic.

"Demetrius."

"Mine is Rufio. Tell me your tale."

He moistened his lips. "I was the slave of Senator Publius Claudius Longinus. When the senator died last year, he had many debts unsettled. He was a very generous man. His family disposed of most of his slaves to meet his obligations. Crus bought me and made me his personal attendant. I'm a scholar, not a foot washer. I'd administered the senator's library. I'd helped him with his speeches. Into the small hours of the morning we would discuss Plautus or Livius and —"

"You're well-versed in the Roman authors?"

"As well as the Greek."

"Continue."

"I was unfit for my new duties. Yet I worked hard to meet these new demands. I—"

"Stop." Rufio held up his hand. "No scholar would work hard at being a menial. He'd do just enough to get by while he maneuvered for a change of circumstance."

Demetrius was only in his early twenties, and his days and nights among the scrolls had not equipped him to be a skillful liar.

"Don't lie to me again."

"It's true. I was a poor personal attendant—but I won't submit to being put on the block again."

"Why not?"

"Because I'm good-looking and I'm Greek. That's enough reason for some to buy me." His young eyes searched the centurion's face for understanding.

"I see. Well, my taste doesn't run to boys or men, Greek or otherwise. I didn't acquire you to grease you."

Demetrius flinched at this typical Italian frankness.

Rufio turned and stared across the lake. An occasional bird swooped low over the peaceful water, rippled here and there by the movement of a fish near the surface. Insects buzzed nearby, and brightly colored butterflies flew out from the arbor to alight on the swaying heads of sweet-smelling flowers. The breeze fluttered his silver hair as he gazed off into the beauty of a Gallic spring.

"It's far too gentle a day to kill a man." Rufio turned to Demetrius. "My sister is newly widowed with a young son. I want him to learn the Latin writers in addition to the Greek. You will teach him."

Disbelief and gratitude ran over one another on the Greek's face until they formed a preposterous expression.

"I don't understand," he said, apparently fearful of some new torment. "I threatened to kill you. How could you send me to your sister's house?"

Rufio smiled at a distant memory. "Flavia knows how make a fist. She's the most beautiful woman in Rome—she needs to know how to defend herself."

"Rome?"

"One thing more. Don't think for a moment I was impressed by your farce with the Gaul. That was a shabby thing."

Demetrius lowered his eyes.

"There was no courage in that," Rufio went on. "You humiliated that poor lad. But it was a useless act and that's how I know your story is true. Only a man without hope would act so hopelessly."

Demetrius dropped to his knees and wrapped his arms around the centurion's bare legs.

"Up!"

He stood. "When will we go to Rome?"

"You'll make your own way. I'll provide you a horse and silver. You held that bow well, so I know — "

"Alone? You'd trust me to go alone?"

"Trust . . ." Rufio said and turned away at the taste of that as if it were a harsh condiment. "The word always threatens to inflame my liver."

"Then how do you know I won't run away? Shall I take an oath?"

"Oath? I've never known a Greek who understood the sanctity of oaths. Greeks are a conniving race from birth. But" — he raised a finger at Demetrius — "I've never known a Greek who didn't pay what he owed. And you owe me everything."

"Yes. But I still might flee. You cannot be sure."

"Then you'll have betrayed me."

A horseman rode out from the fort and approached the bower. Rufio, alone now, leaned with an outstretched arm against the trunk of an oak and watched the rider come.

The soldier was still several hundred feet away when Rufio recognized him. He smiled and sat on the hillock.

The rider reined up and stared down with a grin. "I knew it was you. The last time I saw you, you were bandaged and bleeding in Spain, but when I heard what happened today I knew it could only be you."

"Hello, Probus." Rufio stood up.

Probus slipped from his mount, and the two men smiled into each other's eyes.

Probus pointed to Rufio's belt. "I remember a time when you threatened to lay your vine-stick across the back of any soldier who left the fort without his sword."

"I'm growing lax in my dotage."

Probus grunted as they sat together on the grass.

"Why are you here and not with the Second Legion in Spain?" Probus asked.

"I wanted to see the land of my youthful adventures one more time."

He scowled. "I don't like the smell of that. You cannot be thinking about retiring. . . ."

"Very soon."

Probus rested his forearms across his knees and stared across the lake.

Rufio knew Probus's disapproval always took the form of silence.

"Cheer up," Rufio said. "We're among the gallant Gauls again. What could be better?"

"The army cannot afford to lose soldiers like you. Savages are out there eager to sink their fangs into the throat of Rome."

Rufio said nothing.

"Do you know who first said that to me? You."

Rufio squinted at the sun reflecting off the water.

"Don't let what happened in Spain bleed you forever," Probus said.

"You know better."

"I don't know better."

Rufio's slate-blue eyes regained their easy smile. "Do you know anything at all, then?"

"I know women, I know war, and I know Quintus Flavius Rufio."

"In that order?"

"In order of importance," he answered, struggling but failing to hold back a laugh.

"You bull-necked Philistine," Rufio said, laughing with him. "How long have you been here?"

"A few hours. I brought twenty recruits with me. A pack of scarecrows."

"What cohort are you with?"

"Third. First Century. And you?"

"Second. I haven't met my men yet. The journey from Spain put me back in the hospital. I escaped this morning."

"How's your back?"

"It's a slow process. What's the matter?"

"Second Cohort you said." He bared a sadistic smile. "With your seniority it must be the First Century."

Rufio stared back warily. "Why?"

Probus continued grinning.

"Oh no . . . the recruits. How many?"

"All of them."

"What? How can that be?"

"Every wretch goes to Second Cohort, First Century. I heard there was some catastrophe that bled it white. Probably stubbed their toes and died."

Rufio stood up and walked to the edge of the trees near the lake. The sunlight pressed onto his face like a sheet of warm metal.

"I'm too tired to train new warriors."

"Tired from what? What are you forty? Forty-two?"

"A hundred."

"A few days with those pathetic stick-men should restore your vitality."

"And I suppose your century is all veterans."

"Iron men."

"You're a foul swine."

Probus joined him at the edge of the trees. "Has there been any excitement along here?"

"When I was in the hospital I was told there were a few raids from across the river. Mostly against the Gauls."

"You know the Germans — they're always thumbing the edge of their knives."

"I'm not sure it's just that this time. I think they might be testing. Opening a vein to see how quick we are to close it."

Probus folded his arms and nodded. "Is there talk of a campaign this summer?"

"I don't know. But I do know this is not the best time to be nursing twenty babies."

5 YOU FALL INTO SCYLLA IN TRYING TO AVOID CHARYBDIS.

Roman saying

I like Probus. I enjoy his company very much. He is a rough man and would not dare show a tender spot, if he has any. Perhaps I am not so sensitive after all. He is precisely what I expect of a centurion. I doubt he would hesitate to flog a negligent soldier. Yet I suspect he would be just as willing to listen to a reasonable excuse. He is as open and straightforward as the head of an axe.

Yet he is not the only kind of centurion here. The one who doomed the Greek slave disturbs me. His appearance seems designed to deceive. No bluff openness reassures. It is as though a silk hanging concealed an uncertain shape. One pulls it aside to see a spear stained with blood. I have never been a man tricked by appearances. Poison is never so loathsome as when contained in the ornatest of vials.

Diocles sat on the ground at the edge of the Praetorium portico. With his back against a column and his knees drawn up, he played with a white flower. He might have been a lovesick suitor hopeful of placing the petals one day soon in the hair of his beloved.

Footsteps roused him. Probus was striding across the courtyard.

"Romans work and Greeks dream," Probus said.

"Life isn't that easy, centurion," he answered and tossed away the flower.

"I'm on my way to see the commander. I was told he likes to get to know his centurions personally. I like that."

"A rare treat awaits him."

"I smell the manure of sarcasm."

"Can you spare a moment?" Diocles touched the ground next to him.

Probus pulled his scabbard forward out of the way and sat down.

"I have a problem. Perhaps you can give me advice on how to solve it. Sabinus wants me to write a history of life in the legions. He believes it's a story that deserves to be preserved. He says you're all remarkable men."

Probus gazed toward the commander's office. "Does he?"

"So how do I go about it? You're the only one I know to ask."

Probus pulled a hand down across his lips as he thought for a moment. "Well, the spine of the legion is its cohorts, and the soul of the cohort is the century. It's there you'll find the essence of the army of Rome."

"There are a hundred men in a century?"

"Eighty. Things have been reorganized over the years."

"And the cohort?"

"Ten cohorts to a legion. Each cohort has six centuries. There's been some talk of reducing the number of centuries in the First Cohort to five and doubling their size, but nothing has come of it yet. The centurions of the First Cohort are the most senior in the legion."

Diocles leaned his head back against the column and thought for awhile. The buzzing of flies was the only sound in the sunny courtyard.

"Suppose I get permission from Sabinus to live with a century. Would that be the way to do it?"

"The perfect way — but the centurion won't like it. That I can promise. The soldiers either."

"And what about you? Could you learn to like it — or at least tolerate it?"

"Devious Greek! You soften me up for the sword thrust. In fact, I'd enjoy it. But it's not a good idea. My men are mostly veterans. You cannot learn how to cook by staring at hard bread. You must watch the kneading of fresh dough."

"But I know no one else here."

"I do," he said, and in his eyes lurked something Diocles found unnerving.

The office of the Legate in the Praetorium was sparsely furnished. Stools were pushed against the right and left walls. Above the seats hung swords and javelins, relics bequeathed by old warriors from forgotten campaigns. Near the wall opposite the door was a desk covered with papyrus sheets and waxed writing tablets. In the far right corner a bust of Augustus reigned from a wooden plinth. Sabinus sat on a stool behind the desk.

"And you spared him nonetheless?" Sabinus asked.

"Yes, commander," Rufio said.

"And do you think that was wise?"

"It's not fitting for me to comment on my own wisdom."

"Centurion Probus told me you're a man of much experience. Today you appear to be wearing it rather lightly."

"I wouldn't disagree, commander."

"Centurion, just explain your thinking in letting the slave live."

"Everyone deserves the luxury of a mistake—especially if he's young. The Greek wasn't raising revolt. He feared brutal Romans with Greek tastes, so he grabbed a bow like a drowning man grabs air."

"Can you be sure of all that?"

"No, commander. Greeks are notorious liars."

Sabinus threw up his hands. "You hurt you own case. You agree, then, that there could have been great danger?"

"Commander, danger is my profession."

"Probus tells me you were badly injured in Spain."

"Yes."

"Are you fully recovered?"

"I'm ready to resume my duties."

"That wasn't the question."

"There's still some pain."

"And why have you transferred here?"

"I served in Gaul years ago with the Sixteenth Legion. I'm more at home here than in Spain—or in Rome."

"Does it concern you to serve under a commander younger than you with little experience of war?"

"If it does, I'm serving in the wrong army."

"By the gods! Is it your special prerogative never to answer a question directly?"

"No, commander. It's the privilege of twenty-one years and seventeen wounds in the service of Rome."

Sabinus hesitated.

"Commander, the day may come when you need my experience. Then I'll show you how to use it without feeling diminished by the need."

Sabinus smiled. "A fair bargain. Now I have something to discuss with you about another Greek, but first you have visitors. The local chieftain wants to see you." He rose from his stool. "He even brought his wife. That's unusual. The sight of her would stretch any man's bow string."

"Are you sure they have the right man? I know no chieftains here."

" 'The Roman who speaks like a Sequani' is what he said. And one thing more—" Sabinus paused at the door and looked back—"If they have any questions for you, give them a treat—give them an answer."

Rufio took two stools from the side of the room and placed them in the center before the desk. When the visitors came in, the sun was behind them in the doorway and he could make out only silhouettes. They entered with the arrogant stride unique to the Gauls.

"Welcome," Rufio said.

"I am Adiatorix. This is my wife."

Both appeared to be in their early thirties.

"Please sit."

Adiatorix was the man to have at your side in a strange forest at midnight. At least six feet tall, he had shoulders as wide as an ox cart and hands that could have powdered marble. Auburn hair flowed to his shoulders, and a heavy moustache drooped past his chin. He wore a yellow and blue striped tunic with a leather thong at the waist, deep blue linen trousers tied at the ankles, and soft leather shoes.

"We've come to thank you for what you did," the chieftain said in serviceable Latin.

Rufio was trying to focus on Adiatorix, but the man's wife presented an enormous distraction.

"And you are . . . ?" Rufio asked.

"Varacinda."

She filled out a short-sleeved blue and red checked tunic. Over it she wore a brown leather jerkin, and her trousers, too, were leather.

"I appreciate your gratitude. What have I done to earn it?"

"You saved the life of my cousin," the woman said. "My uncle says you are the bravest Roman in Gaul."

Varacinda's hair had the sheen of gold coins held in the palm at sunset. Long and dense, it was swept over and back as though she were perpetually caught in the wind.

"The armorers," Rufio said.

"My uncle told me you spoke to him in a way that touched his heart and then you faced that desperate slave unarmed."

Rufio leaned back against the edge of the desk and folded his arms across his chest. He idly thumbed the ring on his left forefinger. "No Roman soldier is ever unarmed. Even naked, he still has his training and his experience."

"That doesn't diminish our gratitude," she answered, scorning the Roman's lessening of his deed.

A slave entered with a bowl full of dates and cut apples. Rufio gestured at the Gauls, and the slave offered them the fruit.

Rufio watched the woman's lips as they changed shape around a slice of apple.

Adiatorix stood up. "Please accept this small token of our gratitude and friendship."

The chieftain removed a gold torque from his neck and gave it to Rufio.

"Thank you."

"I know Romans don't wear these things as we do, but keep it as a symbol."

Rufio looked to the woman. "And thank you also."

She gazed at him in supreme self-assurance, like a horse half-broken but never really tamed. Her high cheekbones gave her a fierce beauty, sharp and cutting.

Rufio looked back to Adiatorix. "Please don't be offended if I tell you that the whole business was for me a small matter."

"No," the woman said. "It was not. You couldn't know how much it meant." She paused, shaken by some emotion she struggled to control. "Last year I lost my sister Larinda. My uncle and cousin and my one dear friend are all I have now, besides my noble husband."

"My wife's sister was visiting a village down the river when the Suebi raided it. She was carried off with several others."

Rufio laid the torque on the table and walked across the room as he stared at the floor.

"Was there retaliation?" he asked at last.

"No," Adiatorix said. "The legion had a different commander then. He seemed more concerned with his political career than with matters of honor. He feared angering Rome by rousing the Suebi to war. He did nothing."

"And you?"

"He wouldn't allow us to take to the field in pursuit."

"I'm sorry."

Then Adiatorix seemed to see Rufio for the first time, or at least to see him in a new way. "You look familiar to me. Have you been in Gaul many years?"

"What is time in this peaceful wilderness?"

"But your mastery of our language . . . That couldn't have come quickly."

"Language is a tool, like a sword. A soldier needs all the tools in the forge."

Adiatorix smiled. "Sabinus warned me that answers from you are as rare as the tears of a wolf." He turned to his wife. "Come."

She took her place next to him.

"Again we thank you." Adiatorix led the way out the door.

The woman paused and turned. "And your name?"

"Rufio."

"I am Varacinda," she said unnecessarily and then stepped into the sunlight.

He gazed after her for a long time, then picked up the torque from the table. Heavy, yet elegantly wrought, the gold ring sported a snake head at each end, one facing the other. Footsteps in the doorway caused him to look up.

Adiatorix was back in the room.

"When I was a boy there was a rebellion by our tribe against the Romans. We lived upriver in a smaller village. Is it possible you fought against my people then?"

He laid down the torque. His eyes answered for him.

"And did you have black hair then and did you ride a golden horse on that terrible day?"

"Yes."

A horrified recognition filled the chieftain's eyes.

Rufio simply looked at him.

"We are all here now. . . ." Adiatorix said.

"All? What do you mean?"

"All the survivors. We joined with this village after that awful day."

"Surely not all can be here."

"Many of the old have died since then—but we who were young are all here."

Rufio turned away, leaning one hand against the table. "I never thought . . . "

"Is it bad or is it good?"

"It's beyond belief. After all this time."

"It must be the will of greater powers than you or I," Adiatorix said, then turned and was gone.

Rufio stared after him with a face as ravaged as though it had been laid open with a sword.

6 A WORD IS ENOUGH FOR A WISE MAN.

Roman proverb

Like the outer side of the fort wall, the inner rampart was constructed of a sloping bank of earthen turves. Here on the inside, stairways of logs ascended the rampart to the walkway above. Up one of these stairs Diocles climbed with the tribune Titinius.

"We have everything here," Titinius said and swept his arm out toward the expanse below. "Our own workshops, bath houses, hospital, even our own veterinarium for our horses. We have granaries that can store enough provisions for over a year. A spring inside the fort supplies more sweet water than even thirsty soldiers can use. We're a self-contained town."

For the exuberant Titinius, his position as tribune was clearly not just another step in a political career. He reveled in his office here. His dark eyes were always alight and he was continually pushing back the hair shaken onto his forehead by his jerky movements.

Diocles gazed out over the fort and pondered a strange reality. No one who had not seen it could hope to comprehend, but now Diocles had seen, and he felt as if he were taking his first faltering steps toward grasping. This vast yet orderly array of buildings pointed to something unique in the world. Other peoples might spawn fine fighters, but what had that to do with this? Even the vaunted army of Alexander — could it be revived — would seem an agglomeration of oafs compared to . . . to what? Compared to some immaterial essence implied by these silent structures. This fort was not a mere legionary camp. Here in the midst of a people who not so long ago might have worn shaggy skins or smeared themselves with mud — here had been projected a visible manifestation of a uniquely Roman thought.

And from whence had that thought come? Diocles placed a hand on the railing and studied the men below. Even in those resolute faces there was no answer. Nor did there seem to be any precedents for an inquirer to study, any gradations to measure. Somehow, out of their own half-barbarous past, a people had made a momentous leap of mind and will that defied intellect. No wonder Romans often behaved as if they believed they had sprung full-grown from the brow of Jupiter.

"You seem lost in thought," Titinius said.

"Lost indeed," he answered with a half-smile. "What's the range of commands here? Explain the hierarchy to me."

"It's simple. The Legate is at the top, of course. Under him is the laticlavian tribune. He has the broad purple stripe on his tunic."

34

"So he's a senator?"

"He will be soon. Beneath him is the Camp Praefect. He's a former Chief Centurion who's spent his whole adult life in the army. We're without one at the moment. Ours retired and hasn't been replaced yet. Then the five angusticlavian tribunes" — he made a mock bow and touched the narrow purple stripe on his tunic — "come after him."

"But the tribunes aren't professional soldiers?"

"Oh, we're soldiers — of a sort — but we're destined for greater things at Rome. Here in the outlands we get our muscles toned. Sometimes we command auxiliary units."

Diocles nodded.

"Then comes the Chief Centurion. He's the centurion for the First Century of the First Cohort. Except for the Praefect, he's senior man in terms of service."

"What of the other centurions?"

"One for each of the sixty centuries. They can be a hard lot."

"In disciplining their men?"

"Among other things. Many are brutal, some less so. But theirs is no easy task. They must hold the line in the face of screaming Gauls or Germans. And they have to pick up soldiers who are squirting soft turds and get them to stand fast."

"Your point is what?"

"The centurions lash out often, but they also absorb much for the sake of the legion. When the blood of battle flows, it's centurion blood that runs most thickly."

"So when Probus told me the century is the focus of the legion, he wasn't exaggerating."

"Ask any common soldier — centurions rule the world. And they often die for it."

Diocles leaned against the parapet and gazed past the ditches and the open field toward the forest beyond.

"Are you ever uneasy out here in this wilderness?"

"What do you mean?"

"There's something terribly lonely here. This fort is an island in the midst of a dark sea. Who knows what monsters might spring forth?"

"You sound more like a Gaul than a Greek," Titinius said with a smile.

"It must be the air. These fields and woods could never soothe. They only threaten."

The tribune's expression showed he was still groping for the Greek's meaning.

"Oh, I know, I know, you're a self-contained world, but it's a dark land beyond this fringe of culture. How can anyone ever be at ease?"

Titinius didn't answer.

"I'm sorry. It must sound as if I'm trying to spoil everything for you."

Titinius laughed in his easy way.

"Go back to your duties, tribune," he said in a lighter tone. "I've kept you long enough from your proper work."

"Sabinus told me to watch over you until you learn to feel more comfortable here."

"Fear not. I'm about to trust my downy skin to one of those tender-hearted centurions who are so admired and abhorred."

"Yes, I know. Which one?"

"It hasn't been settled yet," he said and gazed across the streets below, busy as always with the movement of men and animals. "Perhaps I'm looking at him now. I hope the gods are looking at me — with favor."

"I thought all Greeks believed they were the favorites of the gods."

"What are those buildings up there?" He pointed to a cluster north of the fort.

"A civilian settlement. Roman traders and merchants. Gallic ones, too. And families of soldiers. Unofficial ones, of course."

"Unofficial?"

"Yes, since soldiers aren't allowed to marry. Didn't you know that?"

"No."

"But one cannot deny nature. So they form their own unions. Rome averts its eyes, and when the soldier retires he'll make a legal marriage."

"What's the term of enlistment?"

"Twenty years."

Diocles tilted his head forward as if he hadn't understood him.

"Twenty years," Titinius said.

"No, no, I heard you. I just . . ."

"These men aren't boys, no matter how young some might be. War is a serious business and these are serious men."

"But twenty years?"

"The Chief Centurion in this legion has been in the army for thirty-six years. It's a pitiless world beyond the marble of Rome. No army of farmers could crush a quarter million raging Gauls, as Caesar once did in a single battle. The day of the amateur spearman is ended."

Soldiers came and went up the stairs and along the rampart walkway as the two men spoke. Diocles now observed their manner and carriage with a new awareness.

"Hello, Probus," Titinius said past Diocles' left shoulder.

The centurion came up behind him.

"It doesn't take you long to get to know people, does it?" Diocles said to Probus.

"The tribunes seek me out for my wise counsel. Can you fault them?"

Diocles smiled.

"I'll relieve you of this burden," Probus said to Titinius. "Come, son of Zeus, we have things to discuss."

Probus led the way back along the rampart and up the ladder to one of the gate towers.

"Get yourself some refreshment," he said to the soldier on duty.

After he had left, Probus pointed to the single stool. "This is the most private place in the fort."

Diocles sat.

"I've spoken to a centurion who's agreed to allow you to live with his century if Sabinus approves."

"Thank you. I—"

He held up his hand. "You may curse me later. It won't be easy for you."

"I didn't expect it to be."

"He's doing it as a favor to me. We've been through many battles together. We've seen terrible things." He paused. "There's another reason, too. He said it might be amusing because you were the first Greek he ever met who didn't know his own name."

Diocles' face went slack.

"Ah, I touched the sore with the needle that time."

Diocles stood and paced the planks of the tower like a nervous animal. "How can I live with someone who just slew that slave?"

"Quintus Rufio never even raised a hand to a slave in my presence. And I've known him half his life."

"Oh, I don't say he did it himself. I—"

"The slave is on his way to Rome as happy as a meadowlark."

Diocles sneered.

"Don't call me a liar, Greek—even in your mind. Do it and I'll break your neck. Now sit and listen."

Diocles lowered himself to the stool.

"There are some things you should know about Rufio before you breathe his air. He's not a man for casual chatter. He chooses his words as carefully as he selects a weapon. I know information is what you want, but be tactful asking for it."

"I will."

"Avoid discussions about his early years in the legions. Don't press him too much on the wars of his youth or his battle scars."

"Most soldiers enjoy discussing those things. You did on the journey from Rome."

"I'm not Rufio."

"How long have you served with him?" Diocles asked in a tone respectful enough to imply penance for his earlier impertinence.

"Many years," Probus answered and sat on the floor.

Diocles rose from the stool and sat next to him on the hard boards. "Go on."

"We were together in the Sixteenth Legion when we were so young we could barely coax our rods to weep." He laughed. "But Rufio was always more skillful than I in finding a soft meadow for his lonely branch."

Diocles smiled but remained silent.

"Eventually we were transferred to different legions. Rufio served in Egypt and in Syria, too, I believe. Sometimes over the years we would intersect with one another. The last time was with II Augusta in Spain." He rubbed the back of his neck as if the memory of Spain made his muscles ache. "Those Cantabri are some of the toughest people I've ever fought. Caesar himself had a Spanish bodyguard. Did you know that? If he hadn't dismissed them, he'd never have been struck down on the Ides. Anyway, there was a rebellion up in the mountain country. After a show of Roman force, the Cantabri asked for a parley. It's not unusual to send a centurion as an emissary in these situations. Rufio volunteered. He always liked the Spaniards — in, fact he's always had a special way with people he helped conquer. Especially the Gauls, but the Spaniards, too." He nodded to himself, as if in confirmation of his own cynicism. "The next morning we found him in a mountain valley with a spear in his side."

Probus stood and stared off beyond the fort toward the distant forest.

"Then what?"

"How he lived I don't know. It was a hideous wound. He got a bad infection and was sick for a long time. He still doesn't look right to me."

"He seemed to be in pain when he climbed those hay bales to stare down the slave."

"Did he? I'm not surprised. And now he tells me he's going to retire."

"Perhaps he should."

"No, it's not wounds or sickness. The betrayal by the Cantabri cut something out of him. I don't know if it can ever be replaced." He dropped to one knee and looked at Diocles. "He was lying on his stomach in the fort hospital and was so sick he could barely open his eyes, but he forced himself to speak. He said, 'Probus, why must the honor of man always be a phantom? Is life no better than lies?'" Probus stood up. "From Rufio, life has drained far more than blood."

7   MAN IS A WOLF TO MAN.

Plautus

I am beginning to get my bearings in this place. Probus was right – it did not take long. The organization of the fort is so logical anyone could learn it with ease. Yet, if it is logical, why has no other army done this? There is a fine library here with a collection of military writings, which I have begun to read. I can find no parallel to these Romans. All other armies, even Alexander's, seem semi-barbarous and inchoate. No other fighting men I can find in my research approach the business of living in a military outpost with such relentless orderliness. What fascinates me most is that they implement their innovative approach to these matters in an off-hand way. The physical components of this fort and their arrangement are, as far as I can determine, unique. Yet these men appear not to revel in their uniqueness. They seem to accept it – even expect it – as a natural quality of themselves. Is this arrogance? Hubris? I do not yet know them well enough to give an answer. Perhaps they are like an eagle, which takes no pride in its ability to fly, for, after all, it is an eagle.

The Suebi prized pastureland. Their lean cattle were ever hungry, and the animals now gorged in the meadow east of the river. No Roman would have gazed at these beasts with any thought of dining. The stringy muscles of the German cattle looked as succulent as the torsion sinews on a catapult. Yet the carnivorous Germans had strong teeth.

Barovistus stood with one foot up on the barrel of a dead tree at the edge of the woods. Before him on the ground sat the Assembly of Warriors. There was no war chief of the tribe, for there was no war. The Council of Elders would allow no man to hold such a powerful charge in time of peace. Yet not long before, in the bloody conflict with the Cherusci, Barovistus had shown himself to be the most audacious war chief in memory. And the memory of the Germans was long.

"So what do the Romans do for us?" Barovistus said. "They give silver cups to our elders and call them Friends of Rome. Friends!" He had the ability to laugh and sneer simultaneously. "Dupes are what they are!"

"Why?" shot a voice from among the warriors.

He stepped away from the rotted tree, as though it represented the dead past. "Because they get soft on Roman bribes while we hunger for the glory of men. Why must we keep miles of land this side of the river uninhabited and empty of cattle? Because the Romans say so. Why can we cross the river only at certain points? Because the Romans say so. Why can we not cross at night? Why must we cross unarmed?" He glared at the warriors.

"Because the Romans say so!" the assembly shouted in unison.

"And why do the Italian dwarfs say so?" Barovistus roared back. "Because they fear us!"

A growl of approval rumbled through the assembly.

"Why should we halt at a strip of water. Do Suebi fear getting wet?' He sniffed loudly. "Well, maybe a few of you do," he said with a smile. "But that's a personal matter."

The warriors laughed and the tension eased.

"So why do the Romans draw a line before us as if they pointed with the finger of a god? Because beyond that line lie green fields and hard Celtic steel and ripe Celtic women. And the Romans forbid us to take them." He folded his arms across his chest. "Who are the Romans to forbid us anything?"

A cry exploded from the assembly.

"They come from their far-off land and point their steel at us and tell us to stay where we are. Are they gods?"

"No," said a voice from the crowd. A veteran warrior stood and took in the assembly with a glance. "They are Romans. If any of you don't know, be assured that it's the next closest thing."

The assembly was suddenly quiet, for the words of a former war chief were always worthy of respect.

The man limped to the front of the group and Barovistus stepped to the side, but not too far.

"Orgestes will speak," Barovistus said to the assembly.

Orgestes paused as he gazed across the turbulent sea of warriors. "Do you think the Romans rule Gaul because of bribes? Do you think silver cups have brought them to our frontier? Are the Celts such fools to barter land for bright metal? The Helvetii and the Averni and the Nervii and so many others? Are you such dull calves that you can believe that?"

"They are here because of their good swords!" shouted one of the warriors and he shook his own spear with its simple fire-hardened wooden tip.

"Their swords?" Orgestes smiled as he ran a hand across his bald skull. "Spanish designs and Celtic steel. Do you think they're here because of the temper of their metal? They face us across the Rhenus because they fight like no others fight in all the world."

"We sympathize with Orgestes and his terrible wounds at Roman hands," Barovistus said.

"My wounds are nothing compared to the death of a people. My father and all his brothers eagerly attacked the legions of Caesar, and all were slain by the great Roman. All cheered and shouted as you do today. All spilled their entrails onto the soil of Gaul."

"Caesar is dead!" a warrior yelled.

"His legions live," Orgestes replied. "And his awesome spirit lives in them."

"Shall we fear the ghosts of dead Romans, Orgestes?" Barovistus said.

Most of the warriors laughed, but others were unsure.

"Who fights better than the Suebi?" Barovistus asked of the crowd.

When they had quieted again, Orgestes stepped toward them. "You're all proud warriors. You fight like bears, ferociously. But the Romans fight like wolves — in a pack, with order, with purpose. In the face of cunning wolves, the most terrible bear is simply dead flesh."

"Orgestes speaks well," Barovistus said. "He's always spoken well. But now is different from then. Our fathers were ignorant of the Romans. We are not. I was a soldier for Rome. I was decorated by the Romans for valor against the Gauls. I know how the Romans fight." With a sidelong glance at Orgestes, he said, "They don't frighten me."

Orgestes stared at him in silent anger, then turned again to the assembly. "My friends, beware the man who observes his father deliver a spanking to a brother and then claims himself to know the feel of the lash."

He turned away and limped off with undiminished dignity.

"A great warrior," Barovistus said to the assembly. "But long since broken by Roman steel. We grieve for him but we cannot let tears rot our spears."

The assembly waited. Barovistus paused and allowed the tension to gnaw at them.

"But no war yet," he said at last, denying them the sweet release they craved. "We need more weapons. We need good steel. So first we'll prick the Roman ox and draw nourishment from its wounds. When we've fattened on its blood, we'll be ready. We'll tear its throat and devour it."

A string of Gallic slaves, seven young men and a girl of about eighteen, stood in a line before the mud-daubed wooden hut. All were tied with a three-foot rope between each of them. They gazed mutely forward.

The Germans had little taste for slaves, though they might keep a female Gaul for work or diversion. This girl, though, was delicate as a spring blossom, and so was worth much. Some leering Roman would pay well to caress such soft petals. For so fine a potential profit, the slave dealer would barter much hard steel.

Barovistus passed the slaves and entered his hut. The slave dealer rose from the ground to greet him.

"Hail, Priscus," the German said to the gaunt Roman.

"Hail, war chief of the Suebi," Priscus said. He reached down and pulled aside a brown blanket. Ten fine Celtic swords lay fanned out on the ground.

Barovistus seized one and drew it from its iron scabbard. A heavy weapon, it had a double-edged, three-foot blade and a rounded point. He tightened his fingers around the bronze grip and cut the air with a slashing "voom" as if he were splitting a Roman skull.

Priscus's lips stretched in a smile, but his eyes had the blank stare of a dead reptile.

"You make a fair deal, Priscus—as always."

"And the Gauls?" he asked in a dry voice.

"All excellent."

"And the girl?"

"What about her?" Barovistus said as he bent down to examine the other swords.

"Is she unsplit?"

"Yes, as far as I know. An unplowed field should bring you a sweeter price."

"Good. I'll be back soon," he said on his way out.

"Stop." Barovistus stood. "Share meat with us. Do you still have the two gladiators with you?"

"Former gladiators. When one travels among the Suebi, one does well to be armed with strong men."

"Well said," he answered with a grin. "Share food and drink now and tell me more about the marble cities."

After feasting on venison and milk, the four men lounged on skins in the hut. Barovistus went to a tub and ladled beer into clay bowls and passed them around. Then he dropped back onto his deerskin and drank with the rest.

"Have you ever been to the fort at Aquabona?" he asked.

"Yes," Priscus said

"Is it a legion or just some cohorts?"

"A full legion."

"Veterans?"

"Most of them."

A scoffing laugh shot from the throat of one of the gladiators.

"A comment, Longus?" Priscus said.

"Veterans or not—what difference does it make? They clean latrines more than they pick up their swords. Soldiers fight when they have to. These Suebi fight because they love to. That is everything."

Longus might have been handsome had it not been for the legacy of an old sword strike to his face. A scar ran from his upper lip back under his left eye to a spot over his ear where the black hair refused to grow. As thick in the waist and hips as he was in the shoulders, he formed a huge tube of bone and muscle.

"Longus is right," said the other gladiator. "We fought more in a month than most soldiers do in a lifetime. They dig ditches and build roads. We killed men."

Barovistus smiled. "Sido speaks well. You are not Italian?"

"My mother was of the Cherusci."

"Great fighters," Barovistus said.

In his early thirties, and so a few years younger than Longus, Sido clearly gloried in his own physical perfection. His torso formed a flawless "V" as it tapered to his narrow waist. His muscular legs were hairless, and they looked as if they could be cut in half and still support him on their stumps.

"Maybe I should recruit gladiators for my army," Barovistus said half-seriously as his eyes ran over Sido's impressive contours.

"Spartacus tried that," Priscus answered.

"Who?"

"Never mind. We must be moving." He rose and gestured to Longus and Sido.

"Where are you headed now?" the war chief asked.

"Aquabona. I'm to purchase a Greek slave from one of the tribunes."

"Greek?" Sido said with a telling hunger.

"Not for you," Priscus said. "You may have one of the Gauls."

Barovistus raised a hand. "No words from you, Priscus, about what you heard in this camp."

"To the soldiers? My tongue is as tight as my purse. Kill them all if you like. What do I care?"

———

Priscus and his group made camp at sundown in a clearing in the midst of the forest. The Gauls were given porridge, and they huddled around a small fire as they ate.

The Romans had a large fire to themselves about twenty feet away.

"Will you sell the girl to me?" Longus asked and bit into a strip of salted beef.

Priscus narrowed his heavy-lidded eyes. "You could never afford her. What you mean is will I give her to you."

"You promised one of the men to Sido."

Sido smiled.

"Only temporarily," Priscus said. "Do you want the girl to keep?"

"I never ask for much," Longus said.

"That's true. And you've served me well."

The eager gladiator's eyes shone like a predator's in the firelight.

"But she could bring a fine price," Priscus taunted.

"Priscus, please . . . ."

"Very well, I'll consider it."

Sido sprang to his feet. "Longus, I'm ready."

The two gladiators walked over to the group of Gauls, and Sido pointed to a smooth-faced boy of about twenty. Longus untied him from the rest and led him into the forest. Sido went to the cart and took a lump of lard from one of the food sacks, then followed Longus into the woods.

The Gaul's arms were pulled forward and his hands tied around the trunk of a tree. He was stripped from the waist down.

Without a word, Longus walked off and left Sido to his play.

A shaft of moonlight slashed like a silver sword through the trees and struck the frightened Gaul. The blonde gladiator removed his tunic and linen undergarment as he gazed at the young man's taut buttocks. Spreading lard around in his hands, Sido began stroking himself leisurely. When he could bear no more, he approached the Gaul, who was trembling. Sido smeared the lard tenderly around his buttocks and down the crevice. Placing his hands on the Gaul's shoulders, he stepped close and kissed him on the back of the neck as he pierced him with ease. The Gaul cried out and pleaded in a language Sido could not understand. Gently Sido stroked him as the Gaul gasped and groaned. But Sido's delicate touch soon vanished as he lost control. His buttocks flexed into enormous knots as he hammered the young man repeatedly into the tree. Even the creatures of the forest paused for a moment, startled in the darkness by the bestial growls of pleasure.

8   TRUTH BREEDS HATRED.

Terence

Not since the summer night that he and Cornelia had lost their virginity in each other's arms had Diocles felt as nervous as he did now. Again he was a virgin—and of a very special kind.

The barracks of the First Century of the Second Cohort—like all the other barracks—was a single story timber building at least a hundred and fifty feet long and some thirty or more feet wide. Along the front wall ran a shaded portico. The building was L-shaped, one end wider and protruding from the rest of the long structure. Along the back ran a narrow metalled street with a second barracks block on the other side. Presumably this housed the Second Century.

A series of wooden trapdoors lay flush with the ground before the portico. Diocles lifted one. Set within the timber-lined hole was a wicker basket partly filled with rubbish. He set the lid back down.

Ten wooden doors ran along the portico. He approached the end door and opened it and stepped inside. He was in a room about twelve feet square. Despite the warm day, the air in here was cool. Wooden shelves and storage bins lined the walls. Along the right wall, shelves at eye level and slightly below were divided by wooden partitions so each soldier had his own storage space. In each niche was a short sword in its scabbard, a dagger, a chain mail lorica, and a bronze helmet. Below were compartments holding a pickaxe, a saw, a woven reed basket and some string bags and leather sacks. A bigger bin overflowed with three-foot wooden stakes with points at each end and a narrowed area in the middle. A large communal bin was neatly filled with cooking pots and utensils, and a separate one held a small stone grinding mill.

Along the left wall ran a series of tall bins holding the soldiers' long curved shields, each one wrapped in a protective goatskin covering. Attached to the wall next to these bins was a wooden rack with about two dozen javelins. Set vertically, each throwing spear was held apart from the others, apparently so the iron heads would not touch each other and suffer damage.

The penalty for theft must have been severe, for nothing here was secured.

Diocles crossed the storeroom and passed through a doorway to a second room beyond. Here were the living quarters of some of the soldiers. As wide as the outer storage area but several feet deeper, this room must have housed eight men. Four pairs of bunks were arranged around the walls. In the far wall was a stone and tile hearth, cool now.

Before it in the center of the room sprawled a low oak table. Scattered across it were empty plates and drinking vessels and several dice. To the right and left of the hearth was a pair of windows. Their shutters were open to ventilate the living quarters. The walls were plastered and unmarred. The clay floor was an unusual construction he had never seen before. Fragments of terra cotta tiles had been pressed into the clay and rammed to produce a firm but not uncomfortable living surface. It was as clean as if it had just been swept for his inspection.

No door connected this room with any others, so he went back the way he had come. He entered the next pair of rooms and found them to be similar to the first. The only difference was in little idiosyncrasies in possessions and living arrangements reflecting the tastes and manners of different men.

He left the soldiers' living quarters and walked along the portico until he came to the end of the building that was wider than the rest of it. He opened the door and confronted a cluster of rooms that clearly comprised the quarters and the administrative workspace of the centurion. Probus had mentioned that he was not certain if Rufio had moved in yet. Diocles stepped into the first room. This was obviously the century office. Along the walls to both left and right stood bins filled with papyrus scrolls and a lesser number of waxed writing tablets. A window let in light from the far wall. About three feet in front of it sat a heavy oak desk and stool. Above the table, a bronze three-wick oil lamp hung from a chain. Near the far right corner sat a bronze brazier to provide heat against the sharp Gallic winters.

He stepped further into the room as his eyes grew accustomed to the dim light. Rufio must have begun to settle in, for a scroll and a bronze pen and inkwell lay on the table. Diocles picked up the scroll. Apparently it was some sort of duty roster. A list of soldiers, each with a number preceding his name, formed the left column. The right side was arranged into a series of columns, one for each of the next ten days. Here the duties of the men were written — "street cleaning," "gate guard," "escort to Chief Centurion," "latrines," "armory," "training area," " road patrol," "leave by Praefect's permission," "duty with Sempronius's century." The most common entry was "in century," presumably meaning that the soldier's duties were left to his centurion's discretion, which Diocles had been told was vast.

While he was reading, a cat jumped onto the table and began licking one of her paws and washing her face. She was a striking animal, with hair longer than what one usually saw. Beautifully blotched with white and black and brown, she seemed very pleased with herself and ignored him completely.

47

He put the scroll down just as he had found it. Adjusted now to the room's half-light, he noticed a marble bust off to the left near the back wall. He stepped closer and was surprised to see that it was not the usual likeness of Augustus. Julius Caesar stared back at him. The large head, the hard cheekbones, the prominent nose were caught just as they must have been. No idealized Hellenic portrait here. The sparse hair combed forward in Caesar's famed vanity. The etched cheeks, and those eyes—eyes wise beyond the borders of reason, wiser perhaps than any other man's had ever been, eyes masterful and tragic and reaching. Diocles averted his eyes, humbled by Caesar. Gazed upon from marble as so many had been gazed upon in life, Diocles looked off toward the window. For a while he stared at nothing and then at last looked back. The makeshift wooden plinth on which the bust rested was draped with a piece of purple velvet, a simple tribute from a possibly not so simple soldier. Diocles had not known what to make of Rufio, especially after Probus had told him of the sparing of the slave. Yet though he could not help being touched by this humble shrine, for the moment his judgment remained suspended. For a soldier, who must travel light, to haul across the empire a marble bust of a man he could never have known—even though that man be Caesar—spoke of subtle essences Diocles was reluctant to attribute to a man who lived with his hand on a sword.

"Welcome."

Diocles jumped and turned around.

Rufio swung into the room with that easy stride Diocles remembered so well from the first day he had seen him. He was wearing his rich blue tunic and seemed fresh and bright, an effect heightened by his fair skin and silver hair. Somehow Rufio always seemed as if he had just stepped from the baths. On the forefinger of his left hand he wore a bronze and cornelian signet ring. Diocles suspected he was something of a dandy.

"Hello," Diocles said, surprised at the deference in his voice.

Rufio leaned back against the edge of the desk and folded his arms across his chest.

"You seem uneasy, Greek-with-no-name."

"Please, may we forget about that day?"

"If I'd killed that desperate Greek, you wouldn't have been willing to forget it."

"Why should I have cared about that slave?"

"If I thought you didn't, you wouldn't be standing in this room now."

Diocles looked at him with a puzzled expression.

"He was a countryman of yours," Rufio said. "A man should always care about his countrymen."

"I'm a citizen of Rome."

Rufio smiled. He reached over the desk and picked up the stool and set it down in front of Diocles.

"Soldiers rarely sit in the centurion's office. This will be your first and last time."

Diocles sat on the stool.

"You wish to share the life of a soldier?"

"I wish nothing of the kind."

It was Rufio's turn to look puzzled.

"I wish to be in Rome tutoring the son of Sabinus."

Rufio's eyes narrowed in a squint Diocles found unnerving. "Then why are you here? You're a free man."

"I shouldn't need to remind a soldier that no man has perfect freedom."

"True."

"It's the wish of Sabinus that I be here. My regard for him is such that the choice is no longer a choice. As it is with you and Probus."

"Probus?"

"He told me you would've done this for no one else. That you agreed for me to be here as a favor to him."

Rufio lowered his arms and pressed his fingertips against the edge of the desk. "Probus is mistaken."

"Then why—"

"Where are your belongings?"

"I come to you a scraped tablet. Smooth wax to be etched by your knowing hands."

"It looks like I'll have to get accustomed to having my life seasoned with your Attic salt." He pushed himself away from the table. "At least until you're too exhausted to open your mouth—in other words, until tomorrow." He looked at the scroll. "If this roster is accurate, this century has no optio. I have no idea why. Originally I was going to inflict you on him. . . ."

"What's an optio?"

"The man who takes command of the century in battle if a German spear sends me to Acheron." He set the scroll down. "So for now you'll learn from me. You'll live like a soldier, train like a soldier, and, if you wish, play like a soldier. There are flocks of prostitutes in the civilian settlement if you—"

"I have a wife."

"Here?"

"In Rome."

The hint of cynicism in Rufio's eyes annoyed Diocles.

"She's there — your needs are here. But do as you wish. In all other matters, you'll do as I wish. And you'll not take the sacramentum. There's no point in oaths if you're not going to be a permanent soldier."

"Whatever you think is proper."

"And of course you'll be paid. Deductions will be made — as they are for everyone else. For food, clothing, weapons, and armor."

"What's the rate of pay?"

"Two hundred and twenty-five denarii a year." He smiled. "You seem surprised."

"That's not an insignificant sum."

"Soldiers of Rome are not insignificant men."

That I never doubted. He gazed at the grooves in Rufio's cheeks. Those scored depths told of more hard-won silver than any man could hope to hold.

"You seem in fair condition," Rufio said and ran his eyes over the meat on Diocles' bones.

"An agile brain is useless in a flaccid body."

"A bit thin, though. How old are you?"

"Thirty."

"For a recruit, you're an antique. But you'll have to deal with that in your own way."

"I'm no idle scholar, centurion. I've tracked and hunted boar and wolves on horseback and on foot."

"With what weapons?"

"Bow and spear. My father taught me when I was young — before I became an antique. With a javelin I can drop a charging boar at fifty feet."

"Perhaps we can revive those fading skills."

Footsteps on the portico diverted their attention.

Rufio looked beyond Diocles' shoulder, and Diocles noticed the humor in his eyes vanish like the sun behind a fog bank.

Ulpius Crus strode into the room, and anger snapped against the tiles with every step.

"Do you mock me, centurion?"

The tribune was in his twenties but he seemed older. His long face was an inverted pyramid, the lower part pinched and hungry for something nature had not given him.

"Mockery is the tool of weaklings," Rufio said. "Therefore, the tribune is mistaken."

"Am I?" Crus paused to catch his breath. "An example was to be made of the slave. That was why I agreed to give him to you."

"You agreed because you had no choice."

"I? No choice?"

"Your careless handling of the slave almost led to the death of a loyal Gaul. You stumbled into a bog, tribune, and I reached down and pulled you out."

Crus gave a scoffing laugh. "You did not—"

"But I expect no gratitude. That's the rarest of virtues. I've fought in many lands and haven't found it. I don't expect it here."

Crus hesitated, clearly stunned by this insubordination.

Diocles suddenly feared for Rufio.

"You walk on fire, centurion. Prepare to be consumed by it. I'm a powerful enemy."

"When the tiny asshole of the baby Crus was still squirting yellow, I was pulling arrows from my body on savage frontiers."

He stared in disbelief. "Mark this day with a black stone."

Crus turned and darted from the room like a thrown spear.

9   MANLY EXCELLENCE FLOURISHES IN TRIAL.

Roman proverb

---

*M*y *judgment is already in question. Centurion Rufio does not seem as cold as I first thought. Neither is he a benign uncle. I do not know what he is. This disappoints me. I thought that here at last was a circumstance without ambiguity. For once there would have been no uncertainties, an absence of those shadings that make life such an effort to comprehend. Here, of all places, one would have expected to find it. A society of warriors — what could be simpler? Are not fighting men the least complex of men? Men strong or weak, brave or cowardly, born under good birds or bad. What a relief it would have been to find oneself in a world where judgments were made with ease. Perhaps we all long for a place where we can decide at a glance what is good or foul. Once in our lives if we could find that secret land. The gods are not so kind. They make everything a struggle, for reasons of their own. I thought that here, in this wilderness, life could be shed of its complexity like the sloughed skin of a serpent. But I fear I have foolishly neglected a basic truth. The army of Rome is, in one respect, like every other gathering on earth — it, too, must recruit from the human race.*

"*W*ell, what do you think, Paki?" Rufio said and reached down and ran his hand through the cat's fur. "Is it time to throw raw steel into the forge again and hammer out something that cuts deep?"

When his hand neared her neck, she tilted her head as an invitation to scratch behind her ear.

"No answer today?" he said and stopped rubbing.

She turned and looked at him with wondrous emerald eyes that angled upward at their outer edges. She stood up and extended her head toward him. He lowered his face, and with her raspy tongue she licked him several times on the end of his nose. Then she lay down again and rested her body against his forearm on the desk and purred loudly.

Though she might not have understood every word he said, Rufio was certain she knew at all times precisely how he felt. And his gratitude to this ten-pound beast was boundless. He stroked her and it soothed him as much as it pleased her.

Finally he stood and, after one more caress along her back, he stepped around the desk and crossed the room to the doorway.

Though it was only midday, the men of the First Century of the Second Cohort had been relieved of their duties and had been ordered to assemble in the open area next to the barracks.

They were arriving now. All wore off-white tunics, some dirty from road repair or ditch cleaning. None of the men had a sword belt, though a few wore their daggers.

They had not yet met their new centurion. Curiosity on the faces of the veterans contrasted with the anxiety in the eyes of the recruits. No doubt the new men had already been battered with horrifying tales of centurion brutality. Soldiers had few pleasures, and torturing recruits was one delight they treasured. Rufio remembered well the time many years before when, as a young soldier, he had asked a recruit if he had reported to his centurion to pick up his masturbation papers. The poor farm boy had had no idea what that meant, but the word sounded important and he did as he was told. The cuffing he got from his centurion was a quick dispenser of wisdom. And Rufio, too, had derived from it some distinction. The congenial lad eventually made many friends, but there was only one man about whom he thought long into the night and despised.

Rufio picked up the three-foot vinewood cane leaning against the doorway and stepped out into the sun. The humor in his eyes seeped back into him as quickly as water spilled on sand.

The soldiers became quiet, and all stood straight and alert.

Rufio stopped before the middle of the line of some six dozen men and looked to right and left.

"I'm Quintus Flavius Rufio," he said in his penetrating voice. "I've served in the army of Rome longer than some of you have been alive. I plan to continue serving until all of you have learned enough to stay alive long after I'm gone."

He knew that statement would rankle the veterans. Experienced soldiers — especially those who had been bloodied in war — were always cocky with a new centurion. That had to be countered. Some centurions, especially the brutal or unsure, went right at the veterans' testicles with some crushing verbal smash. He knew better. A quick flash of the gelding knife was usually enough.

"A centurion's record of service is important to his men," he went on. "If you wish to know mine, come and ask me or catch me in a tavern in the settlement. It might cost you a cup of wine or a sweet cake, but I'm easily bribed."

"Like all centurions," came a grumble from one of the veterans.

Rufio acted as if he hadn't heard it. "Arrange yourselves in order of seniority. Then count off and remember that number. If I shout your number in battle and don't hear an answer, you'd better be dead."

He could distinguish veterans at a glance, but he wanted a precise idea of each man's relative experience within the century. The men broke up and shifted until the most senior stood to the left and the recruits finished the rank off to the right. Then they counted down.

"Those of you with the thickest calluses have heard a centurion tell you to forget everything you've learned because now you were going to be remade in his image. That's the counsel of an idiot. Forget nothing. But there's always more to learn."

"Is that true of centurions, too?" one of the veterans asked, probing for some hint of the centurion's mettle.

"Of course. That's why a centurion is the wisest man on earth."

The soldier smiled.

"Two things are unacceptable to me, and they won't be endured in this century. The first is theft. If you don't respect the property of your comrades, you don't respect their dignity. A man without respect for his friends' dignity is useless as a warrior and worthless as a man." He paused for a moment. "The second thing I detest is a man who lies to conceal his mistakes. If a man fears to confront his own errors, how can he face a horde of charging Germans? Physical courage without moral courage is a hard scabbard with a weak sword. Violate either of these two principles and I'll break you down to kindling and throw you into the flames."

He paused while that sank in. "There's going to be one more soldier in this century. He's a Greek writer and a scholar, but he's also adept with a weapon or two. And he's a citizen of Rome. He'll write a history of life in the army of Augustus—as Polybius did for the army of Scipio. He'll be a soldier in all ways, except he won't take the sacramentum. Treat him as well or as badly as you'd treat anyone else." He laid the vinewood cane across the palm of his left hand. "I see only a few of you are wearing daggers. Swords are not necessary within the fort, but I want that dagger nailed to your hip. We're soldiers first. And even if you're bed wrestling with a Gallic beauty, I want sword and dagger nearby."

"Question, centurion," said one of the veterans.

"Speak."

"I'm new to Gaul. Is it true that a hard Roman sword fits most snugly in a soft Gallic sheath?"

A wave of laughter rippled through the line of men.

Most of Rufio's face remained immobile, but his eyes smiled. "Yes—and you might be lucky enough to find out. But with that face, I doubt it."

All laughed even more loudly than before.

"Now," he said to the entire century, "the day is young and the remainder of it is yours. You may go to the baths or relax in your own fashion. I enjoy being loathed only by well-rested men."

Even the veterans smiled at that, and the recruits were already at their ease.

"One more thing," Rufio said. "The soldier who made the remark about centurions and bribes step forward."

The century was suddenly as still as a dead man's ashes.

A soldier came out from the veterans' end of the line. He was in his late twenties with curly black hair and a half-boyish, half-rakish face.

"I made the remark, centurion."

"Name."

"Lucius Valerius."

Rufio placed his right hand around the young man's throat. Without strain, apparently without any effort at all, he lifted him off the ground with one hand. It seemed an impossible feat, but there it was for all to see.

"Mumbled remarks are the words of a coward," Rufio said so only Valerius could hear. "There will be no cowards in this century."

Red in the face and hungry for air, Valerius pulled at Rufio's fingers.

"Drop your hands," Rufio whispered. "I once crushed the windpipe of a Syrian bandit with one squeeze. Surely you can outlast a Syrian."

Valerius lowered his hands by a tremendous act of self-discipline.

"Keep them down," Rufio said.

Valerius dug his fingers into his palms as the sweat popped from his face. He strained to maintain control.

The whole century seemed to be holding its breath as well. Even the veterans moistened their lips and sucked in air as if they, too, were being squeezed.

The eyes of Valerius were beginning to glaze when Rufio finally set him down.

Gasping, he struggled to stay on his feet but fell to one knee.

"If you wish to speak, speak with the full force of your voice. Century dismissed."

The legionary workshops were housed within a timber building in the central range of the fort east of the Principia. It was sited far from the fort hospital so the noise did not annoy the patients. Square in plan, it was a well-built structure arranged around a central courtyard. Rufio passed by the plank-covered rubbish pits out front and went through the courtyard. A rectangular wooden water tank filled the center of the yard. It was fed by a timber aqueduct and drained into a clay-lined ditch that carried fouled water beneath the building and under the Porta Principalis and so out of the fort.

The rank smell from the tannery was thick enough to build a road on. Rufio sliced through the reek and passed the carpentry shop and entered the armory.

Here the smell greeting him was much different. The sweet pungency of burning charcoal blended with the aroma of hot metal. Instantly it recalled to him his early days in the army when he had gone to pick up his first set of armor. Without thought, he inhaled deeply and savored the sharp smells that revived the fragrant hours of youth.

The pounding of iron on anvils was loud but not unpleasantly so. He passed among oak tables covered with swords and iron tools, bronze and iron helmets and chain mail loricas. Horse bits and harness fittings filled wooden bins, and iron wagon tires lined one wall. The Roman armory officer in charge was not present, but a half-dozen Gauls worked at that superb metalworking that was one of their greatest talents.

When the chief armorer saw Rufio, he set down his tongs and hammer and hurried over to him. It amazed Rufio that anyone could work among these flying sparks without a tunic. Perhaps all that hair protected him. His upper body, including his shoulders and back, was as woolly as the torso of an unsheared sheep.

"Centurion Rufio!" the Gaul said with genuine pleasure.

Rufio looked at him in surprise.

"You saved the life of my son. Can I not show you the respect of knowing your name?"

He was much more fluent in Latin now that an arrow was not pointed at his son's head.

"And you are . . . ?"

"Hetorix, chief armorer."

"Well, Hetorix, I need a new sword."

"Swords are my life."

Rufio had no way of knowing how good an ironworker Hetorix was, so he decided to test him. He reached over to his left hip and pulled his sword from its scabbard.

"What do you think of this one?"

Hetorix took it and examined it, then looked at Rufio in surprise. "This is a very old weapon."

He sat on the edge of a table and laid the sword across his lap. His hands ran over it with the comprehension of those of a Greek surgeon examining a diseased organ. The two-foot, double-edged blade was scored in countless places. The edge was nicked and gouged, and the flat of the blade had many pits where rust had begun to feast and then had been removed. The bronze and hardwood guard was battered, and the octagonal bone grip, with its four carved finger contours, was beginning to split. The round hardwood pommel was still serviceable, but it too bore the scars of years of hard use.

"You're not old enough to be the original owner of this weapon," he said as he pulled at his chin. "The quality of the metal tells me that. It's good, but we do better now. I'd say this is at least forty years old."" He looked at Rufio for confirmation.

Rufio was always impressed by professionalism. He knew he had found his man.

"You know your metal. It belonged to my father."

"Ah."

Rufio took the sword from the armorer's lap. "He wielded it against the Nervii."

"He fought with the great Caesar?"

"Yes. The blood of many Celts tempered that metal."

"And that's why it's survived so long," Hetorix answered in solid rejoinder.

The two men's eyes took each other's measure.

"I want to retire this sword and get a new one. You're the man to make it."

"Of course I am. It'll be better than that one" — his marred and darkened face creased in a rough smile — "but perhaps not so heroic."

"Definitely not."

"Come, I'll show you how we do it. Are you familiar with the working of iron?"

"Only when it enters someone's body."

They threaded their way among the tables and came up to one of the forges.

"We heat the iron billet slowly with charcoal until it glows like a maiden's blush," Hetorix said and pointed at the hot red slabs. "We've learned that the charcoal is the secret. It mixes with the iron and hardens it and helps the blade keep its edge. When we're done we have good Celtic steel. After we hammer out the blade we temper it by plunging it into cool water"—he pointed to several wooden tubs—"and then we have a blade that is hard and true. But it's brittle. So we heat it again and let it cool slowly. The brittleness flees like a young girl's sighs, but the hardness stays. And with this steel you Romans guard the edges of the Empire."

Rufio untied a leather sack hanging from his sword belt and took out a block of very dark wood.

"Can you use this for the guard and the pommel?"

Hetorix took the heavy piece of wood and hefted it, then examined the grain. "Beautiful. What is it?"

"Ebony. I brought it back from Egypt."

"Ah—yes, I should have known it. But I haven't seen much of this. I'll dull many edges working this noble wood."

"How much for the whole business?"

"Five denarii—not a small amount, I know, but—"

"I'll give you ten for the best sword in Gaul."

"Give me eight," Hetorix said, "and I'll give you the best sword on earth."

10   THUNDERBOLTS THAT STRIKE BLINDLY AND IN VAIN.

Pliny

The sun had set by the time Rufio finished meeting with the other five centurions of the Second Cohort. As the senior centurion in the cohort, Rufio would command all six centuries in battle. Two of the centurions had served with him in other legions, and they had been happy to see him. That had lifted his spirits. And they were in need of lifting. His back wound was pulling him down, and the appearance of Adiatorix had revived the pain of an ancient agony.

The sound of a galloping horse stopped him along the Via Praetoria. He turned and looked back up the street. The hoofbeats told of trouble racing through the night air. It was odd how the tension of a rider conveyed itself to his mount. This horse sensed much.

"Centurion!" the rider said as he pulled up before him.

In the bright moonlight, Rufio recognized Titinius.

"What is it?"

"Orders from Sabinus. Report to the Porta Praetoria. The Gauls are howling and reaching for their spears. The chief demands to speak with you. Take my horse."

Titinius dismounted and Rufio sprang into the saddle. He reined about and galloped off toward the main gate.

The invigorating wind buffeted his face and the ache in his back was gone. He pulled up before a cluster of men just inside the gate.

Torches held by several soldiers blazed in a semi-circle before a pack of angry Gauls. Sabinus stood calmly in front of them as Adiatorix argued and pounded a fist against his own chest. Four centurions flanked Sabinus. All were wearing their swords.

Rufio slid from the saddle.

"Quiet!" he shouted above the Celtic din. "Respect for the Legate of Caesar!"

The Gauls stopped as if they had been struck in the face.

Rufio strode across the open ground toward Sabinus.

Clearly pleased that Rufio had come, Adiatorix stepped forward, but Rufio placed his hand against the Gaul's big chest and pushed him back. He walked by the chieftain as if he did not exist.

"Commander," Rufio said.

"The Gauls have a grievance and they wish to address you. Adiatorix believes you will speak for their cause."

"Does he?" Rufio said and turned to face the chieftain. "My loyalty is to my commander and my cause is the will of Caesar. Now what is your complaint?"

Stunned by Rufio's response, Adiatorix hesitated.

"Speak, Gaul, or go."

"A slave dealer is on his way to Aquabona. We had word from a village downriver. He brings with him many Sequani slaves—people from our own village. We demand these slaves be restored to their homes."

Rufio turned to Sabinus. "May I speak, commander?"

"Yes."

"Who are you to demand anything?" Rufio asked the chieftain.

"We're a noble people loyal to Rome."

"You're a conquered people. You may demand nothing. You may request."

"Then we request," he said, biting the words to death in his mouth.

"And Rome declines," Rufio answered. "Slaves are the lawful possessions of their owners. The soldiers of Caesar have no legal right to interfere."

"You had the right before these people were enslaved. But that commander didn't act and then stopped us from acting."

"There's no need to repeat the story. That was unfortunate—but a chieftain of the Sequani should be wise enough to know he cannot recover the past."

"I misjudged you," Adiatorix said. "I was childish enough to hope you might speak up for these people."

"They're not my concern."

"They are loyal subjects of—"

"They're property! Like a saddle or a dog. Are there no German slaves in Gallic huts? Are there no German heads in jars of cedar oil above Gallic doors?"

Adiatorix glared at him in useless rage.

"You play the game, Chief, and when it fails to go your way, you call on Rome to smash the dice."

Adiatorix whirled and vanished through the gate like a fierce wind. His men hurried behind.

Some of the younger soldiers holding torches laughed, as young men will, but the centurions remained silent.

"Thank you, Rufio," Sabinus said and dismissed his men.

"Commander," Rufio said, as Sabinus was about to head for the Praetorium.

The Legate looked back over his shoulder. "Yes?"

"This is not the end of it."

"I know," he said and turned and walked off into the darkness.

Of the many rooms in the barracks allotted to the centurion, Rufio had chosen a pair with a southern exposure as his primary living and sleeping quarters. He tossed his dagger belt onto a wicker chair and stepped up to the brazier in the corner. Adorned with lions' heads, it was a pleasing sight after the snarling Gauls. He rubbed his hands together above the embers to melt away the chill.

The walls were adorned with Oriental tapestries he had brought from the East. Below them were racks holding scrolls of military writings and other histories he had collected during his years in the army, and which he still studied.

He took a glowing ember with a pair of tongs and lit the three oil lamps hanging from the bronze stand near the couch. The clever arrangement of the lamps softened the shadows and made the room pleasant and cozy.

He returned the ember to the brazier, then lay down on the couch.

"Neko," he called out, but the man was already on his way in.

"Thank you," Rufio said when the Egyptian handed him a cup of heated wine. "Do you always read my mind?"

"Yes."

"What do you read tonight?"

"Weariness, I think."

"Did you call the augurs? You don't need a haruspex to read that."

"Perhaps not."

"Tonight the slave-owning Gauls were screaming about slavery. What do you think of that?"

His full dark lips widened in a smile. "Do you expect the Gauls to be logical? Do you expect them to be Greeks?"

"Of course, he had a good point, but I wasn't in any position to concede it to him."

"I'm sure you acted in your usual judicious manner."

"Tell me, if I gave you your freedom, what would you do?"

"I would thank you and go and get you another cup of Setian wine."

Rufio gazed at him with mock disappointment. "Don't you think that would make you a fool?"

"But is it not so that the fool is happier than the wise man?"

Rufio laughed even though it hurt him to do so. "It is so, Neko, it surely is. And it's just as sure that it was a happy day for me when I plucked you from the Nile."

"Like Moses."

"Who's that?"

"A Hebrew prophet."

"Well, you don't look the part. Go to the first barracks room and bring Lucius Valerius to me."

Rufio set aside the cup and stared at the ceiling. He grunted when Paki bounded onto his stomach. She walked up to his chest, then settled down and began kneading her claws into his blue tunic. Her purring was as loud as muffled thunder.

"You'll draw blood soon, my girl," he said as her sharp claws sank through the wool to his skin. He placed two fingers under her chin and scratched, and her eyes narrowed to slits of contentment.

When he heard the metal studs of Valerius's sandals snap against the floor tiles, he picked up Paki and set her on the end of the couch. He took an armless wooden chair from against the wall and placed it opposite the wicker one.

The two men entered and then Neko withdrew.

"Reporting as ordered, centurion," Valerius said in a neutral voice.

"Sit."

Being asked to sit in a chair was a privilege bestowed only on women and honored guests. Valerius seemed surprised—and wary. The glances he shot around the room showed he had never before been in the centurion's living quarters.

Rufio sat across from him in the wicker chair.

"I need information. Before I begin training tomorrow, I want to know the history of this century."

"May I ask the centurion why he picked me to tell him?"

"Because I want to know. Tell me about the centurion."

"Titus Herennius was a fine soldier. But he was long past his day. Old injuries and sickness dragged him down. He was eager to retire. He fought at Actium. Did you know that?"

"No."

"He didn't have the energy anymore to discipline. But we didn't need it—we were a disciplined century. But then something odd happened. It's hard to believe, but you can—"

"If I didn't believe you'd tell me the truth, I wouldn't have ordered you here."

Valerius hesitated.

"Patience is not your new centurion's strongest quality. Tell me the story."

"There was a Gallic boy about eleven or twelve who liked to watch us train. He'd sit near the parade ground outside the fort and stay with us for hours. Even veterans can be flattered by that—though they'd never admit it. We adopted him as one of our own. Everybody took to him. He was a wonderful boy."

Valerius frowned and averted his eyes as he gathered his thoughts.

Rufio remained silent.

"One day we were marching near the lake. The boy was marching along next to us. We had the cobbler make him a pair of army sandals and Hetorix hammered out a dull-edged sword for him. He was as proud as any boy could be. While we were marching, a raven fell out of the sky—just dropped dead and hit him on the shoulder. It startled him but that was all. Yet many of the older soldiers said it was a bad omen. Everyone was quiet the rest of the day . . . ."

"And then what?" Rufio said after Valerius had paused too long.

"The next day was no different than any other. But the day after that the boy was not around. Herennius and a few of us younger men went into the village to see if anything had happened. We found his mother and father bending over him in their hut. His body had broken out into a mass of suppurating sores. He was burning up and delirious. We got one of the camp doctors—he's Greek and a good one. But no treatment worked. The next day he began vomiting green slime. He died that night."

Rufio interlaced his fingers in front of his waist. "It's a sad story, but there are many sad stories in life."

"No, there's more. The next day the optio fell off his horse and broke his neck. Twelve years in the legions and he breaks his neck. Two days later a soldier choked to death on a piece of salted fish. Three days after that, two soldiers drowned while swimming in the lake. Sank like stones. No one could explain it. Then the idea spread that the century was cursed. Twenty-two men died of accident or sickness within a month of the raven's fall."

"And what do you think?"

"I never placed much trust in omens. I do now."

"And Herennius?"

"That was the worst of all. He began to waste away. He was a tough old boar, but he just started to disappear. The flesh melted from his body. The doctor was baffled. Herennius had no pain but he had no will left, either. He was shriveling to a husk in front of us. One day during a break on the march, he let us rest longer than usual, so I went to look for him. He was sitting against a tree—as dead as dust, eyes wide open. I never want to see anything like that again."

"Has anyone died since?"

"No, but the damage is there. There's a disease of the heart among the men that's spread like foul humors. Some in the century are even saying we don't belong here. Leave Gaul to the Gauls they say, or to the Germans or to whoever else wants it." He paused. "But don't ask me who said that, because I've forgotten."

"I wouldn't even consider asking." He stood up. "Thank you. Go to bed."

11   USE MAKES MEN READY.

Roman saying

I *am about to become a soldier, and the anxiety I feel can barely be put into words. I am an outsider pushing at the door of a closed society. These are not men like Greek hoplites, who trudge off to battle in the sunny interlude between when they plant their seeds and the time they harvest their crops. They are here in the sweetness of spring, but they will also be here when the snow falls. They do not march out to protect their vineyards or wheat fields. These men are a professional army who must stand resolute and untiring for the finest years of their lives — some for their entire lives. Decades of training and experience are given over to preparation for war, deterrence of war, prosecution of war. What will such men make of me? Suddenly I am so frightened I can hardly breathe. Sleep is impossible. I feel I am about to be consumed.*

Diocles thought he would get an early start by arriving at the barracks before dawn. Everyone was dressed and washed, and the aroma of hot wheat porridge and bacon hung in the air.

"I'm Diocles," he said and he took a tentative step through the doorway.

Most of the seven men gazed at him with that half-surly, half-indifferent look reserved for any outsider. It was the price to be paid by anyone attempting to enter a world where experience counted for much.

"Come in," a soldier sitting on a stool said in a friendly tone. "That's your bunk."

Diocles laid down the leather sack that held some personal items.

"I'm Valerius," the soldier said. "The tesserarius. These wild hairs from a sow's belly are the best tent group in the legion."

A few managed to force a nod.

"Unless you're aiming for Vestal Virgin, take off that ridiculous tunic and put on the one there on the bunk."

"But it's been sun-bleached as a symbol of my goodness and piety," he said and reached for the off-white one.

Several of the soldiers cracked their cheeks in a smile.

"Fine. That means there still might be hope for us to have our character improved."

Diocles peeled off his tunic and donned the slightly darker one. Also on the mattress were a bronze helmet, a pair of military sandals, a belt and dagger, and a bronze water flask.

The leather sandals had thick soles studded with dome-headed nails. The upper parts sported a confusing array of thongs. As Diocles bent over, he shot a glance at the feet of one of the soldiers to see how they were fastened.

The dagger was formidable looking. The double-edged leaf-shaped blade was about ten inches long with a strengthening ridge down the center. A thin sheet of bronze overlaid the handle and the scabbard was hammered from the same metal. Rectangular plates of tinned bronze decorated the leather belt. He fastened the belt around his waist with the dagger at his left hip, like everyone else.

"No sword for you yet," Valerius said in answer to Diocles' questioning look around. "Not until you learn how to use it."

The water flask had been filled by someone, a thoughtful touch that surprised him. He tied it to his belt by the strap around its neck.

"Helmets on and let's face the sun," Valerius said.

The helmet was heavier than Diocles would have thought, and it was fitted inside with an iron skull plate. Fortunately, the helmet was lined with leather. He pulled it on and fastened it under his chin by the leather ties attached to the cheek guards.

The century began assembling in the open space between the two barracks blocks. The puffy-eyed soldiers were yawning and loosening up when Rufio emerged from the building. Diocles knew that by now he should not have been surprised by his appearance. He looked as if he had just been scraped and buffed. Didn't he sleep rumpled and messy like other men? Maybe he simply leaned himself against a wall at night like a spear.

He stood before the center of the rank with his hands on his hips. Diocles had noticed that the centurions wore their swords on their left hip and their daggers on their right, opposite the way of ordinary soldiers.

"All awake?" Rufio asked. "Good. Today we march. There's an auxiliary fort about ten miles north of here. We march there and back, military pace, six hours. Health check—anyone ill or injured, step forward."

No one did.

"Good. Iron men. Let's march."

When the men, six abreast, filed through the Porta Praetoria, the pink sun was just topping the trees on the horizon. The column turned onto the metalled road and headed north.

Diocles was not accustomed to such early rising. He struggled to stifle a yawn when he noticed Rufio glance his way.

The damp air invigorated as only a spring morning could. After the fetid alleys of Rome, Diocles had forgotten how miraculous the effect of sweet air could be.

The century passed the civil settlement north of the fort and moved into the countryside, though they remained on the stone road. Like the recruits, Diocles had no idea how to march. Yet the new men were given no instruction. Apparently they were expected to pick it up by observation. Even more obscure was the reason for marching. It had always seemed to him an idiotic way for men to walk.

Yet as the morning wore on and the column began to generate its own rhythm, the purpose of marching became obvious. Rather than being wearying, it was effortless once one got the feel of it. In some odd way, the legs took on a life of their own and swung forward without any conscious exertion at all. One's mind could focus on other things, such as observing the terrain for enemies, and still the legs carried one forward in a way in which indifferent trudging never could.

And there was a mental component as well. Diocles found the metallic cadence of the hobnails on the stone strangely compelling. It would have been no less so for the other men, though perhaps all were not sharp enough to realize it. Yet all must have felt it. The snapping rhythm of the nails was not simply the feet of men — it was the march of Rome. Relentless, reasoned, filled with the surety of its own destiny. True, there had been other marching feet down the centuries. Yet this was not the headlong rush of Xerxes and his ravening Asiatics. Nor was it Alexander and his amazed troops kicking in the doors of collapsing empires without thought or purpose. Something far different was rolling through the Gallic countryside.

Mid-morning came before Rufio called the first halt. The column left the road and relaxed on the grass of a shady grove off to the right.

Diocles pulled the leather stopper from his flask and took a small drink. "What is it?" he asked when Valerius sat next to him with a puzzled look. He noticed several purple bruises on the soldier's neck.

"I don't know," he said, shaking his head. "I was ready to hate that motherless swine and then he does this. I don't know."

"Does what?"

"Gives us six hours for a five-hour march. That's the standard — twenty miles, military pace, five hours. But he gives us six."

"Is that bad?" Diocles asked and reached down and rubbed his feet.

"He probably did it for the recruits. I've never known a centurion to put any slack in the rope—for new men or anybody else." He shook his head again. "I don't know."

"I'm surprised he's not riding. I've seen his horse. It's a beautiful animal. Small, though."

"It's Numidian. No one breeds horses like the Africans. Rufio knows his mounts. It's unusual for a centurion to have his own horse. He's probably traveled with that stallion all over the empire. I've heard old soldiers say a Numidian can live on grass alone. Survive without grain."

Diocles gazed toward the edge of the glade. Rufio was sitting on the ground apart from the men with his back to them and staring into the distance. He seemed like the kind of man who would own such a horse. Life lived to its limit.

"I want to hate the bastard," Valerius said. "He almost strangled me yesterday."

"Why?"

"I made a remark about centurions taking bribes. By the gods, they all take bribes! If you want to avoid some dirty job or go on leave, you have to bribe them. It's part of the system."

"They why complain?" Diocles asked with annoying Greek fatalism.

"They get paid more than fifteen times what a common soldier gets! Yet every time you need a favor, you have to give them a sweetener. Blood-sucking leeches."

"You gave yourself a title earlier. What was it?"

"Tesserarius. I'm in charge of assigning work parties for different jobs within our century. The name comes from the fact that it's also my duty to get and pass the watchword for the day. I get it on a tessera from one of the tribunes. Then I countersign the tablet and send it back. It changes every day."

"Sounds like an important position."

"I get one and a half times the pay of an ordinary soldier. But I'll never rise any higher. I speak my mind too much."

"Discretion is one of the noblest virtues."

"See that sandy-haired fellow? That's Metellus. You saw him in the barracks. He's the signifer for our century. He carries our standard in battle—ours is a silver boar—and he's in charge of the century money accounts. Soldiers' savings and deductions from their pay and things like that."

"Speaking of that, when do we see silver?"

"The next stipendium is in about three weeks. May, September, and January. Seventy-five denarii for your blisters. But you won't get any this time. Recruits get no money until they're entered onto the books as trained soldiers. That takes about four months. They got traveling money, though, before they left home."

Diocles looked at his swelling feet. "I think I'm being underpaid."

The sudden intensity in Valerius's eyes caused Diocles to turn and follow his gaze.

Rufio was on his feet and staring like a predator at some black speck on the road in the distance.

"Century up!" the centurion said without looking at his men.

"He is cautious, isn't he?" Diocles said.

"Yes," Valerius agreed, in spite of himself.

A cart full of people, driven by a middle-aged man with a dagger in his belt, came into view. Two riders followed.

"Just slaves," Valerius said. "They must be the Gauls that all the noise was about last night."

"There was trouble?" Diocles gazed at their hopeless faces.

"Adiatorix wanted them freed. They came from his village originally. The Germans snatched them awhile ago."

"Why? To trade?"

"The Suebi piss on Roman money, but they like Roman goods. The hairy-faced barbarians don't know the first thing about making iron, but they know how to raid and rob and then barter for what they want."

"There's a young girl with them." Diocles watched Rufio approach the cart. "What's he doing?"

"I don't know. It was Rufio the chief asked for help."

Diocles snapped around in surprise. "And did he give it?"

"No. A centurion's loyalty is to his legion—not to this fallen race. What's wrong? You look disappointed."

"Do I?"

Rufio let the cart and riders pass and they traveled south down the road.

The century fell into line again, but now Rufio had them march next to the road rather than on it. At first this seemed a sweet release from the hard stone, but soon Diocles' thighs and hips ached as he struggled to march over the uneven ground.

"We should be at the auxiliary fort soon," Valerius said when he saw the sweat running down the Greek's face.

"My head feels like it's baking inside this helmet."

Valerius laughed. "We don't usually march with our helmets on."

"What's an auxiliary fort anyway?"

"A small fort for a troop of foreign soldiers who serve Rome. This one holds an ala of Gallic cavalry. Five hundred strong."

"They're not citizens, then?"

"No, but they will be on discharge."

A cool breeze heavy with the scents of spring flowers caressed Diocles' grateful face.

"Even the Germans are enlisted sometimes," Valerius said. "Caesar himself used German cavalry against the Gauls. We have our own cavalry — about a hundred and twenty scouts and messengers. But the Gauls and Germans are better horse-fighters."

"So you use whatever works best. . . ."

"It's the Roman way."

As the century marched on, Rufio took a position near Diocles and Valerius. The man seemed tireless. His face looked as cool and dry as if he had just risen from a nap in some shady bower.

He turned and gazed back over his shoulder.

"Century halt!"

Diocles had heard nothing, but now he detected hoofbeats. He looked back the way they had come. A horseman was racing toward them up the road from the south.

"Titinius," Valerius said while the rider was still a good distance off.

"You have a sharp eye," Diocles said.

"Mostly for young ladies."

"Quiet in the ranks!" Rufio ordered.

The tribune reined up his lathered mount in front of Rufio.

"The century is ordered to return to the fort immediately," the tribune said. "We found three murdered Roman traders on this side of the river."

"Germans?" Rufio asked.

"Looks like it. Money was still near the bodies. Sabinus wants to take counsel with his senior centurions."

"Are there any other centuries out?" Rufio asked with obvious concern.

"All are in but you."

"Good." Rufio ordered the century about.

"Do you want me to ride with you?" Titinius asked.

"No. Go back to the fort and tell Carbo we're coming in now."

As they began the march back, Diocles turned to Valerius. "How did he know where to find us?"

"Rufio had to give a report to the Chief Centurion on where we'd be. We keep records on everything. Documents are the blood of our army."

Diocles scanned the forest off to the left, but no hostile horsemen were visible.

"What will happen now?" he asked and continued to search the woods for lurking enemies.

"Difficult to say. Sabinus is no slug, like the last commander. He may act. Trouble is coming, don't doubt that. And with Germans it always gets worse before it gets better."

12 TO EVERYONE, HIS OWN IS BEAUTIFUL.

Roman saying

The soldiers of Rome are a diverse lot. The impact of Rome has been so great throughout the Italian peninsula that the term "Roman" has come to signify far more than the citizens born on the banks of the Tiber. Judging from the variety of accents here, I would guess that few of these "Roman" soldiers call Rome their home — or, indeed, have ever even been there. I questioned Titinius about this and he confirmed it. He says the centurions prefer to recruit lads from the farms rather than the cities. The country boys are stronger and healthier than those who must daily inhale the effluvia of Rome. Licinius, lean and wiry and eager, comes from a farm outside Mantua. Plancus, a good-natured ox of a youth, hails from a small village near Neapolis. The short but formidable Arrianus comes all the way from Venusia. Now they are all citizens of a single community, the arrogantly self-contained world of the Roman legion.

An afternoon breeze slipped in through the window and soothed the back of Rufio's neck. He paused in the notations he was making and savored the spring air's caress. When he picked up his pen again, he was interrupted by footsteps in the outer room.

There are many varieties of beauty. The man coming through the doorway possessed the sort only a soldier of Rome could love.

Rufio stood at the approach of Sextus Rutilius Carbo, Chief Centurion of the Twenty-fifth Legion.

"Sit down, centurion," Carbo said in a voice informed with the gentle nuances of cinders being crushed in an olive press. He scooped up a stool and dropped it in front of Rufio's desk.

"May I sit?" he asked unnecessarily.

Carbo sported a patch over the place where his right eye had once lived. The patch and thong were cut from a single piece of leather and dyed bright red. A scar snaked out from beneath it and crawled up toward his scalp. Only a fringe of silver-white hair protected his head from the weather. Yet a head such as that needed little protecting. The bald dome squatted on the neck like a capital on a marble column. It seemed as if could sit there forever — and it probably would.

To Rufio, every wound was like a torque of silver awarded for valor, but he knew many felt otherwise. Facial disfigurement was considered especially appalling, even disgraceful, particularly by civilians, so great was the Italian obsession with physical beauty. Even some political and religious offices were barred to those maimed in this way. Rufio was certain Carbo would never leave the army.

"I've checked the service records of all my centurions. Only four have ever fought Germans. You are one. How would you advise Sabinus?"

To be asked for an opinion by a man such as Carbo was an honor.

"As much as you or I might like to, we cannot go to war over the three merchants. If a full-scale bloodletting is the only answer to every outrage, we've lost all flexibility. And you have to stay flexible and keep your ability to maneuver—even against barbarians."

"You sound like a politician."

"My experience has been that soldiers are better at politics than politicians are at soldiering."

Carbo snorted in agreement. "What would you do then?"

"We could send two cohorts for a sharp strike. Bloody their face."

"And you'd offer that advice to Sabinus?"

It was clear that Carbo was testing him.

"No, I would not."

Carbo folded his arms across his chest. His dull red tunic looked like it had been new when Romulus was still swinging from the nipple of the wolf. With his big torso and thick bowed legs, he hid the seat beneath him. It seemed as if at any moment the stool might slide upward and disappear between his buttocks.

"Why not?"

"Because that's exactly what the Suebi want us to do. They know we won't send out a full legion for the dead traders. They're trying to lure out a smaller force and then annihilate it."

"Then what would you tell Sabinus?"

"To wait for a bigger provocation and hit them with eight cohorts. Hit them hard and give no quarter."

"Good." Carbo stood up. "That's exactly what I advised him. There's talk in the legions and in Rome that Drusus is planning a campaign for this summer."

"Drusus is the man to do it. But even if there's no campaign, we cannot sit on our shields if the Germans cross the river. If they march, Sabinus cannot wait for orders from Rome. The time is coming to hurl those savages back into the forests that vomited them out in the first place."

Carbo walked across the room and pushed the stool back against the wall. "There's a rumor in camp that you plan to retire." He straightened and looked back toward the centurion. "If war comes, I need you."

Rufio nodded but said nothing.

"Stand by me and I might even celebrate by buying a new tunic," Carbo said and turned and walked toward the door. "I know that would please you."

Rufio smiled at Carbo's back as the Chief Centurion waddled on his bent legs out of the barracks.

"Neko," Rufio called after Carbo had gone.

As usual, the Egyptian appeared as swiftly as a specter.

"Find Valerius and bring him here."

When Valerius arrived a few minutes later, Rufio did not offer him a seat.

"You're the optio of the First Century."

"No, centurion, I'm the tesserarius."

"You're now the optio. Double pay of course. You may move into these quarters or stay where you are — the choice is yours."

Valerius looked stunned.

"You're a very experienced soldier and you're one of the few people I know who'd have the courage to call me a fool if you thought I deserved it — or allow himself to be strangled if I ordered it. So I'm taking a chance on you. Don't add yourself to the long list of people who've disappointed me. Dismissed."

He just stood there, dazed.

"Well?" Rufio asked.

"I don't . . . I . . ." He cleared his throat. "Thank you."

"The centurionate is within your grasp if you learn to put a rope on your tongue."

"Yes, centurion. Any other orders for the day?"

"Go celebrate."

Valerius was barely gone when Titinius came in. He did not seem pleased to be there.

"What is it?" Rufio asked in exasperation. Did no one realize how much clerical work the command of a century entailed?

"Sabinus demands to see you immediately."

The centurion rose without a word.

"Don't you want to know why?"

"Do you want to tell me?" Rufio said, surprised to find an ally among the tribunes.

"It's Crus," Titinius answered with the expression of someone who has just chewed on a bitter root. "He wants your balls."

Sabinus was seated at his desk when Rufio arrived. He had his chin in his hand and seemed absorbed with some distant problem.

"Commander," Rufio said, rousing Sabinus from his preoccupation with raging Germans.

He looked up in annoyance. "When you took that slave from Tribune Crus, all you did was create problems. The slave dealer came here to make his deal with Crus, but of course there was no deal to be made — thanks to your beneficence."

"If I hadn't spared him, Crus would have killed him, so the slave dealer would still be out of a deal."

Sabinus ignored the logic of that. "Add to it that Priscus and his two over-muscled gladiators barely got here with their lives — or so Priscus claims. Crus insists the least we can do is offer Priscus protection from the Gauls — that we owe him that for his trouble in coming here. And, of course, I'm responsible for the welfare of Roman lives here. Gallic ones, too, for that matter."

Rufio gazed at the handsome young Legate. The burdens of command were pulling him down like a dozen mail loricas at once. He was clearly less than pleased that Rufio had added one more. Yet despite being the focus of his anger, Rufio found he was beginning to like the new commander very much.

"Do you understand what I'm saying?"

"I understand you, commander, but I thought I'd already been suitably reprimanded for the folly of generosity."

The muscles of Sabinus's jaws looked like they were about to burst the skin.

"Are there more like you, Rufio? Tell me now so I can fall on my sword and end the dread."

"My mother told me I was unique."

"The gods aren't that kind. I ordered you here to call on your experience with the Gauls and ask you if Priscus is truly in danger."

"Yes, he is."

"They'd slay him to free the slaves?"

"Who are 'they'?"

"Adiatorix and his people, of course."

"How would you know it was he? He could say it was Gallic bandits who did it and then fled into the wilderness. Would Sabinus retaliate against a possibly innocent village?"

"No, Sabinus would not."

"The Gauls are capable of slaughter and worse."

Sabinus sighed and passed his hand across his forehead.

"Where are Priscus and the slaves now?" Rufio asked.

"Here — within this fort."

"They should stay here for a while and leave at night. The Gauls wouldn't expect that. They can be very simple in these matters and that just wouldn't occur to them. Priscus would be out of the region before the Gauls woke up."

"Very well. Now, something else — off the official record. Am I obliged to give them a military escort? Crus implies that I am."

"Crus is wrong. If you were obliged to provide soldiers to everyone who felt threatened by a Gallic snarl, you'd thin the cohorts to skeletons. Who'd be left to bribe the centurions?"

Sabinus gave him an amused look.

"Commander, there aren't enough soldiers in all of Gaul to give bodyguards to every Roman trader. If you see a Gaul draw his bow, then naturally that's another matter."

"All right. Two things more. First, in case you're blind to it, Crus is no admirer of yours, so — "

"Do you mean my affection is unrequited?"

"So," Sabinus continued, "be more tactful. You may not care for him — frankly, I don't care for him very much myself — but he is the laticlavian tribune."

"Yes, commander."

"Second, Varacinda, the wife of Adiatorix, is here to see you. We don't need an augur to tell us why."

"The slaves."

"Apparently Adiatorix thinks your intercession might be gotten by a more tender approach."

"Is this really necessary, commander?"

"I thought it politic to agree to it. It's your own fault. The incident with the slave now annoys you as much as it annoys me."

"Yes, I — "

"They see you as their spokesman now," Sabinus said and rose and walked across the room.

Rufio stared after him.

"Such a simple people," he thought he heard Sabinus say as he disappeared through the doorway.

Varacinda stepped into the room. She took long strides, as though even walking were for her an aggressive gesture. Again her reddish gold hair was swept to the side, as if she had just stepped out of the wind. This day, though, her eyes seemed less bold than they had before.

"Thank you for seeing me, Centurion Rufio," she said and stopped in the center of the room.

Rufio placed a stool in front of her.

"Thank you. I'll stand."

She moistened her lips as she gathered her thoughts — or her courage. She wore a black leather jerkin over a bright green tunic. Her leather trousers were tied at the ankles in typical Gallic fashion, and Rufio could see her toes bunching nervously in her soft leather shoes.

"Speak to me, Varacinda." Rufio leaned back against the desk and folded his arms. "I have other responsibilities to attend to."

"I don't know how to begin," she said with a fear that was baffling.

"Then let me. You want me to try to arrange for the release of the slaves."

"Yes," she answered in a near-whisper.

He hesitated, a sudden thought flashing across his mind. "Adiatorix doesn't know you're here, does he?"

"No."

"Why are you here?"

She wet her lips again. "To plead with you to get me back my sister."

He dropped his arms. "Are you sure?"

"I saw her in the cart on the road. Surely there must be people you love. You must know how I suffer for her suffering. I want my baby sister! I want her! I want her!" The words rushed out of her now. "Don't tell me about slaves and property. About rules and laws. This is my sister! She's beautiful and fragile and she'll be violated. You know that. You saw those gladiators. She'll be pinned and rammed by some foul Roman bull. By all the gods you believe in — "

"Woman, what do you expect from me?"

Then Rufio, the man of war who had trod the wildest edges of the earth, was stunned by the simple words of a Gallic woman.

"I want you to ask the slave dealer to take me in her place."

At last he understood what he saw in her eyes.

"I cannot do that," he answered, masking his awe at this woman. "You're the wife of a chieftain of the Sequani."

"I'm a desperate woman who would rather be the toy of a brute than see a tear on her sister's cheek."

"Get out of here."

She did not move. Fury and fear and desperation shot from her eyes.

"Get out!" Rufio heard himself shout.

By a titanic force of will, she held her emotions taut. "I thought you were different. After what you did for my cousin, I thought you were more than a Roman."

"Woman, no one is more than a Roman."

She stepped closer, the hard-boned beauty of her face inches from the creased face of the warrior.

"You're not special," she said as she fought to stop the tears from spilling out of her eyes. "I thought you were, but you're a wolf like other wolves. You tear and you eat and you toss aside. I hope you die slowly and in agony."

It was a horrifying curse, and it seemed to shock even the woman who cast it. She spun around and vanished before Rufio could take another breath.

13 THE ASS RUBS THE ASS.

Roman saying

The bathhouse was one of the few stone buildings in the fort. Sited near the intervallum, that space between the rampart and the camp proper, it had been built on a grade that fell away toward the wall, so the continual streams of flushing water could be dumped. The effluvia rushed off in closed channels and ran out under the side gate.

The late afternoon sun heightened the rich color of the building's red roof tiles as the two soldiers approached the entrance. Diocles longed to purge himself of the dirt and aches of the march. Valerius seemed unaffected by the exertions of the day.

They entered the building and went into the changing room. Here the discipline and rigor of life in the legions was forgotten. Talking and shouting rocked the walls of the big rectangular room. Some soldiers were dressing or undressing, but others were lounging around and swapping lies about wars or women. Several sat on benches and played board games. Off to the right, four men squatted on the flagstone floor and played dice. The spot they had chosen was very appropriate. In the wall next to them, seven arched niches housed statues of favored deities. Occupying the central niche was that most elusive of goddesses, Fortuna, whom they now tried to woo or whom a few cursed as a whore.

Valerius and Diocles stripped and hung their clothes on a rack and entered the latrine to the left. Capable of accommodating at least fifty men, the room was noisy with the flush of flowing water. Large stone benches with holes lined three walls. Beneath the seated soldiers, bent forward now in silent contemplation, a vigorous flow of water flushed away the sewage. In front of each seat was a small hole in the stone floor where one could set his personal stick and sponge. Also cut into the floor in front were a pair of deep channels which flushed with a constant flow of fresh water. Here the men could wash their sponges after they had cleaned themselves.

Valerius picked up an iron stylus that was lying on one of the benches. Into the plaster wall he etched the date. Then beneath it he scratched: L VALERIUS OPTIO.

"Now I'm immortal," he said with a smile.

The two men relieved themselves and went back through the changing room and into the coolness of the frigidarium. They washed their hands and face and took a quick cold plunge bath.

Refreshed, they entered the pleasant warmth of the tepidarium. Flues beneath the floor and within the walls carried in heated air from the perpetually stoked furnaces.

"Did you hear what happened when we got back this afternoon?" Valerius asked and sat on one of the benches.

"No."

"The wife of Adiatorix went to Rufio about those slaves."

"The ones we saw on the road?"

"Yes, they're here now. The slave dealer and his men were almost caught near the woods by some Gauls and barely escaped with their lives."

"How do you learn these things so quickly?" Diocles asked in amazement.

He laughed. "I have friends in every cohort. And Titinius and I have shared a meal or two."

"So what did Rufio do?"

"What could he do? He sent her on her way with a slap on her sweet ass — and that's a sweet one. Have you seen her? Give your eyes a treat sometime."

"Do soldiers ever think about anything but carnal pleasures?"

"Not often."

After producing a couple of mild sweats, Diocles and Valerius went into the next tepidarium, this one warmed not with dry air but with steam. The lounging soldiers in here were quieter than those outside. Valerius stretched out on a bench, and Diocles sat and rubbed his blistered feet.

"Will we march again tomorrow?" he asked.

The new optio shrugged.

"Well, if we do, I think I'll choose to fall on my sword."

"That would be a clever trick. You don't have a sword."

"Then I'll fall on my head," he said and sprawled on the bench with a groan.

He dozed off and was roused after a time by Valerius pulling on a toe. They moved off toward the hot room.

"Dry or steam?" Valerius asked.

"You sound like a cook," Diocles said and led the way to the steam.

The caldarium was tiled with black and white mosaics of leaping fish, no doubt to distract one from the steam's stifling tyranny. Diocles lay down and felt his pores open and expand in luscious agony. As the grime was drawn from him, he thanked the gods he had been born in Rome. All his life he had felt pulled between his ancestry and his upbringing. But at this moment he reveled in being a Roman. Other peoples simply did not bathe enough. No one else on earth—not even his blessed Greeks—understood these matters. Only the Italians grasped the supreme virtues of cleanliness. And only they were brave enough to endure this purging which was both savage and sublime.

"What of the war counsel?" Diocles said with an almost unbearable effort.

"I don't know the details, but I hear that Carbo told Sabinus to wait for a major breach." Valerius rolled over on his bench and peered through the steam. "One thing you'll learn is that the best soldiers are cautious about drawing their swords. And they come no better than Sextus Carbo."

"Why the caution? I'd have thought the opposite."

"Good soldiers know that an army about to go to war is like a boulder on the edge of a slope. It's slow to get moving, but once it starts rolling, there's no way to turn it around—at least not without people getting crushed."

Diocles pushed himself up on one elbow. "And . . . ?"

"And Carbo won't urge war until the Germans draw so much blood that Sabinus has no choice but to fight to a conclusion. Carbo won't risk his men in a weak effort."

"And how is someone as young as you so wise in these matters?"

"Young? Life out here ages us quickly. Look at Rufio."

Valerius rose and Diocles followed him into the adjoining room, a combination unctuarium and hot plunge bath. The two men lay face down on tables as the attending slaves hurried over.

"Gently," Diocles ordered.

One of the slaves, a young man of Eastern origin, took his curved bronze strigil by its wooden handle and scraped the dirt and sweat from the yielding flesh. When he had finished one side, Diocles rolled over on his back and the slave continued his ministrations on the front.

"You have a delicate touch," Diocles said.

The young man smiled with pride.

When the thorough scraping was finished, Diocles slid off the table and crossed the semi-circular room to the bath. He eased himself into the steaming water with a sigh and allowed it to carry off the rest of those impurities that so foul the noble body of man.

In the meantime, the slave had cleaned the table. When Diocles reluctantly emerged from the water, the slave dried him with a towel and then told him to stretch out again.

He curled his forearm under his head as the slave massaged him with mint-scented oil. He moaned with the deep and relentless kneading of the muscles. Occasionally the slave would add more oil from a round bronze vessel hanging from a chain at his hip. Diocles groaned as the massage became even more vigorous, and he was convinced that this was almost as glorious as sexual love.

When at last the slave had finished, he left and returned with a dark salve with which he treated Diocles' blistered feet. Moved by this thoughtfulness, he promised the slave a sestertius on his next visit.

When the two soldiers returned to the changing room, they felt as grand as gods and fully as beautiful.

"Do it, Sido!" a soldier yelled.

The blonde former gladiator, stripped to his linen underwear, stood in the center of the room. Legs wide and braced, he gripped a large steel billet from the armory and focused all the strength of his upper body on the hopeless task of bending it double.

Soldiers cheered or hooted as wagers were tossed about. Sido stopped his exertions and asked for a rag. He tore it in half and wrapped a piece around each end of the slab and began again. A sheet of sweat made his skin shine like alabaster. He grinned as he warred against the steel. Clearly he gloried in the glistening magnificence of his own body.

A groan shot up from the doubters as the steel started to give. Like human resolve, once it began to yield, it failed quickly. A roar from the winners rocked the room as Sido flung away the vanquished metal.

"If you think that's power," Sido said after he caught his breath, "look at Longus."

The other gladiator was hanging up his tunic as the eyes of the soldiers sought him out. He turned around as they stared.

"Show them, Longus," Sido said. "Show them true greatness."

"Why fill them with envy?"

"Show us what?" one of the soldiers asked.

With fake reluctance, Longus stepped toward the center of the room. He clearly felt he had much to be proud of. He peeled off his undergarment and posed grandly with hands on hips.

"That's not possible," Valerius said as gasps escaped from the men. "Is it?" He looked at Diocles.

The Greek just shook his head in wonder.

"In the name of Mars," Valerius said. "It hangs halfway to his knees."

"That's no man," Diocles said. "That's one vast penis with a dwarf dangling from the back of it."

"It's as thick as my forearm," Valerius went on. "What must it be like when it's hard? What could a woman do but scream in terror?"

Several soldiers stepped closer to get a better book. Longus laughed as he held his penis in front of them and flopped it around, as big and limp as a dead weasel.

When Diocles had hunted wolves in his youth, his father had told him of the sixth sense a hunter has. The glare of unseen eyes exudes a force a hunter senses in his soul. Suddenly he felt again that strange discomfort. He snapped around.

Against a wall, Rufio stood with his arms folded and stared at Longus with eyes empty of love.

14 THOUGH THEY ARE SILENT, THEY CRY ALOUD.

Cicero

The slanting rays of the sun made Rufio squint as he walked toward the middle of the fort. The stables were situated in the central range of buildings, parallel to some of the barracks blocks.

In front of one of the wooden structures a soldier armed with a sword stood alone, eyes glazed by guard duty. He revived and straightened at the approach of the centurion.

"Easy duty tonight, soldier?" Rufio said.

"Yes, centurion."

"You look tired."

"Road repair today. The stones get heavy after a while. Even for me."

"They certainly do. Cohort and century."

"Third Cohort, First Century."

Rufio frowned. "Probus should know better than to post a tired man to a boring duty. I'll have you relieved."

"Thank you, centurion," the soldier said in surprise and gratitude.

"How are the slaves?"

"Quiet. No trouble." He hesitated. "I feel sorry for them. Their homes and families are so close. . . ."

"Where's the owner?"

"Here," a voice said from the shadows.

Rufio looked beyond the soldier.

"I'm Priscus," the man said and came out of the stable.

"I remember you. We met on the road."

"Ah, yes."

"I'm here to make a purchase."

That lit the fire in his heavy-lidded eyes.

"I want to buy the girl. Give me a price."

"That's rich," he answered and pulled on his chin. "Perhaps too rich for a simple soldier of Rome."

"You're boring me. . . ."

"The rugged palate of a rough man might not appreciate—"

"Two thousand sestertii."

"She's worth rather more. You saw her. You know what I mean."

"Three thousand."

Priscus shook his head with a smile and held up his hand. "I'm teasing you, centurion. I'm planning to give her to Longus, one of my men. Not permanently, of course. But he wouldn't want her forever anyway. And he's a loyal servant and I'm feeling generous."

"Four thousand sestertii. And she's worth more to me as a virgin."

"Perhaps. But there are some men who'd prefer her after she's had a good stretching. I'll sell her later in Rome. And the men will bring a good price on the farms. There are no herdsmen better than the Gauls."

Rufio stepped toward one of the stable doors. "Stay here," he said when Priscus tried to follow him.

"They're my property."

Rufio looked at the soldier. "If he moves, break one of his legs."

"I'd be happy to break them both."

Rufio went inside. A long central corridor was flanked on each side by a row of stables. He walked along the stone-flagged corridor toward the sound of muffled voices. When the Gauls heard the hobnails of his boots scrape the stone, they became quiet.

He found them in a stall about halfway down the building. The seven men were tied together, but the girl was fastened separately to a tethering post. The stone floor of the stall was clean but bare.

He went to the end of the building and got some fresh hay and threw it onto the stall floor.

"This will make it more comfortable," he said in Celtic.

The Gauls seemed bewildered.

"Have you eaten?"

"Yes," one of them answered.

The girl huddled by the post, her long blonde hair half-covering her face, as if that might somehow shield her.

Rufio knelt next to her. She trembled like a twig in a winter wind.

"I won't harm you." He drew his dagger and cut the thongs from her swollen wrists.

She peered at him from behind her veil of hair.

"What's your name?"

"Larinda."

He leaned closer. "Have you been to the latrine?"

She shook her head no.

"Would you like me to take you?"

"No," she whispered and pointed with embarrassment to the drain in the floor. The flagstones around it were still wet.

He pushed back the hair from her face. She was about eighteen years old. Very different from her sister in appearance, she was captivating in a smooth and yielding way, with soft features that seemed about to melt.

"I spoke with Varacinda today," he said. "She asked me to tell you that she loves you very much."

85

The girl's green eyes filled with tears and her lips quivered, but she refused to weep. "Tell her I love her, too." Suddenly she gripped his forearms. "I'm so afraid. I fear some man will buy me for his pleasure. I've never had a man before. What will happen? Will he ravish me?"

It was an obscene remark to come from so innocent a mouth. Rufio curled a finger beneath her chin and brushed her cheek with his thumb. "Perhaps the gods of Rome are not so cruel."

Priscus was still outside, sitting on a water trough, when Rufio came out.

"Six thousand sestertii," Rufio said. "You'd be wise to accept."

"She's not for sale. I told you that."

"Would you rather have Longus kill her?"

"You exaggerate. There never yet was a field that wouldn't accept a plow."

"Soldier!" Rufio said.

"Yes, centurion."

"No one except Priscus is allowed in with the slaves."

Then he turned and walked away.

"We'll create no disturbance here, centurion. We're not so foolish."

Rufio paused and looked back over his shoulder. "How foolish you are remains to be seen. You'd be wise to remember that many of us are fated to become the food of Acheron."

With that reference to one of the rivers of Hell, he turned and walked off into the dying light.

———————

Neko led Diocles through the centurion's sleeping quarters to a room beyond.

"Centurion Rufio says you may use this room for your writing." Neko lit a bronze oil lamp and set it down on the desk.

The room was about eight feet by ten and apparently had been built as a storeroom. Now it housed a writing desk, a wicker chair, and a bronze brazier. Some shelves had been set up along two walls to hold papyrus scrolls.

Diocles picked up a scroll that lay open on the desk. He realized with amazement that it was Lucretius's masterwork of Epicureanism, *On the Nature of Things*. The exuberant foe of the grim Stoics, Lucretius had attacked with vigor the mystery of Nature. Whether or not he had succeeded was still being debated. Yet none could deny the brilliance and originality with which he had grappled with the riddle of life.

"Will there be anything else?" Neko asked.

"How long have you been with Rufio?"

"Many years. I was a teacher once, before that, long ago."

"He puzzles me."

Neko's full lips widened in a grin. "He puzzles himself."

"Has he always been a soldier?"

"Can you imagine him as anything else?"

"Tonight my powers of imagining have vanished."

"Then let me tell you. He is a great soldier and he is a great man."

Diocles pulled out the wicker chair and sat down. "Why?"

"He is a great soldier because he is strong and wise. And he is strong because he is wise. His strength grows out of that wisdom."

Neko paused, but Diocles said nothing and waited for him to continue.

"And he is a great man because he is truly brave. I don't mean the bravery of thrusting swords—I mean the courage to face within himself that which is unfaceable. He has done that. That is his greatness and his tragedy."

Diocles stared at him in confusion.

"You see," Neko went on, "Rufio is not just a man who reads Lucretius. He is also a man of war capable of things you dare not even imagine. Rufio is two different beings fused into one. He is like a centaur—he thinks and speaks with the reason of man, and yet he is forever on the verge of raging and lusting and trampling. He struggles with these two beings within himself every day of his life. Out of that terrible war comes the extraordinary creature I know as Rufio. He is the greatest man I will ever know."

Diocles gazed at Neko for a long time after he had finished. The love in the man's eyes ruled out the possibility that Neko was leading him on. Yet it all did seem rather overstated. Like their temples and monuments, the words of Egyptians always seemed a bit outsized.

"Thank you, Neko. That will be all."

The Egyptian withdrew.

Diocles rolled up the scroll. Beneath it were several sheets of papyrus with what looked like fresh writing. It contained a collection of military anecdotes, each one revealing some stratagem used to thwart an enemy at the moment of crisis. They were not uniquely Roman, nor were they drawn from any particular period of history. Rather, the incidents apparently had been selected solely for their instructive value.

Diocles smiled. It was another example, if one were needed, of the relentless Roman pragmatism.

"I recommend the story of Gracchus and the Lusitanians. Few tales of war are more telling than that."

Diocles jumped at the sound of Rufio's voice, though he was not sure why.

"I thought you might like to have a quiet area where you could write at night."

"Thank you. Won't I disturb you here?"

"I sleep only three or four hours."

He came over to the desk and picked up a waxed tablet.

"Rufio . . ."

"M-m-m?"

"Are you writing a book?"

"Compiling one, you could say. Though I'm throwing in a few stories of my own."

"A book on war?"

"War is my life," he answered, his eyes as cold as slate. Then he turned and walked away.

Diocles felt uncomfortable. Rufio seemed irritable tonight.

"How did you like the feats of strength?" Diocles asked.

"Very impressive," he answered from the other room. "If you like freaks."

Diocles went to the doorway. "Have you ever seen anything like Longus?"

"Friend, no one has ever seen anything like Longus."

Rufio went into the small alcove where his bed was and sat on the edge and glanced down the tablet.

"I'd hate to be the receptacle for that one," Diocles said. "I saw a rhinoceros once in Rome—"

"Talkative tonight, aren't you?" Rufio said in annoyance. He breathed on his signet ring to warm the stone, then pressed it into the wax and set the tablet aside. "The fact is that the Sequani girl is going to be the receptacle for that monstrosity. If she survives it. I tried to buy her but the dealer wouldn't deal."

Diocles sighed and looked away.

"She's a slender and delicate flower the gods should never have grown," Rufio said. "Beauty is the cause of much ugliness in the world."

"Perhaps I can get Sabinus to buy her. He can offer more money than you could."

"Money wasn't the issue. Besides, it no longer matters. They left at sundown. And good riddance." He lay back on the bed and stared at the ceiling.

Diocles turned away and went back to the small room. The night was a warm one and the place seemed airless. When he sat at the desk, he realized he was far too tired to produce anything useful. Yet Rufio expected him to, so perhaps he should try.

Paki sprang up onto the desk from out of the shadows. She sprawled on the papyrus sheets and gazed at him with that profound skepticism with which cats have always tormented the human race.

He scratched her under the chin, and she began purring. Then he turned to look again at Rufio.

The room beyond was almost dark now. Only a single oil lamp was burning. Rufio sat on the edge of the bed in the flickering yellow light. He was slumped forward, his arms folded across his knees and his forehead resting against them. He seemed overwhelmed by some vast and insurmountable exhaustion.

Diocles turned back to his work. He picked up Paki and set her to one side of the desk. She ignored the indignity.

He dipped his pen into the small bronze inkpot and held the point above the paper, but no thoughts would come. He heard Rufio get up and walk toward him.

"Can you swim?"

"Like a sturgeon."

"Tomorrow any recruits that cannot swim will be taught. I want you to be one of the instructors. I won't have men in my century who fear fighting near water. We never know where we might have to make a stand for Rome. And their—"

"I taught the son of Sabinus to swim in one day."

"Good. The feet of the new men could use a rest, too. The cool water of the lake will soothe them. Teach them quickly. I want to begin weapons training as soon as possible, now that war with the Germans is imminent." He turned back toward his room.

"Imminent?" Diocles said in surprise. "I thought it was uncertain."

"No longer. Priscus the slave dealer told us so—though he didn't realize it."

Diocles gave him a puzzled look.

"Priscus would never have come this great distance for those few pathetic Gauls."

"There are more then?"

"There must be more to make it worth his expense. He must have made an arrangement with the Germans to dispose of their captives after the battle. The Suebi don't care to keep slaves."

"This is incredible. But surely you don't mean Roman captives."

"Oh no. The Gallic cavalry at the other fort. And any Gauls from this village who fight by our side and are taken in battle."

"Did you tell this to Sabinus?"

"No, but Carbo will have figured it out. If it were up to me, I'd have laid the head of a hot pilum across Priscus's balls until he told us everything."

Diocles looked away and stroked the cat as he absorbed all this.

"It's warm in here tonight," Rufio said. "I need air."

Diocles listened to his fading footsteps and thought of the barbarian race beyond the river. He stopped petting Paki, and she reached out and began licking his hand.

He smiled to himself as he gazed at the cat. Every man, no matter how clever or sophisticated, feels a childlike pride when an animal takes to him without reason. No one is immune. Diocles was wise enough to know that everyone longs for love without conditions. All seek it in their mates, their friends, their comrades in battle. So few find it. Perhaps Rufio had forsaken the quest among men and had found it here at last with this gentle beast.

Suddenly he felt agonizingly weary. He placed his forearm on the desk and laid his head down on it next to the cat. He fell asleep in an instant.

A hand on Diocles' shoulder roused him from his slumber. He looked up and saw Rufio standing over him. There was something different about him. His hair was not as neat as it usually was, and it seemed damp with sweat.

Diocles had no idea how long he had been sleeping, though somehow it seemed very late. When he sat up, he felt as if liquid lead were rolling around inside his head.

"Time to go to bed, soldier," Rufio said pleasantly.

Yet Rufio's face did not seem pleasant in the uncertain light. The expression was taut, and the eyes . . .

Diocles' memory shot back to a moment in his youth. He and his father were returning at night from a hunting excursion. They were carrying torches along a trail in the woods when his father pointed out something that Diocles thought he saw again at this instant—the fierce and ominous eyeshine of a wolf.

15 DEAD MEN DO NOT BITE.

Roman saying

It is difficult to believe than any man could be so tired. I am exhausted always. Every part of my body cries out with weariness. Formerly it took time to fall asleep. Now just the sight of my bunk causes my body to slump. Some of the recruits are even worse than I. The veterans, though, seem impervious to effort. All are in fiercely sound condition. I have never seen such a gathering of fine physiques, all capable of limitless endurance.

Hunger, too, is my constant companion. I could eat the sandals off my feet if I dipped them in fish sauce. Yet we eat much and well, at least as well as the Gauls – perhaps better. But the endless drilling keeps me permanently hungry. Valerius says that nothing a commander does is more important than providing his men with plentiful and wholesome food. Obviously Sabinus concurs. Soldiers will complain about anything, and yet I have never heard a single word against our food. We eat better than any ordinary inhabitant of Rome. Never in my life have I consumed so much meat. We have our own herds and flocks, and there is a limitless supply of animal flesh. Pork is a favorite, along with poultry, and we also relish beef and mutton and veal. We eagerly pull sturgeon and pike from the stream nearby. We have a smokehouse and a salting room within the fort to enable the stockpiling of provisions in case of some emergency or disaster.

Of course, our wheat stores are also vast. "The rock road on which we walk" is how Valerius refers to the humble grain. We have as much bread as we can eat – wholemeal only, at the insistence of the senior centurions who, I am told, maintain that it prevents constipation. I can verify that.

Each tent group prepares its own meals, and I am becoming quite adept with the quern-stone and roasting pot. Since we have an unending supply of milk from our herds, I have also learned to be a cheese-squeezer of no small talent.

These seemingly menial chores – which in Rome would of course be performed by slaves or women – the soldiers undertake with vigor. I could not understand this at first. However, I have since learned that among Roman soldiers one should cultivate thinking in a manner precisely opposite to the way one normally does. These men would feel demeaned only if they lacked the skills for these tasks. In all of their abilities they take enormous silent pride. Never have I known a society of men who so embodied this consummate manly completeness.

The predawn light had barely begun seeping into the barracks by the time all the men were up and dressed. They washed, rubbed their teeth clean with burnt nitrum, and then visited one of the latrines near the edge of the fort. By the time they returned, the two men assigned cooking duty for the day had the big pot at the hearth bubbling with porridge. They made some wheat pancakes as well and covered them with sliced apples and honey.

Now they relaxed over their meal, stretching and belching and breaking wind with indifference, like any group of men freed of embarrassment by the absence of women.

"Nothing like the first fart of the day," Metellus said with a laugh after one of the men almost tore a hole in his tunic with an especially devastating roar. "Sorry, Greek," Metellus added to Diocles, eating his breakfast on the bunk next to him.

"You should be," Diocles said. "We Greeks do not fart. Occasionally we do pass overheated air, but not until we've discussed it for three days and then put it to a vote. And, of course, after we've determined that no one will take us to court over it. Then we gracefully raise a cheek and smoothly vent our woe."

Everyone laughed, a few men choking on their porridge as they did so.

"And I suppose Greek farts don't stink," Metellus shot back.

"Air as sweet as an Arcadian breeze."

"I knew having a Greek around would raise our level of culture," Valerius said as he came through the doorway.

Diocles lowered his eyes. "I accept your judgment with humble pride."

"Humble pride?" Metellus said. "What does that mean?"

"Another Greek sophistry," Valerius answered.

"Sophistry?" Diocles said. "Where did you learn that word? I must have scratched it on the latrine wall."

"That must be why I associate it in my mind with squeezing out a turd."

"Your mind squeezes out turds?"

"To make a proper place for your wisdom."

"As if it could fit!"

"Certainly it will. I keep it stuffed in there with that other tiny collection — *Tales of Spartan Lovers.*"

Metellus spit out an apple laughing at that.

"Enough philosophy for today," Valerius said. "Metellus, have the century assemble next to the barracks in a half-hour. Diocles, come with me. Bring your cloak."

Diocles gulped down the rest of his porridge and followed him out. Valerius paused in the storage room and pulled two javelins from a rack on the wall.

"Take this." He handed one to Diocles. Then he took his sword belt from one of the bins and buckled it on. "We're riding down to the lake."

They left the fort and passed through the gate guarding the bridge at the outer ditch.

"The men have already accepted you."

"Have they?" Diocles tried to conceal his pride. "Why?"

"Most Romans envy Greeks for one reason or another. But one thing we hate about them is the way they complain so much. Greeks are always whining about something. But not you. Your feet look like rats have been chewing on them — but not a word. You bear pain like a Roman."

As a learned and sophisticated Greek, Diocles knew he should not have been moved by this, but he now felt as if he were growing inches by the moment.

"Thank you."

"You could've thrown gold at them and they would've been unmoved. But those bleeding blisters have bought you much."

Diocles smiled and gazed at the road ahead. "Why are we going to the lake before everyone else?"

"To find a safe spot for the new swimmers."

The sun was rising over the water by the time they reached the bank of the lake. The pink disc spread its light across one of those hazy spring mornings that could shoot life into a dying man. The cool air made the skin tighten and almost quiver, and the birds filled the ears with songs that seemed to have no purpose other than to delight the soul of man. On such a day as this, sin could not exist on earth.

The two men dismounted.

"Take your pilum and feel around for any holes." Valerius removed his sandals and sword and dagger belt and stepped into the water.

Diocles did likewise and thought he would die of shock, the water was so cold. Yet he dared not protest and soil his newly won reputation. Then he smiled to himself and wondered if that was precisely what Valerius had in mind.

"Invigorating, isn't it?" the optio said and waded through the icy water.

"I don't know. I'm too numb to be able to appreciate it.'

"Now don't go Greek on me."

Diocles poked around with the butt of his spear, and all seemed smooth and solid beneath his feet.

"This looks like a good spot to turn men into fish," Valerius said after a thorough sounding. Then he returned to the bank.

Diocles gratefully followed. They stuck their javelins into the ground and dried themselves with their woolen cloaks.

"The fort is an amazing place," Valerius said. "But sometimes it's good to be free of it." He stretched his arms and sucked in as much air as his lungs could hold.

Diocles threw his cloak over his shoulder and scanned the wilderness. Suddenly he tensed and squinted into the distance.

"What is it?" Valerius asked, buckling on his dagger belt.

Diocles pointed south over the trees.

Buzzards were circling in the blue sky.

"More Roman traders?" Diocles asked.

"Maybe." He put on his sword belt. "Maybe dead Gauls. The Suebi might have crossed the river during the night and raided again." He grabbed his horse's mane and leaped into the saddle.

"Shall we tell Rufio?"

"We'll see for ourselves first," he answered and pulled his javelin out of the ground and galloped off.

Diocles jumped onto his horse and followed, gripping his javelin in his left hand. His heart pounded and his mouth was as dry as leather as he raced after Valerius. The palms of his hands were sweating on this chill morning.

He saw Valerius pull up and he slowed his horse and came up beside him.

"By the gods," Diocles said and stared at the carnage before him.

Three men lay riddled with arrows around a smoldering campfire. A single stout shaft had felled Priscus, three had cut down Longus, and five Celtic arrows had been needed to drive Sido to the earth.

The slaves were gone, as were the horses. The cart sat off to the side of the camp.

"The Gauls are a terrible race," Diocles said. "They could've simply overpowered these men and freed their people."

"Mercy is not to their liking." Valerius slid from his horse. "We have to make a report to Sabinus."

"Wait." Diocles dismounted. "Impress him with a good one. Let an old animal tracker see if he can figure out what happened here. Stand off to the side."

Diocles examined the ground. The grass was still damp and retained the impression of several feet. He circled the camp and observed the flattened blades of grass and eyed angles and distances. After he had made a complete circuit, he studied the bare ground near the fire and returned to a spot on the grass he had already examined. He sank to his knees and lowered his face to within a few inches of the grass. When he stood up he was drawn and pale, like a child who has been compelled to witness some obscene act.

"This . . . This is the act of a single man."

Valerius looked at the bloody men and then back at Diocles. "How? Can you say?"

"We can go closer now."

They stepped nearer to the contorted men.

"A single trail of footprints leads across the grass from that group of trees," Diocles said, pointing. "There are no horse tracks, so he must have come on foot. Apparently he was walking quickly—the footprints in the grass are far apart and—"

"Or he could have been tall—like Adiatorix."

"Yes. He stopped right there, where you saw me on my knees. It looks to me as if Priscus was on guard while Longus and Sido were sleeping. Priscus was sitting by the fire and might have heard something. He seems to have turned around while still sitting. You can see the marks where his heels scraped the dirt as he turned. He took one shot straight through the heart. He probably made some kind of noise as he died, because Longus and Sido jumped up. They both grabbed their swords and charged. Longus was closest to the attacker and he was shot first. He took three arrows in quick succession—his footprints in the dirt are clear and regular and then they stop where he fell." Diocles paused for a breath. "And then there was Sido. That man was a titan. The attacker fired one or two arrows as Sido charged him— probably the two arrows in his stomach. That staggered him. Look at the prints. But he continued coming. Then the attacker fired two more arrows into his chest. That knocked him down. But by some miracle he pushed himself up—you can see his handmarks in the dirt. He was shot full of arrows but still he charged, probably screaming in rage. He was almost within arm's length of his attacker when the final blow struck."

Diocles looked down at the fallen Sido. An arrow had been driven with terrific force straight through his left eye, the iron head protruding now from the back of his skull. His mouth gaped and his tongue lay slack within it. His sword was still in his hand.

"And then there is one final incredible thing," Diocles said. "The slayer stood here as solid as a marble column and never wavered. One clean set of footprints in the grass, no blurring. No hesitation or retreat.

He stood here and drew and fired and drew and fired. They charged him and he never moved. Sido closed within inches and still he did not move. He faced them all and struck them down. What kind of man could do that? Is he greater than a man?"

Diocles dropped to the ground on his haunches and pressed his head forward against his knees.

"It's a pitiless world we live in, my friend." Valerius placed a hand on one of Diocles' shoulders.

"But must it be?"

"I don't know. And the gods refuse to tell us."

Diocles rubbed his temples with the heels of his hands. "Where do you think the slaves are now?"

"With their families. Adiatorix will claim he has no knowledge of how their owner died. Gallic bandits he could say. And who could prove him wrong?"

Diocles pushed himself up. As he did, he felt something hard against the palm of his right hand. He dropped back down and ran his fingers through the grass inside the slayer's footprint. Something shiny caught his eye. He pulled it from the grass and suddenly he felt sick.

"What is it?" Valerius asked.

Diocles stood, his hand clenched.

"What is it?"

He opened his hand. In the center of his palm lay a dome-headed hobnail from a Roman military sandal.

The two men stared at each other in silence.

Valerius reached out and took it. The small bit of metal spoke volumes. Then he tossed it away.

"Neko said—"

"Yes." Valerius gazed at the corpses. "Gallic bandits must've done this. At least ten of them."

Then he gave Diocles a look that needed no words, and the two men turned away from the dead.

16   THE LANGUAGE OF TRUTH IS SIMPLE.

Roman saying

I fear that my account of life with the Twenty-fifth Legion will turn out to be a failure. I am becoming increasingly fond of these men. As anyone with sense knows, fondness is the slayer of honesty.

Rufio is another matter. The feelings he arouses in me are such an unsettling mixture of uneasiness and admiration and horror that I dare not set them down further.

Rufio sat astride his black horse and gazed with satisfaction at his men around the lake. The new swimmers appeared to be making a fair measure of progress. The mid-afternoon sun had warmed the water, and the recruits — once reluctant to enter the cold lake — could not now be kept out of it. Even more remarkable was their trust in allowing Diocles to take them to a depth where they could no longer stand. The Greek instilled a quiet confidence in them that could not be bought for any amount of silver. Rufio, specialist in war, was always impressed by a man whose talents were not all of one kind. Diocles possessed a wider range of shadings than he seemed inclined to expose to the flinty-eyed gaze of centurions. His slight build and ordinary face concealed the unselfconscious authority with which he now calmed the nervousness of these young men. And he seemed always as ready as a conjurer to surprise with some unsuspected talent or perception. But wasn't that always so with Greeks?

The veterans of the First Century swam or lolled about in the sun. Ordinarily they would have been assigned to other duties while the recruits were being taught something new. Carbo had insisted that they be sent to the Third Century of the Fifth Cohort to help repair part of the north rampart. However, Rufio had objected and, despite Carbo's growls, had gotten his way. What he was constructing here was just as important as walls. He was building comradeship and cohesion in a shattered century. In ordinary circumstances, new men were most effectively trained in isolation from the arrogance of veterans. Now, however, matters were different. Even the old hands had been frightened by the apparent displeasure of the gods toward their century. It had far to go before it was again a fighting force worthy of its legion. So, despite Carbo's snorts and grunts about idle soldiers, Rufio had prevailed.

Hoofbeats from the south caught Rufio's ear. Because of the uncertain movements of the Germans, Rufio had placed pickets around his men. Now Metellus came riding in from the south sentry line. The smile on his face showed that the matter was not a pressing one.

"The wife of Adiatorix is in the glade beyond the lake," Metellus said. "She wants to speak with you."

"With me or with any centurion?"

"With Centurion Rufio," he said with a smile. "And she's alone," he added with a raised eyebrow.

"Go take a swim." Rufio turned his stallion about. "I'll have someone relieve you."

"Not for me. I never let cold water touch my skin. Only warm water and warm women."

Rufio galloped off.

Varacinda was sitting on a white horse in the half-light of the glade. She was dressed as she had been the first time he had seen her, with blue and red checked tunic and brown leather jerkin and trousers. A mix of sunlight and shadow dappled her face as she watched Rufio approach.

"Hello," she said hoarsely and then cleared her throat. She seemed as taut as stretched leather. She dismounted and approached him.

He slid from his horse and took a few steps toward her.

She stopped several feet in front of him and stared into his eyes in silence. She seemed shaken by some unbearable emotion. Yet the force of her character steeled her. She would not relent for anyone.

"I came to tell you that my sister is back with me."

"Yes, I know. Gallic bandits, I hear. Sabinus wasn't pleased by that, but he has more pressing concerns."

"He won't seek to reclaim the slaves?"

She seemed afraid to take another breath.

"Why should he? The owner is dead. And if there are heirs, they couldn't easily prove their claim." He folded his arms across his chest. "The slaves now belong to themselves."

Her blue eyes blurred with moisture and she blinked several times to clear them.

"My sister told me only a god could have slain those awful men."

"And did she see a god?"

"It was dark and she could see no face, but she saw those evil men fall. And when a voice told my people they were free, they rushed forward to thank him but he vanished — as only a god can."

"The gods of the Celts are indeed great."

"Yes, they are, but this was a far more wonderful god than ours. It could only have been Mars, your terrible god of war."

"Why should a god of Rome free Celtic slaves?"

"Yes . . . why? Yet when he spoke to my people in their own tongue, he spoke in the accent for Rome."

Rufio said nothing.

"So you see, he must have been the great warrior god of Rome. I don't know how to speak to a Roman god, so I've come to ask you to speak to him for me. Please tell him" — she hesitated as she pulled her shaking body under control — "please tell him that what I owe him is beyond measuring. Tell him that if he were a mortal I'd give him the breath from my body if it could help him to live forever. Tell him" — her voice began to crack — "tell him that on the day of her last breath, Varacinda of the Sequani will still speak his name with honor."

She turned and Rufio stared after her. Tall and taut, she strode away, her reddish gold hair falling carelessly down her back. She took the reins and curled her fingers around one of the corner pommels, then paused. She turned her head and looked back at him. The reins slipped from her fingers and her chin quivered like a young girl's. Suddenly she bolted toward him. She fell to her knees at his feet and seized his right hand and pressed it to her face. Out of her throat shot a feline wail, and she wept deeply and uncaringly, soaking his fingers with her tears.

Rufio touched the back of her head as she kissed his other hand again and again.

"Do not kneel, Varacinda."

He reached down and grasped her beneath her armpits. The palms and heels of his hands pressed against her ribs and the sides of her breasts as he pulled her up.

Her chest heaved as she tried to stifle the sobs. This was not a woman who cried easily, and she seemed unaccustomed to the violence of weeping.

Rufio smiled in reassurance.

With all the tears, her blue eyes seemed like gems lying at the bottom of a lake.

"I want to repay you for what you've done," she said with sudden coolness as she tried to reclaim her role as the wife of a Celtic chief.

Rufio gazed at her in fascination. Retreating now was the passionate woman who had allowed a Roman to touch her near her nurturing core.

"You owe me nothing."

She turned away and walked off a few paces. Then she sat on the grass and held her hand out toward him. "Come sit with me for a moment."

Rufio ignored her hand and sat across from her.

"My husband told me what happened those many years ago," she said with surprising gentleness.

Rufio had nothing to say to that.

"She'd want to see you," Varacinda went on. "I know it."

"To curse me?"

"She'd never do that. She's a woman now. Come to the village with me."

"No!" Rufio shouted and looked away.

"Her parents died about a year ago. They were very old. Adiatorix and I now look after her. Until she takes a husband."

"Is she well then?"

"Oh yes, very well." She smiled. "And so beautiful she makes other women cry."

"What's her name?"

"Flavia."

"A Roman name?!"

"Her parents named her after the clan of the Flavii. You needn't ask why."

"To haunt me," he said bitterly.

"No, no, you see everything the wrong way."

He stood up and walked toward his horse.

"Wait!" she said and ran after him.

He stopped by the side of his mount.

"Do you want to see her? Tell me the truth."

He stared at the side of his saddle for a long time. Finally he turned and looked over his shoulder. "Yes, but I'm far too much of a coward to speak to her."

Varacinda hesitated, and then seemed to reach a decision. "I know how you can see her. But you must keep a secret. You must promise me."

"All right, I will."

"There's a cove at the edge of the lake near the village. Sheltered by many trees. The women from the village go there to swim and bathe. I'll send you word when she's about to go down there. You may see her there. And you must promise never to tell any of the soldiers of that spot." She smiled, her white teeth catching a ray of sun that slipped through the trees. "Or else we could never use it again."

Rufio stared back at her. Even when she smiled, the half-wild look remained. The high cheekbones, the taut, tight beauty — a rare creature, this Varacinda of the Sequani.

"I promise my silence." He paused for a moment. "I know a merchant in Cremona who's rich beyond counting. He speaks Greek like an Athenian, he has a beautiful wife who loves him deeply and three handsome sons who honor him. I've always considered him the most fortunate man I know. But no longer." He jumped into his saddle and reined about. "Adiatorix is."

With that, he galloped off, leaving the startled figure of Varacinda standing alone in the shady grove.

————

The roaring half-circle of campfires lit the clearing near the lake. The soldiers had finished their meal of smoked venison, hard cheese, and bread. They were weary from swimming all day, but refreshed by the food and the blazes. Alert but mellow, they could absorb anything that made sense, and they were inclined to resist nothing unless it proved painful. They were precisely as Rufio wanted them.

Valerius had told the century Rufio was going to address them. They now looked at the centurion expectantly as he stepped out of the darkness and into the arc of fires.

The century rose as one man, but Rufio waved them back down. His gaze glided across their faces. Scarred veterans stared back, men who had suffered great wounds and trials. Other veterans faced him, too — soldiers who by odd casts of fortune had never known war. Sweating through the peaceful toil of army life, they had built bridges and roads and aqueducts — and even an occasional city. And there were the recruits — fresh-faced and fearful, awe-struck by tales of centurions who crushed failed soldiers like grubs beneath their feet.

These were Rufio's men. To their centurion they looked to preserve their lives until they had served their twenty years. In a wild land and among barbarous men, they must trust him to be their guiding brain, their leading sword, their final shield. It was a sobering responsibility — even for a god of war.

"Have you eaten well?" Rufio said.

They nodded or mumbled yes.

"Good. Men who eat poorly make war poorly and make love poorly. We're Romans, so we cannot allow either of those two things."

An easy laugh rolled through the group.

"Two topics are on my mind tonight. The first is honor." He clasped his hands behind his back and stared at the ground as he strolled in front of them. He seemed to be gathering his thoughts. The long pause, with its tension and anticipation, opened their minds as easily as a finger lifting a lid.

"Honor is your greatest strength," he said and turned his gaze upon them. "Some of you might think courage is. Yet a courageous man can also be a swine, but an honorable man cannot be a coward. Honor carries bravery with it like a scabbard carries a sword. The existence of one compels the existence of the other."

He took a breath and retraced his steps in front of them.

"Some of you might have served in the East, so you know how soldiers there are often billeted in cities. There they grow soft, they violate women, they extort money from the local people. They seek pleasure and ease—and they create hatred and contempt. They dishonor themselves"—his gray-blue eyes were suddenly as hard as slate—"and they dishonor Rome. Degrade these Gauls and you'll destroy much. You'll betray the legacy of Caesar." He extended a hand in a gesture of reasonableness. "If you want something from the Gauls, bargain fairly. You're paid well enough to do that. If you want to sample these beautiful Gallic women, then do it—but take no women against their will. If the Gauls come to you for help, listen to their troubles. You'll gain far more with your patience than with the edge of your hand. I know—the Gauls are quick-tempered and impulsive. Insolent and selfish and shortsighted. We trust them at our peril. These things are all true—sometimes. But remember this, too—the Gauls are a great race. Not as great as Romans"—Rufio smiled—"but then who is?"

The men laughed and the tension eased.

"And remember this," Rufio said, changing the tone again. "Anyone who dishonors Rome will stand before me alone"—he paused and glared at them—"and we'll permanently resolve that matter between us."

He turned away and drifted to the edge of the firelight. The soldiers had to strain to see him. He turned and came back into the glow of the flames.

"The second topic is you." His voice hit them with the force of a ram. "The soldiers of Rome—the spine of the Empire. Why are you here among these forests and valleys? Sometimes you must ask yourselves that question. I know that. You've had much sorrow in this century. But before I answer, I'll ask another question. How is a city on the Tiber able to rule the wilderness of Longhaired Gaul? The answer is as clear as carved marble. We succeed because we are not Greeks." He glanced at Diocles in the front rank of men. "Greek, why is Greece the footstool of Rome?"

Caught off guard, Diocles hesitated.

"Surely you know," Rufio said.

"I'm a simple man. I look to my centurion to tell me."

"Then I will," he said to the entire century. "The answer is that to the Greeks there are no such people as Greeks. There are Athenians and Corinthians and Spartans. Petty squabblers. No cohesion, no purpose. No vision of themselves as the creators of some further greatness. But we" — his voice rose and his arm swept across the crowd — "we are all Romans. Whether we were born in Rome or Venusia or Cremona. The ore might come from many mines, but we're all forged of the same steel. And the driving heat of that forge is the citizenship of Rome and the irresistible force of her destiny."

Rufio stalked before the front ranks of men. "And here we are — among these dark forests that most Romans will never see. And before we came, what was here? Savage tribes tearing each other. Wars and threats of wars and fears of wars. And even we weren't immune to the Terror of the Gauls. We all know how one time long ago the Gauls poured into Italy and sacked Rome itself. But now? Now the Gauls pay tribute to Rome — and yet they prosper. They rear their children in peace, they tend their farms — and Romans needn't fear Gauls climbing through their windows at midnight. And why?"

"Tell us why, centurion," Metellus shouted.

"Because *we* are here! We guarantee the peace of Gaul and the safety of Rome."

The men were growing excited now, and they shifted about on the grass.

"But what of the Germans?" Valerius asked. "Can you speak of them?"

"The Germans," Rufio said in a way that showed that here was not a taste to his liking. "We all know their gentle ways and their faithful friendship. We know how they joined with the Sequani in a war against the Aedui — and how when that was finished they turned on the Sequani and slew them like dogs and stole their land. They now stand ready to flood across the river. Eager to steal whatever they can carry and to destroy everything that has been built from the time of Pericles to this moment." He paused, then said, "But they do not — because *we* are here!"

He stepped closer, as though the fierce energy of his own person could shoot and crackle like lightning into his men.

"A thousand years from now, when another Livius writes the history of this age, who will be remembered? The great Caesar, of course. And the noble Augustus. And Vergilius and a few others. But most will be forgotten." He stared at his men with unashamed arrogance. "But *we* will be remembered. Our names might be lost but our impact will survive. Men of the future will write of our deeds with awe and wonder. They'll speak in amazed voices of the daring and brilliance of the army of Rome. And here we stand. Will you be worthy of the praise of distant ages?" He drew his sword and held it vertically before him, the tip level with his eyes. "All civilization, all learning, all that we've created — all is balanced on a swordpoint. The survival of all that we love is guarded by the swordpoint of Rome. Dare we let it go?"

The men were on their feet and roaring, Diocles among them, swarming around Rufio before he could loose another breath.

17   TO HOLD A WOLF BY THE EARS.

Roman saying

Barovistus sat astride his horse on a ridge. The breeze fluttered the golden hairs that fell out of the knot at the top of his head. He breathed deeply and stared into the limitless expanse of the German hinterland.

"You spend much time on your horse these days," Orgestes said when his black and white mare reached the top of the ridge.

Barovistus looked at him, then turned away and said nothing.

"The young men want war," Orgestes said. "Most of the older men, too. All because of your words. And yet you sit here alone."

"A war chief is a lonely man. Lonely in any army. The Romans have war chiefs they call centurions. Men of great power, great strength. Men of great loneliness."

"What's your plan?" Orgestes asked, refusing to sympathize.

He continued staring off beyond the meadows toward the dark forests. "The Romans have cut out our vitals. With their silver cups and soft garments they've made us soft. They try to destroy in us what it means to be Suebi. They want our men to be like women. And when they've weakened us, they'll smash us and hurl us far back into the heartland from which we came."

"Why should they do that?"

"Because they fear us. They know that one time long ago the Teutones and Cimbri almost marched on Rome itself."

"Then the answer is to show them that they have nothing to fear."

Barovistus looked at him as if he were mad. "They have everything to fear. We are men of blood and war."

"Yes, but—"

"The fox devours the hen as we'll devour them. This is the purity of what we are. This is what it means to be Suebi. It will never mean anything else."

After a pause, Barovistus said, "You stare but do not speak."

"What is there to say?"

"What would you have us do?" Barovistus shouted with sudden anger. "Lie on silks in marble cities? Grow flabby like women? Be like Romans?"

"Is that what you think I want? You're the fool's fool. And you have no excuse. You served with them—you know better. Do you think the legion beyond the river is filled with flabby women? They're warriors trained and drilled in all the ways of war."

"They're small and slight."

"They'll have your head upon a spear."

"And what a sight it would make," he answered with a fierce grin.

"If we close with them there will be no letting go. The Romans will destroy these young men without mercy."

"No. One of us is greater than three Italians. They're dwarfs. We'll hack them down like the farmer hacks wheat."

"And if we fail?"

"Death in war is not failure. It is greatness."

"Death in war is just death."

Barovistus turned away.

"What's your plan?"

"First to show the Sequani they must not fight by the side of the Romans."

"They are allies."

"We'll make the cost too high." He folded his hands on the horse blanket in front of him. "We'll choose a village—one far from the fort—and we'll destroy it. We'll slay every fighting man and sell their women and children to Priscus. Then we'll put it to the torch. We'll show the Sequani the simple choice—abandon the Romans or submit to be slaughtered." He clawed at his dense golden beard as he stoked his inner fires. "Then we'll attack the ala of Gallic cavalry at the fort north of Aquabona. I'll lead this attack myself. Five hundred men means hundreds of swords and horses to be plucked like fruit."

"And what of the Gauls there? They're great fighters."

"We'll slay them all. That'll draw out the Romans and we'll face them at last. And we'll take no captives."

18   FIRE TESTS GOLD. ADVERSITY TESTS STRONG MEN.

Seneca

If any soldier enlisted simply to be a fighter, he would have been wiser to choose marriage. Military duties comprise only a small fraction of the activities of a legionary. Paperwork seems to be the primary task of the Roman soldier. The immense tabularium in the Principia houses most of the documentation for the legion. Service records, official correspondence, copies of orders – all are tended by a tireless army of clerks.

Of course, there are manual duties as well. The Roman obsession with hygiene ensures that a large number of soldiers are scrubbing something, somewhere, at any time of day. Surprise kit inspections have so become the norm that they are no longer surprises. They are expected at all times and are prepared for incessantly. And when the men are not scouring their own quarters, they are cleaning their centurions' rooms. Rufio, however, has Neko, his Egyptian slave, to do this for him.

Outside the fortress there are as many tasks as there are inside. Work parties are continually engaged in felling timber or making charcoal. At the edge of the civil settlement is a sawmill operated by men from this legion.

Soldiers are also tasked with bridge building and repair – which they do with speed and skill – and are called on to show the Gauls how to drain some of the fetid marshes around here. For some reason, the Gauls seem to have problems with this and need to be retrained all the time. They are an impatient race and are not inclined to focus their attention on something that does not show immediate results. The Gauls are incomparable stock raisers and metalworkers, but hydraulics eludes them.

A vineyard extends beyond the rear rampart and, as is to be expected, the soldiers tend this with extraordinary dedication. We have herdsmen to tend our animals, as well as trackers and hunters to supplement our meals with game. The most skillful butchers I have ever seen are soldiers in this legion. Nothing is wasted.

Guard duty is another preoccupation. There are guards stationed at the gates, on the walls, and inside and outside the Principia. The Praetorium, Sabinus's house behind the Principia, has its own guards as well. Soldiers guard the granaries, the artillery sheds where the catapults are kept, and the armory. Guards are even posted at the hospital.

In the settlement, officers supervise the markets to keep swindling to a minimum. Nonetheless, sharp practices do go on.

Sabinus himself is not without responsibilities to the local populace. He must arbitrate disputes among the Gauls, or among Gauls and Romans. He must also protect them from bandits and invaders. Because Roman soldiers are the finest practical engineers anywhere, all civic building projects fall within

the Legate's sphere of command. Even natural disasters are his to subdue. Should famine strike, the fort granaries must feed the local people.

To be a roman soldier is a privilege accorded few, but with that comes a responsibility far heavier than any lorica of mail.

"The Saturnalia is over," Rufio had said after the balmy day of swimming, and soon Diocles knew exactly what he had meant. Every morning for the next week, the recruits were out early on a route march. When they returned, they had to clean the stables and stack bales of fodder. By mid-afternoon, when they were convinced they had reached their limit of endurance, they were led out on a second march. The first few days of this brought them almost crawling back to the fort at the end of the day.

Diocles had not been aware that he had at his command such a marvelous range of obscenities that he now poured—silently—on the silvered head of Rufio. Yet by the end of a week, the edge seemed to be dulling on this ordeal. Once his muscle aches began to ease, the rationale for this regimen became clear. The brisk marches over roads and hills strengthened legs and increased endurance. However, a man fought also with his arms and back. What better way to prepare him for the weight of shield and sword than to condemn him to the rank realm of those tireless dung producers?

The full century went out on the first march of the day, but the veterans were assigned other duties in the afternoon. It surprised Diocles that twenty or more soldiers in the century were excused from normal fatigue work of all kinds, though not from drilling. Then Valerius explained that these were the specialists who had more vital tasks. These fighting men were also blacksmiths, tanners, wood-cutters, wagon makers, butchers, charcoal burners, hospital orderlies, clerks of various kinds, and so on. It was the earliest goal of a private soldier to so distinguish himself at his duties that his centurion might choose him to be trained for one of these specialties. In this way he would become an immunis and so excused from normal fatigues. Diocles the scholar would have considered this a sadly humble goal. Diocles the soldier now gazed upon it as though it were the entrance to paradise.

After a second week of marches, the skin of his feet was as tough as the leather that surrounded them. A once-tortuous march over roads and valleys seemed more like an outing than an effort. The shoveling out of the stables had blessed his palms with calluses as rough as the

footpads of a dog. Bales of hay he had dragged around like slabs of marble were tossed about with increasing ease.

"Weapons training starts today," Rufio told the assembled recruits at the beginning of the third week, and the excitement could be tasted. Though Rufio had said that battles were won more with pickaxes and turf cutters than swords, these tyros yearned to be warriors. As in all armies in all times, those most eager to draw blood were those who had never smelled it.

Behind the fort spread a flat parade ground. Here the commander could address the cohorts from the stone tribunal at one end. The area was also used for cavalry drill in good weather. Abutting it on the north side was a smaller area of level ground where several dozen stout, six-foot-high stakes had been sunken into the earth. Diocles noticed they were heavily battered.

Rufio led the recruits across the parade ground to the staked area. Metellus and Valerius were off somewhere else.

A mule cart rolled up behind them and Rufio pointed to it.

"One sword and shield for each man," he said. "Then stand before your enemy."

The cart was filled with long wicker shields and wooden short swords identical in size to the standard equipment of the legionary. When Diocles pulled a practice shield down from the cart, he was startled by how heavy it was. The sword, too, weighed so much that he could not imagine how anyone could ever learn to wield it. No wonder Herakles had preferred a club.

Diocles approached one of the stakes, and the mid-morning sun was beginning to bake him inside his helmet. Some sort of bug bites on the back of his neck had started to itch. He wiped the sweat from his face and positioned himself before his oaken enemy.

"Are the shield and sword too heavy for you?" Rufio stood before them with his vinewood cane in hand.

They shrugged or mumbled in reply.

"Never lie to your centurion. Of course they are. They weigh twice as much as real weapons. Learn to use these and the others will seem like toys. You're all asking yourselves why you must wear helmets today. The helmet increases your weight and changes your balance. If you learn to fight without it, you'll have to learn all over again how to fight with it. I don't want to teach you twice." He tapped his chest with the tip of his cane. "I'll be your weapons instructor. I'm told there are many good ones with this legion, but I'll train you myself. If you have a question, ask. Only weaklings are afraid to ask for help. I'll have no weaklings in my century."

The recruits shifted their feet and a few of them looked at one another.

"You have two weapons. Both are important. Without your shield to protect you, your sword will be useless — because you'll be dead. But your shield is more than protection. It's an offensive weapon, too. A real shield has an iron boss in the center. That's not just to protect your hand, it's for striking your enemy as well. Is anyone here left-handed? No? Good — that makes things simpler. Now the first thing to learn is how to stand. A downed soldier is a desperate soldier. Nothing you learn today will be more important than how to stay on your feet. Place your feet about shoulder-width apart."

He pointed at his own feet with his cane.

"Bring your left foot slightly forward. Now slide your right foot backward. Keep the toes of your right foot in a horizontal line with the heel of your left foot. Flex your knees a bit and shift your weight to the balls of your feet."

He showed them with his own body.

"Here you have the most stable fighting stance there is."

The awkward recruits looked skeptical.

"I know it feels unnatural, but soon you'll be doing it in your sleep. Practice it at odd moments during the day."

"When do we get those, centurion?" Diocles asked.

Laughter sneaked out of the throats of the recruits.

"We have a wit among us," Rufio said. "Aren't we a lucky century? Remember — never keep your feet parallel beneath your body. You're living men, not statues. The Germans are big and muscular and they'll try to tip you. If you go down, you might not get up again. Any questions?"

There were none.

"Now the second point. When you approach the enemy, always keep your files straight. You probably think that's easy. It's not. Because your shield is in your left hand, your right side is partly exposed. Without thinking, you'll begin to drift to the right to get the protection of the shield in the left hand of the man next to you. I don't want to see that. The entire front rank will start rolling and the files behind you will get ragged and try to compensate. Soon the whole century will be fading to the right. That can throw the entire line out of position. The Germans look for that. If they see it, they'll rush men to their own right and try to flank us on our left. If they do — well, then our loved ones wonder why we've stopped writing."

Rufio paused. Diocles watched him as he allowed his words to seep into his men.

"Once you close with your enemy — or he closes with you — strike that first blow. Extend that shield arm sharply and drive that boss right into him."

He picked up a shield and showed them.

"Smash him back, break his momentum. Do it now."

They thrust their wicker shields against the oak stakes.

"Good. Good. I like the way you did that. Do it again — a little more sharply. Do it with confidence."

Diocles and the others drove their shields into the wooden enemy.

"Good. Better. The next thing to remember is to pull your shield back just as quickly. Don't leave it out there so a German can grab the top edge and pull it forward and away from you. Try it. Good. That's it. Thrust and retract. Again. Excellent. Again. Keep it vertical when you pull it back. Again. Again. Again. All right, rest."

They lowered their shields and paused to catch their breaths.

"I didn't say offer yourselves up for sacrifice!" he shouted. "Keep those shields up!"

They flinched at his words and jerked up their shields.

"Never lower your shields until the enemy is off the field."

They held them up until their arms began to shake from weariness.

"All right. You may rest them on the ground."

They hesitated at first, as though fearful their centurion were laying a trap for them.

"Swords are the permanent mates of your shields. Never divorce them."

He bent down by flexing his knees and picked up a wooden practice sword without taking his eyes off his men.

"If you drop your sword, retrieve it like that without lowering your head. Never take your eyes off the enemy."

He stood up straight.

"Drop your swords and do as I did."

They imitated him.

"Well done." He held the wooden weapon out toward them. "The Spanish sword. It's better than Roman swords were, so we adopted it long ago. Made now of the best Celtic steel. It's the finest weapon of its kind."

"Question, centurion," a recruit named Licinius said.

Rufio nodded.

"Do the Germans use these swords, too?"

"Only if they get some of ours. Most Germans have no swords at all. They rely on their spears. But when they do use steel, it's usually a long Gallic cavalry sword with a rounded tip. They attack with a slashing sweep." He turned his gaze to the entire group. "A race's personality can usually be seen in its weapons. The Germans' swords are big and brutal and they flail wildly with them. They're like their owners — power without discipline. A Roman's sword is like the Roman mind — sharp and straight and to the point."

Rufio was subtly shaping the recruits' perception of themselves. Diocles marveled at the deftness with which Rufio's words were used for purposes other than the immediate topic at hand.

"We've conquered many peoples in many parts of the world," he went on, his eyes seeming to reflect inward as he reached for some hallowed memory. "If you could speak to them, they'd tell you that it's not because we're the best horsemen or archers. Or even the best spearmen. It's because the Roman soldier is the most highly trained and most disciplined swordsman on earth. Once we lock with our enemy we're invincible."

Far more meaning weighted Rufio's words than that carried by technical facts. His voice was heavy with feeling and purpose. He spoke of the weapons of war not simply because it was his job to do so. Rather, it seemed as if these frightening tools represented something of his undiluted self — as if the elements in him had been rendered down to their thickest essence and had been found to be the blood of Mars. That a man so sharp and lively of mind and so attractive of body should find his greatest fulfillment in the clash of armies was to Diocles painfully sad.

"How do we use this gift from Spain?" Rufio said. "Its primary purpose is the thrust. It's not an axe. Thrust quickly and deeply into an enemy and withdraw just as fast. I never want to see any of you slash with this weapon unless there's absolutely no danger to you from that action. When you raise your arm to slash, you expose many of the most vulnerable parts of your body. Let the Germans slash. You keep your sword low — no higher than your hip — with the blade parallel to the ground or angled upward."

He showed them with his wooden weapon.

"Hit with your shield, then step in quickly with your sword. Thrust with confidence. Ignore the chest — too much bone. Pierce the stomach or the intestines. Keep an eye on the armpit — always a vulnerable spot on an enemy who raises his sword to slash. The throat, too, and the face can be good choices if your opponent is not too tall. Step back quickly after your thrust so that when he falls he cannot pull you down with him."

"Question," Diocles said.

Rufio nodded.

"What if he's down but not dead?"

"Leave him. Don't waste time finishing him off. The fighting man on his feet behind him is a greater threat to you than a bleeding man on the ground. Look to your right and left to see how your comrades are. If they're not in trouble, close with another of the enemy." He looked around. "More questions? All right, grip your sword firmly but not too tightly. Raise your shield, close with your enemy, and strike a blow for Rome."

Diocles stepped toward the oak post, struck it with his shield, and thrust the tip of his sword hard against its wooden bowels.

"Good," Rufio shouted and walked among them with his cane. "Step back and attack again. Continue attacking and retreating until I tell you to stop."

Grunts of exertion mixed with the clatter and thud of wooden weapons as the men assaulted their unyielding enemy.

From the corner of his eye, Diocles saw Rufio come up beside him.

"Go for his face!" Rufio ordered.

Diocles thrust upward at the top of the stake, then withdrew.

"He's looking to his right at Licinius," Rufio said. "Flank him on his left."

Diocles swung around to the side and struck the post with his shield, then thrust his sword at the middle of the stake.

"Don't gloat—withdraw!" Rufio ordered.

Diocles leaped back.

"He has a shield across his upper body," Rufio said. "Go for his legs."

Diocles closed again. He slammed the stake with his shield and cut sideways at the phantom legs.

Rufio's cane sheared down across Diocles' sword arm. "DON'T SLASH!" he roared and Diocles howled in pain. "Pick up your sword!"

Diocles reached for his weapon and glared in anger at Rufio.

"Don't look at me!" Rufio yelled and he snapped the end of his cane across the bridge of Diocles' nose. "Face your enemy!"

Diocles grabbed his sword with his half-numb hand and again assaulted the wooden stake.

"Thrust into his thighs!" Rufio shouted. "Cripple that savage."

Through tears of pain, Diocles attacked and withdrew and attacked again. Finally cries and yelps down the line told him that Rufio was no longer behind him.

Movement off to his right caught Diocles' eye. A bald soldier with a red leather eye patch had sat down on the rim of a water trough at the edge of the parade ground. He leaned forward with his forearms on his knees and watched.

"Is the battle over?" Rufio said and brought his cane down with a crack across Diocles' shoulders.

Diocles grunted in pain but made no protest as he turned back to the stake and assaulted it again.

Streams of sweat burned his eyes as he attacked the immortal enemy. Occasionally he had to stop and massage the tightening muscles of his right hand. Then he resumed his war.

An arm came around him from behind and he flinched as though from a blow.

"You're holding it like you're gripping a timid maiden," said a gravelly voice, and Diocles turned to see the one-eyed man standing behind him.

With callused hands, he took Diocles' fingers almost tenderly and loosened them on the contoured grip of the sword.

"There," he said. "You want to hold it, not crush it."

"Thank you."

The man turned away and walked back toward the fort.

"Retreat and rest!" Rufio shouted about the din.

The men stepped back but were careful to keep their shields up.

Diocles watched as Rufio walked among them and checked their stance and bearing. Apparently satisfied, he stood before them again.

"You acquitted yourselves well, but not nearly well enough to have survived. The Suebi are about to charge again. Get ready for the second wave."

The soldiers tensed.

"Here they come. Hit them!"

19   DRIPPING MOISTURE HOLLOWS OUT A STONE.

Roman saying

Valerius stood before Rufio's desk early in the morning and tried to stifle a yawn.

"Do your new responsibilities exhaust you?"

"No, centurion. I had an erotic dream last night and I still haven't recovered."

Rufio laughed and shook his head. "After the sword drill this morning, take the century on a three-mile march. Armor and full packs. When you get back, release the veterans to their other duties and take the recruits to the hospital. I've arranged with the chief bandager to begin their lessons in wrapping wounds. After their meal, give them another sword drill. Make it a hard one. They can take it. Questions?"

"Diocles has some kind of skin rash. He's scratching all the time."

"Send him to me."

Valerius left and Diocles came in a few minutes later.

The flesh below his eyes was a hideous purple from Rufio's blow across his nose. He was scratching at the back of his neck.

"Yes, centurion?"

"Do you have a skin disease?"

"No, centurion. Bites. I think there are fleas inside the fleece of my mattress."

"That's easily fixed. Go to my sleeping quarters and bring the chest next to my bed."

He did as he was ordered and placed the small wooden chest on Rufio's desk.

Rufio flipped it open. He removed four old wreaths of dead oak leaves that lay on top and pulled out several strips of cedar.

"Take these. Open the stitching on the side of your mattress and slide these inside. Fleas hate cedar. They won't annoy you again."

"Thank you," he said without feeling.

"You didn't come in to write last night." Rufio placed the wreaths back in the chest.

"Too tired, centurion."

"I thought maybe your hand was cramped."

Diocles said nothing but stared toward the window beyond with eyes as blank as river stones.

"Dismissed."

Diocles turned and went on his way.

"One thing more, soldier," Rufio said.

Diocles stopped in the doorway and turned around to face his officer.

"Petulance is a quality I despise."

"Yes, centurion."

"Go."

———————

Metellus was, in Diocles' opinion, the most intelligent man in the century, after Rufio. This was not surprising. In battle, it was his task to use the century's standard—theirs was a silver boar—as a signaling device for the deployment of the troops. Victory or defeat might turn on quick signaling by the standard bearers. He was also in charge of the century's accounts—pay, soldiers' savings, and the like, so he had to be skilled in basic mathematics.

Metellus surpassed these lower limits of expertise. Quick-witted and clever, he viewed the world with a perpetually half-amused, half-bemused expression that hinted at a sharp insight into the foibles of man.

In appearance he was un-Roman, with sandy hair and light skin. He rather resembled the Gauls, among the women of whom he was reputed to have more sated lovers than any three ordinary men.

This morning he was looking annoyingly superior as he leaned against his bunk and gazed at his Greek tent mate.

Diocles ignored him and picked up his newly issued lorica of mail and lifted it over his head. He lowered it to his shoulders, and it seemed to want to pull him to the ground. It felt as if it weighed at least twenty pounds. He began buckling on his dagger belt, but Metellus stopped him.

"Loosen the belt." He reached out and grabbed the mail on each side above the hips. He pulled it up slightly. "All right, now tighten the belt."

Diocles did so.

"There," Metellus said and he let the few slack inches of mail fall over the belt. "Now part of the weight is shifted to your hips. You don't want to end up a hunchback."

"Will you show me how to do this?" Diocles pointed to the pile of equipment on his bunk.

Metellus started pulling the items together. There were two large sacks. A cloth one held a cloak, an extra tunic, and fresh linen underwear. A leather sack carried a slab of bacon, a lump of hard cheese, three days' rations of hard-baked wheat biscuits, and a flask of acetum, the vinegary wine that was their daily issue.

Metellus took the long, T-shaped pole that each man was issued and tied the packs to it. Then to the crossbar he tied a heavy pickaxe, its edge protected by a bronze guard, and a turf cutter, a small saw, and a sickle for foraging.

"This basket it for moving loose dirt when we entrench and the strap is for shifting turf," Metellus said and fastened them on. He added a small bronze cooking pot and a bronze skillet that he tied to the pole by the leather loops on their handles.

"Shields today?" Metellus asked the optio across the barracks room.

Valerius thought for a moment. "No, next time. But everybody carries two pila. Would you pass the word for me down the barracks?"

Metellus nodded as he picked up Diocles' kit pole. "Carry it over your left shoulder, your pila over your right. Hold everything loosely or else your hands will give out before you've gone a mile."

"Thank you," Diocles said and rested the pole against his shoulder. The weight almost staggered him.

"You'll get accustomed to it," Metellus said.

"More easily than I'll get accustomed to Rufio."

Metellus folded his arms and gave him that bemused look.

"Don't stare at me like that," Diocles said like a cranky schoolboy.

"So he tweaked your nose and rubbed your fur the wrong way. How tragic. The Germans would never do such a thing, would they?"

Diocles turned away, uncertain whether to feel angry or foolish.

"You were reared in Rome, weren't you?" Metellus asked.

"So?"

"Then you have no excuse for being ignorant of one of the oldest of Roman sayings."

"Which is?" Diocles asked as Metellus walked away.

"He who loves well chastises well," he said over his shoulder and he went out the door.

Diocles' lips parted, but he said nothing. He just stared after him in embarrassment and confusion.

————

The grove of trees near the cove was so dense that little light penetrated its depths. Varacinda sat on the grass in the shade as Rufio approached on foot.

She stood up and smiled. Dressed in black, she seemed more a creature of the forest than the same kind of being as Rufio. She walked ahead of him through the trees.

He heard splashing and laughing. Soon he could see a break in the trees, and they stopped about ten feet from the edge of the woods.

Six naked young women, ranging from about eighteen to twenty-five, swam in the blue water or lolled on the bank. At the sight of them Rufio found himself suddenly growing in the most obvious place. He shifted his weight and extended the leg nearest Varacinda to conceal it. She looked at him with eyes that told him she was not so easily fooled.

"Not all obey the command of the centurion," she said with a smile.

He turned toward the lake again. He was about to ask her to show him, when she pointed and said, "Flavia."

A young woman was stepping up out of the lake directly in front of them. She faced them unseeingly. Water slid from her as she emerged as gracefully as Venus rising from the Cytherean Sea. Her pink skin contrasted with the long black hair that hung down her back and with the black triangle exposed now in innocent allure at the summit of her thighs. She strode toward them, her heavy breasts rising and falling. She stopped a few feet up the bank and lay down on a blue cloak to dry in the sun. As she leaned back on her elbows, her breasts fell softly to the sides. She extended one leg and kept the other bent at the knee and allowed the spring sun to caress her.

Rufio felt nothing so crude as animal arousal now. He was stunned by something he had not felt in more years than he could count—he was strangling on a lump in his throat. Decades of erosive guilt had not prepared him for this. He lowered his head and closed his eyes. The sound of a musical voice caused him to look up.

Flavia was speaking to the others. She seemed to be the natural focus of the group. All had gathered on the grass and were talking in that uniquely animated way that young women do. One of them leaned forward in a conspiratorial fashion and said something in a mock whisper. They all laughed and as they did they looked eagerly to Flavia, as though deferring to her even in laughter. Her head was back and she was laughing with them.

Rufio turned to Varacinda. His throat was as tight as a fist.

"They each know how special she is," Varacinda said. "No one can say why. She simply is."

"Yes," he managed to whisper.

"Come to the village and speak with her."

"Thank you for showing her to me," he said and turned away.

"Don't you see?" she said, hurrying after him. "I've shown her to you in this way to show you the glory of what you did. The gods must favor you for giving so beautiful a life—"

"No," he said and left her standing behind him. "They've marked me as food for Acheron."

20   **WOE TO THE SOLITARY MAN.**

Roman saying

---

*H*ow different is this army from all those that have gone before. One consults the histories and finds mad hordes cutting swaths through virgin lands or else kicking down the walls of dying empires.

The Roman army is not one of these. This army builds – builds as much as it trains, and far more than it fights. Today I learned the quarrying of stone for road repair. It sounds boring. It was fascinating! These men are startlingly competent craftsman who can cut stone as neatly as a cook cuts cheese. Rufio led the entire century out to the quarry a few miles above the fort. Even the men normally excused from fatigues – the artisans and clerks as well as Valerius and Metellus – were ordered out. I was surprised to hear no complaints, but it may have been fear of Rufio that encouraged this restraint. When we reached the quarry, Rufio removed his weapons and peeled off his tunic. He stood before us near-naked in the hot sun and said he wanted neat stones, not torn tunics. He ordered us to take them off and get to work. Of course, he would never admit that he ordered it so we could also be more comfortable.

Rufio himself showed me how to quarry stone. He looked for a natural crack and with an iron mallet and chisel he made several holes along it about a foot apart. Then he took a heavy long-handled hammer and drove wooden wedges into the holes. We then doused the wedges with water. They slowly swelled and split the rock like magic. We trimmed the stones and slid them down the rock face toward the ox-carts by a wooden chute earlier soldiers had put in place. While we were doing this, I sneaked a few glances at Rufio. He has a magnificent body, superbly contoured. He is not the biggest man in the legion, but none is more nobly assembled. He glistened in the sun as his muscles rolled smoothly in the heavy labor. His skin seems too small for him and gives his body the appearance of a fierce tightness about to burst its confines. Clear, too, are the relics of his life, for everywhere he is adorned by savage scars. Not one does he have on his back. At no blow had he turned and fled. Every sword strike he had faced as it came.

When the sun began to die and we finished for the day, I looked myself over. I was filthy, scraped, and bruised. My hands were blistered and my back was stiff and aching. And I felt absolutely wonderful. As I picked up my tunic, I saw Metellus using one of the chisels to carve something into the vertical rock face. I walked across the rocks and saw that it was a huge phallus with an enormous set of bloated testicles. A good luck symbol. When I asked him what sort of good fortune he hoped for, he scowled and said, "The good luck never to come here again."

Ah, these indolent officers.

"What do our spies tell us?" Sabinus asked. "Sit down and give me the details."

Crus took a stool and set it in front of the desk. "There are definitely large-scale movements of Germans in the hinterland. The different Suebian tribes—we call them pagi—are moving together. They could be preparing for war."

"Carbo believes Priscus was in the pay of the Germans and that they're planning war."

"Priscus? That's absurd."

"He has his reasons for believing it. But never mind that now. Tell me about our sources of information."

"The troops who collect the tolls on the Rhenus bridges hear about everything that goes on in the eastern forests. They've heard from merchants and from friendly Germans that the Suebi are on the move."

"What about spies closer by?"

"I have two traders in the civil settlement I'm paying for information. They travel across the river and barter with the Germans. They say German passions seem to be boiling over a high flame."

"Are these men reliable?"

"I believe so. One is a former soldier and one is a German."

"Tell me more about the Germans themselves."

"A crude and brutal people. They're not a people I'd care to spend an evening with. They—"

"Spare me the moral commentary. Give me the facts."

"Yes, commander. They're mostly stock raisers, though they do some farming as well. It may be that they hunger for these fertile Gallic fields."

"What's wrong with their own soil?"

"Nothing, but this land is already cleared and planted. Their technology is very primitive. They make no iron themselves. They'd prefer to take this land rather than have to clear their own. They cannot read and write, and any appeal to moral or spiritual values will be lost on them."

"Crus," Sabinus warned.

"They have little government," he went on quickly. "Just a council of leading men—nobles of a sort—and an assembly of warriors. They also have a war chief, but only during wartime or when war is imminent."

"And what do we sell them in peacetime?"

"We don't sell, we barter. The Germans have no use for money. They see no point in it. They cannot grasp—"

"All right, what do we barter?"

"Luxury goods and iron."

"And in return we get what?"

"Cattle and slaves."

Sabinus leaned forward and rubbed his eyes with the tips of his fingers. "Well, we should—"

"But there's no such thing as peacetime, commander. There are only lulls between wars. Pillaging is their way of life. The greater the booty, the greater the prestige. To the Germans, there's no merit in restraint. There's glory only in the savage prosecution of war."

Sabinus stood and Crus did likewise. Sabinus massaged the muscles in the back of his neck as he walked around the room. "Then how do we deal with them?"

"Carbo could tell us how, commander. It's the wisdom of those who are in a position to know that diplomacy with the Germans is a contradiction in terms."

"And what's your opinion?"

"If they reach for their spears, we cannot deflect them with words."

Sabinus sat on the edge of his desk. "Has anyone asked Adiatorix his views?"

"I did. He agrees with our spies." Crus looked uncomfortable. "He was rather hostile to me—over the slave incident, I suppose. And he seems to have befriended that arrogant ass Rufio."

"Ah yes, your favorite centurion."

"That pompous Adonis. I don't care how many battles he's fought. The bloated pustule—I'd like to squeeze him until he pops."

"Not an action I'd advise, tribune."

"My two spies know him. One of them served with him in another legion years ago. He says Rufio always thought he was superior—as if he were some sort of eagle compared to the rest of us crawling worms."

"Perhaps he is superior, tribune."

"Only in arrogance. Someday I'll drain him like a boil and the legion will be the better for it."

"Ah, Crus," Sabinus said and turned back to his desk to retrieve some papers. "What a world it would be were it not for your charm."

———————

The civilian settlement near the fort had grown up haphazardly over the years, and now it spread out in an amorphous fashion northeast of the fort. A military center has many needs, mostly of the flesh, and a town had arisen to sate those cravings. Food shops of various kinds lined the stone-paved streets. Stores selling textiles or metal goods competed with them for space among the jumble of wooden buildings. Taverns and bakeshops were common and often sat adjacent to small inns catering to merchants traveling around Gaul or headed for Suebian lands. And there were brothels, the number of which never seemed to be sufficient to meet the need. Even a few Italian women were to be found here, but most were Gauls. And though they were hardly the dew-dappled flower of Celtic youth, to most bored soldiers they were preferable to solitary release in darkness.

Diocles explored the town in the late afternoon. He noticed there were as many Romans here as Gauls. Many of them, he had been told, were retired soldiers. Upon leaving the army, they had at last been able to marry their common-law wives, usually local women. Then they had settled down near the fort in the area in which they had served and where they felt more at home than among the alien byways of Rome.

Diocles came to the corner of a busy street. To his left was a butcher shop selling salted beef and pork, as well as live and fresh-killed poultry. On the corner to his right sat a sizable tavern—a yellow amphora was painted on the wall outside.

He wandered over. Several crude wooden tables with rough-hewn stools were set up outside the open door. Probus and several other centurions were sitting at one of these and talking and drinking. Diocles could see a small L-shaped counter inside abutting one wall. Wide-mouthed pots of wine and Celtic beer were sunken into the stone-tiled counter, and the tavern keeper used a ladle to draw the drinks. On the wall behind him were several shelves filled with tiny loaves of bread and some sweet cakes. A few tables smaller than those outside filled the rest of the tavern.

A striking red-haired woman leaned over a balcony and called down to him. Her wide-necked tunic billowed open as she bent over and smiled. He had to admit to himself that there were some things in life, especially those that came in pairs, which were certainly worth hard coin.

"Some other time," he said good-naturedly. He went inside and bought a cup of beer and came back out and sat alone at one of the tables. He noticed Ulpius Crus sitting at another table and talking with two men.

In front of the tavern, children played in the street, as they seemed to do in every street in every town on earth. Women came to the stone fountain to fill their jugs and chase the stray cats that sat on the edge to marvel at human labor.

A string of stepping stones stretched across the street. In a rainstorm a pedestrian could avoid the water rushing down the street by walking across the high stones. Situated a foot apart, they allowed the passage of the wheels of the occasional cart or military wagon.

He nursed his beer for a while and then went to the table where Probus sat.

"Excuse me, centurion," he said to Probus. "May I speak with you for a moment?"

"Even the Greeks seek my wisdom," Probus said to his fellow centurions and they laughed. He stood up and Diocles pointed to a table far away from all the others.

They sat but Diocles could not find the proper words.

"What is it?" Probus asked, clearly eager to rejoin his friends.

"I need your advice. I want you to tell me what's wrong with Rufio."

"I already explained to you what happened."

"No. No tales of Spanish treachery or wounds in the side. That's not what I'm talking about. And you know it."

Probus stared at him over his drink.

"Listen to me," Diocles said. "Yesterday Rufio went off into the woods while the rest of us were drilling. I saw him go. When he came back, he seemed to be in a daze. Rufio!"

Probus shrugged.

"Then later I saw him in his quarters. He hadn't heard me come in—this is the man who could hear a leaf fall. He was sitting on the edge of his bed. His face looked like it had been struck by lightning."

Probus pushed his drink away and stared down at his hands. He rubbed his thumbs back and forth over his thick knuckles. "If I knew, could you give me a reason why I should tell you?"

Diocles stared off at the children playing in the street. "Rufio has hurt me. He's laid into me with that vinestick again and again. He's insulted me and berated me. Sometimes just the sound of his voice infuriates me. Yet when he's absent from the century for a day I can hardly wait until he returns. When he's gone, I feel so vulnerable I cannot bear it. It's as if a shield has been pulled away and I'm standing there naked. Some of the other soldiers—even some veterans—have admitted the same thing."

The centurion gazed back at him with an expression deepened with much understanding. "Go on."

"I try to stay angry but I cannot. He hits me and abuses me during training and I want to kill him. Then I cannot resist helping him organize the book he's writing. He smiles at me and it's like a blessing from Caesar."

"He's had that effect on many people."

"Do you remember when you were eight or nine years old and there was some boy a few years older whom you suddenly took an intense liking to? For reasons you couldn't explain—even now—you found yourself liking this other boy so much that you'd be in ecstasy if he chose you as a friend. . . ."

Probus remained silent.

"When you're a child, these feelings fall away quickly. But when you're an adult, they adhere like the robe of Nessus. I want to be his friend. I want to help him and I don't know how."

"No one can help Rufio," he said, and the certainty in his voice chilled Diocles.

"Tell me why."

"Even Jupiter cannot change the past and it's the past which cuts him. It doesn't scar him, because the wound has never healed. It just cuts and cuts."

"Nothing could be that terrible," Diocles said, but he realized he sounded very naïve.

Probus took a deep breath, and when he began to speak, the voices of the children faded in Diocles' ears. As he focused on Probus, his surroundings receded. Slowly he was transported to a time far removed from the present.

"It was about twenty years ago and not far from here," Probus began. "I was very young and hadn't been in the army long. My centurion sent me as a messenger on a mission to another legion. On the way back I got lost. So they sent out someone to find me—a black-haired young soldier named Quintus Rufio. I guess you could say that everything that happened was because I was stupid enough to get lost. You cannot imagine how many times I've tried to rewrite that in my mind."

Diocles watched him as he paused to take a drink. He thought he saw the centurion's hand tremble.

"After a while Rufio did find me and we rode back toward our legion. What we didn't know was that while we were out a local rebellion had broken out. Some Roman revenue farmers were bleeding the people white and the Gauls had had enough. They were killing every Roman on two feet. We were riding back near a village downriver from here when a flock of Gauls swooped on us. We had good mounts but the Gauls had us surrounded. There was nowhere to go but straight through the village. They were waiting for us there, too. A handful of Gauls lined up and blocked our way with spears. Even the women were out shooting arrows at us or throwing rocks. We had no choice but to ride straight toward the spearmen. Most of them backed off in the face or our charge, but at least one held his ground. He was braced to run Rufio through, when Rufio scooped up a spear that one of the Gauls had dropped. He let if fly at full gallop and with incredible force. It was an awesome throw. The head drove straight through the Gaul and nailed him to the wall of a hut while he was still on his feet. He hung there as dead as a deerskin. Suddenly there was this horrible scream and a woman came running toward Rufio. We found out later she was the dead man's wife. She was unbelievably beautiful and howling with the kind of anguish only a young widow can know. She must have been close to nine months pregnant and she waddled as she ran. She grabbed her dead husband's spear and lunged at Rufio. She caught his horse in the withers. The terrified animal reared and when it came down its hoofs came down right on this hopeless woman."

What could only have been tears glazed Probus's eyes. They seemed so out of place in this man that they frightened Diocles.

"You cannot imagine. The woman seemed to explode. Her belly burst open and blood was everywhere." He stared at Diocles in horror. "And she was still alive! Rufio had fallen off his horse when the animal reared and when he got to his hands and knees he was right beside her on the ground. I jumped down from my horse next to him. You could see the baby half hanging out of the woman's torn body. The woman was shrieking in agony and the baby was flailing and twitching. Rufio whipped out his dagger and cut a strip of cloth from his tunic. He reached inside the woman and tied off the cord and cut it and pulled the baby out. It was a little girl and she was wailing and covered with blood. The woman was struggling to raise her head. Rufio held the baby toward her and she reached out and managed to touch the infant. It seemed to me that she smiled through her pain, and then she died."

Probus's eyes flashed anger at Diocles for demanding from him this terrible tale.

But Diocles still could not speak, even to console.

"And all at once the war had stopped. There wasn't a sound in the village. They stood around stunned and silent. Rufio got to his feet, and everyone shrank back from him. As if he was some demonic creature spat from the mouth of Hell. A middle-aged couple was standing near us and Rufio stepped toward them and handed the baby to the woman. He found out later they were childless and had long since despaired of having children. He went back a few times with money and goods for them and the baby. But he was posted to a different legion not long after that. As far as I know that was the last he saw of them." Probus paused to moisten his dry lips. "The day it happened — and for three nights and days after that — I had to stay with Rufio constantly to stop him from throwing himself on his sword."

Diocles turned away and stared at nothing. His own sheltered existence in Rome seemed absurd in the face of all this. He felt like an actor mouthing silly lines while the brutal drama of life raced along in these barbarous outlands.

"And the worst thing of all," Probus said, "is that it should happen to him. If Rufio is capable of love — and I don't know that he is — it's these Gauls he loves. Sometimes it's true that the conqueror does feel much for the conquered. More than anybody, we Romans have that weakness. Sometimes we hide it with arrogance or a show of contempt. But the weak spot is still there."

"It's not weakness, my friend, it's greatness."

"Rufio's problem is that he's always been a solitary person. He's never been one to confide in others. When an infection like this eats at you and you cannot drain it off by sharing it with someone, it just sickens you forever."

"You're a wise man, Gaius Probus."

"Just a soldier."

"What I don't understand is what could have happened to him this week. How do you know it has anything to do with this at all?"

"I'm just guessing. But I don't know anything else that could have hit him like Jupiter's bolt."

"But what exactly?"

"Maybe he met someone from that old village. It's deserted now — we passed it on the way here. Maybe the people who lived there joined with this one later. They do that sometimes. It could even be that he saw the little girl herself — the woman, I mean. She might still be alive. Twenty years is a long time, but people do live to be twenty."

"But wouldn't he be happy to see her?" Diocles asked, desperate to use the magic of logic to abolish Rufio's pain.

"And how would you feel, my sensitive friend, if you were to gaze into the eyes of the woman whose parents you slew?"

21   THAT MAN IS WISE WHO TALKS LITTLE.

Roman saying

"The pilum." Rufio held the spear aloft. "In a trained hand, a weapon of irresistible power. Today we'll learn how to break a German charge."

Diocles watched as Rufio hefted the javelin at its balancing point. Again he felt toward Rufio that eerie fusion of admiration and repellence. He held the deadly tool as naturally as a father coddling his child.

"The Germans rarely have armor. Few even have shields. As with all weapons, the pilum's power is related to the absence of a defense against it. The Germans know this — they think about battle all the time. More than they think about food or women — which is how we know that Germans and Italians are not related to each other. . . ."

The recruits laughed.

"So what's their defense against the pilum? Any guesses?"

The recruits arrayed before him on the training ground were reluctant to chance a reply. Like recruits everywhere, they would rather have been silent than risk sounding foolish.

"The answer is simple," Rufio said in his most easy-going way. "They attack immediately and try to close with us before we loose our pila. Just as the Nervii did along the Sabis against Caesar. The Germans charge wildly not just because they like the roar of battle. They charge because they dare not wait for us to attack. Without armor, they cannot afford to wait for a shower of pila." He paused, then said, "For they know that many will fall beneath that lethal rain."

There was silence for a moment, then Diocles said, "Question, centurion."

Rufio nodded.

"Won't the Germans throw their javelins at us?"

"Good question. If they do, you have the finest shield in the world to protect you. But they won't. Few of them have swords, so if they throw their spears they have nothing. I've seen German warriors who've lost their spears resort to throwing rocks. No, they hold onto their spears as long as they can."

"Thank you," Diocles said.

"When the Germans charge, they'll come at us in a giant wedge. They'll try to split our line in the first rush. They know it's their only hope. They'll try to panic us and scatter us before we can close with our swords. If they have cavalry, they'll try to flank us at the same time. And be warned — the German cavalry are excellent. Caesar often used

have her dough kneaded. Rufio insists we meet the legitimate needs of our Gallic friends." His smiled in the afternoon light streaming in from the street. "I try to comply as often as possible. I demand of myself nothing less than the severest exertions."

Diocles laughed as he watched Metellus leave the tavern. He was growing fonder of him by the hour. Valerius was Rufio's perfect choice to keep the blade of the century keen, but Metellus was just as vital. He was a corrective to too much seriousness, ever the one to hold the follies of life in perspective. Diocles had never believed that wisdom existed solely among the scrolls of Greek sages, yet he had not expected to find it here among such men in these remote Gallic fastnesses. He smiled to himself. He had come a long way for it, but he was now certain it had been worth the trip.

He was startled to hear Rufio's named mentioned in the tavern.

"Oh yes," Bassus went on to his German companion. "I know him well. Crus is right—he's an empty braggart."

The German, a middle-aged man with yellow-brown hair and beard, smiled.

"A swaggering ass," Bassus said. "Thinks he's the spawn of Jupiter."

With a flash of anger such as he had not felt since childhood, Diocles jumped up and approached Bassus. Yet he had no idea what to do when he reached him.

"What?" Bassus said, looking up at him.

The ex-centurion had an oblong face with features much coarsened with time. Many scars adorned it.

"Quintus Rufio is my friend," Diocles said with a pride that surprised him.

"Your bad luck."

"You're an imbecile." He turned and walked away.

Strong fingers jerked his tunic back at the neck and an arm shot up between his legs from behind. An iron hand crushed his testicles and the other one lifted him off the ground by the neck. Diocles howled in pain as his vitals were wrenched. Like a broken toy, he was hurled through the air and into the street beyond. His face broke his fall.

He vomited from the horrific pain in his groin. No one dared to help.

Through the dirt and the tears, he saw Bassus approaching. He fumbled for his dagger.

A grunt shot from his lips when Bassus kicked him in the center of the forehead. His head snapped back and the rear of his skull hit the street. His eyes were open but only half-seeing. He gazed uselessly into the afternoon sky as he lay there like a crushed dog.

Bassus laughed as he seized the front of his tunic and sliced it down the center with the dagger. Diocles fought feebly as Bassus cut off his belt and tore his clothes from him and threw them aside in the ultimate childish humiliation. The Greek tried to cover himself, but it was the desperation of a naked man in a nightmare.

"Enough!" shouted a voice that filled the entire street.

The power in that single fearless word shot strength into Diocles' limbs. He succeeded in pushing himself to one elbow.

A cloaked woman sat astride a gray horse ten feet away. She was glaring at Bassus. She was tall atop the horse, with long hair as black as the rivers of Hell.

Bassus laughed as he tucked Diocles' dagger into his belt.

With deceptive ease, the woman swept a bow from her shoulder and slid an arrow from a leather quiver hanging down her back.

"Away!" she said and drew the bow.

"Hurt a Roman?" Bassus said, still laughing.

A soft "f-i-i-i-it" from the arrow was the only sound as the iron head sliced the centurion's face and shot off into the distance beyond.

The blood had not yet streaked his cheek before she had fitted a second shaft and drawn the bowstring. She lowered her aim to his chest.

Bassus stared in disbelief and backed away, dabbing his cut face with the back of his hand. Then, with a hollow laugh, he wheeled about and returned to the tavern.

The woman slid from her mount. She set aside her bow and removed her cloak and draped it over Diocles

"Are you a soldier?" she asked in Latin graced with a Celtic trim.

"A poor one," he whispered and gazed into her striking face.

"I'll take you home." She slipped her arms beneath him and around his back and lifted him as easily as if he were a child.

22   DO NOT SPEAK AGAINST THE SUN.

Roman saying

Valerius was spitting fire. "That stinking pus-bloated pig! I'll carve him like a slab of rotten meat!"

"No." Diocles slumped on the edge of his bunk. "It's not your fight."

Diocles' tent mates had gathered around. There was no teasing, even though he had been rescued by a woman. In the ranks now there was iron solidarity.

Metellus came up with a cloth soaked in vinegar to disinfect the cut on his forehead.

"Besides," Diocles went on, "he's too much for any one man."

"Then Valerius and I will cut him down together," Metellus said.

Both the veterans and the new men looked at Metellus. For some of them it was the first time they had ever heard anger in the signifer's voice. His eyes now seemed miles from their usual smile.

"What's this?" the voice of Rufio said from the doorway.

Diocles turned his head away when the centurion came into the soldiers' quarters.

"Bassus!" Valerius shouted. "That sow-sucking swine."

"Bassus? He still lives here?" Rufio stepped up to Diocles. "You don't look so bad. I've seen Bassus beat tyros into jelly."

"But his balls might never work again," one of the new men said with innocent sincerity.

"Harems in the East are always looking for men light in the groin to fill a few select positions," Rufio said. He swept his gaze across the men like an iron rake. "I want no vengeance here. You'll maintain discipline." He glared at Valerius. "Inform the rest of the men."

"It's the honor of the century," Valerius said. "Herennius would have—"

"Are you disputing me, optio?"

"No, centurion."

Rufio turned and as he left he touched Metellus on the arm.

"So what happened?" Rufio asked when they reached his office.

"I wasn't there, but I understand that Diocles was defending your honor."

Rufio stared at him in surprise, then gestured to a stool.

"Thank you." Metellus sat down. "Apparently, Bassus made some unkind remark about you. Diocles objected."

Rufio leaned back against the front edge of his desk and folded his arms. "I was the optio in Bassus's century many years ago. He tried to break me a hundred times. Like most cruel men, he hates a man greater than himself."

"All the men of the century—even the new ones—were ready to bleed for Diocles' honor."

"By the gods, they're good Romans!" Rufio said, snapping his head to the side with a smile. "They're becoming a unit now. In a few more months, they'll be a fighting unit."

"Your campfire speech must have worked."

"Metellus . . . ." Rufio gave him a penetrating stare. "You don't think that. No speech by an officer will ever get a man to expose his bowels to the enemy's steel."

Metellus gazed at him with his bemused smile. "Then why?"

Rufio sat on the corner of the desk. It was a flattering informality.

"Because in order to win, a man has to know why he's fighting. You've been in the army long enough to know that. And to be victorious, he has to be fighting for something real and immediate and valuable to him personally. And the greatest of those things is freedom. That's what I was hammering into them. And that's why a handful of squabbling Greek cities were able to unite for once and crush the Persian horde. Free soldiers always fight better than an army of slaves. What were those pathetic Persians fighting for—to be dogs at the feet of Xerxes? The Greeks were fighting to stay free men."

"I see."

"Did you know that the word freedom exists only in Latin and Greek? I mean political freedom—the liberty to speak and argue with praetors and senators and consuls. The freedom to go before courts of law and seek justice. To write or sculpt or sing whatever songs please us. You won't find that word in Egyptian or Celtic or Syriac. Mention liberty to those people and they won't even know what you mean. They won't even be able to guess."

"I had no idea."

"And we're fighting for even more than that—we're fighting for Rome. Not the wealth of Rome but the ideal of Rome. Civilization instead of barbarism. A greatness that other people cannot even dream of. It's Vesta's flame—so sacred it's almost beyond imagining. Rome is an idea that exists beyond our own short lives. Beyond time itself."

Metellus gazed off toward the window. "I never thought of myself as fighting for a timeless ideal."

"You are. And, of course, a man also fights for the men at his side. He fights well because he fears if he doesn't, the men on either side of him will be struck down. Or because he fears being seen as weak or cowardly in their eyes. Only when a man's concern for the lives of his friends and his fear at the loss of their respect are greater than his fear of the enemy — only then will he be a soldier." Rufio smiled. "Warriors are everywhere. But soldiers?" He tapped the desk with his knuckles. "Only here."

"You left out one thing. He also fights if he fears the scorn of the leader he admires. If he fears the loss of the praise of the officer he respects. Isn't that so?"

"Yes," he said with the wisdom of a dozen battlefields.

A long silence followed.

"Did you know Bassus was one of Crus's spies?" Metellus asked.

Rufio gave a disgusted laugh. "I shouldn't be surprised. Crus leans against the hollow strong man. What about Diocles?"

"Bassus pounded him into the ground, then stole his dagger and tore his clothes from him."

"Bassus was always an expert at making a man feel like a worm. I'm surprised he didn't beat him worse."

"That's the final flourish — a young Gallic woman stepped in and stopped it. Sliced Bassus's cheek with an arrow. Then she brought Diocles back. She was just leaving the fort as I was coming in. A wild beauty from the forests of Gaul. Diocles said her name is Flavia, of all things."

"Of all things," he said and looked away.

"Do you know her?"

"When she was very young. But she doesn't know me. Take Diocles to the hospital and have the doctor poke at him."

Metellus pushed the stool against the wall and turned to the door.

"The Greek doctor," Rufio shouted after him. "I don't trust that Roman meat cutter."

The afternoon sun balanced for a moment on the horizon. As a final beneficence, it shot an orange sheet of painless flame along the wide street. Rufio squinted and sat on the edge of the stone fountain and played with the cats that had gathered. Some meowed and jumped into his lap when he produced chunks of dried fish from a little sack. Other cats sat at his feet and waited their turn with that serenity that mystifies dogs.

The children were fascinated. A small knot of them stood watching a few feet away. The boys seemed puzzled. Several of them were ten or twelve years old — the age when they would just as happily have tortured a cat or tied a rock around its neck and tossed it into a river. That this man, obviously a soldier, would take his dagger and cut small slivers of fish for the fuzzy kittens at his feet seemed very strange indeed.

"Make a friend of a cat and you make a friend for life," Rufio said and he motioned for the children to come closer. He smiled at them and one or two dared to smile back. A few of them looked half-Italian, children of retired soldiers who had been held to Gaul by a Gallic smile.

"But they won't care about you once they're full," one of the older boys said. "Will they?"

"What do you think?" Rufio asked with a raised eyebrow and he glanced among the children.

In silent answer, a large gray cat that had eaten his fill jumped into Rufio's lap. He reared up and placed a paw on each of Rufio's shoulders and licked his face. After a while Rufio had to push the cat away as his skin began to hurt from the rasping tongue. The cat settled down on his lap and purred in contentment as his eyelids drooped.

Rufio passed out pieces of fish to the children, and even the older boys could not resist the pleasure that comes from an animal's trust. Soon they had all picked out a cat as their own.

A little girl of about five, more timid than the rest, stood playing with her fingers at the edge of the group. Rufio gestured to her. Slowly she came up to him. He sat her on his knee next to the gray cat and handed her a piece of fish. It seemed huge in her little hand. She held it out about an inch away and the big cat stretched his neck and took it gently from her fingers. She laughed and looked up at Rufio with a smile that could have touched a tyrant.

He slid her from his knee. "Here," he said. "Open your arms."

She held them wide and he draped the upper body of the cat over her shoulder. Then he wrapped her arms around the cat's middle.

"He told me he wants to be your friend," he said with a smile.

She turned away, carrying the cat that was almost as long as she was. She walked off down the street and giggled as the gentle old mouser licked her ear.

"You have a tender hand with children," an accented voice said from behind him.

"Even the iron men of Rome were babies once," he answered and turned around.

Flavia stood before him. Behind her, a gray horse stood at the end of the slack reins in her hand. Flavia's hair fell to the shoulders of her short-sleeved red tunic and matched the color of her trousers. Her hair was just as black as the day decades before when Rufio had first seen it.

She wore a black leather archer's bracer on her left forearm and a bronze torque on each biceps.

"You're Rufio, aren't you?"

"And how do you know that?" he said in Celtic and tried to conceal his unease.

"The man in blue with the silver hair—you're the soldier who saved the son of Hetorix."

"I simply stopped a Greek from being a fool."

"Modesty from a Roman. . . ." She smiled a smile that wrapped around him with its warmth.

Pride stained with guilt seared him with an almost pleasing agony as he searched for the little girl he had swept from the abyss.

When she turned away, he found his voice.

"I'm told you helped one of my men today."

"The Greek?"

"Yes."

"He's not a very good fighter," she said with a sigh. "But he's a very nice man."

Suddenly her expression tightened as though hit by a chill air.

Rufio turned. Outside the tavern up the street, Bassus and a few others were laughing over something.

"I must go," he said as he slid off the fountain. "Bassus and I have a matter to discuss."

"Be careful with him."

"Thank you," he said, and it was extremely pleasant to say these simple words to her.

"It's just that"—she hesitated—"Adiatorix and Varacinda told me you were a noble man."

"Go home now, Flavia." He turned away. Halfway up the street, he paused and looked back. She was still staring after him. She seemed as tall as a willow, the low sun throwing her into sharp relief. Finally she turned and mounted her horse and was gone.

With the end of the sun came the end of the day and all the shops along the street were closing. Yet the tavern was still crowded with Gauls and off-duty soldiers as Rufio stepped up to the wide doorway. Inside, the big figure of Bassus could be seen in the half-light. The tavern owner had lit an oil lamp, and Rufio could also make out another man with him, apparently a German. A pair of willing women hung over the two men. Though occasionally pushed away, these aging nymphs would swoop back and cling as tenaciously as a couple of birds digging their talons into a windy escarpment.

"What do you want?" Bassus said as Rufio stood before them.

"You have something that belongs to one of my men." He held out his hand. "I'll take that dagger now."

Bassus's eyes widened. He stood up and pushed the woman aside. "I didn't recognize you. Your hair has changed."

"The cares of war."

"Trogus," Bassus said to the German. "Don't interfere."

Rufio glanced at him. The German's eyes shone with all the cunning of his savage race.

"Fools and I have nothing in common," Trogus said.

Bassus stepped around the table. "Rufio despises me — do you know that, Trogus? Said I was too brutal with my men. Too eager with the vinestick. He doesn't know that tyros are like unripe women. You beat them until you break them — then you can bend them any way you want."

"You'll never change," Rufio said with contempt. "Did you think you could curse the sun? Did you believe I wouldn't demand a reckoning?"

"For a Greek?"

"For my soldier, you rank maggot."

Bassus pulled Diocles' dagger from his belt and advanced on Rufio. "This will be as sweet as sin."

Rufio slid his dagger from its scabbard. With a snap of his wrist he flung it into a nearby tabletop.

"I've never touched Roman steel with Roman blood," he said. "I won't do it now."

He reached down and grabbed a stool. With a crash he smashed it into the table. Pieces of wood flew everywhere. A few more blows against the table and all he had left in his hand was a short stout leg.

The soldiers and the Gauls stepped back, and the two women and the tavern keeper scurried to the rear of the room. Trogus stayed where he was, his eyes eager and excited.

Unlike most bullies, Bassus was no coward. He looked disappointed. The younger and smaller centurion seemed badly overmatched.

"Slide that blade between my ribs," Rufio said. "Do what you've always dreamed of doing."

Bassus lunged for Rufio's heart.

Rufio glided to the side and Bassus pierced the air.

With a short stab, Rufio thrust the end of the stool leg straight at the centurion's mouth. Bassus grunted as the jagged wood shredded his lips like steel raked across dough. Blood streamed down his chin.

"Not as bad as having your balls crushed, is it, Bassus?"

The big man charged again.

Rufio ducked beneath the blade and slashed upward with the stool leg. Bassus's cheek shattered. He howled in rage and lunged once more. His other cheek collapsed beneath a second savage blow. Weak in the legs, he staggered back for breath. Tears of pain mixed with blood on a face that was suddenly unrecognizable.

With hair still unmessed, Rufio stood before him. "Do you think stealing a man's pride is nothing? Do you think a man's honor is to be kicked aside like a turd?" His eyes glittered with a ferocity that would have frightened his own mother. "Now you yourself will know," he said and glared at the face crushed by wounds no surgeon could ever heal.

Bassus groaned in despair and stabbed at his enemy's chest.

Rufio struck at the lunging wrist. The bones shattered like nutshells and the dagger clattered to the floor. Beyond reason now, Bassus grasped at Rufio with his other hand. That, too, splintered and cracked beneath the stool leg.

Mindlessly, Bassus sought to envelop him with his useless arms. Rufio sprang to the side. With the force of a Celtic swordsman, Rufio slashed down behind the centurion's ear. Though only wood, the leg rang with a metallic twang as it hit the bone. A groan poured from his mouth and his legs buckled and he hit the floor with his face.

But Rufio had long ago mastered the arts of death. He knew that Bassus lived, and that was as it should be. Lessons are lost on the dead.

"Let the word go out," he said, only a few beads of sweat on his forehead betraying his exertions. "The men of my century are inviolable."

He plucked his dagger from the table plank and picked up Diocles' weapon as well. Then he turned his back with insolent supremacy and walked off into the deepening night.

23   **THE SUN SHINES FOR EVERYONE.**

Roman saying

The dawn gave way to one of those spring mornings when it is impossible to believe that all the gods are not sweet and wise.

The First Century was assembled on the parade ground, and all were crisp and alert. Word of the events of the previous evening had spread through the legion like fire through straw. No member of the century believed that Rufio had done what he had done solely for one man. He had made a stand for all of them.

Rufio dismissed the veterans for their morning weapons drill. All soldiers, regardless of their length of service, drilled at least once a day. Like every centurion in every legion, Rufio believed the Roman aphorism that by doing nothing men learn to act wickedly.

Valerius went off with the veterans to supervise them at the oaken stakes, while Metellus had the century accounts to attend to. Rufio now had the recruits to himself. He knew that without the buffer of the junior officers the new men would feel even greater unease under the gaze of the omnipotent centurion.

"Relax," he said and led an old mare by the reins to a spot in front of them. The horse wore the four-horned Celtic saddle the Romans favored.

"I'm excusing you from morning weapons drill—though you'll sweat this afternoon. Today you'll learn how to mount a horse cleanly. Most of you will never have to ride in battle, but one never knows. Every soldier must be competent to handle an animal in an emergency. First you'll learn to mount slowly, then swiftly. After a few days of this, we'll start over again slowly, but with full armor and weapons. Within a week you'll be able to leap into a saddle as easily as if it were your bed."

The new men did not seem intimidated by the horse. This was always the case with recruits, and this innocence amused Rufio. He knew from experience that no aspect of training blessed the feeble body of man with more bruising and battering than basic horse training.

"This old trooper is a very docile beast. Relax and watch."

He held the reins in his left hand and gripped the horse's mane and seemed to float into the brown leather saddle. "As you can see, man and horse were made for each other." Then he gracefully slid from his mount.

The recruits seemed more at ease than ever.

"Diocles," Rufio said. "Show us how it's done. For now, I'll hold the reins. Mount slowly."

Rufio knew that Diocles had experience hunting from horseback, though the other men probably were unaware of it. So the ease with which he could mount would give them added confidence. When dealing with animals, confidence was everything.

Diocles smiled and nodded. He sprinted toward the horse and sailed into the saddle. Startlingly, he kept sailing. Right over the top he flew and slammed into the ground on the other side, hitting his shoulder hard.

"See how easy?" Rufio said.

Stunned, Diocles pushed himself up from the dirt and rubbed his shoulder.

Then the old horse swung her head around and gazed at Diocles with eyes heavy with equine despair. The men roared.

"Now," Rufio said. "Who's the next young Perseus to tame this savage steed?"

———

The Italian custom of the early afternoon nap had taken hold even at Aquabona. As the seventh hour of the day ended, the legion belched from its midday meal and retired to its bunk to refresh itself. Of course, guards and lookouts were always on duty to maintain that relentless watchfulness that so often thwarted the enemies of Rome.

Rufio strolled up the Via Praetoria. A soft breeze blew across the drowsing fort. He often thought that his willingness to endure decades as a soldier — and there was always much to endure — was due to his ability to take pleasure in every aspect of the soldier's life. He loved the pulsing complexity of a legionary fort, with its vast energy and power brought under reasoned control. Yet he also enjoyed these gentle moments. To him the fort at rest was a lovely thing. The clean streets unmarred by traffic. The quiet of a spring afternoon. Even the most raucous soldiers asleep now, as innocent as children.

For this life, he knew he had been born. What could he possibly hope to achieve by leaving it?

He crossed the Via Principalis and entered the Praetorium. He greeted the duty officer and the soldiers on guard in the forehall and passed to the metalled courtyard beyond. He crossed it to the hall at the opposite side and went through to Sabinus's office. Ulpius Crus was bending over the Legate's desk and making a heated point. Sextus Carbo stood off to the right.

"Reporting as ordered, commander," Rufio said.

Sabinus was angry and clearly in no mood to try to conceal it.

"I've been informed that you attacked and nearly killed a former soldier of this legion. Someone who now provides us with information about German activity beyond the river."

Rufio said nothing.

"Well?" Sabinus said.

"Commander?" Rufio asked.

"Is it true?"

"The commander has been misinformed." Rufio glanced at Carbo, but the Chief Centurion's face was a wooden mask.

"You deny this?" Crus said.

"Most definitely, tribune."

"Explain," Sabinus said and flicked a finger at Crus for silence.

"The former centurion named Bassus attacked one of my men and beat him and stole his dagger. I confronted him and demanded he return the weapon. He tried to place it in my liver."

Sabinus looked at Crus.

"Then you don't deny you tried to kill him," Crus said.

"Of course I deny it. He's still alive." Rufio looked at Sabinus. "Does the commander believe that Bassus would still live if I'd wished otherwise?"

"The Legate of Augustus doesn't know what to believe."

"Commander, if I wanted to slay Bassus, I'd merely have to brush him aside like a flour grub to do it."

Sabinus turned to Carbo. "And what have you learned of this?"

"I spoke to some of the Gauls and soldiers who were there and I went to the village to see the Gallic woman who rescued the soldier. Everything Rufio has said is the same as what they told me."

Crus looked like he were about to be consumed by his own acid.

"Rufio, why do problems forever swirl around you?" Sabinus rubbed his forehead as if it pained him. "I'd think a seasoned soldier of your standing would content himself with the easy road. Why these continual skirmishes and wars?"

"They choose me, commander. I don't choose them."

It was clear from the expression in Sabinus's eyes that he liked talking with Rufio and despised it at the same time. "Is it the Fates, then?" he asked in exasperation. "Is that your view?"

"I have no view. I long ago abandoned any attempt to reason it out."

Sabinus toyed with the bronze stylus in front of him. He seemed to turn inward toward his own thoughts. An insect in the room buzzed in the ears of the three men standing before their commander. At last Sabinus laid down the stylus and looked up.

"Rufio, a centurion is a powerful man. Physically he's stronger than most. In terms of authority, he rules his men more absolutely than the Senate rules Rome. Most important, he carries within him wisdom that can be acquired only at the most terrible human cost." He stood up. "There are sixty centurions in this legion. I cannot afford the time to put out fires they carelessly start. It's their task to put out fires for me. Isn't that so?"

"That is so, commander."

"I have Gauls to keep happy and Germans to keep at bay. Don't add to my concerns."

"I'll put my full attention to it, commander."

"Dismissed."

When Rufio reached the door, Sabinus called after him.

"The soldier you avenged — whoever he is — I'm sure he's grateful you made a stand for him."

"Not for him, commander. For the Twenty-fifth Legion."

"Yes," Sabinus said and the hint of a smile narrowed his eyes. "Be assured, centurion, that the Legate of Augustus is grateful too."

———————

The Scorpion was a frightening thing. The Spanish sword or the Celtic bow could be admired from an aesthetic viewpoint, but the Scorpion was pure function. One could not pretend it was anything but an engine of death.

The recruits assembled on the parade ground and awaited Rufio. The Scorpion was set up before them. Diocles ran his hand along it and used his agile Greek mind to attempt to figure it out.

This wooden catapult clearly operated on the same principle as the bow, yet it looked much more lethal. Fastened to its own wooden stand, the weapon rose about as high as his waist. The two curved wooden arms in front were more or less horizontal, with a vertical strut in the back to adjust the angle of flight. Each of the arms nestled into an upright bundle of torsion ropes at the front. Firmly secured with iron bolts into a wooden frame, these densely packed cords were made from animal sinew. A wooden, open-topped chute, supported by the adjustable strut, extended back from the frame. Within it lay a wood and metal slider that could be moved forward to engage the heavy bowstring. A lever at the rear on the right could draw the slider and string back to launching position. A ratchet on the left prevented slippage or accidental discharge. The force generated for this terrible tail-sting must be incredible.

Rufio appeared with a round basket under one arm. Coming up behind him was a mule wagon piled high with hay bales and driven by one of the soldiers from the stables.

Rufio directed a few of the men to set up some bales in a man-size stack about two hundred feet from where the rest of the recruits were assembled. Then he dismissed the soldier with the cart.

"The more that a soldier can lengthen his arm, the better. Far better to kill at a distance than to wait for your enemy to close with you and then taste his spear." He set down the basket and pulled from it a stout projectile. "Today we'll learn to use the Scorpion's sting."

The heavy dart was passed among the men. Diocles examined it. The brutal-looking missile was about a foot long, a third of its length being a pointed iron bolt, pyramidal in cross-section. A wooden shaft comprised the remainder of the dart. Three leather flights were inlaid at the tail to direct its travel.

"Every century is issued a Scorpion. We'll learn to use ours as well as any century in the legion."

He took another dart from the basket and placed it into the slider of the weapon.

"Nothing is more demoralizing to a charging enemy than to see his comrades in front of him cut down before they're even near their foe. In war, the mental factor is as important as the edge of your steel. Cripple your enemy's resolve and it's better than if you cut out his bowels. A dying man can still kill, but a broken and frightened man can only die."

Rufio pushed the slider forward until it engaged the heavy drawstring.

"One man can operate this weapon, but I want two of you on it at all times. One loads, one shoots—if the shooter is killed, the loader takes his place."

He cranked the slider backward. The mechanism made little noise other than the metal pawl of the ratchet engaging the wooden teeth of the wheel. The curved arms were drawn back and the torsion ropes twisted.

"Caesar's men used the Scorpion very effectively at Alesia. They needed it. They were outnumbered five to one."

When the string reached maximum draw, Rufio leaned forward and took aim by adjusting the angle of launch with the vertical strut. Then he straightened up and faced his men.

"No man can withstand the Scorpion."

He triggered the release without bothering to look back downrange. The string snapped violently forward and the heavy weapon leaped from the ground with the sudden release of so much tension.

But downrange there was nothing. The stacked bales looked untouched.

"Diocles, retrieve the dart."

He ran to the bales, but the bolt was gone. He turned back and shook his head at Rufio. The centurion stood there with folded arms, and the look of impatience on his face encouraged Diocles to search harder. Suddenly he felt as if his stomach were falling through his bowels as he saw an annoyed Rufio approaching.

"What's the matter with you? Where do you think it went?" He walked over to the stacked bales.

Diocles felt foolish as he noticed the rear tip of the shaft almost flush with the face of one of the bales. The bolt had pierced the packed hay as easily as a finger jabbed into a pile of sand.

"Did you think I missed?"

"No," Diocles lied. "I just didn't see it."

Rufio gave him a look that bored through his skull, and Diocles turned away and rejoined the other recruits.

Rufio came back and returned the bolt to the slider on the catapult. "The soldier who shows the best natural talent will be given charge of the Scorpion. Veteran or not, it doesn't matter. He'll learn how to care for it, how to repair it, and how to use it to make a pointed statement for Rome."

For the next several hours, Rufio instructed his men on the use of the Scorpion. Despite their initial fumbling, his patience seemed limitless. However, Diocles had long since concluded that his centurion was by no means the most patient of men. The effort for him must therefore have been enormous. Far more admirable to Diocles than the understanding instructor was the restless and impatient one who succeeded in bending that restlessness to his will.

Only once did Rufio's impatience slip its harness. The attention of Licinius had lapsed and he was joking about something with the man at his side. Rufio lashed out with his vinewood cane across the young man's shin. He shrieked and the pain drove him to his knees. Rufio said nothing, but laid his cane down and continued his lecture on how vital it was to keep the cords dry at all times, as the sinew quickly lost its powers of torsion when wet.

When Diocles' turn came at the Scorpion, he could not suppress the exhilaration it so readily gave. So much power brought within the span of the human hand. He felt ashamed at the pleasure he derived from driving the bolts again and again into the stack of hay across the parade ground. The mind of the scholar should have been immune to such primitive passions. Yet the declension of nouns was never like this. On the other hand, the yielding bales of hay had no face. And they surely did not bleed.

24 IF YOU WANT PEACE, PREPARE FOR WAR.

Vegetius

---

*T*oday we put to good use the stones we had cut. Our century repaired a section of road north of the fort. There was an eerie feeling of participation in a historical purpose, for this was a road that Caesar had built during one of his great campaigns.

A surveyor from the First Cohort came with us to ensure the obsessive precision Romans demand of themselves. His surveying instrument is an interesting tool. It is called a groma. It is made of bronze and is composed of a pole about four feet high that sticks in the ground. An arm swings out from the top and at the end of this is a pivot where two thin bronze arms are joined to each other at their centers to form an adjustable cross. A plumb line hangs from each of the four slender arm tips. Valerius told me that the groma is used for laying out the grid for a field camp. How it works I have no idea.

One point made clear to me is that the military success of Rome owes much to these metalled roads. The speed with which we can travel is astounding. The weather is irrelevant, since the stone drainage channels carry off the rain. And the durability of the roads is incalculable. This one needs repair only because Caesar's troops were forced to lay it down in haste in the heat of a military campaign. It looks like it could endure forever.

At the end of the day I noticed Valerius off by himself working on a stone with hammer and chisel. When he finished, he called to me to help him. We lifted the heavy block and fitted it as the final piece of the western drainage channel. Into its outer vertical face, Valerius had cut :

LEG

XXV

RAP

COH II

> Q RUFI

He looked at me and said, "Rufio is wrong. Ages to come won't forget him. A thousand years from now, people will know that the men of his century walked this way."

For a moment the levelheaded optio looked wistful. His eyes were softened by a pure and elemental pride such as I had never seen in a man's eyes before. He seemed embarrassed and turned away. As he stared off at the road beyond, I smiled at his back and felt privileged to share with him this silent moment.

"The Gauls have grown careless," Barovistus said. "They look more like sheep than men."

The Suebian war chief was down on one knee and gazing across the slope at the village below. Several dozen conical huts, stone and wood and roofed with thatch, spread out in an irregular fashion not far from a gurgling stream.

"It looks perfect," Barovistus said. "Give me details."

Racovir smiled and knelt at his side. "I knew you'd be pleased.

The most trusted of the war chief's young leaders, Racovir was only a few steps from greatness. With the hard looks of a forest god, he lacked only the scars of battle. His hair, as fair as sunlight, was pulled up and knotted at the top in the usual Suebian style. Though he wore black Suebian trousers, his tunic and cloak were the dark Roman red he favored.

"Sapped by peace. " Racovir pulled at a short beard the color of brass. "I'm told no man here has borne arms in many summers. They're as soft as the flesh of a woman's belly."

"How many warriors?" Barovistus asked with the caution of the seasoned war leader.

"Seventy or eighty. The chief is a frail graybeard." He sneered. "He trusts the safety of his people to the arms of Rome."

"Who did they think you were?"

"A cavalry officer from one of the auxiliaries."

"Attack in two days. By then, I'll have destroyed the Gallic ala north of Aquabona. How many men will you take?"

"Allow me seventy and I'll eat them to the bone."

"The children and women will go to the slave dealer. And as many of the men as you take alive. Slaughter the animals and burn the village to the earth. Remember to let a few women escape. They must spread the tale like swamp air spreads death." He smiled. "Fear is a wonderful disease."

———————

The ferrous smell of the armory filled Rufio's nostrils as he waited in front of the armorer's cluttered worktable. From the back of the shop, Hetorix carried two objects wrapped in white cloth. He laid one down on his table and presented the other to Rufio. The centurion slipped off the cloth and looked at the most beautiful sword he had ever seen.

"Does it please you?" Hetorix asked with a smile.

Rufio laid the flat of the blade across his left forearm. The gleaming metal had been forged and worked with a master's touch. No impurities were visible in its skin. The edge had been honed with a fanatic's precision, and then the entire blade had been polished to a soft sheen. The hand guard was carved from Rufio's ebony and fitted on its underside was a recessed bronze plate where it would abut the scabbard. The grip was cut from bone into eight sides and fashioned with four finger contours. It was topped by a round ebony pommel, smoothly polished and fastened to the tang with a small bronze knob.

"I dulled many tools on that ebony," Hetorix said good-naturedly.

Rufio hefted the weapon. It seemed to balance itself in his hand.

"Beauty is not its only virtue," Hetorix said. "I promise you it'll withstand the trials of war. The grip is ox bone. A young male's thighbone seasoned five years. It'll take a shock or two."

"Yes." He laid the sword down and pulled the cloth off the other object. The scabbard glittered before him. Over the wood and black leather sheath had been fitted an embossed bronze faceplate. He took the scabbard and held it in the glow from one of the forges. Above decorative whorls and flourishes, the graceful figure of Victoria, wings at rest, had been intricately hammered into the bronze. She was flanked by the eagle of the Twenty-fifth Legion.

"For a work like this, I owe far more than eight denarii."

He took the leather money pouch from his belt and scooped out some coins. Hetorix reached over with his massive hand and closed Rufio's fingers back around them.

"How can I take money from a man who gave me my son?"

"Will you take my thanks?"

Hetorix smiled a broken-toothed smile. "I will."

Rufio smiled in return. "Do you have any old swords you haven't reworked yet? I need them for training."

"I have a few dozen I haven't gotten to. I'll clean them up and dull the edges for you. I can have them ready in a few hours."

"Thank you." Rufio picked up his new sword and slid it into the scabbard.

"May it guard you as well as you guard Gaul."

Rufio nodded and left the armory without saying anything more.

———————

Sabinus stood on the rampart walkway and inhaled the smell of bread coming from below. A group of stone ovens was built into the inner turf rampart, and there always seemed to be soldiers there baking bread for their centuries.

Sabinus savored the smell. Why was the aroma of baking bread always so reassuring to the troubled heart of man? Did it remind him of home and peace and family? It was like a drug, its soothing powers that great.

Sabinus pulled himself away and stared toward the dark Teutonic forests. Of course, they were far beyond the horizon, but he could see them in his mind. Hatred of the Germans had an honored history at Rome. About a hundred years earlier, the Cimbri and Teutones had ravaged Gaul. Some people claimed these marauders were in fact Celts, but no one really knew. Whoever they were, they slaughtered every Roman army sent against them. When they turned toward Italy itself, panic swept the land. Then, in battles without quarter, the fabled Gaius Marius shattered them. With an army ferociously disciplined and trained, he marched off to meet them and cut them down. At Aquae Sextiae, the Teutones fell like trees, two hundred thousand slain. Then at Vercellae, the Cimbri, too, fed the earth with corpses beyond counting.

And now the Germans were pressing once more. Like the tide, they always came around again. Not as regularly, but just as surely. Always pushing, testing, forever hungry for that which was not theirs. And Rome was not unique here. Sabinus knew enough history to know that every civilization had had its Germans. It was as if the most perverse gods had decreed it. Every culture rich and grand must have some rapacious horde clawing at its gates. Over and over the cycle went on. Could there never be any peace? Always there were rough-skinned men eager to kick in the door and seize whatever they could carry — and to put to the sword or the torch whatever they could not lift.

He turned and went down the steps leading from the rampart and walked to the Principia.

"Get me Carbo," he ordered one of the tribunes as he crossed the forehall. "And that German spy Trogus," he shouted back over his shoulder.

There was something comforting about the appearance of Sextus Carbo. When he stood in silence before the desk of Sabinus, the Chief Centurion seemed as solid as a walled city.

"I want the latest reports from the toll-takers and the customs officers at the Rhenus bridges," Sabinus said.

"Some written reports just came in about an hour ago, commander. No unusual movement beyond the river."

"Any increase in the trade in slaves or weapons?"

"None reported."

Instead of being satisfied, Sabinus felt uneasy.

"Sit down, Carbo."

The centurion placed a stool before the desk and enveloped it with his bulk.

"I feel them, Carbo. They're reaching for their spears, and here we wait. The murder of the traders was no whim. It was a taunt."

Carbo remained silent.

"Your own view? You're not here to pose for sculpture."

"My view, commander, is that peace to the Suebi is the time spent resting between wars."

"Then say that! Say it without my having to prompt you."

Carbo was unruffled. "Decades in the army have taught me caution in the presence of my commander."

"Forget caution. I need your experience and your wisdom."

"You have my experience and my loyalty and my sword."

"Thank you," Sabinus answered with a smile. He was never able to stay angry for long. "This is what I want. Starting now — this hour — I want four daily scouting patrols across the river, not just one. We have good scouts, do we not?"

"Men specially trained for it."

"Good. I want them to range as far eastward as they can and still return before sundown. I want to know what's happening out there. Second, I want you to send one of your best centurions to the cavalry fort in the north. I'll have a letter for the ala commander explaining my concerns and ordering him to be prepared for immediate movement. Do you know if he's a Gaul or a Roman?"

"Ala commanders are always Romans. I know him well."

"Good. Whom will you select to go?"

"Me. I always trust myself best."

"Take the First Cohort with you."

"Three centuries should be enough." He stood up. "One of my centurions has a broken foot and another has some kind of bowel sickness. Another just retired and hasn't been replaced yet. I'll leave their centuries here."

"Very well. Prepare for your trip."

Carbo was almost at the door when Sabinus called after him.

"Commander?" he asked, turning.

"I need you, Carbo. Stay healthy."

His huge face split in a grin. "Commander, I plan to die healthy."

———

After a full hour with Trogus, Sabinus was still perplexed. He had assumed the man was a Romanized German, but that did not really seem appropriate garb to hang on him. Nonetheless, one could not maintain that he was a coarse-mouthed barbarian. He was too cultivated to be a forest-prowling Suebi, but too — too something — to be just another eager aspirant to Roman citizenship.

The two men, dressed in white tunics, reclined on couches in Sabinus's living quarters and dined on smoked fish. Sabinus had decided to meet with Trogus here in the casual atmosphere of the Praetorium in the hope of reading his man more accurately. It had been a vain hope.

Sabinus gestured to one of the slaves, and he refilled the bronze goblets with the straw-colored wine from Latium that Sabinus favored.

"So you're convinced that this Barovistus is determined on war?" Sabinus said.

"He hungers for these plump green fields." Trogus set down his cup. "You must understand that the Suebi are bred to war. If Gaul were a desert, they would want that, too."

There was a hint of pride in Trogus's half-smile that Sabinus did not like.

"You are Suebi. Why are you different?"

Trogus vented a laugh that was unreadable. "I was meant for nobler efforts than spilling my entrails in a war for Gallic dirt."

"How many men do you think he can gather to him?"

"I'd estimate he can have at his command — within a month — two thousand warriors."

"That's less than five cohorts."

"Don't be so relieved," Trogus said with that annoying half-smile. "Two thousand armed Suebi cannot be judged in Roman terms."

"Then how should I judge them?"

Trogus shrugged but said nothing.

"Are all of them battle-hardened fighters?"

"Oh no. Many are surely young and untested. But isn't that true of your men as well?"

Sabinus eased back down and draped his arm over the end cushion on the couch. "Would you be willing to return to the other side of the river to verify all this?"

"Certainly. As long as the gratitude of Caesar continues to be spoken in Roman gold."

25   THINGS ARE NOT ALWAYS WHAT THEY APPEAR TO BE.

Phaedrus

I am amazed that there is not more petty squabbling among the soldiers. Opportunities for amusement are rare out here and boredom is an insidious instigator. True, discipline is severe. One day on the way in from a route march, I saw a soldier leaning forward against one of the training stakes and being savagely caned by his centurion. I was told he had lost his dagger in a game of dice. Nonetheless, the threat of the vinewood is not enough. Self-discipline must also restrain the unruly nature of man.

I hear there are forts with small arenas for gladiatorial combats or wild beast fights, but we have none. Off duty soldiers spend most of their leisure time sleeping or gambling with their tentmates. We have horse races on the parade ground, and they are well attended. Wrestling matches are the favorite forms of competition. I cannot imagine more enthusiastic spectators than these.

Official festivals are an important part of everyone's relaxation here, as well as an opportunity for moderate revelry. Augustus's birthday and the anniversary of the founding of the legion are two of the most notable. There is also the Rosaliae Signorum, as deeply felt a religious festival as I have ever attended. This feast is for the purpose of venerating the standards. The golden legionary eagle and the silver capricorn of the Twenty-fifth Legion, as well as the standard of each individual cohort, are set up together outdoors by the senior signifers, and the entire garrison is mustered before them. After words by the commander, the standards are anointed with holy oil and adorned with woven crowns of roses, and public thanksgiving is made. One might not think of soldiers as religious men, but the cult of the standards means more to them than any soft-bellied civilian could ever imagine. They are kept, along with a statue of Augustus, in a shrine in the Principia next to Sabinus's office. Beneath the shrine is the strongroom housing the legionary treasury. Guards are posted at the shrine all day and all night, and this is not just to make sure the money is safe. The veneration of the standards binds these soldiers to each other with a tie of iron.

Occasionally we are entertained with plays — of a sort — by troupes of traveling mimes and what are rather broadly referred to as actresses. Actually, these well-rouged nymphs can swiftly drain a man's testicles and his purse with equally wondrous facility.

And, of course, there are the brothels. The number of prostitutes living in the civil settlement could capsize a bireme. Never in my life have I seen so many doubtful maidens in so small an area at one time. There seems to be at least one prostitute for every strand of pubic hair of every soldier in the legion. Naturally, the men make good use of them, a fact about which only a Stoic with a dead branch would complain. Yet I sometimes think that if any of these cohorts should give way before the charge of an enemy, it will not be because of a lack of training or a failure of discipline. It will be a collapse brought on by simple copulatory exhaustion.

Diocles silently thanked Rufio for all those rank hours spent shoveling out the stables. The shield he was expected to wield must have weighed about fifteen pounds. Just a few months earlier he never would have been able to manage it.

A damp breeze was blowing down from the north when the recruits assembled on the parade ground. The sky was darkening, but Diocles could not imagine anything as trivial as weather having any effect on Rufio.

Diocles rested his shield on the ground in front of him. It was curved and stood slightly over three feet high. The edges had an oval contour, but the shield was squared off at the top and bottom. Because of the curvature, Diocles suspected it was not a solid slab, but several thinner layers of strip wood glued and laminated together. The shield was covered with calfskin, and a bronze rim reinforced the entire edge. The number of the cohort and century had been scratched inside the top rim. A spindle-shaped iron boss was nailed to the center. The leather covering was dyed bright blue. Two painted pairs of large white wings flanked the iron boss. Shooting out from the center toward the four corners were four lightning bolts.

Thunder threatened in the distance as Rufio directed every man to take a sword from the cart. Diocles knew enough about the customs of other peoples to be intrigued by the Roman attitude toward weaponry. Coolly professional, the Romans had no hoary legends or pious rituals on the subject. If the Spanish produce a superior blade, adopt it. What matter where it comes from? The Roman's weapon matched his outlook on life, which is to say it cut very deep indeed.

The swords distributed now were not in the best condition. Their edges were gouged from much use, and an occasional rust pit showed here and there.

"I want every man to work at the stakes just as he did with the wooden swords," Rufio said. "Work at your own pace. Don't disappoint me. Show me what you've learned."

The young soldiers attacked with confidence. Iron bosses slammed home hard, and swordpoints thrust at the wooden torsos. They thrust and circled and thrust once more. Again and again they sought to achieve maximum effect with minimum effort. "Battles can last for hours," Rufio had drilled into them. "Squander your strength and you squander your life."

Rain began to pelt the young warriors, but Rufio gave no order to halt. He stood in the thickening mud with folded arms and got as wet as everyone else. Soon the parade ground was as slick as grease. Some men fell as they lunged. They pulled themselves from the sucking mire and attacked again.

The storm worsened and the spring rain soon had everyone shivering. As all knew, the immense forehall of the Principia was designed to be used for training in foul weather, but Rufio seemed to have forgotten that. So the mock battle continued, accompanied now by grumbling that several men did not care to keep to a whisper.

Some of the soldiers' lips were turning blue from the chill when Rufio said, "I believe I hear a murmur of complaint."

The men paused in their miniature war.

"I'll make a bargain with you," he went on above the pounding rain. "We can return to the fort and drill indoors—if one of you can promise me the Germans will attack us only at noon in June in sunshine." He placed his hands on his hips and waited.

The shivering men could only stare at him in silence.

"Fight!" he shouted in an angry guttural.

They wheeled on their wooden enemies and savaged them.

The harsh contact with the stake felt good to Diocles, especially when he pretended it was Rufio.

After another half-hour of this ordeal, the centurion barked an order for them to stop.

"I want those weapons cleaned and dried. I want to see no rust. Then one last order—everyone is to go to the baths and cook himself until he's crisp."

The men looked at one another and smiled.

"Well done," Rufio said with satisfaction.

He turned and led them back, slicing through the mud and rain as if he did not feel either.

Perhaps, thought Diocles, he really did not.

———————

Among the centurion's cluster of rooms at one end of the barracks was a room set aside for the signifer, where he could tend the century accounts. Rufio had decorated it with tapestries and rugs he had brought from the East. A desk squatted at the far end. Its front had been adorned by some ingenious craftsman with a relief of Herakles slaying the Nemean lion. Racks overflowing with rolled documents lined the two walls flanking the desk.

For the past several weeks, most of the talk in the barracks had been about money. Now the thrice-yearly payday had come and Metellus was awash in paperwork.

"I'm the only one who can compete with their preoccupation with fornication," Metellus said to Diocles, and he unlocked the ironbound money chest on the floor next to the desk. "Only the veterans get paid today. The new men aren't entitled to a stipendium until they take the sacramental oath when their training is done."

"But don't they need money, too?"

"They were given seventy-five denarii in traveling money when they enlisted. More than enough to hold them over." He placed a bag of silver in front of him and organized the documents on the desk. "First tent group!" he shouted, and eight veterans hurried through the doorway.

They joked and jostled one another and commented on each other's ugliness and on how much silver it would take to find a willing Gallic bedmate.

"See what I mean?" Metellus said to Diocles. "Italians and lust—a matched set."

Diocles smiled but was careful not to laugh aloud.

"Remember, Salvius," Metellus said to the burly soldier before him. "This has to last until September. Spend it with care."

"Yes, Metellus," he said with fake seriousness. "With a good officer like you, we need no mother."

"Get out of here, you rank stag."

Diocles looked down at the papyrus sheet. Beneath the name of Lucius Salvius was a column listing bedding, rations, boots, arms, and Saturnalian feast, with corresponding figures for some of them, no amounts for others. There was even an entry for burial club. Perhaps, Diocles thought, a man fought with greater valor if he knew he would be taken care of if he fell for Rome. Toward the bottom, the expenses were totaled. Underneath were notations of the remainder on deposit, the previous balance carried over, and the total present balance.

"I don't understand," Diocles said. "Why didn't you give him all he's entitled to?"

Metellus gestured the next soldier forward as he spoke.

"Out of his seventy-five denarii, I hold on to sixty-two against future expenses and as a forced savings. That way these stoats cannot squander their money on mindless debauches. Isn't that right, Primus?"

"Oh yes, Metellus," answered the scarfaced soldier now standing before him. "And we love you for it."

"When they come to retire, they'll thank their officers for their foresight," Metellus said to Diocles. "Now, they'd prefer to piss in my ear."

After the entire century had been paid, Metellus spent time going over all the accounts once more.

"I was taught mathematics by a Greek. I take pride in never making a mistake in these matters."

As Metellus was finishing, Rufio walked in. He seemed distracted and distant.

"I want all the recruits advanced twenty denarii," he said and threw a large bronze key onto the desk

He turned and left as quickly as he had come.

Metellus stared after him for some time.

"What is it?" Diocles asked.

"Herennius would never have thought to do that. Rufio may be a centurion, but he remembers what it's like to be a recruit. How miserable you feel when you see the other men get paid. How you feel like only half a soldier. He knows the recruits couldn't have spent their traveling money yet. And he also knows that's not the point."

Diocles picked up the key. Scratched on one side was Q FLA RUF.

"That's the key to his personal strongbox," Metellus said. "In the floor of his living quarters."

"It's his money, then?"

"Yes. How could anyone claim this century is cursed? I say we were all born under very good birds indeed."

The spring storm had fled as quickly as it had arrived. Varacinda sat on the damp grass near the swimming cove and brushed up some small white flowers that had been flattened by the rain. The glare of the sun off the beads of water on the grass was as cutting as the edge of a knife, and she squinted and looked away.

Flavia placed a hand on her shoulder and sat down next to her.

"You seem troubled today," Flavia said with a voice that could have soothed a torrent.

Varacinda looked at her with the fear and helplessness of a small child who has somehow lost her clothes and has no idea where she put them.

"What's wrong?" Flavia asked.

"I feel so bad," she answered with guilty eyes.

"Tell me why."

"Last night . . . last night I dreamed of a Roman. We did things in my dream—intimate things—and I loved it so."

The younger woman stared at the older one with bafflement. "What does it matter?"

Varacinda sank her teeth into her lower lip and looked away.

"What does it matter?" Flavia persisted, placing her hands on Varacinda's forearms.

"Because I'm awake now," she whispered. "And every time I think of that dream I grow wet inside."

Flavia laughed with that wonderfully musical laugh of hers.

"Stop it!" Varacinda shouted as she glared at her in a flash of anger.

"Oh Vara," she said, still laughing and wrapping her arms around the other woman's shoulders. "I've had dreams like that, too."

"But not about this man."

"How can you know that?"

Varacinda stared at her.

"We're not stone, Vara. We're women. And as much as men may drive us mad, there are some who can also drive us wild. So what does it matter that we dream of them?"

"But I'm married. I love Adiatorix more than my life."

Flavia took her right hand and leaned forward until she was just a few inches from her face. "Adiatorix is a great chief and a noble warrior and a loyal husband"—Flavia squeezed her hand tenderly and whispered—"but he's not entitled to the secrets of your dreams."

"Oh Flavia, I love you so very much."

Flavia's blue eyes smiled her love in return.

Varacinda shook her head in wonder. "I wish I could be like you."

Flavia's dark brows knotted in puzzlement.

"You take everything so easily," Varacinda said. "All of life's passions and troubles. You're very much like your name, you know—more like a Roman than a Sequani."

Flavia placed the palm of her right hand against Varacinda's face and pushed her back onto the grass. And then they both laughed together like children.

26   AMID ARMS THE LAWS ARE SILENT

Cicero

Rufio had slept just a single hour. His breakfast had tasted like leather and mud. Every sound annoyed him this morning, and the skin on his arms felt itchy and tight.

He reined about and stared down from the low rise. His century stretched out on the stone road below. That soothed him. Still six short of a full century, but they would do. Seventy-four men in full armor, gear-heavy cross poles held in one hand and extended over a shoulder, two pila in the other hand and resting on the opposite shoulder. Covered shield hanging down the back. Twelve pack mules laden with equipment and provisions. Metellus riding at the head with that relaxed competence he wore so well.

The rising sun brightened their off-white tunics and lit up the bronze helmets. The shattered century of Herennius was a dying memory. Yet there was still much for them to learn. And there was little time.

Rufio turned his black stallion toward the hinterland as Valerius came riding up.

"An east wind is coming," Rufio said.

Valerius looked off at the blue sky. He wet some fingertips and held them toward the east.

"I can't feel it."

"It's coming. The wind of death."

Valerius stared at him in silence.

"I can sense these things. I always could. Every since I was a boy."

"What do you feel?"

"Tragic nights. Endless weeping in darkness."

"But we are here," Valerius said with the confidence of youth. "You came back at the perfect moment. Just in time to save your Gauls."

"My Gauls?"

"Oh yes," Valerius said with a grin. "It's in your eyes every minute of the day."

"Today I want the men to learn everything they can about a marching camp. I want them to be experts by tomorrow."

"Not much time."

"The barbarians are out there. Waiting." He stroked his horse's mane as he stared far off.

"Soon do you think?"

"At any moment. I've sensed it before. In Syria, in Spain, in Gaul when I was young."

He took the iron helmet hanging from a corner pommel and put it on and tied the thongs.

"Do you think I could develop this sense?"

"It will steal your sleep and haunt your dreams." *But it keeps my men alive.* And Rufio thanked the gods for it.

———

Three hours before sunset, Metellus stuck the shaft of the century standard into the turf of a broad meadow bordered on the north by a stream. On this spot Rufio's tent would sit. A perimeter was marked off and camp construction began. One third of the men lined the outside edge. They thrust the sharp butts of their pila into the ground next to them and leaned their shields against them, then faced outward, searching for unseen enemies.

The remainder of the men began trenching. Still in full armor, they dug a ditch about three feet deep and four feet across at the top to form the perimeter of the camp. The loose soil was piled behind the ditch into a rampart. They then lashed together sets of three four-foot wooden stakes they had brought with them. Tied at their narrow centers, they formed six-pronged obstacles that were lined up atop the rampart to form a low but formidable palisade.

The gateway had no gate but merely an opening. However, the left and right ditches and ramparts overlapped, with the left ones curving inward and around and behind the right ones. In this way, an enemy who made it past the pickets and gateway guards could not rush straight into the camp but had to go around a bend. With his shield in his left hand, he would be unprotected on his right, the side facing the rampart and its defenders. He would not get far. With their characteristic penchant for nicknames, the soldiers called this curving gateway the clavicle, after its resemblance to a small key.

Valerius ranged about, instructing and encouraging the recruits. He carried the optio's symbol of office, a long staff with a bronze knob, and he occasionally struck a veteran across a thigh for being too eager to let the recruits do all the work.

When the trench and rampart were complete and the pack mules safely within the camp, the tents were pitched. There was still plenty of time before sunset to cook the evening meal and lean back on the grass with a cup or two of Celtic beer.

Diocles sat with some of his tent group around a small fire in front of their eight-man goatskin home.

"Why are you staring at me like that?" he said with the irritability that weariness brings.

Metellus rested back on one elbow and gave him that infuriatingly bemused look. "I've been watching you for the last two hours. You entertain me."

"Perhaps I should learn to juggle, too," he said with a scowl.

Valerius came up and sat on the grass.

"Our Greek friend thinks we're fools, Lucius."

The optio grinned but said nothing.

"The Attic sage believes we like to dig holes and kneel in dirt for no reason."

"I never—"

"Don't bother to deny it. Sour confusion—that's how I'd describe your face since we started the camp."

"Am I that obvious?"

"Never consider politics," Valerius said. "You lie too poorly."

"But what is all this?" Diocles asked with a sweep of his arm. "This trenching and mounds and sticks."

"Do you thinks it's for nothing?" Metellus said.

"What purpose can it serve? It's a house of straw. Whom could it keep at bay? A three foot ditch and a little mound and these bundles of stakes . . . ."

"You tell him," Metellus said. He reached for a wineskin and squirted some acetum into his mouth.

"It's a camp, not a fort. " Valerius took off his helmet and laid it on the grass beside him. "If the enemy appears, we'll meet them on the open field."

"They why bother with all this? It took hours. We could've gone much further if we didn't have to stop so early to do this."

"Would you sleep just as comfortably in an open field."

Diocles said nothing.

"Or are your dreams just a little sweeter when your skinny Greek torso is surrounded by a ditch and rampart and guarded gateway?"

"So this is just for peace of mind?"

"Don't be a fool. The palisade keeps spies and bandits out. Scavenging animals, too. And it keeps our own animals from straying."

"And it discourages deserters," Metellus said. "Though I cannot imagine anyone deserting Rufio."

"Do you feel better now?" Valerius asked with a mocking smile.

Diocles stood up and gazed down the line of tents. They extended as straight as a sword blade, ten small tents in a row with Rufio's larger tent at the end. In front of each, every soldier's shield leaned against a pilum in an inverted "V". A helmet rested at the apex. All was at the ready.

"Sit down," Valerius said.

Diocles obeyed.

"I'll tell you a story," the optio said. "About, oh, forty years ago, Caesar and his troops bridged the Rhenus. He could've built boats— much more easily than a bridge. In ten days his men finished it. Ten days. And he did it for no other reason than to cow the Germans. They'd never even seen a bridge before."

Valerius gestured for Metellus to pass the wineskin and he took a drink.

"Guess what he did then. " Valerius wiped his lips with the back of a hand. "After marching through Germania for a few days, Caesar returned to Gaul. And then he destroyed the bridge." He leaned back with a smile.

"I'm missing your meaning. He didn't want the Germans to follow him. . . ?"

"Follow him?" Metellus said, laughing. "The Germans were shaking in awe. Here was a structure they couldn't even have imagined and he destroyed it as if it were nothing. To show them he could build it again in an instant if he wished."

Diocles remained silent.

"That was Caesar," Metellus said with reverence. "The Germans trembled in their forests like whipped dogs, and he hadn't even had to strike a blow."

"This isn't just a defensive structure," Valerius said. "It's a moral blow at all who oppose us. Every day, no matter how far we've marched or how hard we've fought, we stop and trench and fortify. We're relentless. Look at the camp through the eyes of the Germans for a moment. You'll fear what you see."

Metellus stood up and slapped Diocles on the back. "Not just a patch of ground, my friend. A sword thrust into the heart of the barbarian."

Rufio walked along the line of tents. The men were resting around their cooking fires. The veterans talked and joked with the recruits, and they smiled in return. Gaining confidence daily from their newfound skills, the new men moved with increasing surety. And the shared toil drew the bond between new men and old ever more tightly.

"Have you eaten well, comrades?" Rufio asked and he stopped before one of the tent groups.

"Always, Rufio," Licinius said with a full mouth.

"You'll sleep soundly tonight. But if any of you hears a strange noise, alert your senior tent mate. In these forests there are no innocent spirits."

Though he was not thirsty, he reached for a skin of acetum and squirted some into his mouth.

"Thank you." He handed back the skin. "Sleep well."

He touched Arrianus on a shoulder and moved on.

Similar chats he held down the line, as he shared food and tales of exotic lands.

No longer did his men flinch at his approach. They looked up with keenness, expectancy. A kind word or a shared morsel from Rufio was now a banquet at the table of Caesar.

Diocles was sitting on the grass in front of Rufio's tent in the fading daylight when the centurion approached. His knees were drawn up with his arms wrapped around them. He stared off into the wilderness.

"Pensive tonight?" Rufio removed his helmet and sat on the ground beside him.

"I suppose. There's so much to learn."

Rufio leaned back on the grass and remained silent.

"I'm a freeborn citizen of Rome," Diocles went on. "Nursed along the Tiber. You'd think I'd know what it means to be a Roman."

"Of course you know."

Diocles shook his head from side to side.

"What troubles you tonight?"

"A month ago I'd have sneered at Valerius and Metellus. Just as so many civilians do when you mention soldiers. And now . . ." He sighed. "I marvel at their wisdom. And they're so young."

Rufio smiled.

"I'm a scholar. A man sheltered by his books. What I know about life — real life — could be balanced on the tip of a pilum." He stood up and stared off toward the darkening east. "I'm soft and weak and I know nothing."

"And you've not yet seen battle. If you do, you'll learn all there is to know about the nature of man. Now go get me my officers. I need them."

When Metellus and Valerius came to his tent, he left the signifer in command and rode east with Valerius.

The meadow sprawled for about two miles beyond the camp before it was broken by woods.

"I want a sentry line a mile out from the camp perimeter." Rufio traced it with an extended forefinger. "I want four men patrolling at all times. Changed every hour so they get enough sleep. I want the password changed every hour, too. They'll be inspected at their posts every half-hour. I'll take the first three hours, Metellus the next two, you the last three."

"Yes, centurion."

"I want them mounted. You know that, don't you?"

"Oh yes," he said with a smile. "Horses hear better than men."

"You and Metellus will sleep in my tent when we're in the field. Get to sleep early — you'll be up early. I'll feel much better if I know it's you who's welcoming the dawn."

"Thank you."

Rufio gazed at the distant forest as he idly thumbed his ring.

"Are you sensing it again?" Valerius asked.

"Yes. I can almost smell those yellow-haired savages."

———

Rufio was up before dawn and patrolling the camp on foot. The night had been quiet and all was well. By the time the sun had topped the trees to the east, the men were cooking their morning porridge.

Valerius was out inspecting the sentry line while Metellus supervised the breaking of camp and the loading of the gear onto the pack mules. The bundles of palisade stakes would be last. Caution always.

Rufio walked among his men and observed their interactions. The gruffness of the veterans had softened now that the recruits had sweated through the construction of a marching camp. And the new men, though still respectful, were no longer overawed by them. It was clear to them that their centurion would not allow them to be abused any more than was necessary to toughen their hides.

While a pair of soldiers folded his tent, Rufio put on his mail lorica and buckled his swordbelt. Lost in his reverie, he dressed without thought. Hoofbeats from the east startled him.

He grabbed his helmet and hurried to the gateway. Valerius was coming in, riding fast.

The animal had barely stopped when Valerius jumped from the saddle.

"What?" Rufio said, putting on his helmet.

"The east wind."

"Where?"

"About two miles northeast. They put a village to the torch. I saw smoke so I went to check it. Orders?"

Rufio smiled at his optio. Never had it occurred to Valerius to leave the Sequani to the wolves. This was a fighting Roman.

"Three ranks," Rufio said and tied the thongs on his cheek guards. "Recruits in the middle, veterans front and rear. Diocles with me."

The men assembled in two minutes.

"Double time. March with valor. Move!"

The men swung into a quick cadence across the meadow. Smoke was darkening the sky to the east.

The plain rose gently to a broad ridge. When the century reached the summit, Rufio raised his hand.

"Dress ranks!"

The line had become ragged on the incline, and now the veterans straightened it out. They pushed in closer, shoving and jerking the recruits into no more than a three-foot frontage for each man, and three feet in front and back to allow room for throwing their pila.

Metellus and Diocles flanked Rufio on horseback at the front. Valerius guarded the rear from his mount.

In the village below, all was chaos. Flames were devouring dozens of huts and seemed to mock the buckets of water thrown at them. The black smoke obscured much, but the shrieks of the women could be heard even from here.

Their cries cut into Rufio. Like the wail of a woman he had heard so long ago.

"Drop your gear!"

The veterans dumped their cross poles with their equipment and swung their shields off their backs and peeled off the leather covers. In their right hands they hefted their pila. The recruits copied their actions.

"Move!"

Down the slope they marched in three tight ranks.

No fighting could be seen. Women and old men were running everywhere, and even small children were dragging buckets. Yet there were no warriors.

"Help us please!" said a graybeard who ran up to the centurion.

Rufio had seen many burning villages. He knew what had to be done.

"Pull your people back. Don't risk any more. Let the huts burn. We'll send soldiers to help you build more."

The stench was overpowering, but it wasn't simply wood and straw. Assaulting the soldiers was the most loathsome odor a human can smell.

"Do it!" Rufio shouted. "Get them away from those flames!"

The old man ran off waving his arms at the women.

"Where are the fighters? Metellus, circle the village. Quickly and report."

Metellus jammed the staff of the boar standard into the ground and galloped off through the smoke.

Rufio scanned the distance but could see nothing.

A dazed young woman, coughing and choking, staggered out of the smoke. She carried a small burnt log and held it out toward Rufio.

He slipped from his horse and hurried to her. When he reached the woman, her legs buckled. She fell to her knees and vomited and dropped the black log at his feet.

He picked it up and had to suck back his own breakfast porridge. An incinerated infant lay in his hands.

Though shaking with rage, he set it down gently.

"Valerius!"

The optio rode up from behind the third rank.

"Hold the men here."

Rufio ran through the smoking village. Past flaming huts and crying women he bolted, but no warriors were to be seen.

He caught up with Metellus at the edge of the village.

"Nothing," the signifer shouted.

Rufio glimpsed a young woman hiding in the shadow of an unburned hut.

"Come," he said. "I'm here to help you."

She stepped forward, a red-haired girl of about eight clinging to one of her legs and sniffling.

"Where are your men?"

"Still fighting," she said and pulled her daughter more tightly to her.

"Where?"

"A short run from here east of the village."

He whistled sharply and in an instant his horse galloped up beside him. Diocles followed quickly behind.

"Show me." Rufio mounted his horse and pulled her up behind him.

"Mommy!"

"Come here, sweetheart," Metellus said and he scooped the girl into his saddle.

The five of them raced off to the east.

It was a startling sight. Seventy or eighty enraged Gauls had beaten back equally as many Germans and pushed them against a low hill. Hemmed in, the German warriors could neither flank the Sequani nor risk turning and fleeing up the hill and being cut down in flight.

Both sides were nearing exhaustion, their arms wielding weapons that seemed as heavy as lead.

"Metellus," Rufio said and pointed behind him.

The signifer turned and galloped off to get the century, the little girl still in the saddle in front of him.

"Thincsus is a poor tactician," Rufio said, referring to the German god of war. He turned to Diocles. "Do you see what's happened here? The Suebi allowed themselves no line of retreat. Savage amateurs."

"What happened?"

"No scouting. No spies. They underestimated the number of Gauls. And the Germans are fighting for greed and glory. The Gauls are fighting for their lives."

"Can we do something?"

Rufio turned to the woman behind him on the horse. Her arms still hugged his waist.

"Is your husband there?"

"I have no husband," she said with fearful eyes. "But my brother fights. He's their leader."

"I'll bring him home to you." He jumped from his horse. "Get in the saddle."

The century appeared, Metellus riding at the right of the first rank, the standard in his hand. The little girl gripped the horse's mane in front of him.

"Valerius!" Rufio boomed. "Twenty men. Veterans. Around the back." He made a hooking gesture with his wrist. "Pila. On Metellus."

Valerius jumped from his horse. In an instant he had selected twenty men from the third rank, and without being told they formed three ranks. At a trot they disappeared with the optio around the right flank of the hill.

On seeing the Romans, the Gauls drew fresh life and threw themselves anew at the Germans.

"No!" Rufio shouted in exasperation.

"What's wrong?" Diocles asked and jumped from his horse.

"They have to disengage. Metellus!"

The signifer dismounted and hurried over, the little girl still gripping his hand.

"We don't have a trumpet, do we?"

"No."

Rufio shook his head in anger. "The next time I go into the field without a trumpet, kick me in the ass."

Valerius and his twenty men had encircled the back of the hill and now appeared at the summit.

"We can't wait," Rufio said. He dropped to one knee before the little girl. "I need you to help me, pretty one," he said gently. "Will you do that for me?" He held open his arms.

She looked up at Metellus as she still held his hand.

"It's all right," he said with a smile. "He's the man we always trust. Go with him."

She smiled and extended her arms toward Rufio.

He carried her to within about a hundred and fifty feet of the battle line and set her down and knelt beside her.

"What's your name, sweetheart?"

"Kalinda."

He smiled and brushed one of her freckled cheeks with his thumb.

She flinched at the rough skin of his hand but then reached up and squeezed his fingers. Her blue eyes gazed at him with an innocent trust that touched him where no sword could ever reach.

"I want you to face those men out there now, and I want you to scream as loud as you can. I want it to start at your pretty little toes and go all the way up through your body and out your mouth. Will you do that for me? I want to help your uncle get away from those bad men."

She nodded and turned and let out a shriek heard as far as the Tiber. On and on it went, a piercing little girl scream that could have shattered tempered steel.

Stunned, the Gauls pulled back and turned, fearful of some new threat to their families.

"Disengage!" Rufio shouted, waving them aside. "Break off!"

He waved his men forward.

The Sequani woman rode up on his horse and he lifted Kalinda to the saddle.

"Take her from the field. Now."

She wheeled and galloped off with her daughter toward the village.

The three ranks of soldiers stopped before him. The veterans stuck the pointed butts of their pila into the ground next to them and the new men did the same.

At the foot of the hill, the Sequani had drawn away and split in half, allowing a clear field for the Romans.

Rufio turned to his men. The veterans were taut and expectant, the recruits terrified. The expressions of the new men were those of children suddenly thrust into the world of adults. Several were shaking so much their mail loricas sounded like the distant rustling of leaves in the wind.

Rufio stepped before them, the first rank of veterans at his back.

"Hear me. These good men will carry you through this day." He gestured to the rank behind him and to the other rank of veterans to the rear. "And remember this—I am with you always."

Like the outstretched shield of Mars, Rufio's voice covered them with its strength and drew them within its protective shade. Several dusty mouths suddenly found saliva. Twenty pairs of eyes began to relax as they gazed at this man, serene in the belief in his own utter invincibility.

The Germans seemed confused. Several warriors clustered around a figure in the center. Wooden spears were their principal arms, and a few carried Gallic swords and wicker shields.

Atop the hill, the twenty soldiers hefted one of their two pila and brought them to shoulder height.

The Germans still had not seen them.

"Metellus!" Rufio shouted.

Metellus raised the silver boar so all on the hill could see it. He kept his eyes on his centurion.

Rufio slashed downward with the edge of his hand.

Metellus lowered the boar in a sweeping arc.

A communal grunt of exertion rolled from the hilltop, and an iron rain crashed into the Germans.

Men screamed in pain and rage. Skulls split and spines shattered. Warriors still standing turned in all directions, but the Gauls flanked them, and the Romans held the field before them.

"First rank, pila up," Rufio ordered.

Each soldier in the front rank jerked a spear out of the ground and brought it to shoulder height.

"Now!"

The second volley sheared into the Suebi. Their unprotected breasts sucked in the Celtic steel. Stout fighters crumpled like collapsed cocoons as howls and groans fouled the air.

"Metellus!"

The signifer raised the boar.

Rufio cut the air, the boar came down, and the second volley from the hilltop tore into the desperate men.

Three-quarters of the Suebi were already dead. Wounded warriors, some with spears still buried in their torsos, dragged themselves across the ground with the futility of pierced insects.

"Surrender or die!" Rufio shouted in Celtic. He gestured to his first rank and each man brought up his second pilum.

The German in the center strode forward and shouted some Suebian curse and threw his sword onto the ground in front of him.

"I want them alive," Rufio said to Metellus. "Keep the Gauls away."

Metellus signaled to Valerius and his men, and in a tight rank they descended the hill behind the Germans. The soldiers still held their pila at the ready.

Rufio confronted the leader as Metellus split the century in two, each half ordered to hold the angry Sequani at bay with their shields.

Valerius and his soldiers surrounded the surviving Germans.

"I am Racovir," the leader said to Rufio in Celtic. "War chief of the Suebi."

Barely able to suppress his rage, Rufio stared into the eyes of the barbarian.

"You're an arrogant fool." He looked to Valerius. "Back to the village."

"Rufio," Diocles said, speaking for the first time since the battle had begun. "What about the wounded?" He pointed to the Germans still groaning on the ground.

"Leave them to the Gauls." He gestured to Metellus, and the signifer pulled the soldiers away.

Rufio turned his back and the Sequani descended on the bleeding Germans and began hacking them to death.

Amidst screams heard only in the alleys of Hell, Rufio walked calmly away and led his men back to the village.

"Stake them out," Rufio ordered when they reached an open space in the midst of the smoldering huts. "Take your young ones away," he said to the mothers, and they hurried off with their children.

Several of the soldiers gathered slivers of wood and scraps of leather. While some of the Sequani warriors held back raging women, twenty-two German survivors were laid out on their backs on the ground. Soldiers drove the sticks into the earth and lashed each German's wrists to them with the leather thongs. They lay sprawled and defenseless.

Except for Racovir.

Rufio dragged a table and some stools from one of the huts and set them up in the clearing. He pointed to one of the stools. Racovir sat.

The war leader glared at the Roman with the sneer of one who had toppled a city, rather than a third-rate tactician who had just burned children to death in a mindless folly.

Valerius was carrying Racovir's long sword, and Rufio took it and laid its blade down across some glowing embers.

"Metellus, set up a sentry line and patrol the edge of the village. I want no surprises." He turned to his men. "Three ranks and stand at ease."

They rested their shields on the ground but never took their eyes off Rufio.

The centurion sat opposite the German. He pulled off his helmet and set it aside and stuck his dagger into the wooden plank between them. Valerius and Diocles stood and watched near one end of the table.

"You're a liar," Rufio said to Racovir. "A war chief? No. A sub-chief of some kind. Nursed on a boy's fantasies of glory and blood."

Like a bolt from Jupiter, the back of Rufio's left hand raked across Racovir's face. His ring laid open the cheek to the bone.

"There," Rufio said. "Now you have your blood."

Racovir stared back with watery eyes. "You're a brave man with soldiers at your elbow," he said in Celtic.

Rufio knew that questioning the Suebi was the easiest of tasks. The Germans lived for boasting.

"Why?" the centurion asked.

"To test the strength of your stunted limbs." Blood dripped from his cheek onto the table between them.

"What else?"

"To see if you'd fight for these dogs."

"Of course we would. You should know that. They're our allies."

"That word has no meaning in Suebian. The Sequani are nothing."

"They beat you to a standstill."

"We were beaten by Romans. Someday we'll have our reckoning with the Sequani."

"You'll see Hell before you'll see that day. Who is your chief?"

"Barovistus."

"Why isn't he here?

"Other battles."

Rufio didn't like the sound of that. "Where?"

"A place of his choosing. Now what will you do with us? Loose these Sequani dogs and let them devour us?"

"What would you do?"

Racovir said nothing.

"Let me guess. You'd tear us apart and hang our heads on oak trees as gifts to your forest gods."

"And what a gift yours would make, Silver Hair."

"But I won't do that."

Contempt for Roman mercy stained Racovir's smile. "I know that. And I should thank you, too. For this." He pointed to his cheek. "Now I have my scar."

"Oh no. For a scar, the wound must have time to heal."

The sneer poured like wax from Racovir's face as Rufio plucked the dagger from the table and thrust the blade through his left eye socket. He twisted it brutally and blood from the German's brain shot onto his hand. Then he wrenched it loose and Racovir's head hit the table with a bang.

Rufio vaguely heard a gagging sound come from Diocles off to his right. The centurion reached across and cut a strip from the back of the corpse's tunic and turned to face the helpless Germans.

They gaped at him in terror.

He bent down and wrapped the cloth around the hilt of Racovir's hot sword and took it from the embers. He approached the Suebi pinned to the earth. The blade glowed an angry red.

"Never cross the river again. If you do, you won't return."

He slashed down at the first captive, severing his left hand with one swift blow.

The stump flailed wildly and squirted Rufio with pulsing blood. He slammed a foot down onto the forearm and pressed the hot blade against the stump and sealed the wound. The man was wailing as Rufio cut the thong on his other wrist.

Down the line Rufio went, slashing and searing and freeing. The sizzle and stink of burning German filled the air. The Suebi began urinating themselves at the shrieks of their comrades and at the Roman's approach. Twenty-one hands he left on Gallic soil. The final warrior was a blonde boy of no more than eighteen who shook as though with palsy. He reeked with the stench of animal terror and his own waste matter as the blood-spattered Roman stood above him.

Down the blade came, first on the left thong, then on the right.

"Go home whole," Rufio said. "Hug your mother and pray you never see me again."

27   IS IT THE GODS WHO PUT THIS FIRE IN OUR MINDS, OR IS IT THAT EACH MAN'S RELENTLESS LONGING BECOMES A GOD TO HIM?

Virgil

The orange sun was dropping behind the horizon when the century entered the fort. The guards seemed especially alert. Rufio sensed distant thunder.

He dismissed his men to their barracks and the baths and rode to the Praetorium.

With his blue tunic and lorica still crusted with blood, he startled the guards at the entrance to Sabinus's residence. One hurried to the commander's office while Rufio waited in a small anteroom lined with benches and lit by a single lamp hanging from a bronze stand in the corner.

He heard running feet and turned to see Sabinus rush in, followed by Probus and several other centurions.

"By the gods!" Sabinus said.

The commander had the look of a man who had just been saved from drowning. He gripped Rufio by both arms.

"We thought you'd been killed."

"We're all fine. Diocles, too."

Probus smiled. "I told the commander the steel hasn't been forged that could cut you low."

"Who's this?" Sabinus touched a bloodstain on Rufio's tunic.

"Racovir of the Suebi. Why did you think we'd been killed?"

"Carbo is dead. Come."

Sabinus dismissed the other centurions and went with Rufio into his office.

A young Sequani warrior was sitting on a bench and being tended by one of the camp doctors. A bloody linen bandage encircled his neck, and the doctor was applying some frankincense to a gash across his forehead.

The brazier in a far corner cut the chill of the early evening, and numerous lamps on the tables and hanging from stands suffused the room with a golden glow.

Rufio breathed deeply. It was good to be home. Then he noticed a red leather eye patch on Sabinus's desk.

"Can you tell us your tale again?" Sabinus asked.

The young man looked up at Sabinus and then at Rufio. "Yes."

"That's enough of that," Sabinus said, waving the doctor off. "I'll send him to the hospital when I finish here."

173

The doctor hurried away.

Rufio pulled up a stool and sat across from the young fighter.

"Tell me, lad."

The boy was no more than twenty and clearly scarred now by something more than wounds.

"They're all dead."

"All?"

"Our cavalry ala and your three centuries."

Rufio looked at Sabinus and back at the young fighter. "Tell me."

His eyes filled with tears and his lower lip quivered.

"You're safe now," Rufio said and laid a hand on one of his shoulders.

The boy cleared his throat. "The Suebi attacked a village near our fort. We could see the smoke. Your centuries were on their way back here but turned around and joined us. We tried to save the village but they slaughtered everyone."

"What about the soldiers?" Rufio asked.

"Overrun. Carbo sent out scouts but it didn't matter. There must have been two thousand Suebi. Many horsemen. They turned our flanks. We were encircled and beaten into the earth. The Romans fought like I've never seen men fight before, but they were doomed."

A slave entered with a tray of nuts and three cups of heated wine.

The Sequani's hand trembled so much he spilled the wine down his chin.

"I was wounded and pretended to be dead. I saw the end. Carbo was among the last to die. He'd taken a spear through the side and was down on one knee. The Suebian chief came up to him and laughed. He threw aside his sword and picked up a tree limb. He broke Carbo's legs first so he couldn't rise. Then he crushed his chest. Not enough to kill him outright. Carbo cursed him as he broke his ribs." Tears filled his eyes. "He died slowly. Died cursing him. I think he strangled on his own blood."

"Any other survivors?"

"I alone," he said and bent over and began sobbing.

Sabinus stepped behind him and placed his hands on the boy's shoulders. "You'll be made a citizen of Rome for your valor, and you'll return to your family."

Rufio stood up and wandered to the window that opened onto the courtyard. He stared into the deepening night.

"Carbo," he said with reverence. "We won't see such a man again."

"Such a man stands before me," Sabinus said.

Rufio turned and looked at him.

"Bathe and eat and rest," Sabinus ordered. "Return in two hours. It's time to go to war."

———————

The scraping and purging of the baths could cleanse only the skin. None of the dark stains of battle could be so easily scoured away. Rufio knew this cruel truth better than any man did. Yet he felt refreshed as he walked through the darkness to the barracks of his century. He wore the off-white tunic he favored in the evening, and he hungered for the comfort of his rooms.

Neko, of course, had not doubted his return. He regarded the killing of Rufio as simply an impossibility. A selection of dried fruits and cheeses had been laid out, and within minutes of Rufio's arrival an hour earlier a cup of heated wine had been in his hand.

He had told Neko to go to bed after the meal, so he was surprised to hear his voice carrying through the darkness. He was arguing with a woman, and they were as angry as a couple of alley dogs biting each other's flanks.

Rufio turned the corner of the barracks and saw the last person on earth he expected to see.

Flavia stood before Neko. He was tying to get her to leave, but he might as well have cursed the stars. Her furious face shone like white-hot metal in the moonlight.

"What's this?" Rufio asked.

A sharp intake of breath was the only sound she made when she saw him.

"Master, this woman won't leave."

Some of his soldiers had come out of the barracks to investigate the commotion.

"Why are you here?" Rufio asked.

"To see you."

Rufio hoped that envious Venus was sleeping, for even in the pale light of night Flavia shamed the heavens.

"Back to your dreams," Rufio said to his men. He smiled at Neko. "I should call you Cerberus, you guard my gate so well."

Neko bowed.

"Warm some wine for our guest."

Rufio's living quarters welcomed them as they entered. The lamps and tapestries and heat from the brazier enveloped them with a warm embrace.

Yet Flavia did not sit but stood in the center of the Oriental rug and stared at him.

"How did you get into the fort at this time of night?" He looked straight across into her eyes, for she was as tall as he was.

"Across the ditches and over the wall."

He gazed at her in amazement, though he tried not to show it. Perhaps she truly was a forest goddess.

"Flavia, the soldiers on duty could be flogged if their centurion learns of this."

That startled her. "I'm sorry. I didn't know that."

"And you could've been killed if you were seen. Especially with that bow and quiver."

For the first time she smiled, as if she knew better than anyone what an unusual person she was and took much pleasure in it.

Neko came in with spiced wine.

"Now to bed," Rufio said.

"When you sleep, I sleep," Neko said. "Not until then."

And he melted into the shadows.

Flavia set her weapons aside and sat on the edge of a couch.

"Stretch out and drink in comfort." He handed her the cup of wine.

She seemed not to hear him. "A story went through our village that you and your men had been killed. When Adiatorix heard it, he looked like he'd been hit by an axe. He said nothing but just stared off toward the forests. Toward the Suebi." She took a sip of wine.

He placed a wicker chair in front of her and sat down.

"And Varacinda and Larinda couldn't be consoled. They held each other's hands and wept. But very quietly—as if your spirit might hear them and not understand why they care for you so."

"I don't understand. Why risk your life to come here to tell me this?"

"No, not to tell you." She set down her wine. "To see for myself if you lived. I didn't believe the rumor. I couldn't believe you'd died. I had to know."

"Why?"

With startling ferocity, she glared at him. "Don't you think I know who you are?"

"Who am I?"

"The man who's haunted me for twenty years. But I knew you'd return. I knew the gods wouldn't let me live my whole life without ever looking into your eyes."

She seemed uncertain. Fearful.

"What do you see?"

"Thousands of times I cursed you. I hated you from the depth of my spirit."

The words were astonishing coming from this striking woman. Her flashing blue eyes and the black river of hair running down her back. The green tunic and black trousers that hid what Rufio had once secretly seen. The black leather archer's bracer on her left forearm. The bronze torques, one on each upper arm, that glittered when she gestured toward him.

"What is there for me to say?" he asked. "Do you think there's been one night in the last twenty years when a wailing baby hasn't tortured my dreams?"

She moistened her lips. She was trembling now. "I cursed you so much. And then you saved Vara's cousin, and Adiatorix told me who you were. Then by a miracle, Larinda was restored to us like a gift from the gods. But she wasn't a gift from the gods but a gift from you. Then I knew I'd committed a great evil in my heart."

Tears in the eyes of this forest spirit seemed more profoundly painful than the open weeping of a lesser woman.

Rufio sat next to her on the couch and reached for her right hand. She slid it into his.

"And then I saw you with those children and the cats. I had to speak with you. I felt so guilty for the demon I'd created in my mind."

"Enough, Flavia," he said and placed the tip of a forefinger against her lips.

"But I was afraid," she said and pulled his hand away. "And then you went to face down Bassus and I stood there staring after you. Certain you'd be killed with my terrible curse still on your spirit."

Her tightly bound tears cut their bonds and slid down her cheeks.

"But you lived. It seemed as if nothing could strike you down. I had another chance. Then today I heard you'd been slain by the Suebi and I couldn't bear it. I still had this ugly thing in my heart. The gods couldn't be so cruel. I had to know if you lived."

"But Neko must have told you."

"I had to see." She squeezed his hand.

"Flavia, Flavia" he said gently.

She leaned forward and rested her head against his chest. "I'm so sorry," she whispered and placed the palm of her left hand against his breast.

He curled an arm around her shoulders and pressed the side of his face against her hair. The last time he had touched her head it had been a tiny thing, wet and bloody. Now her hair was fragrant with cedar oil and fresh blossoms.

She was young enough to be his daughter, but he felt no fatherly feelings now. Yet an incestuous shame threatened this moment. He had created her almost as much as her parents had. What right did he have to draw such feelings from her touch? But he could not deny himself. He slid a hand along her throat, and the simple throbbing of her pulse beneath his fingers flooded him with a pleasure more sublime than the touch of any other woman ever had.

She reached up and wrapped a hand around his fingers. When she felt his ring, she pushed back a bit and took his hand in hers.

"Who's this?" She placed a fingertip on the winged figure incised on the cornelian.

"The goddess Victoria."

She smiled into his eyes. "She's brought me victory tonight."

He could have stared at her forever.

"You won't leave here again?" she asked.

"Leave where?"

"Gaul."

She seemed so vulnerable now. Not at all the arrow shooting woodland warrior others saw.

"I must obey the will of Caesar."

"But is Caesar not like a god? And the gods have willed your return." She sat up straight, her blue eyes inches from his. "It could have been no accident. It's destiny."

He brushed her cheek with his thumb and smiled.

"You cannot leave me again," she said, half-commanding, half-pleading.

Was this a daughter speaking to a father, or was it something else?

"It's time to go," he said. When they stood, she kept her hands in his. "I'll take you home now."

"I feel so safe here."

In this fort? Is that what she meant? Or in his hands? He did not dare to ask.

28   WORSE THAN WAR IS THE VERY FEAR OF WAR.

Seneca

Sabinus's office was much changed. Comfortable chairs and couches had been brought in, and oil lamps had been hung from stands or set on tables around the room. Despite the late hour, trays of fruit and still-warm bread had been placed on the seat cushions, and the two glowing braziers cut the Gallic chill.

Rufio had been in the offices of many commanders, and they had always seemed to revel in Spartan fantasies of self-denial. The taste of Sabinus was much more to his liking.

All six tribunes were present, but Crus and Titinius were the only ones Rufio knew. Sabinus was bending over a table and staring at a map.

Diocles came running up behind Rufio as he went through the doorway.

"I don't know how I'll rise in time for drill tomorrow," Diocles said.

"You're excused from drill." Rufio pointed to a small table off to the side with papyrus and pen and ink. "Your true task is here. Observe, record, and be silent."

"Rufio," Sabinus said. "Join us."

He stepped up to the table with a look that betrayed his opinion.

"What is it?" Sabinus asked.

"Our maps are poor. Don't rely on them. Crus, what about your spy?"

"Trogus should be here by tomorrow."

Bruttius Macer, the senior surviving centurion from the First Cohort, came in. Illness had spared him from the fateful trip that had destroyed Carbo and his men.

"You and the rest of the First Cohort will remain in the fort," Sabinus said. "Rufio will help me plan this campaign."

Disbelief and anger twisted Macer's face. "Commander, my illness is almost gone. I—"

Sabinus held up his hand.

"Who is he?" Macer asked. A scar-faced old warrior, he clearly resented the favored newcomer. "My seniority—"

"Doesn't interest me," Sabinus said. "This decision is to preserve your health and your life. Dispute me again and tomorrow you will be an optio in the Eighth Cohort. Dismissed."

The tribunes were stunned as the veteran left the Praetorium, but Rufio appreciated what had happened. Sabinus had just shown that he

179

grasped the most elemental fact of command: Authority is never something you are given — you must take it.

"I dislike standing," Sabinus said. He pulled a chair up to the table. "Now, Rufio, sit and tell me what you believe the Germans will do."

Rufio slid a chair over to the table and sat down.

"Their plan is clear," he said. "They're raping the Gauls in the outlying areas to provoke us. They know we'll take the field to protect our allies. There the Suebi hope to destroy us."

"I know you've fought the Germans before. What are our choices?"

"No choice. We meet them in battle."

"There's a legion at a fort about a hundred and fifty miles west of here. And they have a unit of Numidian archers. Should we summon them now or wait?"

"Don't summon them at all. Not enough time. My guess is that the Suebi will stop their outrages for about two weeks. Barovistus won't want to risk any more injuries to his warriors if it isn't necessary. But if we don't take the field within that time, he'll begin again. If the Gauls are battered enough, they might change sides. It's happened before."

"But the Suebi betrayed them before."

"The Celtic memory is short."

"Crus?" Sabinus turned to his senior tribune.

"Rufio is right. If the Gauls defect and the Germans flood across the river, all Gaul lies before them."

Sabinus folded his hands on the table and stared at Rufio. "So perhaps this is a historic moment."

"Yes," Rufio said.

"And how many cohorts can we risk?"

"We should leave one here. What remains of the First. The rest march on the Suebi."

A slave came in with a pitcher of Celtic beer, and all but Rufio and Sabinus sampled some of the brew.

"But what if nine cohorts aren't enough?" Sabinus asked.

"They must be enough," Rufio said. "There's no choice."

"All right," Sabinus said. "What now?"

"Summon the senior centurion from each cohort."

"Titinius," Sabinus said with a jerk of his head.

Rufio touched the tribune's sleeve as he went by. "Including Macer."

Titinius turned to Sabinus.

"Do it," the commander ordered, and Titinius was off like Mercury.

Accustomed to the unexpected, the centurions soon assembled. Sabinus had them relax on the chairs or couches in a semicircle around the table and a few sat on the floor.

Macer was clearly surprised to be back. "At Rufio's insistence," Sabinus told him and he gazed at the new man in a different light.

Several slaves came in and passed around the bread and fruit and drink.

Sabinus gestured to Rufio to take a place beside him at the table.

"Now, centurion, tell us how to make history."

Rufio gave him an ironic smile, then turned to one of the slaves. "Spiced wine."

When the slave returned, Rufio took a small sip and set the cup on the table.

"How many of you have fought Suebi?" he asked.

Only Probus and Macer gestured back.

"Well, we have a bit of work ahead of us." He looked to Sabinus. "Do we know anything about a war chief named Barovistus?"

Sabinus turned to Crus.

"A respected fighter," the tribune said. "Trogus tells me he served in an auxiliary unit."

"Thank you, Crus," Rufio said and nodded in appreciation.

The tribune smiled back uncertainly.

Rufio wet his lips with the wine. "Barovistus probably thinks his experience with us gives him an advantage. It doesn't. I'll explain why in a moment. But first we have to consider what the Germans are likely to do on the battlefield. Their tactics are simple. If they meet us in the open field, they'll amass as many men as possible and crash into the center of our line. If they have cavalry, they'll try to turn our flanks at the same time. Crus, make sure you find out from Trogus how many horsemen they can field."

"I will."

"And our own cavalry?"

Crus looked at a sheet on the table in front of him. "One hundred eleven."

"That's nothing. We'd better pray that Mars is on our side." Rufio took another sip of wine. "The Suebi know if they fail in this first attack, they're doomed. That's why they'll do everything they can to avoid meeting us in the open. They'll try to maneuver us into an area next to some woods and attack us from there. They know how difficult it is for us to form an effective line in the forest. We cannot allow that to happen."

"Then what if they refuse to give battle?" Sabinus asked.

"We refuse to take the bait. They're desperate for war. They won't allow us to retire from the field and simply walk away. Their hunger for blood and glory is their greatest weakness. And one of our best weapons."

"What about their weapons?" Diocles asked.

Several of the centurions turned toward the Greek upstart.

"A good question from our scholar," Rufio said. "They'll have swords and armor from our own dead soldiers and from the slaughtered Gauls. But most will have neither. Just fire-hardened spears. No helmets. Maybe a few shields. They fear pila most of all because they have no protection. So they'll try to close with us before we can throw and cut them down from a distance."

"And if they do close with us?" Sabinus asked.

"They'll come at us with their spears. Most of the Suebi won't risk throwing them because they have no other weapons. I've seen Germans in battle without spears have to resort to throwing rocks."

"Our own shields and armor?" one of the military tribunes asked.

"Good protection against their spears, so they'll go for our faces and throats and legs."

"You haven't told us how they behave on the battlefield," Titinius said. "I've never even met a German except for Trogus."

Rufio smiled as he chewed on a piece of crusty bread and washed it down with wine. "Romans have been underestimating the Germans since before Marius. The Germans fight like demons. They're powerful and ferocious. But their size works against them. They tire quickly and they do poorly in the heat. A screaming and charging Suebi soon becomes a whipped dog on a hot day."

"Where will Barovistus be?" Sabinus asked.

"At the head of the charge. I said that his experience with us won't matter. There are two reasons. The first is that our tactics are as flexible as a Numidian bow. He has no idea what we'll do on any given day. And it's not possible that he's familiar with all our tactics anyway. The other reason is that once the battle begins, he'll have as much control over his men as he would over a pack of mad dogs. The Germans do what they want on the battlefield. They'll never look to him for guidance. They just pick out enemies opposite them and charge like madmen."

Silence hung over the room for a moment, then Crus said, "Are you sure we have two weeks?"

"Only fools are sure," Rufio said. "But that's been my experience. We should train hard for another week, then march. As soon as we leave the fort, Barovistus will know. He certainly has spies in the civilian settlement. He'll be waiting for us."

For another hour the discussion went on, the other centurions questioning Rufio further on German attitudes and tactics. When the meeting finally broke up, he was drained. It had been one of his most exhausting days in many years.

"I hate war councils," he said to Sabinus after the other centurions and the five military tribunes had left. "The timid always infect the daring."

Sabinus leaned back in his chair and took a sip of wine. "Rather than the daring emboldening the timid?"

"It's odd, but it never happens that way. That's why Caesar rarely held war councils. Timidity spreads like foul humors until everyone is vomiting fear. A single drop poisons the well."

"Be we had none of that tonight," Crus said.

"No, these are good men." Rufio looked at Sabinus. "You're a fortunate commander."

"I know that. Tomorrow I want a full report about what happened today between your century and the Germans. Now go to bed."

"Thank you, Rufio," Crus said with the newly discovered delight of a young man beginning to find his way at last. "Get some rest now."

"Tribune, sleep has never been my friend. I doubt he'll be one tonight."

It was a few hours after midnight when Rufio crossed the fort grounds to his barracks. The seventh and eight hours of night were among his favorite times. He inhaled deeply the damp air, and the darkness softened by moonlight made the world seem a far more serene place than it would ever really be.

The chatter of insects and the soft rush of water rolling through the drainage channels created an oddly soothing mix. Guards on the ramparts stared into the distance, alert to the phantoms of the night. Rufio's footsteps caused some of them to turn and look down. He waved to them at their lonely posts. Even hardened soldiers, cloaked now by darkness, took boyish delight in being acknowledged, and they waved back.

Only a single lamp burned in Rufio's sitting room. Neko, ever faithful, had nonetheless lost his battle with Morpheus and lay curled in a small chair.

Rufio took a blanket from his bedroom and draped it over his old friend and then extinguished the lamp.

The brazier in his bedroom was warm, and three lamps welcomed him with their glow. He unfastened his dagger belt and tossed it aside and removed his sandals. He noticed one of the hobnails was missing from the left sole and made a mental note to have it repaired. He pulled off his tunic and underwear and then stretched until he could almost reach Olympus. He moaned with pleasure, relishing the freedom of his nakedness.

A glint of something on his pillow caught his eye. He stepped closer. A bronze torque lay in the center. He lifted it as delicately as if it would break and sat on the edge of the bed and examined it in the lamplight. She must have placed it there when he went to get his horse to take her home.

She seemed suddenly present again. He pulled a blanket across his naked lap. Without thought, he held the torque to his nose, but no scent could cling to the metal. Sized to fit below one of her biceps, the bronze armlet could easily fit a man's wrist. Onto his left wrist he slipped the coil.

He threw aside the blanket, extinguished the lamps, and slid into bed. He stared into the blackness and prayed to Victoria that she grant him not only primacy in war, but victory in the dangerous realm of the human heart. And the wisdom to use every victory with honor.

29   THE GERMANS HAVE NO TASTE FOR PEACE.

Tacitus

Wailing women screamed for blood. Hundreds of them swarmed Barovistus and demanded Roman heads.

From a distant ridge, Orgestes watched the frenzy in the village below.

"They have no idea. Their husbands or sons without a hand are better than no husbands or sons at all."

Beside him sat the young warrior who, by some inexplicable fate, had been returned whole.

"I don't understand," the boy said. "Why did the Roman do what he did? He must have known he'd just enrage us."

The old chief gazed at him with fatherly patience. "Of course he knew that."

"Then why?"

"First, for vengeance. To retaliate for what our men did to the Sequani. Second, because he knew it would enrage us. He did it to show his contempt for our rage."

The boy looked at him in silence.

"Suebi flesh is feeding the worms of Gaul to show that he scoffs at our fury. This is a terrible man we'll face in battle. He'll give no quarter."

"Then why did he spare me?"

"Who can ever hope to understand these Romans?"

Sabinus walked the training ground outside the fort where soldiers assaulted the wooden stakes. The parade ground, too, was filled with men sweating through the most intense weapons drill of their lives.

He turned at the sound of an approaching horse. The majestic figure of Adiatorix rode up, dwarfing the roan between his legs.

"Hail, Sabinus," he said, the first time those words had ever come from the Gallic warrior.

"Hail, Chief."

Adiatorix dismounted and led his horse by the reins.

"We grieve for the loss of your fallen brothers," Sabinus said, referring to the slaughtered Gallic cavalry.

"And we honor the Romans who stood by them to the last. Carbo is with the gods."

Sabinus smiled. "That would amuse him greatly."

"Will you walk with me now?"

They began to trace the edge of the training ground, the horse walking behind them.

"How will you fight the Suebi without cavalry?" Adiatorix asked.

"We do have some. We'll make do."

"Their task is to patrol and scout. I mean horse fighters."

"We'll fight on foot."

Adiatorix paused in his walk and stared at Sabinus. "That is no answer."

"It's the only one I have."

Adiatorix looked away, absently pulling at the drooping ends of his moustache.

"Give me one moon," he said. "I'll have here five hundred of the finest horsemen in Gaul."

"You're a loyal ally, Chief. But we cannot wait. If we do, more Sequani will die."

Sabinus pointed to a bench from which centurions could observe the weapons drills. The two men sat, while the roan grazed nearby.

"Chief, who is Flavia?"

The big Celt gazed down at the smaller Roman. "A woman from our village."

"I heard a rumor she was in the fort last night."

Adiatorix smiled but said nothing.

"Do you know why that would be?" Sabinus asked.

"We heard a story that Rufio and his century had been killed. She probably came to find out for herself. That's Flavia's way."

"I don't understand. Does she know Rufio?"

"For many years."

"No. He just arrived."

"Twenty years ago they met."

"You speak in riddles," Sabinus said, laughing. "She cannot be more than twenty herself."

"Yes."

"Is she his daughter?" he asked in surprise.

Now Adiatorix laughed. "Flavia's feelings are not those of a daughter."

"You know her well then?"

"She's my sister—not by blood, but by love. She has no other family."

"I'm as confused as a drunken mime. What can Rufio be to her?"

"The ghost of yesterday. And the longing of today."

"But she's only half his age."

"Surely the Legate of Caesar is wise enough to know that the human heart moves not according to the sun and moon. It moves by the mysterious spirit that lives within it." He placed a hand on Sabinus's right shoulder. "I haven't thanked you for allowing the slaves to return to their homes."

"It was a greater power than I who took a hand."

"Varacinda believes it was Mars."

"Perhaps it was."

Adiatorix took an enormous breath and let it out slowly. "I owe you a great debt. I'll repay it now. I'll tell you how Flavia came to be. And how her every waking moment is now filled with thoughts of a man who once haunted her dreams."

30   PEACE IS THE BEST THING THAT MEN MAY KNOW. PEACE IS BETTER THAN A THOUSAND TRIUMPHS.

Silius Italicus

The clang of swords had awakened Rufio. The recruits were training just outside the barracks. The entire fort rattled with drilling soldiers and space was scarce.

Washed and refreshed, Rufio stood back and watched Valerius raise a sweat on the new men. Gone were the wooden weapons. Real swords tipped with leather flashed in the morning sun.

Valerius saw Rufio and came over.

"Thank you," Rufio said. "I haven't slept this late in ten years."

"I saw no reason to wake you."

Rufio watched the ten pairs of dueling soldiers. They were clearly as eager to perform well for Valerius as for their centurion.

"It means a great deal to me to have a weapons officer like you."

Valerius smiled.

"Where's Metellus?"

"Out of the fort at the moment."

"Where? I approved no leave."

"I did. There's this young lady — "

"Sweet Venus's tits! Does he have to drain his balls every day? We're on the eve of battle and he — "

"Rufio," Valerius and held up a calming hand. "This isn't lust. It's a pure and special thing. I've seen the lady. I understand. You would, too."

The impish look in Valerius's eyes cooled Rufio's anger. "What are you talking about?"

"She's enchanted him. Dazzling blue eyes, red hair, freckles." He smiled. "About eight years old."

Rufio burst out laughing. "The little girl from the village?"

"A delegation came today to thank Sabinus. The girl's mother is the sister of the warrior who led them in battle. Her name is Calpurnia."

"A Roman name?"

"Her father was a retired centurion. She came with her brother and daughter."

"Kalinda."

"That's her. As soon as the little girl saw Metellus, she flew to him. Her hand slid into his and wouldn't leave it."

"That old rake. Who would have thought?"

"Her mother seemed taken with him, too. And when he spoke to the mother, he was different. Restrained. That child gazed up at him with those adoring eyes — it was like a spell. He wanted to help them rebuild their homes. I told him to be back by sundown."

"It's all right then."

"I've known Metellus four years and I've never seen that expression on his face. He's melted many women, but today he melted like butter when that little hand touched his again."

Rufio turned back to his men. "They look good today."

"They're driven to please you."

"Any sign of that German spy?"

"Not as far as I know."

"I'll go into the settlement to see if he's been around. I'll be back by the sixth hour." He turned away but stopped. "Valerius," he said, looking back.

"Yes?"

"You're my right hand. And Metellus is my left. Know that."

He turned and walked off and heard Valerius thank him above the banging of the swords.

———————

Rufio sat at a small table outside a food shop along the main street. He finished his second honey cake and watched the women carry their pitchers to the well. Their children played around them, and the cats observed everything, as they always did.

Occasionally one of these graceful Gallic women would glance his way, and he would smile back with that penetrating and passionate gaze unique to the Italian male. Forgetting her husband and children, she, too, would smile, and for a secret moment they would share a safe and hidden fantasy known only to themselves.

Hobnails on the paving stones distracted him. Diocles approached his table. He looked exhausted.

"Rest is a great elixir," Rufio said. "You should sample it."

He sat and rubbed his eyes. "I slept poorly last night."

Rufio said nothing.

"I'm baffled and I need your help. I've been wandering about all morning seeking inspiration, and all I've gotten is tired."

"How may I help?"

"My writing has hit a wall. I realized last night that I understand nothing."

Rufio went into the shop and got a cup of beer. He placed it on the table before Diocles and then sat back down.

"Refresh yourself and tell me your woe."

He took a long sip. "I always assumed the core of my book wouldn't be a description of battles but the nature of the fighting man. But it's not to be."

"You mean you created a theory before you had facts. And now reality refuses to agree with your prejudices. So you grab a stout hammer to bang the facts into shape to make them fit. Like a true scholar."

"You're not helping me," Diocles said with a sour look.

"What can I possibly give you?"

"Insight. I'm looking for the warrior ethos. The spirit of men in war."

"You'll not find that here, my friend."

"But it must be here!"

"Why?"

"The empire stretches as far as the reach of Jupiter. It was won by arms."

"True."

"I'm seeking the warrior spirit but I cannot find it. Last night after the fight with the Germans I expected drinking and celebrating. A bonding of men. But the men were quiet. As subdued as if we'd just come back from road repair. They cleaned their weapons and went to the baths and ate quietly and went to bed."

Rufio looked away. A pretty dark-haired woman approached the fountain with two pitchers. A familiar little girl followed behind with an enormous cat draped over one of her small shoulders. She saw Rufio and pulled excitedly at her mother's sleeve and pointed at him. The woman nodded and smiled, and Rufio smiled back.

How could he explain that this was what Romans lived for? Not for twisted fantasies of death.

"Rufio?"

He looked back at Diocles. "You're among the wrong people if you're seeking a warrior ethos."

"Why? Everyone knows that Romans are the most warlike people on earth."

"What everyone knows is usually false."

"No, I'm certain that —"

"There's a distinction to be made here and you're not making it."

"What distinction?"

"You said Romans are warlike. What Romans?"

Diocles hesitated.

"If you mean politicians seeking plunder and fame, then you're right. They all dream of military victories. They hunger for war. Riding to greatness on the backs of my men. Greedy patricians fit your definition. Not Roman soldiers."

"But look at the triumphs staged for your great commanders. Parades that last for hours. Celebrations that go on for days."

Rufio smiled and helped himself to some of Diocles' beer. "You've proved my point. 'Staged' is the right word. If Italians were a warlike people, those revels would be spontaneous. They're not. You wouldn't need parades and spectacles and free food and drink to get people into the streets. . . ."

"Go on."

"Italians celebrate victory in war for the same reason other people do—it makes them feel superior. More important for Italians, though, is the fact that then they can relax and enjoy the finest things in life. Their wives and their children. Their mistresses and their friends. Fresh bread and rich wine. Military glory means little to ordinary Italians." He dismissed it with a wave of his hand. "That's a myth created by decaying Greek kingdoms beaten on the battlefield."

"You're turning my whole world upside down."

"I'm not saying most of our people don't take pride in our victories and like to brag about them. Of course they do. People always like to share in the triumph of others. War without wounds. But that's as far as it goes. Why do you think we have a professional army? Because most Italians want nothing to do with war. Why should they?"

"I don't understand. I—"

"What is there to understand? Who wants to be cut up or killed? Who looks forward to chopping men in half? And Roman soldiers are the least belligerent of all—real soldiers, not retired consuls looking for fame. The days when cities were bursting with booty and making soldiers' mouths water are long over. We want to serve out our enlistment in peace. And to be so great at waging war that no one dares disturb that peace."

"But surely you must admire the great warrior peoples."

"Where do you think you are? Sparta?"

"Don't you admire them?"

"I admire their valor, but then I'm finished."

"I thought they'd be your idols."

"The Spartans? Their whole society dripped with war. No Italian would admire that. It's ridiculous."

"But—"

"Warrior societies are the bleakest on earth. Athens waged war, but she wasn't a warrior society. And look what she created. And see what we've created since then. We're the light of mankind. The Spartans? They stood fast at Thermopylae and saved us from Xerxes' savages. We honor them for that. But that's all."

Diocles just stared at him.

Rufio laid a hand on one of his forearms. "Warriors who treasure peace are far greater than warriors who live for war. And remember this — warrior peoples produce little worth having. And almost nothing worth saving. All they create is ashes."

After a long silence, Diocles said, "What happened yesterday?"

"With the Germans?"

"Yes."

"I don't understand your question. You saw what happened."

"Did it have to be that way?"

"No, we could've turned around and let the Sequani die."

"That's not what I mean," he said with a touch of anger.

"Ah, well, I could've released those barbarians to go home and get more weapons to return and slaughter those people. Or I could've killed them all. I chose to do neither."

"I'm sorry. It's just that it's not what I'd imagined it would be."

"War is never what people imagine it to be."

Diocles gazed into his eyes as if he were searching for something he feared to find.

"What is it?" Rufio asked.

"Last night I went through your books for accounts of other Roman battles. Campaigns from long ago. . . ."

"And you found them."

"Yes . . . and they're all horrible. Just like yesterday."

"What did you expect? Greek myths?"

"I don't know. The savagery. Ferocity the average person cannot even imagine. Why?"

"Do you really want to know? Or do you just want to sit there and try to improve my character?"

Diocles' jaws clenched but he said nothing.

"Well?" Rufio asked.

"I want to know."

"Because that's how we survive. Do you think those seven little hills on the Tiber are protected by the hand of Jupiter? They're not. It's the sword of Mars. Do you need a list of all the invaders who've marched up and down the peninsula?"

"No."

"These wars weren't like your little Greek wars—skirmishes settled by trading a piece of ground or turning over a handful of tribute. Ask Pyrrhus. Ask Hannibal. These were wars of annihilation. These were the wars we survived. Again and again."

"But what—"

"Look what happened after Cannae. We were bled white. Hannibal thought we were a cold corpse. It was time for us to negotiate. He was certain of it. But we did not. Hannibal was baffled. Every power on earth would've bent its knee to him then. But we did not. Defeat isn't defeat if you don't admit defeat. To us it's simply a delay on the road to victory. That's what Cannae was to us. We sucked back the blood in our throats and fought on. And where is Carthage now?"

"Barely a memory."

"These were wars that didn't mean just a loss of dignity if we were beaten—but slaughter, the end of us as a people. We didn't fight for land or tribute or some foolish treaty. We fought to crush the enemy's army in open battle. To demolish it as a threat to Rome. That was the forge we were tempered in. So since those early days we've fought every war as ferociously as if it could be our last. And that fury has always brought us victory."

"But is there no other choice?"

"If you have one, tell me what it is."

Diocles was silent.

"If we fail, who'll weep for the children? Shall we ask mercy from the Suebi? Or even from the Gauls? Almost four hundred years ago, the Gauls sacked Rome. Today you sit peacefully in Gaul itself and sip your beer. Why? Is it because they honor us?"

Diocles didn't answer.

"Is it?" Rufio demanded.

"No. It's because they fear us."

"Now you've learned something. The denarius or the sestertius isn't the coinage that matters. The Roman legion is the currency of the world. Never forget that."

"But what about now? We're not fighting for our lives anymore."

"We're *always* fighting for our lives. Our soldiers are outnumbered everywhere. We're stretched as tight as the skin on a pig's ass."

"Even if that's true, what does—"

"We don't have the luxury of defeat. There are hungry hordes at every edge. If we show weakness in the face of insolence, we might as well cut out our own bowels."

"I'm not convinced. According to our own histories, we've gone to war over simple insults. Slaps in the face. Whole armies have clashed over questions of so-called honor. It's madness."

Rufio took a long, slow breath to help calm his impatience with the obstinate Greek.

"Consider this," Rufio went on. "You own a beautiful villa outside Rome. Someone breaks into it and steals your silver and beats your children and rapes your wife. What do you do?"

"Tell me."

"You hunt him down and beat him into the ground and slay him like the dog he is."

"All right. I agree."

"Now suppose someone else breaks into your villa to steal your silver. He ignores your family but on the way out he smashes the busts of your ancestors. What do you do?"

Diocles was silent.

"You do the same as you would to the rapist," Rufio said.

"Why?" Diocles asked, clearly appalled.

"Your honor has been violated. And your honor is everything. If you don't retaliate, no one in your family is safe. A man who won't defend his honor won't defend anything. The savages will smell your fear a mile off. They'll descend on your loved ones and plunder or destroy all you cherish. That's why we let no insult go unanswered. Why we'll march across wastelands to avenge a wrong. Our survival depends on it. If we refuse to defend our honor, Rome will soon be as lifeless as the rubble of Carthage."

"This is a world beyond my comprehension."

"Many things are beyond your comprehension. And you've never even seen a city sacked."

"I've read the accounts. The slaughters."

"Is that how you see it? A city at war with us is a savage animal. It has to be brought to heel or killed. If they refuse to surrender on reasonable terms, then the ram hits the wall. And as soon as it does, the deal is cancelled."

"And then you're free to do as you want? Is that how you justify it?"

"Justify? Do you justify killing a dog at your throat? If I have to watch some of my men die storming a stronghold, I'll slay every man inside and sell every family into slavery so it doesn't happen again. I'll spread terror throughout the countryside if it means frightening them into submission. If it means I'll have to write fewer letters to mothers whose sons died in my care."

A long silence followed.

Finally, Diocles said, "What Racovir told you—"

"Was only half true. Barovistus was testing us, but he already knew in his rank heart what our answer would be. He attacked our allies. He knew we'd march. We'll always march. Nothing will stop us but annihilation."

Diocles turned away and stared at nothing.

"Look out there. " Rufio pointed toward the busy street. "If the Suebi pour across the river, all those women will be widows. And some of them will die, too, and their children will be orphans. Have you ever held an orphan in your arms?"

"No."

"I have."

With troubled eyes, Diocles rose from his seat. He was across the street when he stopped and came back.

"I almost forgot. Valerius sent me to tell you that Trogus has returned."

"Good." Rufio downed the rest of the beer. "Let's go see what the German traitor has to say."

31 BY COMMON DEFECT OF NATURE, THE UNUSUAL AND THE UNKNOWN MAKE US EITHER OVERCONFIDENT OR OVERLY FEARFUL.

Julius Caesar

"Two thousand fighting men?" Sabinus was saying as Rufio went through the doorway into his office.

"Yes," Trogus answered from his chair across from the Legate.

All the tribunes were present, flanking Sabinus on either side as he sat at his desk.

Rufio stayed toward the back of the room and motioned for Diocles to do the same.

A slave entered with a drink for Trogus.

"What about cavalry?" Sabinus asked.

"About one hundred. Perhaps one hundred and fifty."

"I'd have expected many more than that."

"You Romans are lucky this time," he said with a dry chuckle. "Last month a disease killed many of their horses. Their good horsemen will have to fight on foot."

"Commander," Rufio said.

"Step up here, centurion," Sabinus ordered. "No formalities now."

"What about equipment?" Rufio said and approached the German.

Trogus looked to the side at the centurion. "Mostly spears. About three hundred good swords. Not too many shields — maybe two hundred."

"How many of these Suebi have fought before?" Crus asked.

"That I don't know. But you cannot be complacent. Suebi warriors cannot be judged in ordinary terms."

"Well, we outnumber them two to one," Crus said. "That gives up plenty of room to maneuver."

"Overconfidence is a toxic potion," Trogus said.

"How long do we have until they march again?" Sabinus asked.

"Odd use of the word — march," Trogus said with his grating laugh. "The Suebi don't know how to march. They do know how to kill. They —"

"Answer the question," Crus said.

"Such things they don't confide to a humble trader. I'd guess about one week. Perhaps ten days."

"What about their spirit?" Titinius asked.

"Barovistus has them boiling. They're ready to drink the lifeblood of Gaul.

Crus had his own small office near that of Sabinus. It was cluttered now with countless documents, and he was bending over a desk covered with papyrus sheets and waxed tablets. From the window beyond, a pleasant afternoon breeze rippled the papers as he gathered some of them. The air's caress was a deceptive one, giving no hint of the coming storm.

"Yes?" he said as Rufio's sandals snapped against the floor.

"A word with you, tribune."

"Sit here." Crus cleared off a chair and took a place behind his desk. "I'm being buried in documents."

"Sometimes peace is more complex than war."

Crus waited for him to continue.

"Seems like a thousand years since the Greek slave," Rufio said.

"Very trivial now, I suppose."

"I'm here to help you."

"Me?"

"Sabinus is going to want to scald you. I'm here to help you prepare for it."

"What are you talking about?"

"Trogus was lying."

It was like a blow across his face.

"About what?"

"The German traitor is no traitor."

"How do you know?"

"I asked him about equipment. Remember? He said they had only three hundred swords and two hundred shields. They slaughtered three of our centuries and cut down almost five hundred Gauls. We don't need Metellus to do the mathematics for us."

"By the gods," Crus said and slumped back in his chair. "Why did none of us notice that?"

"All of you were too eager to believe what he said. When it comes to Suebi, I'm eager only to discover their lies."

"And the two thousand warriors?"

"You can be certain there are thousands more than that. And don't forget about the cavalry. Trogus said they had a hundred and fifty horses. What about the butchered Gauls? Five hundred cavalrymen. Where do you think their horses are now?"

"He lied about everything."

"Spies are always a risk. Now you've learned that."

"I've been a fool. What did Sabinus say to this?"

"I never carry tales about my tribunes."

Crus stared at him in surprise.

"Better for you, tribune, to hand him the rod yourself. Take the flogging like a Roman."

"Thank you. Will we still take the field?"

"Of course we will. We're Romans."

"How on earth will we overcome them? We have so little cavalry. No archers. . . ."

Rufio stood up. "Perhaps we can rely on Caesar's Luck. It always worked for him."

For the first time since Rufio had met him, he saw Crus smile.

"Rufio, you cannot convince me you've ever relied on luck for anything."

"Rely? No. Fortuna is too fickle. But there are other goddesses who care about us. We must pray to them tonight."

32 A GERMAN . . . THINKS IT SPIRITLESS AND SLACK TO GAIN BY SWEAT WHAT HE CAN BUY WITH BLOOD.

Tacitus

"What troubles you?" Varacinda asked and sat on the grass beside the lake.

Flavia lay stretched out on her back and was staring at the sky. Instead of her usual short tunic and trousers, she wore a short-sleeved long green tunic belted in the middle and extending to the middle of her thighs. As always, she wore a black leather bracer on her left forearm.

"One moon ago, I ate well and slept well. I was happy with that. But now. . ."

"But aren't you happy now?" Varacinda asked with a smile.

"Oh yes." She rolled her head to the side and gazed at her. "But I hunger so. It's driving me mad."

"But what a luscious madness it is."

Flavia smiled and extended an arm.

Varacinda lay down and rested her head on Flavia's breast above her heart.

Flavia curled her arm around her and pulled her close. "I couldn't live without you."

"You never have to," Varacinda said and slid an arm around her.

"Oh, Vara, what shall I do?"

"Take each day as it's given to you."

"I worry about him so."

"You're being silly. No man in Gaul needs your worry less."

"But I fear he'll leave again and this time not return."

Varacinda ran a hand gently up and down Flavia's bare left upper arm, then pushed herself up and looked down at her.

"Where's your other torque?"

Flavia smiled.

"Then that will protect him. Have no fear."

"There's a terrible battle coming," Flavia said and squeezed her friend even more tightly.

"I know."

"That awful Suebi spy isn't to be trusted. He's evil."

"The Romans have no choice about him. If a Roman spy crosses the river now, the Suebi will kill him. They'll kill any Roman they see."

Flavia jumped up and smiled that reckless smile that so many found unsettling. "But they won't kill us. We'll go into Germania."

Varacinda looked at her in alarm. "Can we?"

"We can do anything. We're Sequani."

"Adiatorix would be furious."

"We'll be back before sundown." Flavia leaned forward and kissed her on the cheek. "Come. We'll help the Romans who risk their lives for us. We'll show them what we're made of in this land."

―――――

The Rhenus was an awesome thing. Spring rains continued to feed its hunger, and the great blue monster rolled on. The banks on both sides dipped at steep angles and formed a sharp green wedge. Tall trees grew almost to the water's edge.

The Roman bridge treated the river's grandeur with scorn. It shot across over a thousand feet, its timber legs anchored deeply in the helpless earth. Crossbars of cut tree trunks braced it against the river's anger.

Flavia gazed down from her gray horse at the majestic sight, while Varacinda refreshed herself with some water from her flask.

Three soldiers milled around outside a small hut at this end of the bridge.

The women urged their horses down the slope to the bridge. The soldiers looked at them as if they were mad. Didn't they know the Suebi were on the move? Unwilling to let them pass, the soldiers threatened everything short of physical restraint, but Flavia's bow and quiver of arrows told them it would not be easy. The soldiers watched them go.

Unaccustomed to bridges, the horses had to be coaxed onto the span. The roadway was over thirty feet wide, the decking a heavy timber lattice covered with thick wattle-work.

The clean smell of the water invigorated them as they rode across, toward the deep forests of the Suebian heartland.

At the other side, they entered a stand of trees, but that soon opened onto a vast green meadow. To the south, a dark thread moved northeast. It had to be a line of men. When the women approached, it seemed to grow larger and crawled like a huge snake toward a distant rise and slid beyond the horizon.

"Warriors?" Varacinda asked.

"Yes."

"It looked like hundreds."

"Many hundreds." Flavia scanned the horizon south to north. She nudged the sides of her mare with her heels and they picked up speed.

They crossed the sun-baked plain to the ridge, and Flavia pointed to some trees. "We'll be safer away from the skyline."

Into the shelter of the forest they passed, but somehow the German woods offered no comfort. It was cool here, and yet now the hot meadow seemed preferable. The rush of the air through the trees made it difficult to hear. The rustling confused their ears, and even the sound of their own horses' footfalls died amidst the noise of the branches. Unlike Gallic breezes, these eerie winds failed to soothe, but sounded like nothing so much as the Suebian gods of the forest moaning for the dead.

They moved on. Flavia's green tunic and Varacinda's black jerkin and trousers helped conceal them in the forest's depths. The air grew colder, and little sun reached the woodland floor.

"How do we know what direction we're following?" Varacinda asked. The anxiety in her voice could not be concealed.

Even Flavia was unsure. She looked up to the towering treetops and then turned in her saddle and could just make out the afternoon sun behind them.

"We're still heading east," she said, her innate sense of direction prevailing once more. "We'll ride on a bit longer."

Though a decade older than her dearest friend, Varacinda obeyed her as if it were the most natural thing in the world.

The endless wind and the swaying of the trees were becoming more and more unnerving, yet on they rode. After another quarter-hour, the woods brightened and they seemed to be coming to an end. Ever impatient, Flavia galloped ahead and burst into the sunlight.

"Oh no," she whispered to herself.

On the rising plain below, the Suebi were gathering. An ocean of them. Like waves, they rolled inward into a great central sea of men.

"Oh Flavia," Varacinda said as she rode up. "Look at them."

"There are thousands," Flavia said in a hushed voice.

Because of the distance, the men seemed to move slowly, but Flavia knew that was an illusion. They hurried toward Barovistus, full of the lust for blood and glory.

"How many?" Varacinda asked.

"There must be ten thousand. How can . . ? Even my Rufio . . ."

Varacinda looked at her sharply.

Flavia quickly turned to her friend, startled by her own words. For a moment, the cataclysm threatening below was forgotten.

"Is he then?" Varacinda asked. "Is he yours?"

"Oh yes," Flavia admitted with a sensual longing. "He has always been. It was fated from the very beginning."

Varacinda smiled and reached across and touched her hand.

"Who are you?" a coarse voice said in bad Celtic.

Flavia snapped to her left. Two Suebian horsemen had emerged from the trees about a hundred feet to the north. One was a blonde youth barely old enough to grow a beard, but he wore a long Gallic sword at his hip. The other was an older warrior with a massive head as bald as a pustule. He held a long spear.

"What do you want?" the young one asked.

"They're spies!" the other yelled. "Get them!"

"Vara!" Flavia shouted and reined her horse about, and the two of them bolted through the trees.

They raced like madwomen, ducking beneath lethal branches as their horses veered around tree trunks and leaped over rotted logs.

The Germans crashed through the woods behind them.

On the women sped, the gods on their side as they sliced through the dark forest.

They flew out onto the plain and across the soft grass. Flavia could hear the hoofbeats fading in the distance. The Suebian mounts were no match for Gallic steeds.

"Flavia!" came a frantic cry.

Flavia looked back over her shoulder as her horse raced on. She stared in horror. Varacinda had fallen behind about a quarter of a mile. Her horse had gone lame. The poor beast struggled to keep up, but it was hopeless. The Suebi were about a mile back and coming fast.

Varacinda stared at her with the eyes of the dead. And then she waved farewell.

And now there occurred on that sunny plain what not even Mars himself had ever seen before.

Flavia reined about and raced back the way she had come. Past Varacinda she shot like a bolt of lightning straight toward the charging Suebi.

She had closed within a quarter mile and they were bearing down on her when she suddenly pulled up. She leaped from her horse and slapped its rump to chase it away. Whipping a handful of arrows from her quiver, she thrust them into the dirt beside her. She swept the bow from her shoulder and plucked an arrow from the ground.

The Germans were screaming now, charging with that hideous Suebian cry that froze their enemies. The young warrior led the charge, his long Celtic sword high in the air. He was a hundred feet away.

Flavia fitted an arrow. A breeze rippled her green tunic, but her powerful thighs and calves rooted her to the ground. As she drew the string taut, the muscles of her left arm knotted and her right biceps bulged. Her eyes narrowed. She let fly.

202

The head sliced straight into the horseman's throat. He dropped his sword and gurgled and choked. He clawed at the arrow and the shaft snapped in half, and he tore at the stump still in his neck. A second arrow pierced his hand, nailing it to his throat, and he tumbled dead from his horse.

Down on her rushed the second horseman. His head gleamed in the sun and his screaming mouth looked like some black abyss. He jammed the butt of his spear into his right armpit and braced himself to run her through.

Flavia nocked another arrow. He was a hundred feet away, but she waited. His horse churned up the turf as she watched him come. Fifty feet and still she did not shoot. She could see the horse's nostrils stretched wide to suck in air, and the hoofbeats pounded in her ears. Still she held. The warrior's howling was now vibrating her breastbone. He was close enough for her to see his brown teeth when she let the arrow fly.

It sheared deep into his chest, ripping through a lung. A scarlet river gushed from his mouth, but still he held his spear. He was almost upon her.

Flavia snatched another arrow. Strong fingers pulled the bowstring to its limit. Her blue eyes glittering like tempered steel, she shot straight to his terrible core. The iron arrowhead crashed between his eyes and he flew from the saddle and sank deep into the blackness of Acheron.

Flavia stared at the fallen men. She lowered her head and took several deep breaths to regain her composure. Then she pulled the rest of the arrows from the ground and returned them to her quiver.

Varacinda ran up. Flavia opened her arms and Varacinda leaped into them. They squeezed each other until they could barely breathe, and Varacinda covered Flavia's face with kisses. Then the wife of a chieftain of the Sequani wept uncontrollably into the bosom of her friend.

33   EVEN A GOD FINDS IT HARD TO LOVE AND BE WISE AT THE SAME TIME.

Publilius Syrus

"Ten thousand?" Sabinus asked.

"Please don't doubt Flavia," Varacinda said. "She has the eye."

"Sit."

"We must go," Flavia said to him across his desk. "I promised we would be home before sundown."

Dusty and sweat stained, they were still the two most striking women in Gaul.

"You took great risks."

"We are Sequani," Flavia answered.

"How may I reward you?"

"Is Centurion Rufio within the fort?" Varacinda asked, and Flavia turned and glared at her.

"Titinius," Sabinus said to the tribune sitting at a small table.

"Commander?"

"Rufio."

When Titinius returned with the centurion, Flavia refused to meet his gaze, but glanced at her torque on his left wrist.

"What's happened?" Rufio asked Sabinus.

"They have a tale to tell you." Sabinus came out from behind his desk.

Flavia saw him motion to Titinius and the two of them left the office.

"There are more than ten thousand Suebi gathering beyond the river," Flavia told him.

"How do you know that?"

"We've seen them," Varacinda answered.

"We've been to Germania," Flavia said.

"I would have died in Germania if not for Flavia."

Flavia shook her head no at Varacinda, but the wife of the chief refused to be silenced. She told Rufio all that had happened, and then slipped from the room.

Flavia steeled herself for his disapproval. No man, no Roman — no one — would ever tell her what she could do.

But no anger came. A look of great sadness clouded his face. The corners of his dark eyebrows turned down in an expression of almost boyish sorrow.

"Oh Rufio," she said and rushed to comfort him.

She slid into his arms. His strong right hand curled behind her ears and she felt his fingers slide along her scalp as he pressed her head to the side of his face. She inhaled deeply of his scent.

"Don't you know you mustn't die?" he whispered. "Then I would die, too. You justify my life."

She tilted her head back and gazed into his eyes. "Your honor justifies you."

"No. You must live for your people. Live for Gaul." He held her even more tightly. "Live for me."

Without warning, she began crying. She pressed her face into the hollow of his shoulder and wept convulsively as the reaction set in from this terrible day.

"Never leave me," she said through choking sobs. "Never abandon me again."

She felt his lips press against the top of her head, and she dug her fingers into his tunic, as if she were about to slide down a cliff face and slip forever into a world without him.

34 YOU WILL FIND IT HARDER TO PERSUADE A GERMAN TO PLOW THE LAND AND TO AWAIT ITS ANNUAL PRODUCE WITH PATIENCE THAN TO CHALLENGE A FOE AND EARN THE PRIZE OF WOUNDS.

Tacitus

Barovistus was sitting on a fallen tree in the forest when the blonde boy approached.

"Sit." The war chief pointed to a spot beside him.

The boy did so.

"You showed great bravery against the Romans."

"Thank you. " He moved his hands back and forth across his knees as he sat in the presence of the great chief.

"Even when that Roman threatened to maim you, you refused to beg."

"I would've traded my hand for one Roman dead."

"No, I need you with both hands. You're a hero and you must help me inspire the other young men."

"I don't feel like a hero, but I'll try."

"That's why you won't fight in this battle."

"No!" he wailed as if he had just been whipped. "I must do —"

"Stop."

The boy was silent.

Barovistus stared at him. In the heart of this dark forest, they seemed to be the only two people on earth.

"I have many young men who are eager to fight. What you saw will move them and what you did will inspire them. I need you for that. There will be many more Romans after these. Do you understand?"

"Yes."

"Rise. Go now. Speak with them and let them draw from your courage."

When the boy passed out of sight, an old woman emerged from the shadows among the trees. She dropped to her knees before the chief and pressed both of his hands to her lips.

"You're a very great man," she whispered and kissed his fingers.

"Don't kneel." He lifted her to her feet.

Her tired eyes gazed into his for understanding.

Barovistus smiled. "He will live," he said and placed an arm around her frail shoulders. "Long and free in these great forests."

"May Thincsus protect you."

She strained to wrap her arms around his massive torso.

He hugged her gently. "May he protect us all."

After the woman left, he walked alone through the woods. Beyond the edge of the forest, thousands of warriors were gathering, but the chief needed a moment away from it. Soon many of those young men would be carrion. The faces of weeping mothers haunted the dreams of even a war chief of the Suebi.

But he was allowed no respite. Hoofbeats caught his attention. He turned and saw Orgestes and another rider racing toward him among the trees.

They dismounted in front of him.

"This lad has something for you," Orgestes said and limped toward Barovistus.

A young warrior approached the chief. He was holding a small wad of red cloth.

"Speak," Barovistus said.

"I was riding along the river when I saw a mounted Roman soldier on the other side. He signaled me to approach the bridge. Then he rode halfway across and waited on his horse. It was a beautiful animal. He wore a helmet but no armor and had a sword and dagger. He—"

"Did he give you his name?"

"No, chief. He was about forty years old. He wore a blue tunic. I noticed he had a Sequani torque on his left wrist. He handed me this."

He held out the small red bundle. But then he hesitated.

"Go on," Barovistus said.

"I'm afraid to speak."

Barovistus smiled. "No need. Only the Romans need fear me. What did he say?"

"He told me to give this to Barovistus the child slayer." The young man lowered his eyes and offered him the ball of cloth.

With hardening face, the chief took the little bundle and unwrapped it.

In the center of the cloth lay a human tongue.

Orgestes looked into the war chief's eyes. "You know who that is."

"Trogus," he said and stared at the shriveled piece of meat.

"But where is the rest of him?" the boy asked.

"In the stomachs of wild dogs," Orgestes answered and waved the lad away.

The boy mounted his horse and was gone.

"This Roman fears you?"

"He's a fool." Barovistus turned away and dropped the tongue to the forest floor.

"If he was a fool, you'd be laughing. I hear no laugh."

Barovistus stared off into the depths of the forest.

"Well?" the former chief said.

"He's a demon, Orgestes. A demon."

35   ONE CANNOT BLUNDER TWICE IN WAR.

Roman saying

I fear for these men. Within days they will march off toward a terrible foe. I am relieved I will not be permitted to fight, and I am ashamed that I feel relieved. I should be at their side with a sword and pilum, but they will not allow it. Nor would Sabinus or Rufio. They see my task as something greater. I fear it is vastly less.

Men are drilling and training in all available space. Seemingly everywhere, I see ranks of soldiers braced against their shields as screaming cavalrymen charge them and veer off at the last moment. The centurions have great respect for the German horsemen, and they are working hard to accustom their men to standing fast before a cavalry charge.

Equipment is being checked, horses examined, provisions packed. Extra wagons and horses are being leased from the Gauls. The soldiers' talent for organization would make even an ant colony envious. Yet all roads have ruts and bumps. Valerius told me Rufio was furious when he learned there were only forty-two working Scorpions, instead of sixty, one for each century. Also, there are no cohorts that are not understrength. Our own century is only seventy-four strong instead of the mandated eighty. Few things anger Metellus, but miserly politicians shorting the troops turn him into a snapping Hydra. In his words, they want to ride to glory without feeding the horse. Later, though, he had calmed down, and I saw him sitting and carving a small doll from a piece of wood.

I need to know more about our tactics before I am called upon to witness and record the days to come. Rufio has been very busy, but he has promised me an evening soon to prepare me for what I will see.

Neko, though, has been generous with his time. We have grown closer lately, as I have sought the benefit of his insight. When he speaks, it is as if he is calling forth the accumulated wisdom of centuries. His people go back so far they seem almost to touch with their toes the shores of infinity.

When I remarked to him that Rufio seemed tense, he quickly rebuked me.

"Tension is an alien emotion to Rufio. What you see is a fierce concentration."

I replied that I suspected that even Rufio would have a restless sleep the night before we departed, and again the retort was swift.

"Do you understand him so little? The afternoon before we leave, he will go into the village. While most soldiers are collecting their gear or settling their affairs, he will sit in some public place – near a fountain, perhaps – and watch the women and children. To remind him of the gentler side of life and the reason why some men must be soldiers. He will dine lightly that evening and will sleep soundly. Only before battle is his sleep serene."

"Why?"

"Because he knows that this is the reason he was born. When he rises, he will be refreshed, and he will pray to his special goddess — Victoria — to lead him through this day, as she has led him through all those that have gone before."

"They've crossed the river!" Titinius shouted and hurried past Diocles and raced toward the Principia.

Having just finished at the baths, Diocles broke into a fresh sweat while running back to the barracks.

The century had already gotten the word. All the men were standing in the dying sunlight and talking in small groups. How human it was, Diocles thought, that in times of crisis—any crisis—people immediately go outdoors and seek others. It seemed to bring both solace and strength. Most of the recruits had gathered around Valerius and were pelting him with questions.

Diocles went to the end of the building and into Rufio's quarters, but the centurion was not there. Again he shivered with that strange vulnerability he always felt at Rufio's absence.

Paki was curled up on his writing table, and he sat down and stroked her. She purred and pressed her head hard against the side of his hand. Never before had it felt so good to him to caress this gentle creature. He leaned forward and so did Paki, and she rubbed the side of her face against his cheek.

"If I don't survive this battle, I want you to take her with you to Rome."

Diocles jumped at Rufio's voice coming from the adjoining room. He rose and went to the doorway.

Rufio was unbuckling his dagger belt.

"I don't accept that you won't survive," Diocles said and suddenly realized how much he sounded like Neko.

"The Fates can be malignant," he answered and dropped his belt onto the bed.

"Where are the Germans now?"

"They crossed about four days march south of the village where we fought Racovir."

He turned away and went into his dining area and Diocles followed.

"What direction are they headed in?"

"North."

Rufio stretched out on a couch, and Neko appeared with a tray of cheese and olives and a pitcher of wine.

"Toward the village?"

"Of course," he answered and pointed to a couch opposite.

Diocles lay down and reached for a cup of wine that Neko had poured for him.

"To kill all those people?"

"What do you think? They know that will draw us out—slay them all and put the village to the torch."

"Does Metellus know this?"

"Yes. Why?"

"Calpurnia and Kalinda."

"That doesn't matter." Rufio reached for some cheese. "We'll be there before the Suebi."

"Can we be sure of that?"

"What's the matter with you?" he said with annoyance.

"It's just that I care about Metellus."

"I care about Gaul," he said, steel in his voice.

Diocles stared into his cup and swirled the wine around. "During training everything seems so simple. But this is real. I feel I'm being sucked into a whirlwind. I'm scared for all of you."

"A whirlwind is a good description."

"Will you tell me how we'll meet the Suebi?"

"Now?"

Rufio sounded impatient.

"If it's not inconvenient."

"Neko!"

The Egyptian appeared and Rufio pointed to the food and drink.

"My office." He looked back at Diocles. "This room is for peace, not war."

He rose from the comfortable couch with its Oriental coverings and went into his office.

Diocles followed. This was not an evening to keep Rufio waiting.

Neko lit the lamps and got the brazier going as the spring day fled with its warmth.

Rufio sat in the wicker chair behind his desk and Diocles sat across from him.

After arranging the food and drink, Neko slipped away like a phantom.

Diocles watched in silence as Rufio sipped his wine and stared off at visions only he could see. At last he set down the cup and looked across at him. Diocles was surprised to see a smile in his eyes.

"I've enjoyed our time together," Rufio said.

The tone of finality chilled Diocles. It seemed like a summing up.

"Have you?" Rufio went on when he failed to answer.

"Very much. If you retire after this battle, will you go with me back to Rome?"

"We'll see."

"Then that means you must live to retire, doesn't it?"

"You'll write a fine book. I'm certain of it."

"I'll try."

"Don't concentrate on me. Shine your torch on the spirit of Rome."

You are the spirit of Rome. "I'll do my best to maintain a balance. And you'll be there to help me."

Rufio reached for an olive but just rolled it around in his fingers.

"Rufio?"

He looked up.

"We'll succeed, won't we?"

"In history? Or on the Rhenus in three days?"

"In battle."

"Rome will succeed. But many will fall."

"Tell me about the Germans."

He set down the olive. "It'll be the most difficult battle of my life. No archers, no cavalry. . . ."

"And the numbers?"

"Not good. But I've never fought a battle where we weren't outnumbered." He smiled. "You seem surprised."

"I am."

"The most important lesson you can learn is that to defeat an enemy it isn't necessary to destroy his ability to fight. It's necessary to destroy his will to fight. Crush his men and he can raise more men. Crush his will and he's finished."

Diocles searched his eyes, but they were unreadable.

"If Flavia is right—and I'm sure she is—there are at least ten thousand Suebi. We'll face them with nine cohorts. That's about two to one against us. So the most important thing we have to do is choose the battleground. We cannot let the Suebi do it."

"But I don't understand how we can avoid being flanked. There are so many of them."

"That's why we cannot give battle except at a site of our own choosing. If the terrain is against us, we have to withdraw. Even if it means that village is slaughtered."

"That's not acceptable."

"You sound like a Roman."

"I am a Roman. What can we do?"

"Anchor our line."

He slid aside the waxed tablets on his desk and put the plate of food at one edge and his glass goblet at the other. He took some olives and set them in three lines between the cup and dish.

"Three ranks," Rufio said. "But this time there has to be some natural obstacle on each flank" — he pointed to the plate and the goblet — "or else the German horsemen will turn our lines and devour us. Without Gallic cavalry on the wings to protect our infantry, we have to wedge ourselves in. It's our only chance."

"Excellent! But can we find such a place?"

"We must. The way Scipio Asiagenes anchored his left wing on a river at Magnesia against Antiochus."

Diocles stared at the three ranks of olives. "Why don't we fight every battle that way? The line looks impregnable."

"No line is impregnable. And there's a major weakness. How do we exploit a break or a collapse in any part of the German line? We'd have to leave our little haven. Move forward and risk our flanks. What if we do it too soon? Or what if they close the breach in their line and then turn our flanks?"

Rufio cupped his hands and curled both ends of the Roman lines inward. Though they were only olives, now they seemed like a circular mass of helpless men.

Rufio looked up at him, and Diocles gazed into his penetrating eyes. There was no fear. Neither was there optimism nor pessimism. Just a ruthless recognition of a terrible reality.

At that moment, for the first time, Diocles began to comprehend the profundity of Neko's love. Truly, what manner of man was this?

"What is it?" Rufio asked.

Diocles looked down at the desk so Rufio could not see his face. He pretended to study the battleground as he attempted to conceal the despair he felt at one day having to return to a life among ordinary men.

"Relax." Rufio pushed a goblet of wine toward him. "I haven't even told you all of it."

"Why three ranks? According to your books, the Greeks fought in massive formations. Eight ranks or more. It seems much safer."

"It is safer. The best thing is that it prevents men from running away. They're packed in that solid mass and can barely move. More men are killed fleeing the battlefield than are ever killed facing the enemy. A huge formation prevents that. And it's much easier for a deep and narrow group like that to stay together when advancing, at least on level ground."

"Then why don't we do the same thing?"

"A big phalanx has no flexibility. It cannot pivot. If you get to its side or completely around to its rear, it's as helpless as a turtle with its legs cut off. Like the Macedonians who faced us at Cynoscephalae. All the turtle can do is die."

"Then why did they use it?"

"They had no choice. Except for the Spartans, the Greeks were poorly trained. Have you ever seen one of those old Greek helmets? Tiny eye holes. They didn't have to see much. Just push forward shoulder to shoulder with their long spears. Some of those spears were twenty feet long. And the helmets had no ear holes. There were no commands to listen to. And that made sense because they were undisciplined. They wouldn't have obeyed anyway. Except for the Spartans, the men in those old phalanxes fought in near-terror and were often half-drunk. Show me a deep formation and I'll show you a commander unsure of his troops. Antiochus at Magnesia fielded formations thirty-two ranks deep. Can you imagine that? The poorer the training, the deeper the ranks. Show me three or four ranks advancing smoothly in open files" — he spread his hands over the desk — "and I'll show you men to fear."

"Tell me more about anchoring our line."

"Now you begin to understand the dangers of immobility. If we have to fight between two barriers, we cannot charge the Germans. We must wait for them to hit us. That's an enormous disadvantage. The momentum of a charge is terrific. And to stand there and wait for it is more demoralizing than you can possibly imagine."

"You don't think we can withstand a charge while standing still?"

"Impossible to predict."

"Aren't there any examples of it in your histories?"

"I know of only one involving a Roman army — Pompeius at Pharsalus. And he was crushed. When I was a young soldier in Syria, I met a retired centurion named Gallus who'd served with Pompeius in the civil war. He told me their army was huge — it certainly outnumbered Caesar's. But their morale was poor. And many of Pompeius's troops were very green. It's always dangerous to charge with inexperienced troops — they cannot hold formation. Pompeius knew this. So instead of charging, he formed his men ten deep and waited for Caesar's charge. The distance between the armies was greater than usual and he believed Caesar's line would break up and get ragged before it reached his wall of men." Rufio smiled. "But it did not."

"Don't stop now. What happened?"

"Caesar halted the charge in mid-attack, ordered his men to dress ranks, then ordered them to charge again."

"Just as you did halfway between the Sequani village and Racovir's men."

"Yes. When Caesar's men hit Pompeius's line, it was devastating. Of course, the battle was much more complex than that, but—"

"But Pompeius never recovered the initiative."

"Exactly. He was routed." Rufio looked away toward some distant memory. "Gallus had served with Caesar here in Gaul. Yet after Caesar crossed the Rubicon, Gallus sided with the Senate and Pompeius. He was wounded at Pharsalus—in the leg, I believe. He was left on the battlefield. After the fight, he saw a group of men picking their way among the dead. He tried to push himself up to face them. It was Caesar and some of his officers. Caesar was searching for old comrades. Gallus thrust the tip of his sword into the ground and managed to push himself to his feet. Caesar approached him as he tried to steady himself. Caesar knew every one of his centurions by name. He came up to him with that incredible smile and placed a hand on his shoulder and said, 'Welcome back, my old friend.'" Rufio turned in his chair and looked over at Diocles. "Gallus wept as he told me this."

Diocles smiled, more to himself than to Rufio. Perhaps that bust of Caesar was not so heavy after all.

"Is Gallus gone now?"

"Oh yes. He died in Antioch about three years after I first met him. We had many long nights together. I spoke with his daughter at the end. She told me he died whispering Caesar's name."

Rufio stood up. "We march in two days." Then he turned and strode from the room.

36 HE CONQUERS TWICE WHO CONQUERS HIMSELF IN VICTORY.

Publilius Syrus

*R*ufio has an endless list of tasks to perform before we march, so I was surprised to see him sitting behind his desk and patiently listening to the lament of a soldier. I stood in the doorway and watched.

Arrianus from our century had brought a friend from the Fourth Cohort. It seems the hapless lad had fallen asleep after dallying with a Gallic woman in the settlement and someone had made off with his sword. He was terrified of returning to his barracks and facing his centurion. Arrianus asked Rufio if his friend might borrow one of our swords until he could get some of his money to buy another.

"You want me to conspire with this careless soldier to deceive his centurion?"

Arrianus did not know how to answer that.

"You were lax," Rufio said to the soldier.

"Yes," he answered in an unsteady voice.

"The vinestick awaits you."

"I know," he said, trying to sound brave.

"Rufio," Arrianus went on, "if we – "

"Dismissed."

Arrianus, as tough and combative as a badger with his fellow legionaries, shut his mouth instantly and turned away.

"Not you," Rufio said to the other soldier as he started to leave.

Rufio stared at him for a moment, then said "Neko" so softly I could barely hear it at the back of the room.

Miraculously, Neko appeared from somewhere behind me and slipped past me through the doorway.

Rufio whispered to him and Neko left and quickly came back with a small sack and gave it to his master. He handed Neko some coins from it, and I heard him say the name Hetorix. Neko hurried off and returned in a few minutes with an excellent sword and scabbard.

Rufio nodded and Neko handed it to the soldier. The boy was speechless. Finally he managed to blurt his gratitude and how he would pay double what it was worth. But Rufio stopped him with a raised hand.

"You owe me nothing except a promise to march with valor for Rome. Return to your century."

Rufio folded his hands on the desk and gazed down at the papers in front of him.

After the lad hurried off, I approached the desk, and Rufio looked up at me. He was struggling to hold back a smile, but suddenly he gave up and exploded in laughter. I could not hold back either and we laughed together at

216

this boy who probably had never had a woman before he had left home to join the army. Then his moment of delight had spawned a catastrophe, only to be magically transformed by this iron-faced centurion. Never had I expected to see tears of laughter in Rufio's eyes, but there they were, and mixed with compassion, too, as he no doubt recalled the days of his own adventurous and perhaps wayward youth. I have seen Rufio with many expressions and in many roles — or guises, for I have never been quite sure — but that was the one that will stay with me forever. That is the way I will always remember him.

———————

Rufio sat outside the tavern and watched the children play at the fountain. He had exhausted his stock of sweets for them and had retreated to a small table in the shade of an overhang.

A cup of beer was set down by his hand. He looked up at a thickset man in his mid-thirties. He was wearing a spattered leather apron.

"To refresh you," the Gaul said with a smile.

He was evidently the owner.

"Thank you."

Rufio noticed a woman standing in the shadows behind the man. She was the dark-haired woman he had seen at the fountain with her little girl and her cat.

"We thank you for what you are about to do," the man said.

"We all have our tasks."

The tavern owner seemed not to know what to say next. His wife stepped up by his side.

No Sequani chieftain here, no golden-haired Varacinda, but tough, handsome people. The spine of Gaul.

The man seemed uncomfortable and turned and went back into his shop.

His wife remained.

Rufio stood to face her.

Lines of care at the corners of her eyes and around her mouth graced her with a mature elegance.

"We fear the Suebi," she said. "But you fear nothing."

"Everyone fears something. But don't fear the Germans. We stand between them and Gaul."

"I know that," she answered with a smile, the lines around her mouth deepening.

"Your daughter is safe. She'll grow up proud and beautiful. Like her mother."

She seemed to peer into his soul. "May the woman you love carry your spirit within her heart until you return."

She turned away but Rufio touched her arm.

"And why do you think there's a woman I love?"

"You have an edge, centurion. But you have a gentleness, too. No man can acquire that alone. He gets it only when he allows a woman's spirit to enter his heart."

Rufio's eyes smiled at her. "What makes you so wise?"

"I'm a woman." She smiled back. "And I'm Sequani."

The most beautiful mixture on earth, Rufio thought.

"Keep safe, centurion, and return to the woman you love."

She turned and walked off into the shadows.

Flavia appeared at the edge of the firelight. The campfire sputtered and crackled, and flecks of glowing wood floated into the night air. She entered the small clearing, awash now in golden light.

Rufio stood next to the fire. On the grass near his feet lay an Oriental carpet, a basket of cheese and fruit, and a jug of wine.

"Do you enjoy sending mysterious messages to unmarried women?" she said with a smile.

She strode toward him out of the darkness with those long and powerful legs and seemed again to be the graceful woodland goddess emerging from the forest.

She stood before him now with that confident smile.

"I wanted to see you once more before I left for battle," he said.

She glanced down at the rug and the meal he had brought.

"I understand."

She took the bow from her shoulder and pulled the quiver from her back and set them on the ground next to his sword and scabbard. Then she sat in the middle of the carpet.

"I'm here," she said and extended her right hand.

He took it in his and sat beside her.

He stared into her eyes for a long time. The warmth of the fire ignited the smell of blossoms in her hair and her own sweet scent. He felt as if he were inhaling an exotic drug.

"I chose this place for privacy," he said, fearing she might misunderstand. "To be able to pretend for one night that there was no one else on earth."

"Do you think I don't trust you?" she said, smiling. "I know you didn't summon me here to seduce me. Other men have tried that. But you don't need firelight and stars." She brought his right hand to her lips and kissed his fingers.

He hooked an arm around her shoulders and pulled her in, pressing her head against the side of his face.

"I'm so proud of whom you have become," he said. "But I don't deserve you in my arms."

"None of us deserves another person's love. But that doesn't matter." She kissed his hand again.

"I saw you once, not far from here. At the swimming cove."

"Yes, I know," she said softly and rested her head on his shoulder and stared into the fire. "Vara told me."

"When I saw you—when I felt you—it was as if Victoria suddenly reached down and pulled the dagger out of my chest. It had been embedded there for twenty years."

"Oh, Rufio, I'm just a woman."

"No, I've known women, I've had women—all over the empire. They seem like shadows now."

He touched his lips to the top of her head and pressed his face against her hair.

She reached up behind her and curled her fingers around the back of his neck.

"I could stay here forever," she said.

He felt his control slipping away and he eased off.

"What's the matter?" she asked, turning half way around.

"Everything is perfect."

She gave him a knowing half-smile. "You said you were proud of me. Do you know how that makes me feel? I grow taller every time I think of it."

He gazed into the staggering beauty of her eyes, and suddenly he felt very old.

"And it's not difficult being taller than an Italian," she said with a teasing laugh, and she tapped a finger against the end of his nose.

He grabbed her hand and held it.

"You're the wisest man I know, but there's something you've forgotten." She leaned so close to him that some of her long black hairs tickled his cheek. "Your pride is precious to me"—her voice was barely above a whisper—"but you're not my father."

Her lips engulfed his as she locked her hands behind his head. She slid her tongue between his lips and sought out his.

He growled from the depths of his hunger and buried his hands in her hair and tried to devour her.

Soon they were both gasping. She pulled away.

"I've never had a man before. I want you to be the only man I'll ever have."

She stood over him and undressed in the flickering light.

Rufio felt as if he could hardly breathe.

She now wore only the black leather bracer on her left wrist and the bronze torque on her right biceps.

"Come to me." She held out her hands.

He stood and removed his clothes. Her longing seemed to envelop him. He slipped into her arms and slid his hands around her hips and onto the cheeks of her bottom. As his full body pressed against her, she moaned.

"I want you within me, my dearest love. So deeply you'll touch my heart."

As they descended to the carpet, they entwined as tightly as if they were a single being.

Rufio struggled to control his passion. He kissed her gently and slid his hands over her breasts and along her legs.

"I won't shatter," she said with an adoring smile.

Yet he knew his own desperate need and he fought to bring it under his command. He slid over her and opened her as delicately as if she were a flower.

She cried out in awe and wonder, the cry a woman can make only once in her life.

She stared disbelieving into his eyes. "More of you," she whispered. "Rufio . . . ."

She grunted as he obeyed. Then a husky guttural burst from her throat, and her groan of pleasure ignited Rufio and he cried out with her.

But it was only the beginning. She could not be sated. Each intense caress of him was more demanding than the last. Each of her cries louder than before. Every shudder more convulsive as she almost threw his body from her. Like the flame of Vesta, she was a fire that could not be quenched. One could only blissfully submit and be consumed within her.

———————

They lay at rest, warmly wrapped in the soft coils of the carpet. The fire still blazed beside them.

"How did you get a name like Rufio," Flavia teased and playfully ran her fingers through his silver hair.

He tilted his head forward and kissed her on the bridge of her nose. "I'm told a red-haired Thracian enchantress lurks somewhere in my lineage."

"I'm sure she was a beauty."

He took a deep breath as he pulled her to him.

"I won't escape from you. And you mustn't escape from me. I command it."

He knew he could never make that promise.

"There's a rumor you're going to retire and return to Rome. I forbid it."

She nestled her head into the hollow of his shoulder and sighed with pleasure.

He could feel her warm breath along his chest.

"Before tonight, I was half a man. I never knew that. All my skills and talents — all incomplete."

"You're more man than any ten men."

"Now I feel whole." He shook his head in wonder. "I always thought I was so wise."

She turned and gazed at him. "The love of a woman makes a wise man wiser."

He smiled and leaned forward and kissed her on each of her dark eyebrows.

"You do know I love you, don't you?" he asked. "That your breath is my life?"

"Of course I know. How could I not? I'm a woman and I'm Sequani." She laughed. "I know all."

He laughed with her.

She laid her head back on his chest and rested a hand on him. "You must stay with me forever."

36 THE HIGHEST SEAT DOES NOT HOLD TWO.

Roman saying

At Rufio's command, I took his horse and raced up a nearby ridge. From this vantage I could take in a long section of the road below. I stared in awe at the most extraordinary animal I had ever seen. Four thousand men, fused into a single being and looking like some enormous mythical beast, bored through the Gallic countryside. Their hobnails snapped against the stone, and the pink early morning sun made the road beneath their feet seem to be paved with blocks of coral.

About half of our cavalry and the Second Cohort formed the vanguard. Behind them came soldiers with tools for smoothing out breaks in the road or for hacking through any obstructions that might lie in our path. Then came the surveyors to lay out the camp. The baggage train of Sabinus and the tribunes followed with a small cavalry escort. Just behind this came the train of pack mules hauling the partly dismantled Scorpions. The tribunes followed, surrounded by a bodyguard of specially selected men. The bearers of the silver eagle and of the capricorn of the legion marched directly behind, accompanied by the signifers and their individual standards. The signifers wore wolf skins draped over their helmets and hanging down their backs, and they carried small round shields instead of the big shields of the infantrymen.

The cornicens with their curved bronze horns and the tubicens with their straight trumpets followed the signifers. Then at last came the cohorts. Marching six in a rank, they split the Gallic wilderness, as unstoppable as one of the iron chisels Rufio had driven between those fractures in the stone so long ago.

The mule train of the legion followed the infantry and carried the rolled leather tents and other paraphernalia of a marching camp. Trailing the animals were the servants.

Because we have so few cavalry to form a rear guard, Rufio had placed one cohort between the baggage train and our remaining few horsemen at the rear.

According to Rufio, poor commanders often ride in the middle of the column to feel safe. This was not to Sabinus's liking. He rode up and down the right edge of the column, encouraging the troops, joking with them, helping the centurions keep the files straight. The men joked back. I have stopped being surprised at the freedom commanders allow their troops in talking back to their officers, even to the point of tossing caustic barbs at the Legate. I am told even Caesar permitted this, so it has a hallowed tradition. I suspect the wisest commanders know that it is like tilting the lid on a boiling pot. It vents excess steam but allows the pot to keep boiling. Crus, too, did the same along the left edge of the column, riding up and down and joking with the men and laughing as they joked back.

At that moment, as I sat on Rufio's stallion, I could have dropped dead and died as a man fulfilled. That is how proud I felt to belong to this unique assemblage of men.

———

"Rufio," Sabinus said from his horse. "What do you make of that?"

Rufio turned and looked back the way they had come. He stood along the road edge, outside the marching column, and could see far to the west. Riders were coming fast. From their height in the saddles and the way they sat their horses, he could see in an instant who they were.

"Sequani."

A cheer began at the back of the column and gathered force and rippled forward through the Romans.

Adiatorix rode at the head of about a hundred horsemen. He carried a carnyx, a high vertical trumpet with the mouth in the shape of a boar.

"Hail, Chief," Sabinus said.

"Hail, Sabinus. These are the best. As many as I could gather. We will face the Suebi together."

"You're a loyal ally, Chief. Divide your men and send half out to each wing. You ride with my decurions at the front."

Adiatorix nodded and divided his men as ordered.

Rufio watched the big Gaul take a place near the head of the column.

"No battle will turn on a few dozen horsemen," Sabinus said to his favorite centurion. "But it's good to have them here."

Rufio smiled. The veteran of countless battlefields knew better. The spirit of the Sequani could not be measured that way.

———

Shortly after midday, the first elements of the legion reached the Sequani village. It seemed as if every inhabitant had turned out to greet them. They rushed the column with food and drink and shouts of welcome. Several villagers recognized Rufio and converged on him with bulging wineskins and baskets of bread. Diocles had rejoined his century and now saw Calpurnia and Kalinda being jostled in the midst of the throng. Rufio pushed aside several men with his vinestick and pulled the woman and her little girl toward him.

"He's farther back in the column with the other signifers," Rufio said.

Kalinda grabbed her mother's hand and tried to drag her along.

"No," Calpurnia told her daughter. "We must not—"

"It's all right. Tell them Rufio said to let you pass."

Calpurnia smiled at him and raced down the column with Kalinda to find Metellus.

"I'd like to see that look in a woman's eyes someday," Valerius said and watched her run along.

"You will," Diocles said. "You'll grow old and wise and have fat babies on your knees."

But Valerius looked pensive.

"What is it?" Rufio asked.

"It's just that I've never been in love."

"You mean you don't love your centurion?" Rufio said in disbelief.

Valerius burst out laughing. "How can I answer that?"

The legion passed the village and continued marching to a large meadow about a mile beyond it. Crus rode ahead and placed a white flag in the spot where Sabinus's tent would be pitched. The soldiers would construct the entire camp around that point, near the brook that supplied water to the village. Here the legion would entrench itself, between the Suebi and the Sequani.

Laid out by the surveyors with its own Via Praetoria and Via Principalis, the camp was a smaller copy of the legionary fort. The troops dug, mounded, and fortified with the spiked caltrops in the same way Rufio's century had done just before the clash with Racovir.

To Diocles, the hours consumed in the camp's construction now seemed like nothing. Soon water carriers would be sent out under guard, as well as foraging parties for firewood and fodder.

By late afternoon the camp was nearing completion. Where, shortly before, the tender breast of Gaul had lain bare before the Suebi, now nine cohorts of the Twenty-fifth Legion interposed their defiance. Four thousand men, Italians armed with Spanish swords and Celtic mail, scoffing at the warrior's ethos, cinching up now for the serious business of war.

38   GOOD LUCK IS THE COMPANION OF COURAGE.

Roman saying

"Come with me," was all Rufio had said, and Diocles immediately obeyed.

Probus rode beside Rufio and Diocles followed, and they left the camp by the eastern clavicular gate. Behind them the noise of hundreds of animals and thousands of men faded away.

The meadow rolled on far beyond the camp, and across this they rode. Rufio and Probus scanned every feature of the countryside. Diocles knew this was a time for him to be silent.

Several hours of daylight remained, and a warm breeze blew across the meadow. Yet Diocles suspected that the niceties of weather were lost on Rufio.

After they had ridden about a mile, Rufio raised a hand and they pulled up. The plain continued indefinitely to the east and off to the north as well. To the south, though, about a quarter of a mile away, it ended. A ridge ran due east and rose about fifty feet, with a sizeable stand of trees at the summit. Rufio stared at it with that burning concentration Neko had described. Diocles was certain that if he held his hands near Rufio's face, he would feel waves of heat.

Rufio looked to the north. The plain went on for miles.

"What do you think?" Probus asked.

"Not good. Anchoring the right is not enough. The left will die out there."

Diocles could not take his eyes off Rufio. The intensity of his expression told of the nimble mind racing through countless battles. Rufio stared into the distance, but Diocles knew from that characteristic squint of his that he was really looking inward. All his reading and experience of war were being searched with the ferocious competence that so defined this man.

"Look. " Probus jutted his chin toward the half moon in the afternoon sky.

"So?" Diocles said.

"We won't have to worry about the Suebi refusing battle," Rufio said. "They believe it's bad luck to fight during the waning moon. They won't wait. They'll attack immediately."

The three men rode on. The terrain became more uneven, but its open expanse still offered no shelter. To the casual wanderer, it was serene. To an outnumbered legion, it gaped like a deathtrap.

Five Roman scouts rode in from the east, and Rufio waved them down.

"Two days away," the decurion said.

"Slower than I thought," Rufio answered.

"They've brought their families," the decurion said in disgust, and then he hurried off with his scouts back to the camp.

A string of obscenities burst from Rufio's mouth before the hoofbeats of the cavalry had died away.

Diocles stared at him in surprise. Rufio was one of the few soldiers he knew who seemed to have little use for profanity, but now he defiled the air to the horizon.

"What is it?" Diocles looked at Probus. "What did he mean about families?"

"Sometimes the Germans bring all their people to cheer them. Wives, children, old men. They think it gives them added power."

"What does it matter?" Diocles asked, but Probus's silent glare suddenly made him realize what he had said.

"What's wrong with you?" Rufio shouted, turning his anger on Diocles. "Are you a savage? I've killed a man before the eyes of his wife."

Diocles was afraid to speak.

"And I slew her, too. Take that to bed with you the rest of your life."

He jerked away and galloped ahead.

"It's all right," Probus said. "Give him a few moments."

When they caught up with him, his fire had banked.

"Do you hear that?" Rufio was facing northeast.

Probus turned in that direction. "Water?"

"By the gods!" Rufio said and raced on.

They followed him, and there ahead, hidden by a stand of trees, flowed a healthy stream, gurgling with spring rains.

"I told you our maps are useless." Rufio slid from his horse. "They don't show this."

He dropped to his left knee by the stream, his right forearm resting across his thigh.

Diocles watched him stare at the flowing water. Then he saw Rufio's right hand tighten into a fist.

"We've got them!" he whispered harshly and the knuckles of his fist whitened. "We've got them all."

Rufio was standing at the base of the ridge and gazing at the summit as Crus rode up. The Numidian stallion grazed nearby.

Crus dismounted and approached him across the grass.

"We'll fight here," Rufio said. "This will be the killing ground."

The tribune turned toward the north and the expanse of meadow. "How?"

"This ridge will be our right anchor." He pulled his dagger and gestured to the hill like a teacher with a pointer. "Along the top, fifty Scorpions just inside the trees. All aimed in front of our right wing. The Germans will hit an iron wall."

Crus turned again to the left. "But what about there?"

"Follow me."

He mounted his horse, and Crus rode after him to the stream about a quarter mile northeast of the proposed battlefield.

Rufio dismounted and let the animal go over to the stream for a drink.

"We'll trench and divert water from this stream" — Rufio pointed to the ground near his feet — "from here to the northern edge of the battleground. Bring it down from here at about a forty-five degree angle. We'll curl it around our left wing."

Crus dismounted. "Can we do it?" he asked in amazement.

"Six feet wide, four feet deep — that'll be enough. When it reaches the left wing of the battlefield, it'll have sharp-angled sides. And a half-foot trench at the bottom — enough to twist an ankle. In the trench we'll place lilies. That —"

"Lilies?"

"Bunches of wooden stakes, iron prongs — whatever Hetorix and his men can put together for us quickly. Clustered like flowers. The trench will be too wide for most of the Suebi to jump. They'll try to wade across. It'll be like slipping into the jaws of a wolf."

"But can we dig it in time?"

"We start now. Dig all night with torches and all day tomorrow. The entire battle will turn on this."

"We need the man here you trust most." He smiled. "I'll get Probus."

"I want you."

Crus just stared at him.

"You'd never let down your legion. I know that now."

Crus turned away.

"Are you equal to that responsibility, tribune?"

He looked back at Rufio. "Why do you believe in me?"

"I know men."

"I've treated you badly."

"Only my enemies have done that. You've never been my enemy."

"But I've been a fool."

"No, you've been young. That's easily cured. You're a patrician. The future of Rome."

"But what of you? You are—"

"Just a soldier in decline."

"You'll never convince me of that," he said with a laugh.

Rufio did not respond.

Crus stared at him for a moment, then turned away and walked to the edge of the stream. He pulled his sword out of the way and sat on the bank.

Rufio joined him.

"We're caught up in the sweep of history," the centurion said.

"Yes, I know."

"And the Twenty-fifth Legion is the pivot."

"I came out here to advance my career," Crus said and gazed at the flowing water. "Now I'm staring down the throats of barbarians. The world is never what we think it will be."

"You'll make a fine career. You'll be a senator soon. Maybe even consul someday. And many years from now, when you're sitting in your villa in the Alban Hills with your grandchildren gathered around, you'll remember none of that."

Crus turned and looked at him.

"You'll remember your days with the Twenty-fifth Legion. Rough men and crude humor and bravery beyond imagination. On a cold winter night at your fireside, you'll remember a warm spring day in the green of Gaul. How you stood fast before those who would burn down all we cherish."

"Above all," Crus said in a low voice, "I'll remember you."

"The petty squabbling of politicians—the empty oaths—all will fade. But this"—he pounded the ground beside him—"this will remain. This will mark your life and define it forever."

"You'll be there with me. With my grandchildren. I want them to know you."

"What remains of me will be in a funerary urn in a tomb on the Via Appia. Perhaps you can come to visit."

"No, no. You must live to be an old man. I order it. Your wisdom cannot be wasted."

"You can carry a fragment or two of it with you."

Crus looked off toward the east, toward the unseen army approaching them.

"This is greater than we are, isn't it?" he said.

"It's greater than everything. It's the fate of the world."

228

39   THE MATTER IS ON A DOOR HINGE.

Roman saying

Cheers greeted Barovistus as he rode among his people. Campfires speckled the rising plain to the horizon, as if the stars had been plucked from the sky and scattered across the land.

Young warriors boasted to each other of how many Romans they would slay. With spears or stolen swords they fought mock battles, then shattered the night with Suebian victory cries. Older fighters entranced them with tales of war from long ago, though they ignored the fact that their foes had been other Germans, not the trained and armored troops now so very near.

Wives nursing their young sat with their men around the fires and the cooking pots. Though enraptured by their heroes, the women looked fearful. To the dark forests beyond the Rhenus, tales had carried of the ruthless Romans. Men who would march to the ends of the earth to crush even the dying whisper of defiance.

Barovistus saw Orgestes sitting alone by a fire and staring into the flames. He dismounted and approached the former war chief.

"Walk with me."

Orgestes rose, and they passed beyond the young men and into the darkness.

"I wish I could teach them to march," Barovistus said. "Or to form a fighting line and obey me on the battlefield."

Orgestes said nothing.

"But they'll be great warriors."

"Perhaps."

"You won't fight in this battle."

Orgestes stopped and turned to confront him.

"Not with your leg," Barovistus went on. "You'd die in an instant."

Orgestes remained silent.

"But there's another reason. If I'm killed, you must lead them. They'll follow no one else but you."

Orgestes drifted away from the chief.

"Well?" Barovistus said.

Orgestes looked back at him. "What are your orders if you're killed."

"Take no captives. I want a Roman head hung from every tree. All must die."

"And the Sequani?"

"Kill any men who resist. Barter the rest. Our men can use the women for their pleasure and then trade them, too. The children they can barter or burn."

"Children?" Orgestes said in horror.

"Sequani rats."

"Pray Mars isn't listening to you now."

"Mars?"

"Pray he doesn't shout what you say into the ear of that silver-haired centurion. The one who destroyed Racovir and maimed our men. The one who tore the tongue from Trogus."

"Why should I care?"

"You invite that Roman's rage. You're mad. You should fear it."

"I fear nothing," he said with a laugh.

"You're the greatest fool on earth."

The half-moon dropped cold light across the Gallic countryside. A sentry line of Sequani horsemen peered into the distance.

Soldiers with weapons and full armor trenched with that controlled silence unique to the army of Rome. A century drawn from each cohort drove pickaxes and shovels into the earth. Torches lined the empty artery that would soon connect the stream with the battlefield to the west.

Rufio rode along the ditch into the woods that concealed its origin at the edge of the water.

Crus was digging with the rest of the men. Like a man lashed by a demon, he wielded his pick furiously. The sound of the horse caused him to look up. His face glistened with sweat in the torchlight.

Crus smiled as Rufio dismounted. "Look at our progress. We should be finished by mid-morning. I never knew men could work so fast."

"Hetorix and his armorers are making our lilies. We'll plant them tomorrow."

"How long do you think it'll be before the Suebi get here?"

"I sent Adiatorix ahead to scout. He's a better judge of the speed of the Germans than we are. He just returned. We'll be able to smell them by tomorrow evening."

Crus leaned on his pick. "What happens when they see the trench? What if they try to fill it in?"

"We're going to scatter the dirt. And they don't have the tools to do anything about it anyway. If they want to turn our flank, they have to cross."

Crus picked up his flask from the ground and took a drink and splashed some water onto his face.

"Have you ever felt more alive than now?" Rufio asked with a smile.

"Never."

40 FORTUNE FAVORS THE VALIANT.

Terence

T*he marching camp is not like the fort at all. True, it resembles it and is laid out in the same fashion, but it crackles with a repressed energy that is almost maddening.*

Yet I still fail to find that bonding of warriors that had lived so long in my fantasies. These soldiers are, if anything, even quieter here than at the fort. At least about matters pertaining to battle. When they speak, it is about women or families or famous dice games where they won fortunes. I hear no tales of past heroics, though there must have been many. Not once have I heard anyone mention the Suebi. Is it because they fear them? Possibly. How could they not fear those barbarians? Yet I believe it is something different. A truth more subtle and oblique, and yet at the same time open and obvious. I think if I asked them why they do not speak of the Germans, they would ask me what would be the point of it. These men have a job to do and will do it the way they have been trained to do it. As Probus once said to me, why howl or whine — that is for dogs, not men. I believe it is this offhandedness, this nonchalance — even detachment — that is one of their most compelling traits. Certainly it is their most ominous.

Sabinus's huge goatskin tent now held the ten most experienced soldiers in Gaul. Around a large table commandeered from the Sequani stood the senior centurion of each cohort of the Twenty-fifth Legion. Though what remained of the First Cohort had been left with its centurions to garrison the fort, Rufio had insisted to Sabinus that Bruttius Macer, its senior surviving centurion, join them on the battle line.

Surrounded by his tribunes, Sabinus leaned over a quickly drawn map. Cups of acetum and loaves of bread had been spread around the table, and lamps had been set along the edge of the map. They flickered now as the night wind rippled the tent flaps.

Diocles stood off to the side in the half-light.

"The day after tomorrow, the world will change for all of us," Sabinus said. "Early in the day — when the sun is in our eyes — the Suebi will offer battle. We will take it."

Diocles was surprised to see that even here all the centurions wore their mail loricas and their sword and dagger belts, as if they expected the Germans to storm the tent at any moment. Sabinus's bronze muscle breastplate gleamed in the lamplight. Nothing was left to chance.

"We'll fight here." Sabinus thrust his dagger through the map and into the table. "Between the ridge and the flooded ditch." He looked at Crus.

"It'll be finished by the third hour tomorrow," the tribune said. "It can be flooded any time after Hetorix and his men finish planting their lilies."

"Three cohorts in the first line, three in the second, three in reserve." Sabinus looked to Macer. "I want you on the left wing. You know how crucial that is."

"Yes, Sabinus."

"You in the middle to hold the line," Sabinus said to Probus.

"Yes, commander."

"And you." Sabinus gazed across at Rufio. "What shall we do with you?"

The other centurions laughed. They knew there was only one place for him — that part of the line that led the battle and dominated its flow.

"Let's see. " Sabinus screwed up his face as if he were straining to think. "How about the right wing?"

Rufio smiled and touched the hilt of his sword.

Sabinus gestured and Rufio joined him on the other side of the map.

The muscles of Rufio's forearms stood out sharply as he leaned with the heels of his hands against the table edge and stared with a typical Rufian squint at the map before him. Only so masculine a man would dare wear a woman's torque on his wrist. It glittered now as the wavering lamplights danced along its contours.

"There are two mistakes we cannot make against the Suebi," Rufio began. "The first is to underestimate them. They're big and very strong. A blow from one is like the kick of a horse. Even more important is the ugly fact that they live to inflict death on their enemies. Love for the heat of battle is a boiling cauldron at their core. It never cools. The Gauls at their most barbaric are Athenian philosophers compared to the Germans. No people — none — takes greater pleasure in the simple act of killing other human beings."

Rufio paused and took a sip of acetum.

"The second mistake is to overestimate them. They have no discipline. Training is unknown. They're like drunken gamblers — hideous and reckless when they're winning and prone to stumble and panic when they're losing. Remember, to beat them it's not necessary to destroy them — we cannot do that anyway, we have too few men. We don't need to annihilate them. We have to break them — shatter their will. Then — and only then — will the poets write of a Roman victory."

Diocles saw Macer and Probus nod in silent agreement.

"Ten thousand Suebi warriors," Rufio said. "Crashing into a line of three stationary cohorts. Who feels comfortable with that?"

It was an awkward question. Obviously no one did.

"Probus?" Rufio said.

"I've dealt with worse."

"That was not the question."

"I don't like it."

Rufio looked at Macer.

"Nor do I," the centurion said.

Diocles watched, fascinated. He knew Rufio hated war councils. Why was he asking for advice?

"Alternatives?" Rufio said.

Probus shook his head. "There are none."

"There are always alternatives," Macer said. "We can charge them first."

"And expose our flanks?" Probus asked. "That's suicide."

"No," Macer said. "Time our charge so we meet them at just the right moment between the flooded ditch and the ridge. Carry one pilum only. We won't have time to throw a second."

"Can we do that?" Sabinus asked in surprise.

"It's worth the risk," Macer said. "We have the finest men on earth. They can do anything."

"That's asking for a great deal," Rufio said. "Precise timing. No hesitation. Iron nerve. I'm new here — are you that confident in these troops?"

"Yes," Macer said with a touch of defiance. "I am."

Probus scratched the stubble on his chin. "That would be something. We would write history here."

"Besides," Macer went on, "thousands of pounds of smelly German muscle and bone smashing into us so early in the morning — we'd vomit our breakfast. The battlefield would get very messy — too slippery to fight on."

Titinius and Crus laughed, and Sabinus looked around at his men. They all nodded their assent.

"Then it's settled," the commander said. "We await the pleasure of no barbarians. Especially those that don't bathe. We hit them first."

Deep-throated murmurs of approval filled the tent.

Diocles, though, was watching Rufio. *You silver fox. You decided all this beforehand.*

A barely perceptible smile pulled at the centurion's lips as he reached down for his cup. He had not asked for the impossible—he had gotten his men to plead for the privilege of doing it.

41 WHEN THEY HAD SEEN BODIES CHOPPED TO PIECES WITH THE SPANISH SWORD . . . THEY REALIZED IN A GENERAL PANIC WITH WHAT WEAPONS, AND WHAT MEN, THEY HAD TO FIGHT.

Livy

---

*N*eko told me Rufio had risen long before dawn. Neko had to prepare his meal very early because Rufio and Probus and Macer were meeting with the other centurions to plan the coming battle. I could kick myself for missing that. Yet I do not dare ask Rufio what transpired. He is so preoccupied with hundreds of details that I am certain if I interrupted him now, he would turn on me with the glare of Medusa.

I decided to stroll through the camp to get a feel for the mood of the men.

It was a cool morning, and I wrapped myself in my heavy cloak. Only a few clouds streaked the sky, but a cold breeze was blowing in from the west.

The men at their cooking fires were more talkative than usual. They seemed to be more excited now that the battle was near — and more nervous. I doubt there was a single one who underestimated the frightening reality they called the Furor Teutonicus. While I walked along the rows of leather tents — as straight and perfect as the barracks blocks in the fort — I noticed a peculiar fact. Every veteran soldier sitting at a fire and having his meal had several younger soldiers around him. Youth generally seeks out youth, but not today. The younger men had been drawn to the experienced soldiers like tender shoots pulled toward the sun. Yet they did not pester the veterans with questions. Mostly they sat near them without speaking and simply drew comfort from their presence.

The veterans were fascinating to watch. A growing tension was tightening their lips and the corners of their eyes. Some ate their meal in silence, but I suspected from their expressions that they were reflecting inwardly and imagining things I dared not imagine. Others were instructing some of the younger soldiers on the proper grip of a sword or how to angle the wrist.

These were hard men — it showed in every crease of their faces. But could they be anything else and survive? This is where the brutal drilling paid back its bounty. The shouting, the thrashings, the threats of savage punishments — all now more valuable than bushels of silver. The scraped knuckles and bruised legs, the sword arms battered and bloody from badly aimed thrusting and accidentally banging into one's own shield — treasured wounds that toughened more than flesh.

Last night I was up late reading in Rufio's tent. Neko had told me Rufio never goes on campaign without several books. I chose Livius and came across a remarkable story that now seems all the more telling. About two hundred years ago, we were fighting Philip of Macedon. Evidently Philip was unsure of

236

the morale of his troops, so after a small skirmish with the Romans he had the dead gathered up and laid out before his men to rouse them to the proper fury. Apparently Philip had not yet seen the corpses himself. Better that he had. The remains looked scarcely human. Long accustomed to seeing men killed by spear points, Philip's troops recoiled in revulsion. Hacked and chopped by the Spanish sword, their countrymen lay before them like butchered beasts, unrecognizable and obscene. The troops' morale crumbled into dust.

Great courage it takes to be a Greek spearman, but how little that seems to me now. Marching shoulder to shoulder and carrying enormous pikes, reassured by the press of one's comrades, shields locked — what is that compared to standing in open files with a weapon no longer than your arm and looking into the eyes of your enemy and stepping forward and cutting him down?

Discipline is severe, but discipline never won a battle — it simply helped an army not lose one. And there is more than training, too, for training is merely technique. The aggressiveness ignited at the training stakes foments a uniquely Roman boldness in attack. This fuses with the driving spirit of Rome to incite in these men a breathtaking audacity — dynamic, irresistible, and ultimately incomprehensible.

"We came to fight the Suebi — not watch them!"

Adiatorix's scowl was as fearsome as the snarl on a Roman theatrical mask.

"I know that, Chief," Rufio said. He pointed to the ground beside one of the cooking fires. "Sit with me."

The Sequani had declined tents and spent the night bedded down with their horses near the Porta Principalis Dextra, the gateway at the right edge of the camp. Morning fodder had been spread out for the animals, and now the warriors were gathered around their fires.

"You and your men are the ones we can spare to do this," Rufio said. "We don't have enough men to fortify the position. The survival of the Scorpions means the survival of this legion. If the Germans turn our right wing, we're all raven meat."

"Just sit there on the hill?" Adiatorix asked in disbelief. "Nothing else?"

"Hold it to the death."

"It's not the Sequani way to be still."

"It's not the Roman way to die uselessly. Are the Sequani so brave they can face the Suebi, but such children they cannot follow a command?"

Adiatorix gazed at him in exasperation. "Life was easier for me before you entered this land."

"I have that effect on everyone. Learn to endure it."

"Very well. We'll protect your Scorpion shooters."

"No matter what happens on the battlefield, you cannot abandon the hill. Everything turns on that."

The three centurions stood in the middle of the proposed battleground and studied it with practiced eyes. Atop the hill, soldiers were reassembling the Scorpions at the edge of the trees and setting them in place. To the north, about fifteen hundred feet from the hill, the trench already hemmed in the killing ground. The lethal ditch angled off toward the northeast and disappeared into the woods.

Rufio dropped to one knee and stared in the direction from which he knew the Germans would come. It would be tomorrow—he was certain. The failing moon decreed it. Even more pressing was their food supply. Like the Gauls, the Suebi could never field a large army for long. There was no word in their language for supply train. They fed off what they could carry and whatever they could forage or steal. Logistics eluded them. For the Romans, the lifeline stretched from the granaries of Egypt to the banks of the Rhenus. It was a cord more durable than steel.

Probus climbed the hill to inspect the Scorpions while Bruttius Macer knelt beside Rufio in the middle of the field.

"You'll be Chief Centurion after this," Macer said.

"That position belongs to you. Your seniority and experience."

"Sabinus favors you."

"Then I'll ask him to favor me by giving it to you."

Macer looked off to the east. "You know, I should have died with Carbo."

"No, Fortuna made you ill then because you were fated to be here."

"A few days ago I thought you were trying to usurp me."

"I've spent my life being misunderstood by others."

Macer placed a hand on Rufio's right forearm in a gesture of friendship that needed no words.

The two men knelt in silence and gazed into the distance, each trying to imagine ten thousand Suebi warriors.

"A wedge, do you think?" Macer asked.

"Ah, the wedge . . ."

"I've often wondered who taught them that. Or if they invented it."

"Neither, I think," Rufio said.

"What do you mean?"

"I think it's an accident. You know that only a few men are truly braver than the rest in any group, no matter how big it is. They're out front. The less brave fall back. The largest number are the really fearful. They fan out behind and are pulled along by the momentum of the rest. It's like a pyramid laid on its side and dragged along the ground. I've never believed the wedge was a tactic. It's the face of human nature."

"Mmmm. I never thought of that."

"But it's the horses that bother me. So many cavalrymen. They can overwhelm us."

"Our men will hold fast. Trust me, I know these men."

"I believe you. But holding fast might not be enough. Last night I fell asleep thinking about this and I had a strange dream. The Suebi charged us on horses with huge foot-long teeth. Horses like no one has ever seen before. When I woke up, I couldn't get that image out of my mind. Then I realized the enormous teeth reminded me of tusks."

"Elephants?"

"Yes. Scipio at Zama had the same problem — being overwhelmed by Hannibal's elephants. Remember what he did? We'll take a hair from Scipio's head."

"It could work."

Rufio gazed down and ran a hand back and forth over the soft spring grass.

"What do you think about before a battle?" Macer asked.

"Too many things." He plucked a blade of grass and stuck it between his teeth.

"You don't confide in anyone, do you?"

"Should I?"

"Not even in a black-haired Sequani forest spirit?"

"By the gods, is there no privacy in this army?"

"Not in any legion I've ever served in."

"Before a battle, I always feel sad. I look at this grass and I know that tomorrow it'll be a hideous sponge soaking up the blood of my men."

He rose and faced east. "Always a wedge first. The stinking pig's head. Then cavalry on the wings. Every time. No exceptions. Which is why I believe that's exactly what Barovistus is not going to do."

Macer stood up and looked at him.

"This German is no amateur," Rufio said. He tossed away the blade of grass and turned to Macer with a smile. "But then, neither are we."

42 MAKE HASTE SLOWLY.

Augustus

Rufio took the sack hanging from one of the four saddle horns and tossed it down to the men in the trench. They cheered him when they opened it and helped themselves to the hundreds of dried figs.

He rode up to a completed section of the ditch. The "lilies" were already growing. Frightening clumps of jagged branches blossomed from the narrow bottom. Even fiercer tangles of sharpened scraps of iron sprouted among the stakes like toxic flowers.

Rufio rode along the edge of the ditch to where a burly Gaul was bending down and fixing in place more of the obstacles.

"How do you like the battle line?"

Hetorix looked up. He smiled when he saw it was Rufio.

"I'm eager to return to my armory."

"Aren't we all? Well done, swordmaker."

Hetorix nodded in acknowledgement and Rufio rode off.

The stallion made its way among the trees toward the stream. Rufio was pleased to see that the diggers were only about fifty feet from completion.

Crus labored in the trench with them. He climbed out when he saw Rufio approach.

"I'd never have thought this possible." The tribune gazed with pride at his soldiers.

Rufio dismounted and let his horse get a drink at the stream.

"We should be able to break through to the water in about an hour," Crus said.

Rufio walked along the edge of the ditch and stared at the stream beyond. He made a fist with his left hand and rubbed his signet ring back and forth against his chin.

"Not yet," he said.

Crus came up to him. "Why not?"

"If the Germans get a spy through our picket line, let them think the trench will be dry. We'll flood it at the last moment."

He went to the edge of the stream and squatted on the bank. The fresh smell of the water invigorated him.

"We'll make a small dam out of planks and place it at the end of the trench. Then we dig from the stream side outward until there's only a thin wall of mud being held up by the dam. We'll attach a rope to it and lash it to a saddle horn. One of our cavalrymen will wait until the Suebi are so close he can smell them. Then he pulls it down and races out of here like Charon is grasping at his heels."

"But what about the German cavalry? What'll stop them from riding him down?"

"The swiftness of his horse."

"Then I suppose I'll have to borrow your stallion."

Rufio smiled.

"After all," Crus said with a grin, "I must have something to tell my grandchildren around my fireside in the Alban Hills."

43   EVERY SOIL IS FATHERLAND TO A BRAVE MAN.

Ovid

"Do you think Rufio has ever been decorated?" Diocles asked.

"For valor?" Valerius scooped some porridge from the cooking pot into his bowl.

"No, for delicacy of manner."

Metellus started laughing and had a difficult time stopping. Diocles smiled at him and at the little family group around the morning fire. Calpurnia was sitting on the ground beside Metellus. She had a round and cheerful face, with just a hint in the cheekbones of that etched sharpness recalling the legacy of her Italian father. Metellus was holding her hand. This was a shockingly un-Roman thing to do. Men were not supposed to show public affection for their women. However, the imminent arrival of the Suebi inclined one to a different point of view.

At his other side, Kalinda played with the wooden doll he had carved for her.

"What sorts of decorations are there?" Diocles asked.

"Torques, crowns, all kinds of things. Some are reserved for soldiers above a certain rank. Some are open to everybody."

"What would mean the most to you."

Valerius set down his bowl and thought for a moment. "The civic crown." He stared into the fire for a few seconds and then resumed eating.

"What is it?"

"It's open to all ranks. To me, it's the greatest honor there is. Something for your heirs to put on your tombstone. It's the award for saving the life of a citizen of Rome. A crown of oak leaves."

Diocles was about to speak, but looked away.

"What?" Metellus asked.

"Rufio has four of those. I've seen them. They're old and dry and he keeps them in a box with cedar."

Metellus nodded, as if in silent affirmation of a judgment he had made long ago.

"Thank the gods he's with us now," Valerius said to no one and everyone.

Diocles gazed down the tent line. Clusters of soldiers sat around cooking fires that seemed to stretch to the horizon. Shields and pila in front of the tents leaned against each other in neat triangles with a helmet at each apex.

What a society this was. What strange values. In Diocles' world, men thirsted for wealth or power or both. Lavish villas and luscious young slaves to warm their beds and the unfaithful wives of other men to sate their cravings. And here? A man's most cherished wish was for a corona of dead leaves. How foolish that was. And how magnificent. More times than he could count, Diocles had been told in Rome that men enlisted in the army because they were failures in normal life. Perhaps they truly were, to their everlasting glory.

"Hello, pretty little lady."

Diocles jumped at Rufio's voice.

The centurion was down on one knee before Kalinda.

"How is my bravest young warrior this morning?" He took her tiny right hand in his.

Calpurnia smiled at them as Kalinda lowered her eyes but sneaked a look up at Rufio and smiled.

He turned to Metellus. "There's much to do."

Metellus rose and Calpurnia stood with him.

"We'll go now," she said.

All the soldiers nearby were staring at Metellus.

To the signifer they were invisible as he slid his arms around Calpurnia and held her close. Kalinda hurried over and wrapped her small arms around one of his legs.

"You'll return to us, won't you?" Calpurnia asked.

"Of course. This silver-haired madman will see to it."

She turned to Rufio and stared at him for a moment, then reached out for his right hand and pressed it to her lips.

"Thank you," she whispered.

Diocles felt sad for Rufio. As if this man did not have enough burdens, now was added one more. How could he bear them? Of this Diocles was certain, the most difficult job on earth was to be a centurion of Rome. Not long ago, he had not known even one. Now a world without centurions was beyond imagining. And a world without Rufio was too frightening to contemplate.

44   DARE TO BE WISE.

Horace

"So now that I've seen the battlefield," Sabinus said, "tell me how we may use it to apply the principles of war."

Diocles looked up from the map. Sabinus swept into the tent followed by his three favored centurions

Probus laughed and Macer turned away with a smile.

Sabinus looked from one to the other as he pulled off his helmet. "Explain why the commander is such a source of mirth to his men."

Rufio set his helmet onto the map table. "Because these crude louts don't know better than to laugh at the Legate of Augustus."

"That doesn't answer my question."

Sabinus sat on a stool at the table and gestured for his men to sit.

Diocles remained standing.

"Now tell me," Sabinus said and rested his elbows on the map in front of him.

Rufio deferred to his older comrade.

"Because there are no 'principles of war'," Macer answered.

Diocles watched as Sabinus eyed the older centurion and then turned to Rufio.

"Actually, my friend Bruttius exaggerates," Rufio said. "There are three — but only three. Feed your men, prevent them from being killed, and kill the enemy."

Sabinus glanced at Probus.

"We're finished," Probus said and folded his hands on the table before him.

Two of Sabinus's slaves came in with bowls of fruit and cheese and placed them onto the map table and withdrew.

"Then I've been misled," Sabinus said.

"Not by us," Rufio answered. "By old men with too much time and too little to do."

"Explain."

"Aging soldiers enjoy sitting around their firesides and expounding on the principles of war as if they were as certain as the principles of mathematics. How could they be? It's nonsense."

"Tell me why."

"Every battle is different. Even the tiniest variation changes the mix. Throws the whole thing askew. Caesar said that in war great events are the result of small causes." He smiled. "Those dullards don't know more than Caesar."

"So the theorizers have nothing to contribute?"

"I didn't say that. But these old men sit in their chairs with a cup of heated wine and concoct grand theories on the basis of one or two favorite battles and try to apply them everywhere. If they favor cavalry, they recite odes to Alexander at Issus. If they prefer encirclement, they sing of Hannibal at Cannae—always a favorite. If ambush excites them, they bend their knee to Hannibal's brother Mago at Trebia. It's ridiculous."

"I'm not convinced," Sabinus said. "You told me you yourself are researching history for a book on tactics. Doesn't that disprove your point?"

"It proves it. If there were only a few principles to apply, I wouldn't have to strain my eyes long into the night searching for some scrap that might help me some day. Instead, I'd just sit down like a Greek geometer and do the calculations. But it doesn't work that way. Mars laughs at that."

"Beware one theory that explains all." Macer said. "It'll lead you to your doom."

"Then why do some believe otherwise?" Sabinus asked.

"They've forgotten in their dotage that war sneers at theories," Rufio said. "And, anyway, it's human nature. Just like the foolish ancestors of our Greek friend here—looking for one great philosophy that explains everything. That's why no good soldier could ever be a philosopher. He knows too much."

Sabinus's eyes narrowed in amusement.

"Keep your sword bright," Rufio said, "and forget the 'timeless principles of war'. And besides, if there were only simple principles to apply, what credit would there be in victory?"

He pulled his dagger and thrust it into the map in the center of the battlefield.

45   HAPPY THE MAN, AND HAPPY HE ALONE . . . WHO, SECURE WITHIN, CAN SAY, TOMORROW DO THY WORST, FOR I HAVE LIVED TODAY.

Horace

Diocles often felt like sleeping after his midday meal, but today sleep eluded him. He decided to walk through camp to help relieve his tension.

The boiling energy of a legion on the eve of battle had now banked to a simmer. He strolled around the camp. The men of many centuries were seated on the ground before their centurions. Every officer hurled his own style of motivation at his men. Some centurions spoke of the glory of Rome, others of the moral hideousness of the Suebi. Some exhorted with tales of heroes from the past. Others chose a more practical approach and inspired with reassurances of Roman superiority in training and equipment and leadership. One centurion, clearly short on charm, told his men that anyone who turned and ran would have to answer to him, and he would personally cut out the heart of any soldier who returned from battle with a wound in his back.

When Diocles reached the center of the camp, he saw about a dozen centurion tents pitched behind Sabinus's tent. They formed a large open rectangle with several tables set up inside its perimeter. Piles of undyed woolen blankets lay atop every table, for cold was considered especially dangerous to the wounded. Stacks of linen bandages sat atop the blankets. Next to the dressings lay stout leather straps. They could have but one use, to prevent soldiers from destroying their own teeth as they ground them together in agony.

Diocles entered one of the tents. Long blanket-covered tables filled it. Neatly arranged on a smaller table off to one side lay a large collection of bronze and brass surgical instruments. Probes, forceps, bone chisels, and hooked retractors crowded together. Ten double-ended scalpels lay beneath them. Bronze-handled, the cutting tools had a removable steel blade at one end and a bronze spatulate probe at the other. A Greek doctor came in while Diocles was examining one and pointed out proudly that his blades had been made in Noricum, which he claimed to be the source of the finest scalpel steel in the empire.

Diocles suddenly longed to be back with his century.

He found them milling about in the open area next to Rufio's tent. When the centurion came out, he signaled for them to sit. They formed a semicircle around him.

Rufio seemed relaxed, just as Neko had said he would be.

"It's been a remarkable journey," he began without preliminaries. "Me from Spain to here, and you from everywhere to me. But our journey is only beginning. The Germans have thrust a spear into the side of Gaul, and we must do what we're trained to do. What we're fated to do. The Germans are mad dogs—blind to reason and ravenous to the point of insanity. They're poised to swarm the fields of Gaul and devour or defile everything in their path. But they're nothing mysterious. They're simply coarse-haired savages who rarely bathe and who eat bad meat and drink cow's milk like the barbarians they are." He paused for a moment, then said, "Behind us lie villages that will vanish if we don't succeed—including villages where some of your sweethearts live. Think of your own Sequani beauty tomorrow as you fasten your sword belt. Remember the look in her eyes when you saw her last. Her life depends on you now. But most of all, think of the man beside you. His life depends on his courage, but it also depends on yours. Don't fail him. Make me as proud of you tomorrow as I am of you tonight. And remember, I am with you always—even across the rivers of Hell."

Rufio stood and his men stood with him. He approached each one and gripped him firmly by the forearms and whispered a word of reassurance.

Diocles waited until the end. He was trembling when Rufio grasped his arms. He looked into the centurion's gray-blue eyes. They were as serene as those of a holy man. Who could ever hope to understand this Roman?

———————

"I could never have imagined this," Diocles whispered.

The soldier and his centurion sat on their horses and stared into a black infinity. Campfires beyond counting shimmered to the invisible horizon.

"Varacinda was right," Rufio said. "Flavia has the eye. Ten thousand at least."

"I feel so small." Diocles stared at Rufio in the moonlight.

"Remember this moment. Preserve it for your history. But it won't matter. Your readers will never believe it."

Diocles looked back at the fires glittering like thousands of nasty yellow eyes. "How can we have any hope at all?"

"Victoria is not a fickle goddess. She didn't bring us all the way to these lands to allow us to crumble now. Not before the likes of these."

He could feel Rufio's revulsion as fully as if it were a tangible force.

"I want you on the hill tomorrow. You'll be able to see everything from there. To fix it in your mind forever."

"I haven't prayed in many years. I'll pray tonight."

A cloud passed over the moon and he could barely make out Rufio as the centurion turned toward him in the darkness.

"If I never see you again after tomorrow, take this." He slid the torque from his wrist. "Take it to my sister in Rome. Tell her . . . tell her I've been forgiven. And that's the symbol. She'll understand."

Diocles held it tightly.

Rufio turned away and stroked the neck of his horse as the moon reappeared and cast its cool light on the man and his beloved stallion.

"One thing more—a promise from you."

"Anything." Diocles watched him staring off into the blackness.

"If I'm killed, search the battlefield for my body. Retrieve my ring and place it in Flavia's hand."

Diocles swallowed to try to clear the lump from his throat. "I will," he said, grateful that the darkness obscured the tears in his eyes. "But why not give it to me now?"

"No." Without another word he reined his horse about and rode back to camp.

46 BRAVERY IS OF MORE VALUE THAN NUMBERS.

Vegetius

Two hours before dawn, Rufio emerged from his tent and studied the sky. As soon as he had awakened, he had sensed a change in the weather. Not a single star could be seen.

He could feel the heaviness in the air, and the wind smelled like wet earth. Rain was an enemy for which he had no counter.

A crisp breeze from the north fluttered his hair as he walked down the tent line. Valerius and Metellus were already awake and in full armor. They had several fires going, and the smell of hot porridge drifted toward him.

Rufio gazed at them with an affection they could not see in the darkness. What comfort he took from these two men. Sometimes Fortuna did indeed smile.

Soon the nine cohorts would assemble, Sabinus would address them, and the sacrificial chickens would be opened and the auspices taken. They would be favorable. Rufio was certain Sabinus had no intention of allowing otherwise.

And then the soldiers of the Twenty-fifth Legion would march to face their foe. The cool gusts from the north were just damp air, but to Rufio they smelled like wind blowing across the turbulent blackness of Acheron.

Diocles wanted to see Rufio one more time. He gulped breakfast with his tent group and hurried in the gray dawn to Rufio's tent.

It was not to be. The Egyptian Cerberus blocked the way. No three-headed hound could have been more tenacious than Neko. He stood at the entrance to Rufio's tent and held his master's helmet. A long and wispy crest of red horsehair adorned it now.

Though not permitted to enter, Diocles was allowed to peek inside.

Rufio was down on one knee in the middle of the tent. A white cloth covered his head, and his mail lorica and sword and dagger glittered in the lamplight. Bronze greaves sheathed his lower legs.

He knelt with head lowered. On a table beside him, a lamp burned and next to it stood a small red porphyry statue of Victoria, wings at rest. The flickering eerie light caused her to seem to move and gesture toward him. Perhaps it was no illusion. Perhaps she was bestowing on him her blessing or speaking to him the wisdom only she could give.

Diocles lowered the tent flap.

"You love him," Neko said. "Though he frightens you, you love him more than any man you have ever known. In a way you cannot describe. Possibly even comprehend. He touches you with a mysterious spirit that makes you yearn inside." Neko smiled. "Why do you cry? He would not want that. Go now. Leave this man to his solitary duty."

Diocles turned away. He walked back to his century, and the camp around him disappeared. He was all alone in the world.

The men were assembling, and Valerius was inspecting everyone, veteran and new man alike. Metellus was pulling the wolf skin over his helmet. The silver boar standard on its long pole was stuck in the earth beside him, and his small round shield lay next to it.

Diocles stood apart from them and pulled on his mail lorica and buckled his weapons belts. When he had finished he was about to wish Valerius and Metellus luck, but suddenly he felt uneasy. In what he knew was an odd descent into irrationality, he decided that if he said something that even hinted of farewell, he would never again see them alive. While they were busy with their men, he slipped away.

He left the fort and passed the mounted men in the picket line beyond the ditch. He waved to them as he went by.

The battlefield was as serene as a Roman garden. Soon its soft green face would wince beneath the feet of thousands of men. The ditch on the left wing was still dry, but he could see activity on the hill to the right and he headed that way.

He climbed the slope and when he reached the summit he was surprised to see that the men and their Scorpions were already set at the edge of the trees. The bolt catapults pointed down toward the right wing, and piles of their terrible stingers lay on the ground beside them.

Adiatorix, too, was here with his horsemen. They stood next to their mounts and peered from the ridge in all directions for any threat to the Romans.

Diocles crossed the wooded hill and emerged from the trees at the eastern edge.

"It cannot be," he heard himself say. He pulled his cloak more tightly around him.

The Germans were already approaching from the east. At this distance they did not even look like men. A roiling black mass rolled toward the Romans. It reminded him of a huge mat of seaweed drifting in on the tide. Their families followed, faint shouts of encouragement carrying on the wind.

At that moment Diocles knew he would never see any of his friends again.

"Don't despair," said someone behind him.

Adiatorix stood there with folded arms and a look of confidence that was baffling.

"It's not numbers that matter," the chief said. "It's spirit. It's will."

"I know," Diocles answered, and was surprised that his voice was barely above a whisper.

"This is not an undefended village. This is a battleground—and yours are brave men."

"Will you stand beside me today?"

"We'll watch the battle together. I'm forbidden to leave the hill, and Rufio told me you are forbidden to die."

Diocles turned away and stared at the German horde.

"Do you believe in an afterlife, chief?"

Adiatorix hesitated. "I'm unsure."

"So am I. But I think Rufio does. I hope he's right."

"At this moment he's concerned more with this life than the one that follows."

"His goddess won't desert him, will she?" His voice was almost plaintive.

But Adiatorix had nothing else to say.

"Here they come!" shouted one of the Romans.

Diocles hurried past Adiatorix to the western edge of the hill.

Again he felt the lump in his throat, but this time with pride. They were magnificent. The nine cohorts had taken the field and now approached the battleground from about a half-mile off. Because the battlefield was so close, they were not marching in the usual column but had already fanned out. Colorful shields, bronze helmets, mail loricas. In three ranks they marched, three cohorts in a rank. Yet it was not what he had expected. The checker pattern he had read about in the histories—the quincunx, like the five staggered spots on dice—was not there. Instead of the cohorts in the second rank lining up behind the open spaces between the three cohorts of the first, the second rank marched directly behind the men in front. Likewise, the men in the third rank of cohorts lined up with the men in the second. The result was that two great roads ran from front to back straight through the Roman formation. It looked shockingly vulnerable to a pair of wedges—the despised pigs' heads—hurling themselves at the twin openings in the line. What would prevent the Suebi from racing all the way to the back and enveloping the entire legion?

"I've never seen that," Adiatorix said when he came up beside him.

"I have faith in Rufio," Diocles answered, the words coming unbidden from some inner depths.

"You would have made a great Roman," he said as he slapped his hand down onto Diocles' mailed shoulder.

"I am a Roman."

Already the roars and yells of the Suebi were growing louder, as they sought to embolden each other and themselves.

But the Italians scorned this hallowed way of the warrior. They marched in silence. Moving forward, they seemed to be a soundless projection of the dark mind of Mars. Neither their anxiety nor their fear caused them to break this discipline of silence. A few simple shouts would have eased so much tension, but they bent human fear to Roman will.

And Diocles had no doubt that the Suebi, with all their noisy bluster, would look upon the muteness of their foe with terror.

47   IN THE TAIL IS THE POISON.

Roman saying

"Let the first man on the right scrape his shoulder on the ridge" — so Rufio had told Sabinus, and Rufio was that man. The Second Cohort marched on the right wing of the first rank of three cohorts. Rufio's First Century held the First Cohort's right flank, and Rufio himself headed the file farthest to the right. Like all centurions, he led from the front.

Each cohort marched six ranks deep on the approach and about eighty files across, though few cohorts boasted full strength. At the right corner of each century strode the centurion. The optio followed at the back, to keep order and push forward — physically if necessary — any lagging warriors.

But Rufio had no thought of that for his century. Though Valerius brought up the rear, it was not necessary. Rufio knew his men feared their centurion's glare of displeasure far more than they feared the Suebi.

The legionaries marched forward as silent as ghosts. Only the rattling of their equipment made these specters seem human. The battlefield was about a thousand feet away. Rufio's keen eyes searched the distance, but the Suebi had not yet come into view.

Metellus marched beside Rufio to receive instructions for signaling. Instead of a pilum, Metellus carried the standard of the First Century.

The Romans moved swiftly, and Rufio knew if they got too close to the battlefield before the Germans appeared, he would have to call a halt. That was the moment of danger. With the cunning of wild animals, the Germans might smell the rank meat that baited the snare.

Rufio looked back over his shoulder. Sabinus rode behind the Second Cohort, the Fifth Cohort following directly to his rear. From this commanding view on the right wing, Sabinus could oversee the flow of the battle and order reserves into any breaches in the Roman line or exploit any opportunities Fortuna presented.

Rufio smiled in admiration as he looked at the young commander. Sabinus wore a scarlet cloak so he was clearly visible to all his men. Rufio knew there was no greater inspiration to a Roman soldier than the presence of his commander. And no greater drive to heroism than the commander's approving gaze.

A select bodyguard of cavalrymen surrounded Sabinus and his tribunes. The cornicens and tubicens marched beside them. Only Titinius was missing. The youthful tribune, along with the remainder of the cavalry, had been entrusted with the safety of the ever-vulnerable left wing.

Rufio turned back to the front as a few raindrops hit his face. He cursed under his breath. He would rather have had the sun in his eyes.

"Where in the name of the gods is Crus?" Metellus said. "Do you think the Germans got him?"

Rufio thought of the day he had first seen Crus, trying to act manly in front of his men and failing. And now he was performing the manliest act of his life, out of the view of everyone.

"We have a dinner planned thirty years from now in the Alban Hills," Rufio said with a gruffness to conceal his anxiety. "That patrician bastard had better not disappoint me."

Metellus looked at him and smiled but said nothing.

The ditch and the hill embracing the battlefield seemed to be racing toward them, now only five hundred feet away. The drizzle was getting heavier, loudly pelting their helmets.

"Listen," Metellus said.

Rufio's left ear was better than his right and he turned it toward the front.

"Hoofbeats."

A horseman shot into view, racing across the plain. A magnificent black stallion streaked toward them like a launched arrow.

"Neptune speaks!" Crus shouted to Rufio as he rode through the gap between the Second and Third Cohorts and back to Sabinus to report.

"The ditch is flooded," Rufio said to Metellus. "Run back and find out from Crus how far away the Germans are."

Metellus did as ordered.

The first Roman rank was only about two hundred feet from the battleground.

"About a quarter of a mile," Metellus said when he rejoined Rufio at the front.

"We'll have to stop. Maybe we can use it to our advantage—make them think we're afraid. Signal Sabinus."

Metellus turned and made three short up and down movements with the silver boar.

Sabinus saw the signal and spoke to his hornblowers. The cornicens blew three brief notes with their curved horns, and the entire legion came to a halt without another command.

This was the moment when the discipline paid off—or failed to. Nothing in all of warfare so shattered the nerves as waiting and standing immobile at the approach of a merciless enemy.

The light drizzle continued. Rufio peered through the rain and at last saw the great dark mass. Suebi shouts and jeers soon shook the air.

"We'll charge when they're two hundred feet from the hill and trench," Rufio said. "By the time we reach them, they'll be where we want them. Get ready to signal Sabinus."

But then the Germans stopped. They stood and hurled taunts from at least a hundred feet east of where Rufio needed them to be before he charged.

"They know it's a trap," Metellus said.

Rufio looked to the hill. The Scorpions were well concealed.

"It's not possible."

A distant rumble rolled toward them.

"And now a thunderstorm," Metellus said. "What next?"

Though his face was wet from the rain, Rufio instinctively licked his lips.

"No," he said. "That's not thunder. It's horsemen."

He spun around and raised his pilum to Sabinus.

The commander shouted to his tubicens and they blew two sharp notes on their straight trumpets.

Every soldier in unison raised his pilum to shoulder height. The wait was over. Death was racing toward them.

"I knew it," Rufio said. "This Barovistus is no amateur."

Twin swarms of German horsemen burst into view. They veered around each flank of their own warriors and converged on the waiting Romans.

Rufio moistened his lips again and squinted, his fingers tightening around his pilum.

The Germans flew across the battlefield like a horde of raging centaurs. Every one flashed a Gallic sword.

An eerie whizzing sound sliced the air and dozens of iron bolts from the hilltop tore into the racing throng. Animals and men shrieked in pain and terror. The horses took the worst of it. Many crumpled with shattered legs and threw their riders. Some horses crashed into each other in their desperation to escape. A second Scorpion volley sheared into them. The animals screamed anew and scattered in all directions, like doomed prey lost in the streets of Hell. The men were howling, too, some nailed to their mounts by iron that had pierced a leg before sinking into their horse's flank.

A huge German in front waved his sword and tried to snatch order from the chaos. Though bleeding from a scalp wound, he raced across the crumbling battle line to encourage by example. But a third volley drove them to the edge of madness. The horses bristled with bolts in their flanks, and some of the Germans had two or three bolts in their back or neck but were still alive. Horses and riders headed for the only line of escape—straight for the two huge gaps in the Roman line.

Rufio let them come.

At least two hundred horsemen had dashed through the funnels before the signal came. The horns sounded, the Romans pivoted, and the pila flew.

The Suebi were shredded in the mouth of the wolf. Centurions shouted orders and the second rank of cohorts closed behind them. The third rank bored in. There was nowhere for the Suebi to turn. In minutes every German was unhorsed, the Spanish swords flashed, and not a Suebi was still on his feet. The Romans kicked aside the dead and stabbed and hacked every screaming man where he lay.

The few surviving horses galloped to safety behind the lines. The Romans wiped their swords and caught their breaths.

Centurions barked commands and the soldiers dressed ranks. A second set of orders boomed across the field. The cohorts drew up into the quincunx, sealing the gaps and forming now for what they did best.

Out on the battleground, the German leader stared at the carnage.

Rufio fixed the face in his mind.

The horsemen who had avoided the trap of Scipio gathered around their chief. He waved his sword and they rushed back the way they had come.

The first rank of cohorts was still fresh. They had merely thrown their pila and had allowed the second and third ranks to chew up the Suebi.

Now the first rank would face the Germans. Thousands of them.

Rufio tightened his grip on his shield and pulled his new sword from his scabbard. He knew that this was why he had been born.

48   DEATH IS CERTAIN, THE HOUR UNCERTAIN.

Roman saying

While the Suebi hesitated, waiting for their leader, Sabinus rode among his troops. The rain drummed against his breastplate and his cloak was soaked, but he felt none of it. He checked the wounded and was stunned to see only superficial injuries. The rout of the Suebi horsemen had been so thorough and their end so swift that not a single Roman had been killed. Yet he knew there were many hundred more cavalrymen to face.

He rode along the front of each cohort and congratulated his men. They cheered him as he passed, but he knew it was they who deserved the cheers. They had stood as resolutely as rooted trees before the vaunted cavalry of the German barbarians. By Jupiter, he was proud of these men! For a fleeting moment his future career shot before him, and he dismissed it as an absurdity. This day was all that could ever matter. Never before had he felt such purity of purpose, so searing a clarity of thought, as he did at this instant. And he knew he would never feel it again. Here in the driving rain in the wilderness of Gaul he felt as hot and sharp and true as a flash of lightning.

Diocles stood in awe at what he had just seen. The German horsemen were retreating now to the safety of their army. Numbed by the ferocity of the Roman defense, they regathered a short distance off.

Even at this range, Diocles could hear the new Suebi widows howling in grief for their men lying in the mud a few hundred feet from them.

The Romans also reassembled. The first group of three cohorts had faced the cavalry with a formation six men deep, but now they regrouped into only three ranks, each cohort about three hundred and fifty feet across—such was the confidence of the centurions that these men in shallow ranks and open files could prevail against whatever the Suebi hurled at them. To Diocles, who could see all the thousands of Germans at a glance, this confidence seemed rash to the point of recklessness. Yet he had learned enough from Rufio to comprehend his reasoning. A six rank formation was a waste of men, since those in the rear could not engage the enemy. The line had to be just deep enough to withstand the impact of the Suebi, but thin and flexible enough to maneuver and to ensure that the maximum number of soldiers was savaging the enemy at every moment. It was a task as maddening as that of Sisyphus.

Diocles threw off his cloak. He was already soaked to the skin, and the wet wool just made him colder.

The happy men he expected to see as he walked along the line of Scorpion shooters were not there. Looks of concern, and even alarm, darkened the soldiers' expressions. They were checking the tension on the torsion ropes of the catapults. Clearly they did not like what they saw. The cords of sinew had softened in the rain.

"The Suebi cavalry won't make that mistake again," Diocles heard Adiatorix say.

He looked to the right to see the Sequani chieftain studying the German multitude to the east.

"They won't attack separately anymore," Adiatorix went on. "Foot fighters and horsemen will strike together. They'll use their mass to try to club the Romans to death. Crush them with their weight."

Yes. The rock of Sisyphus.

49 WARS, THE HORROR OF MOTHERS.

Horace

The warriors in the German left wing, opposite the Roman right, peered through the rain at the hilltop. Fearful now of the Scorpions, they hesitated. Their cavalry had withdrawn from the front line, and now only men on foot faced each other across the battleground.

Rufio's mouth felt like road dust, as it always did at this moment. His heart pounded and the hammering seemed to race all the way to his skull and thump inside his helmet. His tongue spread the last few drops of saliva across his lips.

The Roman horns shrieked. Rufio and the other centurions yelled, their men roared with them, and then the legion charged.

The once-mute soldiers howled with the throats of maddened beasts as they raced across the battlefield. Stunned, the Suebi recoiled. Like the surface of a lake hit by a wind, the barbarian line seemed to ripple backward. German leaders shouted encouragement and then faced the Romans and charged without their men. Shamed by their leaders, the Suebi in the front line found their courage and launched themselves at the Italian madmen.

Holding their shields above their heads, they dashed toward the charging Romans.

A volley of Scorpion bolts shot down from the hill. They had no effect. The few that reached the Suebi skidded harmlessly off the raised shields. The cords on the catapults were so soaked their powers of torsion were almost gone. The lethal engines had become useless toys.

Just before the collision, the Suebi slowed, evidently expecting their opponents to do likewise so as not to lose their balance. The Romans did not.

Rufio hit the man opposite him with terrific force. He heard the German's breastbone crack under the impact of the shield boss. The barbarian fell backward and Rufio was suddenly standing on both of his thighs. Into the unprotected stomach sank the Spanish sword. The German exhaled with a deep hiss, and Rufio leaped beyond him.

A beardless Suebi faced him. Armed with spear and wicker shield, he yelled the Suebian war cry and closed on the smaller Roman.

The German spearpoint sought his eyes, but with a flick of his wrist Rufio cut it like a celery stalk. Suddenly weaponless, the young warrior pulled his shield before his face and upper body. Rufio thrust his sword into the German's left thigh. The leg buckled, and Rufio slammed his wooden shield outward against the wicker one. It flew from the German's grasp and Rufio sank his swordpoint into the naked throat.

Rufio looked to his left. Arrianus was battling a huge German. The young soldier blocked a tremendous overhand sword slash that split the bronze rim of his shield. He lunged at the German but lost his footing in the mud. Down on his face he went, his shield beneath him. The German grinned at the little Italian at his feet. A downed man was a dead man.

"Son of a whore!" Rufio shouted in the few words he knew in Suebian.

Startled, the barbarian turned to this new threat.

Rufio slashed sideways as though wielding a sickle and took off the top of his head with a single cut. The German crashed to the ground like a chopped oak.

Rufio helped Arrianus to his feet. He paused for breath and looked down the line. The Romans held. But holding would not be enough.

"Rufio!" Metellus shouted from his signaling position in the second rank.

The centurion spun to the right. Straight over his fallen comrades a German charged, gripping a Roman sword and shield.

The sight of the stolen Roman weapons — perhaps Carbo's own — roused Rufio's darkest self. He charged the German through the driving rain.

The Suebi was at least a half-foot taller, but Rufio hit him like a stag. The German stumbled as Rufio's shield boss crashed into the other shield. A cut from the left Rufio easily blocked, and then the centurion thrust to the right. The blade sliced across the German's ribs and he screamed in rage. He raised his weapon for an overhand slash and Rufio sank his sword into the German's armpit. A groan more like a wail of sorrow than of pain echoed from some dark abyss.

Rufio sprang forward and brought his left foot down onto the German's right one and again hit him with his shield. Even with the shouting and clanging all around them, it was a thunderous blow. The German toppled backward like a collapsing column. Pinning his foot, Rufio cold hear his anklebones shatter and snap as he fell. Rufio kicked aside the shield and loomed over him. And now the world became silent. The battle had vanished. From the panic in the German's eyes, it seemed like he was begging, but Rufio could hear no sound. He ignored the gape of terror and slashed down into the center of the face. The German's head split like cheese. Again and again Rufio chopped the skull into fragments, into crumbs, into nothing.

50   VIRTUE IS A THOUSAND SHIELDS.

Roman saying

Sabinus streaked across the battleground. The space between the first and the second ranks of cohorts was his domain. From here on horseback he could take in the entire battle line and move easily across the field. Encouraging here, directing there, he seemed to be everywhere at once.

Rufio's right wing was solid as steel but had made no advance. Probus's cohort in the middle had taken terrible punishment, the huge German wedge threatening to break through. The line had sagged, but the men had rallied and straightened out their ranks. Yet they were still enduring a savage hammering. The German reinforcements seemed endless.

Sabinus rode toward the northern end of the battlefield to get a closer look at the crucial left wing. Even in the heavy rain he could make out the big figure of Macer slamming and thrusting into the Germans before him.

Sabinus caught up with Titinius and they rode together to the edge of the field to check on the flooded trench.

The sight was horrific. Dead Germans clogged the water and floated on the surface like a school of poisoned fish. Many were riddled with pila. Those that had escaped the spears and had reached the inner edge had been struck down as they had tried to claw their way out. Dozens had had their heads crushed by Roman shields. Others had been hacked into chunks of carrion.

"Are you all right?" Titinius asked.

Sabinus wiped away the heavy saliva that preceded vomit.

"I'm fine. Well done." He turned and rode back to check again on the middle of the line.

The stamina of the legionaries surpassed that of the Suebi, but the warriors on both sides were tiring. Ten minutes of heavy fighting pushed even the fittest men to their limits of endurance.

As though by tacit agreement, both sides began to ease up. The Germans pulled back, and the outnumbered Romans were too few to pursue. The centurions shouted commands and the legionaries dressed ranks and took a breath.

"What happened to their horsemen?" Diocles asked Adiatorix as they both gazed across the plain below.

"I was wrong. They lost too many to the catapults in the first rush and decided to hold back. Now that the Scorpions aren't working, we'll see them again."

Diocles studied the battlefield. The Suebi line had withdrawn about two hundred feet to the east, but several thousand eager warriors from the ugly mass beyond were moving forward to join it.

The reordering of the Roman line was far different. Horns blared and the Fifth, Sixth, and Seventh Cohorts from the second rank marched forward between the gaps in the first rank and replaced the exhausted front line. The cohorts of Rufio and Probus and Macer pulled back, the uninjured men helping the wounded and carrying the dead. Diocles could see Sabinus and Crus riding about and directing everything within their line of sight.

"Why doesn't the tired rank move all the way to the rear?" Adiatorix asked.

"Sabinus is keeping the last three cohorts fresh in case he needs them. They're called reserves. The Suebi don't understand reserves."

"Neither did the Sequani when we fought the Romans."

"That's why you're speaking Latin now."

Sequani women drove carts out from the village and passed through the gaps between the last three cohorts. They pulled up to the second rank to pick up the crippled and the dead to carry them back to camp.

"At least the rain is letting up." Diocles knew he was grasping at any help from Fortuna he could find.

"Look."

Adiatorix pointed to a mist gathering over the stream northeast of the battlefield.

"Jupiter's death!" Diocles shouted. "Is there no mercy? These are honorable men. Must they be abandoned?"

"Don't speak against your gods."

"I'll speak against anything! Our men need to be able to see where the Suebi throw their weight. If the fog drifts over the killing ground, it'll be no different than if our soldiers were fighting with their eyes gouged out."

"Look there! Something is wrong."

One of the tribunes was galloping toward Sabinus and Crus. He pulled up, spoke for a moment, and then the three of them raced off toward the Fourth Cohort at the northern edge of the field.

51 THIS VAST EMPIRE OF THEIRS HAS COME TO THEM AS THE PRIZE OF VALOR AND NOT AS THE GIFT OF FORTUNE.

Josephus

Sixteen men from the Second Cohort had been killed and fifty-two wounded seriously enough to be evacuated. One hundred and fourteen suffered smaller injuries they endured now in silence. Rufio's own century had lost one veteran and two recruits to German spears and blades. Each loss, fatal or otherwise, was a sword slash to Rufio's soul. Yet he bore it with a face of iron.

After the kindhearted Sequani women had carted away his wounded, he and the other centurions of the Second Century walked along the line of their resting soldiers. Smiling and heartening them, the centurions seemed to be different beings from the same demons who beat their men with sticks when training.

Valerius and Metellus helped, too. They gripped other soldiers' arms in solidarity and offered water from their own flasks to those who had used up all of theirs.

Rufio watched and he knew there was nowhere else on earth where a man could so cherish other men as in a legion. As in this legion — where he so profoundly loved these two remarkable young soldiers.

"Not a scratch on you!" roared a familiar voice. "Still the favored of the gods."

Rufio turned to see Probus coming toward him. His old friend sported a gash under his left eye from a German spearpoint, and a bloody strip of linen bound a sword cut on his right forearm.

"What's the tally for the Third Cohort?" Rufio asked.

"Eighty-seven killed and a hundred and thirty-four of the wounded taken from the field."

"All right. I'll ask Sabinus to detach three centuries from the Sixth Cohort to give you more muscle. When you hit the Suebi again, you'll need it."

"What do you think?" Probus gestured toward the Germans.

"Tougher than most."

"The man of many words. What about our chances today?"

"What kind of question is that?"

"I mean what do you really think?"

"I think I won't let a little red-haired girl stand by and watch her mother raped in front of her."

"Did you look out there?" Probus pointed east again.

Rufio turned and squinted through the light rain at the advancing fog.

"The gods are testing us," Probus said.

"I'm tired of being tested," he snapped.

An approaching horse distracted them.

"Macer is down!" Titinius shouted as he rode up.

"Valerius! Take command."

Rufio and Probus raced north across the field.

Macer was lying in the mud before the Fourth Cohort. Crus was kneeling behind him and cradling his head in his lap. Sabinus was beside him and had placed one of his own red cloaks over the chest of the fallen soldier.

Rufio and Probus ran up and Sabinus moved back, deferring to the unique bond among centurions.

Rufio dropped to his knees beside Macer.

"Not good," Macer whispered.

His breathing gurgled as if a stream ran through his chest. The flesh of his face was as white as cotton.

Rufio pulled up the cloak. Macer's mail lorica was clotted with blood. A spearpoint had been thrust against his right breast, and by a fluke a few of the mail rings had snapped. The point had gone in deeply.

"How goes the battle?" Macer managed to ask.

"Well," Rufio lied. "One more blow and we'll have them."

"Perhaps Fortuna did save me for this day."

"There's no doubt. It was the will of powers greater than you or I."

Macer extended his right hand, and Rufio took it in his.

"Rufio," he gasped as he pulled his comrade's arm.

Rufio leaned closer and brought his left ear to Macer's lips.

"I'm afraid."

"Fear not, my friend," Rufio whispered. "All centurions live with Mars in paradise." He gripped Macer more tightly. "Wait for me there."

Macer smiled weakly and died holding Rufio's hand.

Rufio touched his ring of Victoria to Macer's pale forehead and then stood, his face as hard as the boss of a shield.

"We've rested enough. It's time to make the mud of Gaul stink with German dead."

52   MAN'S FIRST HAPPINESS IS TO KNOW HOW TO DIE.

Lucan

Fog had enveloped the entire Suebi army except for the thousand or so warriors directly confronting the Romans across the battlefield.

"Perhaps the gods have blessed us and taken them from our midst," Sabinus said with an ironic smile.

"Easy victory is no blessing," Rufio answered.

The commander and his centurion stood between the first and second ranks of cohorts and gazed at the gray-white shroud concealing those who hungered to destroy them. The Suebi visible outside the fog bank milled around a few hundred feet from the Romans and began hefting their weapons and shouting curses.

"They're trying to get themselves excited again," Rufio said. "To smother their fear with bluster."

"It's odd, but I've never thought of the Germans needing to deal with their fear."

"All men need to deal with their fear."

The Romans in the Fifth, Sixth, and Seventh Cohorts already had their shields up and their swords in their hands, while the Second, Third, and Fourth rested.

"The horses this time?" Sabinus asked.

"Yes."

"Both flanks?"

"No. Their mounts aren't sound enough or trained to leap the trench. Barovistus knows that. He'll hurl all of them at our right wing. Pressing our shoulder to the hill will help us, but that's all. Help isn't deliverance. And it certainly isn't victory."

"Did you see him out there?"

"Oh yes. I want to see him again."

Clusters of Suebi made mock charges across the battlefield and then withdrew, apparently attempting to goad the Romans into breaking formation.

The legionaries stared back in silence and kept their line as straight as a spear shaft. They waited for their commander.

Sabinus mounted his horse to get the view and the mobility he needed. He gestured to the cornicens behind him, and they raised their horns to their lips. He took a deep breath, then swept his hand downward.

The horns shrieked and the frontline Romans yelled and charged.

Again caught off guard, the Germans flinched but then checked themselves and threw their mass at the attacking Romans.

The clash was deafening, as if every metalsmith on earth had seized his tools and gone mad.

The Romans crashed and lunged into the slashing Germans. With the smell of their comrades' blood still in their nostrils, the Romans fought with staggering ferocity. Screams of agony made the mind reel. So quickly did the Germans fall that the legionaries stood atop the corpses to reach the enemy, the short Italians fighting on stepstools carved from the dead.

Hundreds of fresh Germans rushed from the mist, but they, too, went down before the Roman swordsmen. Centurions roared commands and the line began advancing over the pavement of German bodies.

The Roman ranks stayed tight as their swords pierced the chaotic Suebi line. Soon the mass of carcasses was so dense the Romans had to stop to pull them aside before they could advance.

The distant rumble of hoofbeats reached Rufio's ears above the tumult.

And now it comes.

Horsemen ruptured the wall of fog and were upon the Romans at once. German riders poured out of the mist by the slope, too, and raced up the hill at an angle and down and around the Roman line. In minutes hundreds of Suebi cavalry had surrounded the entire front rank.

Gallic swords in the hands of the horsemen slashed down into the Romans' backs. The Germans on foot took heart and counterattacked in the front with startling vigor. In moments the legionaries were sealed off, crushed without mercy between the hammer and the anvil.

Some of the Roman cavalry on the left rushed to their aid, but they soon disappeared within the German horde, as though overwhelmed by a toxic sea.

Rufio turned to Sabinus, but he was already signaling. The horns blew and the three cohorts from the first clash charged the barbarian horsemen.

Blinded by their own frenzy, the German horsemen ignored the Romans who now stood behind them. But the legionaries surged with the confidence of bloodied troops and with the rage of men who had lost their brothers. They hit the Suebi hard.

Rufio slashed at the leg of a horseman about to spear a Roman. The German howled and turned to see his knee dangling from his thigh by a few of strings of muscle.

Rufio ran his sword into the belly of the horse and the animal crumpled. The German jabbed at him with his spear, but Rufio knocked it aside like a twig and thrust the blade of Hetorix straight into the German's mouth.

The fog had completely enveloped them now. The Romans kept their line straight by feel and by hearing and by training.

"Eyes front!" Rufio shouted to the soldiers before him. "We'll take the horsemen!"

The men of the Fifth Cohort attacked the Suebi warriors with renewed energy.

Rufio spun toward hoofbeats to his right. A horse's head pierced the fog and he split its skull with a single blow. He leaped aside as the animal fell. A cursing German clambered to his feet and lunged with a long sword. It skidded off the boss of his shield. Rufio slammed the shield into him and sank his sword into the German's bowels.

Horrible cries from the horses came to Rufio through the fog. His chest heaving, he paused for a moment to catch his breath. Now the barbarians were learning what professional soldiers always knew — horses are superb at seizing ground but almost useless at holding it. They skitter and bolt and lose their nerve, like children in a storm.

"Arrianus!" Rufio shouted to his left.

"Here!" he answered from the depths of the fog.

Rufio heard his grunt of exertion and the scream of a horse before it crashed to the ground.

The Roman line moved forward, climbing over fallen horses and slain men. The panicked animals were racing about, even those with riders now beyond control. The legionaries slashed at their legs and punctured their stomachs, and the dying beasts tumbled to the earth. Unhorsed and stunned, the Suebi became easy prey for the Roman blades.

As quickly as it began, the torrent receded. The cavalry charge had spent itself. The odor of wet horses and their reeking entrails clogged the air. The second rank hacked its way through the last survivors and soon bumped into the three cohorts in front of them.

The Fifth, Sixth, and Seventh Cohorts had absorbed a pitiless beating, and many of the legionaries leaned on their shields in exhaustion.

Rufio strained to see through the fog. The Germans were gone for now, staggered by the failure of the encirclement and by the counterattack from the front rank. But they had not gone far. Rufio could hear them moving about in the mist, perhaps only a hundred feet away.

Taking advantage of the lull, he ran down the line and instructed the centurions in the front to pull back their centuries. The second rank would relieve them. Despite their weariness and wounds, the first rank managed the operation almost as smoothly as if it were a drill.

Metellus appeared beside Rufio. He had discarded his small signifer's shield and carried a big legionary one.

"Where's the standard?" Rufio asked in surprise.

"With Sabinus. Visual signaling is useless now. I'll fight by you."

Rufio smiled and gripped his right forearm. "Have you seen Valerius?"

"He's a wall of iron at the back. A couple of German horsemen got through to the rear and were about to trample one of the new boys. Valerius charged them both and cut them down like they were dead wood. Horses and all."

"By the gods! The civic crown for him."

"What now?" Metellus tried to peer through the fog.

"One more big push, I think. They need a success. I know the Germans. They'll lose heart soon if they cannot get a small taste of victory. Their next attack will be everything they have."

"Cavalry?"

"I don't know. We've killed so many, but there could be more. We might not be able to withstand another horse assault like the last."

"But we have reserves."

"Sabinus would never commit them in this fog where he cannot see. The risk is too great. He has to hold them back." Rufio took a deep breath and let it out slowly. "It's up to us."

The Suebi were getting noisier. The clatter of equipment told Rufio they were preparing their assault.

"We won't charge into the fog," he said. "We'll wait for them to come. Pass the word down the ranks and along the files."

Rufio turned to the soldier behind him and told him the same. Then he sheathed his sword and leaned his shield against his left leg and rested for a moment. He rubbed his aching wrists and forearms. They had endured much over the years and he was feeling it now.

The Suebi were almost ready. The rising pitch of their voices was enough to tell him.

He thumbed his ring and then hefted his shield and pulled out his sword.

"Comrades!" he shouted loudly enough to be heard throughout the Second Cohort. "Our loyalty is to the spirit of Rome and our cause is the will of Caesar. For them we face the barbarians. For the safety of all we love we'll hurl these savages through Avernus's foul mouth and deep into the abyss of Acheron."

Like a rising swell, a roar began among the troops until it crashed through the fog like a torrent.

And then the Suebi charged.

Never had the men of Augustus fought as the Twenty-fifth Legion fought that day. Calling on some mysterious inner reserves, they battled the Germans to a standstill and began pushing them back.

But the barbarians seemed willing to sacrifice an entire race simply to tire the Romans. Hundreds of Germans died in minutes, but still they came.

Rufio surged ahead, stabbing and chopping and battering them to death, and yet more rushed forward out of the fog. He knew that soon his men would be unable to lift their shields or wield their swords. Confronting him now was the most terrible irony of his fighting career. The Romans' skill at killing—the endless, bottomless killing—was about to bring on their exhausted collapse.

And then he heard the last sound he wanted to hear. Hoofbeats.

He looked at Metellus

Spattered with German blood and surrounded by bodies, the signifer leaned on his shield and struggled for breath. "Where are they?"

Rufio was not even sure which direction he was facing in the dense fog.

"The right flank!" he yelled as the invisible horses thundered toward them. He would be the first to face them. One more time he looked at Metellus, so Roman eyes would be the last eyes he would see on this earth. Suddenly in his mind he saw his sister sitting in her garden in Rome and the adoring face of Flavia smiling at him in the firelight.

And then the horses were upon him.

Adiatorix burst out of the wall of fog, his sword slashing down into the Suebi before him. Screams of pain and panic shattered the air as the Sequani horsemen crashed into the flank of the German line. Heads split and limbs flew. Pieces of German hit Rufio's helmet as Adiatorix and his warriors flailed into their hereditary enemies.

The Romans cheered their gallant allies and reached within themselves for a strength they did not know they had. They tore into the barbarians.

Down the Suebi went like wheat. And then they lost their nerve. Chopped to pieces in front and not realizing in the fog how few Sequani there were on their flank, they broke and ran. That was their downfall.

The Romans and Sequani pursued, attacking their unprotected backs and feeding the soil of Gaul with dead beyond number.

When the Romans were too tired to kill any more, Rufio called a halt.

"Dress ranks!" he shouted.

The other five centurions and the optios helped to get the troops in order.

The men of the Second Cohort seemed to be in some eerie netherworld. The fog was thin enough for the legionaries to see each other, but far too thick for them to see beyond it.

"Where are we?" Valerius said as he hurried up to the front rank. "I cannot get my bearings."

Rufio looked around. Ahead he could hear the Germans falling over each other in their headlong dash to safety. From off to his left came the sounds of fighting. Yet the faint noise seemed to drift in all the way from the edge of the world. How could everyone be so far away?

"Chief!" Rufio yelled.

Adiatorix rode up.

"Can you sense where the line is?" he asked, so confident was he in the intuitive powers of the Celts.

For a moment Adiatorix seemed to commune with the very forces of nature.

"Northwest," he said at last and pointed in the direction of the distant fighting.

But how could that be? "Let me borrow your horse."

Adiatorix jumped down and handed him the reins.

Rufio rode along the front of the cohort and instructed everyone to be quiet. Then he passed into the deepest fog.

After the chaos and carnage, the silent invisibility soothed him. He moved slowly toward the far-off clanging.

Soon he heard shouts and screams. Without warning, the mist parted and he stared in disbelief.

The Third and Fourth Cohorts were at least a quarter mile away to the left and fighting for their lives. In its savage counterattack, Rufio's cohort had surged far beyond the battle line and now stood behind the Germans.

It seemed as if the entire Suebi nation had launched itself in one final assault against the legion. The Roman line was bending but still it held. Yet it would not hold much longer.

Rufio's hands trembled. But it was not in fear but in anticipation. A soldier could live a hundred lifetimes and never see this moment.

The entire battle turned on this, and with it the fate of Gaul. The fate of the Celts, of the northern approaches to Italy, perhaps of the empire itself for a thousand years—all turned on the decision of an unknown centurion in the fog of Gaul.

Without orders or permission, in the fraction of an instant, he decided. He raced back to his men.

He gathered the other centurions and described what he had seen. And then he stunned them.

"We'll pivot the whole cohort. In silence. The goddess has given us this chance. We must take it now. It won't come again."

Rufio looked into each of his officers. In their eyes shone a full awareness of the enormity of what they were about to attempt. The entire right wing of the legion would swivel toward the rear of the Suebi like a closing jaw. A jaw with teeth of Celtic steel.

"The poets will sing forever of this day," the centurion said to the entire cohort. "And you'll speak of it with awe. Thirty years from now your eyes will grow moist and you'll say *I marched with valor. I marched with Rufio.*"

Even some of the hardened veterans coughed back the emotion in their throats.

Rufio pressed his ring to his lips. "May Victoria keep you safe. And remember, I am with you always."

He handed the reins to Adiatorix.

"Do you have a carnyx, chief?"

"We do."

"I want you to carry it. Blow it on my command."

"I will."

"Line up your horsemen on my right. We'll approach at a quick walk until my signal. Wait for it. And when we close the mouth, don't close it all the way. You know why."

Wise to war and to the terrors of man, Adiatorix nodded.

"I'll always remember this," the chieftain said. "Always remember you. Never before have I served under another."

"Come, my friend. We'll march together into history."

He raised his hand and waited for perfect order. Then he slashed downward and the line began to move. As straight as the spoke of a wheel it swung around, pivoting to the left. The three ranks swept through the fog as quietly as possible. The rattling of their equipment would soon be smothered by the clatter of the battle line.

They pierced the mist and gazed upon their beleaguered comrades. Probus still held the line, but the Suebi were threatening to overwhelm it. Yet the monstrous swarm of barbarians was disordered and inchoate. It was as if Barovistus, desperate now for victory, was rolling against the legion a writhing colossus of muscle and bone.

Rufio stared at the horde that hungered not just for the slaughter of his brothers but for the destruction of everything he cherished on earth. His eyes were slits in a mask of iron.

"Now," he said softly.

Adiatorix blew the Celtic horn and the Second Cohort leaped onto the back of its prey.

Down upon the German mass sprang the men of Rufio. All weariness gone, they thrust and slashed into the Germans' unprotected spine.

Probus's front line cheered and found new strength as the trap began closing on the Suebi.

Assaulted from all sides, the barbarians squandered what little formation they had. Almost instantly they became a churning morass of panic stricken men, abandoning the attack and scrambling to escape.

The jaw of the wolf was closing. Yet off to the right an opening presented itself. The tip of the mouth had not yet shut. Toward this gap at the end of the line the Suebi poured.

There waited the First Century and the avenging Celts.

Rufio and Adiatorix let them pass and expose their defenseless backs. Then the Romans and the Sequani chopped them to the earth. Never had Rufio killed with no compunction as many men as he did this day in the mud of Gaul. His hands bled from the friction of his weapons as he pierced and slashed without mercy.

What began as a panic spiraled into a rout, and the dreams of Barovistus died without honor among the entrails of his men.

53 WITHOUT SUBSTANCE, HONOR AND VALOR ARE MORE WORTHLESS THAN SEAWEED.

Horace

A hundred feet outside the camp gateway, an exquisite white and black mosaic of Minerva, hauled all the way from Italy, supported the chair of Sabinus. Stuck in the ground around the tile platform were the standards from all the centuries and cohorts and the eagle of the Twenty-fifth Legion.

Sabinus, in full armor, took his place in the chair. Crus stood to his right. The six surviving senior centurions stood behind their commander. Sabinus had wanted Rufio to take a position to his left, but he had declined any such distinction and stood with the others. Diocles took a place behind the centurions. The late afternoon sun had finally broken through and now formed a golden corona behind them.

Sabinus had polished his bronze breastplate, but the tunics and mail of the centurions were still splattered with mud and with the blood of their enemies.

An older German and two unarmed warriors rode up at a trot.

"Dismount," Sabinus commanded in Celtic.

They did as ordered.

"Never approach the Legate of Augustus on horseback."

They stood before him in silence.

"I am Marcus Aemilius Sabinus. You may speak."

"I am Orgestes of the Suebi. We would like to remove our wounded from the mud and carry them back to our own lands."

"You may. And clear the field of your dead. I won't have these Sequani smelling rotting German for the next six months."

"May we take our weapons?"

"One spear for each man. No steel."

"Our horses?"

"No Gaul would want those sad creatures. Take them. But" — he raised a finger — "first get fifty men and kill all the crippled horses on the field. I won't have them suffer."

Anger burned in Orgestes' eyes, but he said nothing.

"Speak, chief."

"What of our suffering?"

"What of it? You've created your own pain."

The two young warriors clenched their hands.

"Keep these men under control," Sabinus said. "Or they'll die at your feet."

"May I have your word that my people may withdraw without hindrance?"

"You may have nothing but my dwindling patience. There are those at Rome who'll say I should have put all of you to the sword. Annihilated you as a race so you never threaten us or our allies again. But that's not my role. Do you understand?"

"Yes."

"One thing more. A question. If I suspect you're lying, I'll kill every wounded man on this field."

Orgestes searched his eyes. "I don't believe you're the kind of man who would do that." He hesitated. "But I'll speak the truth."

"Barovistus — was he killed?"

"You want the body of our leader?"

"I want an answer."

"He lives. He has a head wound, but he'll survive. We won't surrender him."

"I don't expect that. Never do we want to see a German face again. Only German backs. Cross the water again and die. Go."

54   IT IS BEST TO ENDURE WHAT YOU CANNOT PUT RIGHT.

Seneca

We have rested for several days now. Sabinus will not break camp until we can move with no risk to our wounded. Our dead have been cremated, and now our doctors are trying to ensure there will be no more for the flames to consume.

I have spent much time in the hospital tents. The remedies of the doctors are numerous and probably of varying effectiveness. Yet I have seen none of the medical chicanery one encounters so frequently in civilian life.

The favorite styptic of the army doctors is frankincense, and our supply has been exhausted. After the wounds are about a day old, the doctors apply other preparations to speed the closing of the flesh. The dressing they prefer is ivy that has been simmered in wine. To avoid excessive inflammation, they replace this later with poultices of shredded raw celery or Achilles' woundwort. The latter is especially favored by our Greek doctor. For those in the greatest pain, there are ominous decoctions of poppy and mandrake and henbane. However, the doctors are reluctant to administer these except in cases of extreme agony. The slightest error in dosage and the patient slips into a sleep from which he does not arise.

The willingness of our men to bear pain in silence is astounding. I can almost laugh when I think of some of my friends in Rome who whine when they are nicked while being shaved. Here in these tents, where men lie cut or punctured, one rarely hears a moan. The men are especially quiet when their centurions are nearby, which seems like always. The officers are constantly checking on their soldiers and on the doctors as well. The centurions are as protective as she-wolves. They freely berate the doctors for not doing enough for their men or for interfering too much.

Rufio seems to live in these tents. I am fascinated to see how he deals differently with different men. Yet there is one constant, and that is that he never speaks about their wounds or the battle. I am certain this is not because of any concern about disturbing them, but that it grows out of that ferocious Roman pragmatism that would consider such discussion pointless.

With the older men, he jokes about the drunken brawls they have been in and the ones they are missing now that they are flat on their backs. He teases them about having limp branches from too many dalliances with Gallic women who drain them dry until they can no longer move.

With the younger men he is like an older brother, gentle and understanding. The boys are eager to talk about their homes and farms and especially about their mothers. He sits with them quietly as they suck back the pain of their injuries. When the doctors are busy elsewhere, he sops up the pus from their wounds until his hands reek from the rank exudate, and then he changes their dressings.

As I watch him, I realize my earlier judgment was correct. Rufio truly would be a failure in normal life. Where else but among the fierce rigors of a legion could his qualities burn so brightly?

———————

Sabinus's tent seemed different now, as tired and spent as the rest of the legion. A couple of slaves were cleaning up the clutter, but Sabinus dismissed them. He pointed to a stool in front of the table where the battle had been planned, and Rufio sat. Sabinus joined him on the same side of the table.

"What we owe you—what Rome owes you—cannot be measured," Sabinus said.

"Never exaggerate the importance of one centurion."

"It's impossible to exaggerate the importance of one centurion," he answered with an ironic smile.

"If I'd not been here, Probus would have led the right wing just as well."

"Probus would be the first to disagree with you. But I'm not talking about the mechanics of battle."

Rufio remained silent.

"Rome owes more to her soldiers than can ever be comprehended by her stupid politicians—of whom I am one."

"I've never expected much from politicians."

"They see you as simple functionaries. Road builders paving the path to their dreams. What those fools don't realize is that you, Rufio— you and your men—you are the dream itself. The dream of Rome."

"Why are you telling me this?"

"It gives me pleasure to tell you. And it's important you realize your value to the empire you serve." He stood up. "Go and rest now. We break camp tomorrow."

———————

A late-morning breeze caressed Rufio's face as he stood beside the hill of Scorpions and stared eastward across the churned up earth. He thought again, as he had so many times, that there was nothing emptier than an empty battlefield.

But the horses were still there, bloated and grotesque. And some Suebi weapons and shields lay scattered about, though they would soon be collected by the Sequani. Yet the Suebi bodies had been hauled off, and soon the land would heal itself. The wounded skin would begin to close, the short memory of man would shame the dead, and the Terror of the Germans would seem as remote as the dark forests they forever prowled.

Rufio turned toward footsteps behind him.

Crus approached.

"Take a day to relax, centurion," he said good-naturedly.

"How did you know where I was?"

"You weren't with the wounded, so I thought you might be here."

"Do you know me that well?"

"I've learned a little," he said with a smile.

"Does Sabinus want me?"

"I do."

Rufio waited for him to continue.

"Have you decided to retire now? I've heard a rumor."

Rufio pulled his scabbard forward and sat on the ground. Crus sat opposite him.

"Diocles wants me to return to Rome with him and help him write his history."

"I understand. It's a noble task."

Rufio's eyes narrowed. "You could say it with a bit more sincerity."

"Could I?"

"I haven't seen my sister in almost three years."

Crus suddenly had an odd look on his face, but he said nothing.

"What?" Rufio asked.

"I've never though of you as having a family. Strange, isn't it?"

"Where did you think I came from?" Rufio said in annoyance.

"I thought you'd sprung fully formed from the brow of Mars."

"Too many have thought that. It's a burden that wearies me."

"A sister, you say?" Crus asked in a soothing tone.

"Until recently, my sister and my mother were the only women I'd ever loved."

"Until recently?"

"Yes."

"Sabinus wants you to stay, but he respects you too much to try to influence you."

"But you don't respect me?"

" 'Mark this day with a black stone, centurion'," he said, quoting himself. "See? I've never respected you." Then he could hold back no longer and exploded in laughter.

Rufio laughed with him.

"Consider it," Crus said. "That's all I ask."

55 TIME REVEALS ALL THINGS.

Roman saying

The story of the battle had sped like a falcon back to Aquabona. It seemed as if every Sequani from the village had hurried out to greet us. Theirs was not simply a celebration of victory. Our triumph over the Suebi was the promise of Sequani survival. Magnificently appropriate was it that Adiatorix and his men had swept in at the crucial moment to help us turn the tide.

Though I had struck no blows, I felt as proud as my fellow soldiers when the Sequani cheered. As we marched up the road toward the fort, I looked at Rufio. He seemed too worn out to smile. Never have I seen him so drained. Of course, he is no youth, but I suspect his exhaustion is not simply a weariness of the flesh. He gives so much of his spirit to everything he does — a fact that not all of his comrades comprehend — that the depth of his depletion is almost frightening. He will be fine in a few days, but in the meantime I yearn to allow him to lean on me. It is an offer I know he would decline.

Yet once I did see his eyes revive. A cloaked woman astride a gray horse waited on a hilltop overlooking the road. It could only have been Flavia. Even at this distance from her, his blue tunic would have stood out. They seemed to see each other simultaneously, and then she turned and raced down toward the fort.

How odd that this vibrant Celtic spirit could soothe the soul of this incomprehensible man.

I feel guilty now for asking him to return with me to Rome.

"The civic crown?" Metellus said with a skeptical smile and sat down on the edge of his bunk. "Are you sure Sabinus has the correct Valerius?"

"I think it's Gaius Valerius in the Second Century," Diocles said. "Excellent soldier."

But their teasing was lost on Valerius.

"What's wrong?" Metellus asked as the optio stared in silence out the window in the back of the barracks room.

"How can I receive an award like that? The same award Rufio has won four times?"

"It's the one you wanted," Diocles said.

"That doesn't mean I deserve it."

"Of course you do," Metellus said.

"An award for valor isn't just a decoration, it's a responsibility," Valerius said. "One you must always live up to. Forever. I've never done that before."

"Then you must learn how," Metellus said and leaned back with that bemused look of his.

"I hear we're being invited to a Sequani celebration tomorrow," Diocles said.

"We?" Valerius asked. "Who?"

"Our century."

"You may drink my share of the beer," Metellus said. "I'm going to ask Rufio if I may go back to spend tomorrow with Calpurnia and Kalinda. Do you know where he is now?"

Valerius shook his head and again stared out the window. "I haven't seen him all afternoon."

Diocles did not answer. He never liked to lie, especially to his friends. A half-hour earlier he had seen Rufio drive a wagon out of the fort. In the back, he saw a basket of food and a jug of wine and a rolled up carpet.

This was one night Rufio deserved for himself.

56   A FRIEND IS ANOTHER SELF.

Roman proverb

"The First Century declines," Rufio said.

The commander looked up from his desk with the same exasperation he had shown the first day they had met.

"Why?"

"I don't believe in selecting units for individual distinction. Mine or anyone else's. There are precedents for it, but I reject them."

"Tell me, Rufio, do you think sometime you and I will be able to concur on all matters for three consecutive days?"

"The auspices aren't good."

"I agree," he said with a sigh. "Fortunately, I have the power to enforce my will. Adiatorix's village wishes to show its gratitude to this legion. It's too small to feed the entire legion or even a full cohort. So he's chosen the century that led the right wing."

Rufio remained silent.

"You'll eat well, keep drunkenness to a minimum, and gratefully accept whatever pleasures the beautiful women of Gaul choose to share with the cheerful young soldiers of the First Century of the Second Cohort." Sabinus's eyes narrowed. "Or, for that matter, even with you."

For once, Rufio kept his sharp tongue in its sheath.

"Any questions?"

"Shall we wear full armor so we look the part?" he said with a touch of sarcasm.

He regretted the words as soon as he spoke them. It was clear from Sabinus's expression that he had not considered it until Rufio gave him the thought.

"No. Helmets and swords should be enough. I mean that. Dismissed."

Diocles was bent over his writing table in the room next to Rufio's sleeping quarters. He must have heard Rufio come in, but he did not turn around. Paki was curled up and sleeping on a stack of papyrus sheets beside his left elbow.

It was unusual for him to be writing so early in the day.

"I want to get this down while it's still fresh," he said in answer to Rufio's unspoken question. "I'll be leaving soon."

When Rufio did not reply, he set down his pen and looked around at his centurion.

Rufio was surprised to see that his face looked haggard.

"I'll write better in Rome without all these distractions."

"I understand."

"I cannot imagine now what that will be like." His voice was unsteady.

"Easier than the life of a soldier."

"The aroma of warm porridge and the clean morning air." He kept his eyes averted. "The crispness of the Gallic countryside as the sun comes up. The snap of our hobnails on the stone roadway."

Rufio smiled and leaned against the doorway. "Odd how the small things are always the most important."

"And the men," he said and looked up for the first time. He seemed suddenly plaintive. "I'll never see them again."

"You'll see Sabinus again. And Crus, too, probably."

"No, our men. This century."

Rufio said nothing.

"Valerius and I marched together on my first day. I liked him instantly. Just as you did, though you pretended not to. I cannot think of not seeing him every morning. And Metellus . . ." His voice was quaking now. "That look of superiority he always gives me. That teasing smile. I think I'll miss him most of all. I think . . ." His voice cracked again. "More than anyone . . ." His chin quivered as he struggled to bring his words under control. "Him most of all . . . no, I'm lying." His eyes were desperate. "It's you. You . . ." His breathing came in quick short gasps and then he spun around and burst out crying.

He wept uncaringly onto the sheets in front of him. Paki licked his ear as he shook.

"What you've taught me," he managed to say through his sobs.

Rufio walked across and wrapped an arm around his shoulders in silence.

"About honor," Diocles said. "About courage. About life."

"I know."

"This is a school like no other." He straightened up and cleared his throat, the tears still streaking his face. "These are men like no other. And who understands them? The politicians? The rabble? They treat you with indifference or contempt—when they think of you at all. And you accept it as the normal course of life. You go off and cut your roads and build your towns and battle the enemies of Rome."

"We have our own codes."

"They're far nobler than any I've ever had."

"Perhaps now you've acquired ours."

Hope shone for the first time in his eyes. "Do you think that's possible? At my age?"

"In the century of Rufio, anything is possible."

"Promise me . . ." He hesitated and wiped his eyes. "I know this sounds childish, but promise me that if I need you, I can reach out in the dark and find you."

"Of course you can. I'm your friend."

Diocles stood and gripped both of Rufio's forearms. "I swear by my ancestors, if you ever need me I'll be there by you. Even across the rivers of Hell."

57 BELIEVE EVERY DAY TO HAVE DAWNED TO BE YOUR LAST.

Horace

"Adiatorix feasting with the Romans," Valerius said with a grin. "Never did I think I'd see this day."

Rufio smiled but said nothing.

The Sequani women laid out food on a great semi-circle of tables in an open area next to the village.

Rufio's eyes were on Flavia as she set down a bowl of meat and cheese on one of the tables. She was wearing her dark green tunic that came to mid-thigh and was belted at the waist. Her bronze torque encircled her right biceps and the black leather bracer covered her left forearm. She had tucked a red flower in the hair behind her right ear.

"The gods favor you," Valerius said.

"More than I deserve."

"The favor of the gods is like the civic crown. A responsibility you must live up to."

Rufio turned to him with a smile. "I see you've thought about this."

"You compel me to."

The tavern owner from town drove up in a wagon carrying large pots of beer. His wife rode with him, and on her lap sat her little girl carrying her cat.

"This is a feast, not a military parade. Let the men put their helmets and sword belts on the tables. They can keep their dagger belts on."

Valerius went to tell them.

Rufio turned back toward Flavia, but soon he felt the pressure of someone else's gaze. He looked around.

The mother of the little girl was standing about twenty feet away and staring at him with a bemused look worthy of Metellus.

Rufio nodded. She smiled and hurried after her daughter, who was chasing the cat as it bounded playfully toward the woods.

"Sometimes we forget how precious life is," Adiatorix said as he came up to Rufio. He took a deep breath of the balmy afternoon air.

"Indeed we do, chief."

"Where's Metellus?"

"He should be along later."

"I'm happy your men are enjoying themselves." He pointed toward the soldiers relaxing on the grass with their food and drink.

284

Only fifty-one men of the First Century were able to share the meal. Five had been killed and eighteen wounded seriously enough to be unable to leave the fort.

Varacinda and Larinda came over, and Adiatorix smiled and walked away.

"My sister would like to speak with you," Varacinda said.

Larinda approached with eyes lowered.

"No need for that," Rufio said and raised her chin with a forefinger.

"I honor you, centurion," she said in the soft voice he had first heard that night in the stable.

"Honors I've had. What I'd like is to see what I haven't yet seen. What you look like when you smile."

He reached out and his scabbed and battered hands enveloped her delicate ones.

Her eyes ignited and her lips widened in a smile that could have melted frozen rock.

"Rufio!" Flavia shouted from across the grass.

She was kneeling at the edge of the woods and talking to the little girl. Her mother was kneeling beside her and looked alarmed.

"What is it?" Rufio said as he ran up.

The girl was gripping her cat tightly.

"She went into the forest to get the cat," Flavia said. "She told her mother she saw men coming."

"Big men," the girl said. "With swords. Hairy men." She made a tiny fist and placed it on top of her head like a knot.

"Suebi?" Rufio asked.

"Yes," her mother said. "I think so."

Flavia sprang to her feet and dashed off toward the trees.

The three minutes she was gone seemed like a year.

"About a hundred on the other side of the woods," she said as she ran up. "Coming this way. About a quarter mile off. What's happening?"

"Valerius!"

Rufio's tone was enough. Valerius dropped his food and ran to him.

"A hundred Suebi. Form up the men."

Valerius was off in an instant.

Sensing trouble, Adiatorix suddenly appeared at Rufio's side.

"What is it?" the chief said.

"A vengeance raid. Barovistus must know it was you and your men who helped turn the battle. He's here to slaughter your people."

Rufio turned toward Flavia, but she had vanished.

"We have enough men to beat them back," Adiatorix said.

"No, you must protect your people. We'll hold them off. Get everyone together and head toward the fort." He looked for his optio. "Hurry!" he shouted to Valerius across the open ground.

"What do you mean?" the chief asked.

"You need a reserve. You people never understand reserves. If the Germans get through us, you'll still be there to make a stand. A rear guard to protect your people."

Flavia came running up with her bow and quiver.

Adiatorix stared at him as if he were mad. "What you mean is you'll hold them off until we can escape. Then they'll overrun you and kill you all."

Valerius hurried over with Rufio's sword belt and helmet.

"We need shields, chief. As many as you can get."

Adiatorix ran toward the village.

"Form a line!" Rufio ordered as his men began assembling. "Three ranks!"

"Rufio," Valerius said.

"What?" he asked and buckled his sword belt.

"We cannot do this."

"Of course we can." He pulled on his helmet. "We're soldiers."

"Seventeen men in a line? They'll flank us in a minute."

Rufio's eyes bored into his. "Have you lost your belief in me?"

It was a terrible rebuke. The shock to Valerius was as great as if Rufio had hit him across the face with a steel rod.

"No, I have not."

"Good." The trace of a smile pulled at his lips. He placed his right hand on Valerius's left shoulder. "I'll see us through this day. Distribute the shields."

Rufio turned toward the east.

"How do you think they'll come?" Flavia asked.

The woods began about a hundred and fifty feet away, but they were split by a small clearing thirty feet across.

"Through that opening," Rufio said. "Passing through the trees would slow them down. We'll be waiting for them."

He looked back toward the village. Adiatorix had gathered his people and some were already hurrying off toward the fort.

Rufio ran over to where his men were getting their shields.

"None for you," he said to Diocles and pulled it from his hand.

"Why not?"

"You won't fight. You must live to write of what you see here."

"You need me."

"Our memory needs you. Stay at a safe distance and lock in your mind all you witness this day."

He turned to Flavia. For a moment, he forgot the world. He stared into her glorious eyes.

"You must go, too," he said.

"No!" she shouted. "I'll fight by you."

She turned and bolted toward the trees.

He ran her down about halfway to the woods and pulled her to him.

"You must defend your people," he said. "If the Germans get past us, you have to make a stand."

"Oh, Rufio," she said and pressed her face to his chest. "You cannot die here today. Then I would die, too."

He held her in his arms. "You must live for your people. Live for Gaul." He smiled into her eyes. "Breath of my life, you must live for me."

He took the red flower from her hair and tucked it behind his dagger belt.

She battled back her emotions and succeeded until he pulled off his signet ring and pressed it into her hand. Then the tears came. She squeezed him in her strong arms and her lips seared into his.

When she pulled back at last, he leaned forward again and kissed her on each of her eyebrows.

"Go now," he said gently. "Don't look back."

He turned away and ran to his men.

The century had assembled into three ranks. The colorful oval shields were dazzling. Red and blue and green hide coverings were decorated with rings and swirls and loops. The shields were smaller than legionary ones, but they had the central iron boss the Romans favored.

Adiatorix stood there holding two swords, a long Gallic weapon and a shorter Roman one.

"We have no more shields," the chief said.

Rufio reached for the Roman sword with his left hand. "This will do."

"I took that from a Suebi. Perhaps it was Carbo's."

"Go now, chief. Your people need you."

The two men locked eyes in the special bond only brother warriors may know. Then Adiatorix hurried away to join his people.

"About a hundred Suebi are coming this way," Rufio said to his men. "They'll be here in a few minutes. They have one purpose, to slaughter these Sequani in revenge. We cannot allow that. Why?"

"The men of Rufio have outlawed German butchery," Arrianus shouted.

They all laughed. They looked more confident than Rufio had ever seen them, so great was their belief in him.

"They outnumber us two to one," Rufio said. "That should make it even. Remain calm. Follow my commands and I'll see you through this day. Valerius will lead the first rank from the right. I'll be in the second rank in the middle. The third rank will follow my lead. We'll meet them at the break in the trees. March!"

The century crossed the open space and halted about fifty feet from the gap in the trees.

Rufio could already hear the Germans. They would never learn to advance in silence. He tightened his grip on the sword in his left hand and pulled the sword of Hetorix with his right.

The Germans came around from behind the trees and entered the break. Barovistus led from the front. A bandage encircled his head. He stopped when he saw the Romans.

"He's stunned," Rufio said. "The lambs aren't here."

The Germans started shouting and waving their spears and swords. Then Barovistus screamed the Suebian war cry and the Germans poured though the opening.

"Hold," Rufio said calmly to his soldiers.

The Germans bore down on them.

"Now!" Rufio shouted as the front of the German wedge cleared the trees.

The Romans yelled and tore across the ground and hit the Germans with the force of a ram. The momentum of the impact was tremendous. The Germans staggered as the Celtic shields smashed into them and the Roman swords flashed and killed.

Startled by the boldness of the attack, the Suebi struggled to pull back and regroup.

Valerius and the front rank sheared forward, climbing over the dead and thrusting and chopping like men possessed by demons.

Then the moment Rufio was waiting for arrived. Barovistus realized how few Romans there were and he ordered his men to flank them.

"Second rank, pivot right, pivot left!" Rufio shouted.

The men on either side of him split in the middle and swung out to the wings, perpendicular to the first rank.

"Third rank, pivot to the rear!"

The third line spun around and in an instant the century had formed a square.

The Germans crashed into it futilely. Their numbers were useless against the wall of shields and blades. The more desperate the Germans became, the more reckless they got, and the Romans cut them down like blind and crippled dogs.

Rufio stood in the center alone, wheeling about, rushing to support every tiring soldier. More than once he slashed past the head of one of his own men and split the skull of a German that was pressing his man hard.

In minutes, more than half the Suebi fell in maddened rushes against the Roman square. Others were already pulling back in confusion and exhaustion.

Rufio looked about for Barovistus. Far beyond his men he saw the last thing he expected to see. Beside the food tables, Metellus was battling two German swordsmen. Blood ran from a wound on his face and he fought without a shield.

Rufio pushed through his men and slashed at the Germans before him, first with one sword and the other. He finally broke through and dashed across the clearing.

Metellus was down on his knees. One of the Germans was dead, but the other hacked at the weakening Roman. The German grinned with the smell of conquest.

Then Rufio was upon him. The German heard him and spun around, slashing down at the shorter Roman. Rufio blocked the blow with his left-hand sword and thrust his right straight through the German's breastbone. It splintered like kindling. Blood exploded from his mouth and he went down. Rufio thrust into him over and over in a warrior's fury until he finally had to stop for breath.

"How bad?" he said to Metellus.

"A cut on my forehead. I'm weak but I'll be all right."

Like a charging bull, something crashed into Rufio and sent him tumbling, both swords flying from his hands.

A grimacing Suebi leaped upon him and pinned him to the ground as massive hands encircled his throat.

Rufio whipped his dagger from its sheath and plunged it into the contorted face. Again and again the blade struck home.

He pushed the corpse away and sprang to his feet. He saw Barovistus launching a spear. There was no escape. It grazed his left thigh and his leg buckled.

Barovistus barreled down on him, a long Gallic sword in his hand.

Rufio looked to Metellus for his sword, but he had fainted and Rufio could not get to it in time.

He turned to face Barovistus from one knee. The German closed in with a snarl of loathing that would have frightened the dead.

Rufio threw his dagger with terrific force deep into the German's stomach. It staggered him, but on he came.

Rufio tried to get to his feet, but his leg failed him.

Looming over him with a face twisted with rage, Barovistus raised his massive sword. Rufio threw up his arm uselessly.

An arrowhead burst through the brow of Barovistus and his entire body rippled like the snap of a whip. For a moment he stared blindly at Rufio, and then his legs seemed to break in half and he collapsed like a shattered icon.

A roar shot up from the Romans at the German's fall.

Rufio's gaze shot across the field and there stood Flavia, magnificent and indomitable, bow in hand and raising a second arrow.

The remains of the German line crumbled. Leaderless, they fell back and ran for the trees.

"Let them go!" Rufio shouted, knowing the Romans were not strong enough to pursue.

A horrible cry shot up from somewhere, and Rufio saw a young blonde warrior bolt straight toward Flavia.

Sword in hand and insane with despair, he rushed to cut her down.

Flavia pulled the bowstring taut and waited.

The German did not seem to care as he closed in.

Flavia drew a bead. And then the bowstring broke. Suddenly the lethal arrow seemed like nothing but a pointed stick.

Rufio pushed himself to his feet, but he could barely hobble. Then he saw Valerius.

The optio had dropped his shield and was dashing across the battleground toward the charging German, but Rufio realized with horror that Valerius would be too late.

"NO-O-O-O!" Rufio screamed with all the pent up anguish of a lifetime.

Flavia braced herself and held the arrow like a knife but it was just a useless twig.

Another cry, a colossal howl of exertion, perhaps a cry from the throat of Victoria herself, shattered the air.

A German spear flew from the left of the field and passed through the air and through the German with the ease of the finger of a goddess. He stumbled a few more steps and crumpled to the earth, the spear breaking beneath him.

Rufio spun to the left.

Still bent double from the enormity of the effort, Diocles slowly stood up to his full height a hundred feet away.

The Romans roared in triumph.

"Help Metellus," Rufio said as Valerius came running up.

Rufio picked up his sword and limped across the field as his men swarmed Diocles and Flavia.

"Form a line!" Rufio shouted.

They did as ordered and he stood before them.

His men dripped blood from many cuts and gouges, but not one had fallen.

"Rufio! Rufio!" Arrianus chanted in his deep voice, and immediately the rest of the men joined in.

"Rufio! Rufio! Rufio!"

He thrust the point of his sword into the ground to steady himself and looked from one to the other of them, and suddenly his eyes felt hot.

"My people thank you for what you've done," Flavia said as she stepped before them. "The Sequani will forever remember this day."

"Kiss her, centurion!" Arrianus shouted. "If you don't, one of us will!"

Rufio laughed and they all laughed with him.

In her own sacred realm, Victoria, too, graced her beauty with a smile.

58   WHO COULD DECEIVE A LOVER?

Virgil

An hour after dawn, the fort pulsed with the energy of a new day. The cool damp air invigorated Diocles like an exotic potion.

He strolled the fort for the final time. The permanent aroma of baking bread already filled him with longing.

He walked by the barracks blocks, noisy with activity. He wanted to visit the men in the hospital once more, but it was too early to disturb them, so he moved on. Past the bathhouse he went and around to the other side of the fort. He stopped before the place where his adventure had begun.

Some of the cavalrymen were leading their horses out of the stable. He went around to the side of the building. With their usual fanatical cleanliness, the soldiers had long since cleared away the old stacks of hay left over from winter. A bare space remained at the spot where Diocles' life had been transformed. Where a strange man, half-crippled by a wound, had climbed some bales and looked into eyes certain of their own death. Where mercy from the hand of the conqueror had begun Diocles' first lesson on the nature of power, and on the power of honor.

He turned away and headed back to the Principia, but he no longer noticed his surroundings.

As usual, Sabinus was at his desk and Crus was bending over it and pointing out something on a document.

"Ready?" Sabinus asked.

"Yes," Diocles answered in a near-whisper.

"Have you said farewell to your century?"

"I did that yesterday. That's why I slept in the Praetorium last night. I cannot bear to see them again today."

"Are you going to sneak out of the fort?" Crus asked in an amused but kindly tone.

"I made Valerius promise me he'd take them on a route march this morning. I'll be gone before they return."

"Always the clever Greek," Sabinus said with a smile. "Let's walk out together."

The three men left and passed the guarded shrine housing the legionary standards. Diocles paused. He stood there for a moment, and then turned away and walked outside.

In full armor, the First Century lined both sides of the courtyard, Valerius and Metellus at either end of the little avenue of honor they had made for him. He stepped into the sun and every man placed a hand on his sword hilt.

He turned to Sabinus and Crus. They smiled but said nothing. He looked back at his comrades. They all smiled at him with affection and with the special respect only Roman soldiers can give.

He swallowed hard and lowered his head. He promised himself he would show no more tears, but he knew he promised in vain.

Flavia sliced with long and forceful strokes through the lake, then dipped beneath the water and swam back in the opposite direction. She pierced the surface and turned and swam to the shore.

She stepped onto the bank, and the late morning sun allowed itself the pleasure of a secret caress. Her hair hung down her back in thick black ropes, and the water rolled off her skin onto the grass. She reached toward the sky and stretched upward as far as she could. As she strained to grasp the heavens, she groaned with the rapture only a young woman can know. Muscled like a female Apollo, but blessed with the softness of Venus, she was a woman for whom any king on earth would have eagerly bartered all the pearls in the sea.

She plucked a handful of yellow flowers and rolled them vigorously between her palms. After sliding her fingers through her wet hair, she lay back on the grass, serene in the unashamed nakedness a goddess preferred.

She felt the hoofbeats before she heard them. She rolled over. Her gray mare was already alert as Varacinda rode out from the trees.

Flavia rose and walked toward her with that powerful stride that was hers alone.

Varacinda slid from her horse and ran toward her. The eyes of the chief's wife were red with weeping.

"He's gone!"

Flavia had no need to ask whom she meant. "Gone where?"

"To Rome," she answered, her chest heaving.

"You're mistaken."

"He left with the Greek a short time ago. One of our people saw him on the road."

"He would never abandon me."

Varacinda's teeth pressed nervously into her lower lip but she said nothing.

Flavia picked up her clothes and dressed and then grabbed her bow and quiver. She leaped onto her horse and raced for the trees.

She tore through the woods and made for a nearby hill that overlooked the road leading from Aquabona. When she reached the summit, she could just make out the small Roman column receding in the distance. The riders were too far to distinguish, but Rufio's blue tunic was easy to see.

Just an escort. He'll be back tonight.

She resolved to wait.

Throughout the day she sat on the grass and her horse grazed nearby. Larinda came with a flask of water and a basket of bread and fruit. They lay untouched beside her while she stared endlessly at the road.

As the shadows lengthened, her body began to feel unbearably heavy. She felt as if she could hardly move.

Below, the road had become a hideous thing, mocking her with its emptiness.

Finally, in the failing light, she pushed herself to her feet. Sensing her sadness, her horse came up and nuzzled her. Flavia pressed her face to the mare's graceful neck and cried softly.

"Did you think a soldier of Rome could not obey a command?"

She snapped her head around.

"Rufio!"

The sun's dying rays fell onto his silver hair and blue tunic and the belt and dagger at his waist.

She tried to speak but no words came.

"I met Larinda in the settlement," he said. "When she saw me, she wept."

"But we saw you leave . . . on the road . . . I saw your tunic. . . ."

"I've been in the fort all day. My tunic?" Suddenly he laughed so loudly he startled the birds roosting in the trees. "That was Diocles. He asked for one as a memento. He needs more muscle to fill it out, but he has time."

Flavia moistened her lips. "What did you mean — not obey a command?"

"You ordered me not to abandon you again. I'm a centurion of Rome — I'm here to show you how a man of Rome obeys powers greater than himself."

"Oh Rufio!" she said and sprang toward him like a deer.

She leaped into his arms and crushed herself to him. She pressed her face against his cheek and felt the pleasant sting of the stubble of his beard against her skin. She kissed his cheek and ear and neck and inhaled deeply of his scent.

"Love me forever," she commanded.

"I will," he whispered as he coiled his arms around her and buried his face in her hair, fragrant now with oil of cedar and the blossoms of spring.

THE END

Printed in the United States
204564BV00002B/5/A